ENGLAND AWAY

John King lives in London. England Away is the third
novel in the loose trilogy that began with The Football
Factory.

ALSO BY JOHN KING

The Football Factory
Headhunters

John King

ENGLAND AWAY

V

VINTAGE

Published by Vintage 1999

9

Copyright © John King 1998

The right of John King to be identified as the author of
this work has been asserted by him in accordance with
the Copyright, Designs and Patents Act, 1988

First published in Great Britain in 1998
by Jonathan Cape

Vintage
Random House, 20 Vauxhall Bridge Road,
London SW1V 2SA

www.rbooks.co.uk

Addresses for companies within
The Random House Group Limited can be found at:
www.randomhouse.co.uk/offices.htm

The Random House Group Limited Reg. No. 954009

A CIP catalogue record for this book
is available from the British Library

ISBN 9780099739616

The Random House Group Limited supports The Forest Stewardship
Council (FSC), the leading international forest certification organisation.
All our titles that are printed on Greenpeace approved FSC certified paper
carry the FSC logo. Our paper procurement policy can be found at:
www.rbooks.co.uk/environment

Printed and bound in Great Britain by
CPI Antony Rowe, Chippenham, Wiltshire

FOR MY DAD, MIKE KING

'The English don't kill people,
unless they fucking have to'

Steve Thorman, the night of Heysel

ISLAND RACE

A STROPPY CUNT in a grey uniform stands in front of me, acting cocky – standing there like a plum. He's looking at my passport. Inspecting the photo but not raising his head to check if Tom Johnson is one and the same. He's waiting for something to happen. Waiting for the face in the picture to lean forward and the mouth to tell him to fuck off. Pull the skull back and nut him on the bridge of the nose. Sending blood down that nice official jacket, running along sharp creases. He's searching inside the lines of my forehead. Reading the script and playing his part. Holding that shitty red passport close, the proud old British version ripped up and burnt by the invisible scum in Brussels. Manky old cunts busy working through the night, nailing us with the European tag. Claiming triple time. No identity and a crisp ironed suit; sagging sweaty skin and pockmarked cheeks. Customs cunt saying nothing, just hanging there, a fucking tart inspecting the photo. Staring into space, the slag. And I can feel my foot tapping and fingers itching, fists clenched, holding back and keeping the violence down. Does he remember something from his hooligan database, or is it a routine piss-take? He raises his head with a blank expression and cardboard stance. Sucking air down so it rattles in his throat. Gagging on bad manners and the smell of a Fisherman's Friend. Giving it the big one. Giving me grief.

– What are you planning to do in Holland then, Mr Johnson? he asks, all curious and suspicious. Full of himself. Full of shit.

I smile my best friendly smile.

(Well, I'm passing through Holland on my way to Berlin, Mr Customs Cunt, where I'm going to see England play Germany and hopefully help turn the place over. That's what. But first

3

I'm going to stop in Amsterdam and get pissed, then service some of those Dutch birds you hear so much about. Not the whores, mind, though I might give them a seeing to as well. Reduced rates for a classic English gentleman. No, I want some of those Dutch beauty queens, with their blonde hair, black armpits and never-say-no attitude to sex. Maybe have a row with the Dutch for a warm-up. Then we're going to do the Germans outside the Reichstag. That's what. And by the way, mate, that wife of yours, she's a right little raver. She fucking loves it, the dirty cow. Last I saw of her, round about nine this morning, after you'd had a wank over the ferry timetable and left for work, she was seeing the England boys off in style. Talk about catching a train. You want to keep your eye on that one.)

– I'm going to Amsterdam for a few days to stay with friends and have a holiday. Visit some of Holland maybe. See the sights and relax.

I watch the rest of the chaps moving away, turning the corner. Acting innocent as new-born babies. Looking at the floor, the walls, finally the ceiling. Makes me laugh how they can waltz through so easy. Blokes like Facelift and Billy Bright who look the part. Bright Spark with his Cross of St George flag under his arm tied together with a thick length of rope and covered in black plastic so it doesn't get wet. These colours don't run. Mark hanging back waving, smiling, laughing. Waiting for me to sort things out and catch him up. Enjoying the show.

I go back to this wanker in front of me. Smile again. A big yellow ball with black strips for the mouth and eyes. Cartoon gun-runner, going the wrong way. Why's he chosen me? Luck of the draw or something more serious?

– Going to test some of the drugs in Amsterdam are we, Mr Johnson? Is that the reason for the trip?

So that's it. Cartoon drug-smuggler. You have to laugh.

(Don't know about you mate, but d'you really think I'd spend the fare just for that? Wise up, giving me hassle when you've let the others through. I should kick you in the bollocks. Kick you so hard your balls jam in your gut and you spend the rest of your life sounding like you've been on the helium. Like we don't have enough drugs at home. But I'll let you off because then I'd miss the fun and games, and your mates would be pissing themselves when I get six months for castrating a member of the civil service. I'm on the move. Amsterdam, Berlin and the Germany-England game. I don't plan on getting nicked before I'm even out of the country. Fuck that. Don't plan on getting nicked at all. It's worth behaving because once we're across the Channel there's no more of your petty rules and regulations. No more Mr Nice Guy. Get to the Continent and that's it. The laws don't count over there because they're made by foreigners. Get out of England and you can do what you want.)

I smile some more. Cheek muscles starting to ache with the effort. Haven't smiled so much since that time me, Rod and Mark got done for a bit of puff he had in the car. Talk about taking the piss. The old bill stopped us because they said Rod didn't indicate. Load of bollocks. Luckily Rod was sober, and we're coming back from a Sunday drink and the old bill tug us because they want the easy life. Can't be bothered raiding Brixton crackhouses and tracking down serial rapists when everyone else is sitting down for their Sunday dinner or on their eighth pint in front of the pub satellite. Maybe they checked us on the computer or something, found out we all had previous, because they only go and charge us. I couldn't fucking believe it. Rod says we have to walk in the magistrate's court stoned. Take the piss. And that's what we did. I was grinning like I'd won the fucking lottery while this old boy's going on about the threat drugs pose to society – 'a very real and tangible threat, because what we must remember is that soft drugs can lead to harder drugs, and before society knows what's happening large sections of the community become ecstasy and heroin addicts, and that means a lowering of moral standards, inevitably resulting in unwanted pregnancies and a rapid increase in lawlessness'. The wanker in the pulpit stops for a breather and tells me to wipe that grin off my face or he'll charge me with contempt. You're not even allowed to smile these days. They take your taxes and all you get back is aggro.

But I'm being polite, that's all. Don't want to wind this

Customs bloke up. He's just doing his job. Flexing dead muscles as he drives the train to Auschwitz. No need for a row. I want to keep him sweet and get moving again. Enjoy myself and see the world. Because travelling with England is always a laugh, no matter who you're playing. Add a friendly in Berlin and the stage is set. I remember the man in front of me and his natural concern at the drugs waiting in Holland, all those unnatural substances pushed by subversive elements within the clog authorities.

– I'm not really into that sort of thing. I mean, each to their own and that, but I prefer a drink.

– A nice pint of real ale always goes down a treat.

– I drink lager myself.

He glares at the passport for a few seconds, then raises his head. He looks me in the eye all hurt, like he's about to burst out crying.

– Of course you do, Mr Johnson.

The man looks hurt. Real ale's the true English drink he says. Lager's just European gas and water mixed through EC filters.

I smile, all innocent. Not a care in the world. Chugging along. Wishing he'd give it a rest. Wishing he'd fuck off and bother some other cunt. His eyes are mean and there's sleep in the corner of the left socket. He's one of those sick sperms that should've been flushed away with the rubber, but instead hangs on under the rim growing in slime. Ends up in a uniform causing trouble. No wonder his missus spends her spare time getting gang-banged by football hooligans on the living-room carpet.

I hear the renegades from the train coming along behind me. Pissed on bottles of fuck-knows-what singing their heads off on the train from Liverpool Street. I don't reckon they'll get out of Harwich the way they're carrying on. Been at the cider probably. They look the sort. We could hear them in the next carriage and Brighty reckoned they were Black Country boys with their farmhand look. Facelift wanted to go and have a word because they were making a racket and he wasn't in the mood, a hangover lingering from last night. We laugh it off telling him to calm down. Take it easy. This is England on tour and you have to know your enemy. All that club stuff goes out the window – most of it, some of it – but it's his first time travelling with England so he's not to know. He's got a few things to sort out and it was the same for me first time I saw England play abroad. You turn up at Liverpool Street or wherever all lairy, but then you get moving and there's other clubs around, and you realise that it's all about people, that you're all basically the same but doing it in different places, that you're all English and patriotic and standing under the same flag. Somehow it works. Give it ten minutes and it makes sense. England, united, we'll never be defeated.

One of the Bully boys is wearing an England shirt. Asking for trouble. Big red face puffed up on the cider and a bottle of spirits, tattoos right up his arms. Covered thick so you can't make out the details. A Union Jack, young Noddy Holder face and several snakes mixing together under a layer of matted hair. He can't wait to get stuck into the duty-free this one. We only left London two hours ago and I'll be surprised if we see him in Berlin. The old bill will be on the look-out for English hooligans, and though we're a few days early the shirt gives the game away. But they're farmhands from the piggery and we're Chelsea boys and that bit smarter. We're taking it slow and easy. The old bill can do what they want and not let you on the ferry. Rights and wrongs don't come into it. Just keep your head down and think of those fräuleins waiting over the Channel. Legs wide open. I can't wait to get away and have some fun. To be honest, I'm sick of working in the warehouse day in, day out. The same old boozers and clubs. All the familiar faces. Same old birds. The football season's over and it gets boring when Chelsea aren't playing. I need a break from London and England, because then when you get back you love your life even better than before.

Some more coppers and Customs appear; smiling and rubbing their hands together. Thank you very much, thank you very very very much. Hurrying now towards Strongbow and his Steve Bull mates, so fucking excited they're almost running to the ice-cream van filling their trousers. Mr Drugs looks over my shoulder and he's not interested in Tom Johnson any more because he knows what to expect from the drunken scum coming his way. He reads his papers and studies his cartoons, and the sad fucker's probably even gone out and bought the fucking video. Replayed it a thousand times with his knob out and the missus banging him off – because here they come . . .

THE FAMOUS FOOTBALL HOOLIGANS.

He hands back my passport and says thank you Mr Johnson. Sorry to have bothered you sir. Enjoy your stay in Holland. He says Amsterdam is a beautiful city with canals and barges and tasty continental breakfasts. They serve fresh bread, ham, cheese and various jams. There's fine architecture that escaped the kind of bombing that wrecked the East End and levelled Coventry. That's what being pacifist does for you. The same goes for Paris. That's what cowardice does. Bunch of wankers the French. It's a private joke that shows unity. Before moving on to the pissheads he laughs and warns me not to overdo things in the bars. Watch those women of the night as well. He starts rambling suddenly saying those darkies are pure filth, getting worked up, pure jungle filth even though they come from Surinam and Indonesia, they'll do anything for a price, and I'm looking at the bloke and have to hold it back. I don't need this. Leave me alone. Just fuck off and leave me alone. He's doing my head in so I push past the cunt. Say nothing and hurry to catch up with Mark and the others. Fucking slag.

The old bill and Customs don't care about me now because they're moving in on the cider drinkers. These men in uniform are all self-important because they know what's what and they've got the intelligence, know their hooligans. Just shows you how intelligent these wankers really are because it's all boot boy vintage recordings. Black and white tabloid snapshots and archive news reels. Customs picking on a few drunks who, if they don't watch their step, are going to be spending their time in the local nick sobering up while the Expeditionary Force filters through and assembles in the half-lit skunk bars of Amsterdam. Hands forming Bomber Command goggles over our eyes, humming the *Dam Busters* tune. Have to laugh. Customs and the old bill. Stroppy cunts the lot of them.

★ ★ ★

8

Bob 'Harry' Roberts hated ferries and hated the sea. Thank fuck he lived in London and not some grim seaside town like Grimsby, where you went to school in clogs till you were eight then the elders sent you to work strapped to the mast of a ten-foot-long fishing boat. He saw himself standing there unable to move, frozen in time and a block of ice, brought back to life by Long John Silver. The captain was hobbling through the rigging with a blowtorch, the one-legged sea dog slicing Harry's ropes with his cutlass, the ancient mariner telling the young land-lubber he was free to go – stuck on a tug miles from shore. He was in the middle of a Force 10 gale helping the fisher folk drag in nets of mutant fish, a North Sea catch of three-eyed monsters, lights pulsating through orange scales, chemical stew boiling under the waves. The young Harry was working through the night to earn enough for a loaf of Hovis. He hummed the tune from the commercial all the way up the fucking hill, past rows of cobbled streets and steaming horse shit. He didn't fancy life in a northern fishing community. It was grim in the North. Give him London any day.

Harry went back to the day Chelsea travelled to Grimsby and won the Second Division championship with a 1–0 victory, Kerry Dixon scoring the goal. They hadn't seen many fishing boats that particular Saturday, and maybe there weren't any steep hills, but never mind, because he'd been pissed like everyone else after a session in Lincoln. Pissed or sober, it was a day he'd never forget. They'd had tickets for the seats, but ended up on the terraces as the organisation inside the ground broke down, Chelsea mobbing the place. No-one was com-plaining, because Dixon, Nevin and Speedie were leading the charge back to the First Division and it looked like they had a team that was going to bring back the glory days, though the old bill had to go and bring on the horses at the end to show how fucking clever they were. Silly cunts almost started a riot. It was magic, getting promoted to the First Division after nearly going broke and down to the Third. They'd spent the night in Chesterfield, in a big pub packed with Chelsea drinking the place dry. There was no aggro, because the coaches often stopped there on the way back from games and everything was friendly enough. They'd had a good laugh chatting up the local girls, Harry and Balti and those Slough boys, the two Garys, Benny with his Crossroads hat. The pub had a late licence and turned into a disco, and they'd had their guts out on the dancefloor like some select firm as the DJ played old singalong Gary Glitter and Slade numbers. There must've been two or three hundred Chelsea in that pub alone and not so much as a broken glass. Funny how it worked. Mind you, there'd been a big punch-up on Morecambe Pier that night, so it was luck of the draw.

They'd had a drink with some striking Chesterfield miners, and he remembered being surprised they were so different from the tabloid pin-ups. He'd always pictured the miners in hobnailed boots and red crash helmets, and there they were, ordinary everyday blokes out for a pint on Saturday night, having a laugh. He'd got talking with these two punks and they were giving him the story on what was happening in the coalfields. He'd listened but not really heard what they were saying. Harry laughed. They were so pissed they'd got the wrong coach back to London and ended up on the North Circular somewhere around Willesden. It was a long trek home at four in the morning because no cab was going to pick them up with their cropped hair and green flight-jackets. Now he was older and wiser and enjoying an easy life in the Premiership. Wreck the old rundown grounds and the club chairmen rewarded you with brand new seats, burger bars and sponsor's lager on tap. Crime definitely paid.

The crossing to the Hook was going to be a nightmare. Harry could feel it in his gut. It was going to be six hours of pure fucking misery. Six hours crouched over a shit-stained bog with the boat rocking from side to side, piss running along the floor soaking his jeans. There was never any paper and always some wanker who had to start banging on the door. He needed a drink to settle his nerves, so broke off from the rest of the boys and headed for the bar, telling Carter to hurry up before the place was packed. He needed some Dutch courage, some Heineken, heading down the steps but stopping in his tracks when Carter said the bar wouldn't open till the ferry was out to sea. It was written down in the rules somewhere, so sorry Harry you fat bastard, you'll have to wait.

Harry shrugged and they went out on deck to get some fresh air and watch the ferry load. He was beginning to wish he'd gone the long way round and taken Eurostar, but then he'd be travelling alone and that wouldn't be much fun. If you were going to be on your own you might as well stay at home in front of the telly. He didn't fancy the tunnel and it would probably be more expensive. He didn't fancy an IRA bomb under his carriage or another fire. Whatever way he got to Europe, though, it was worth the aggravation. Harry had been to Spain, Portugal, Belgium and France, and he'd liked them all. He enjoyed the extended drinking and the food, the clean streets and laid-back manner. There was a different attitude somehow, even if it was only what you saw as an outsider. Probably if he lived in Lisbon or somewhere similar and he was decorating houses like he did in London, then the fumes would smell the same and there'd be all the usual problems, but that was why you went away in the first place. If the language was different it meant you had a breather from all the propaganda being pumped your way through the media. It was a break from the non-stop doom and gloom. A big plate of paella and a nice jug of sangria and Harry was happy. That's all you needed in life. Food and drink and a decent shag every so often.

The European birds were sound as well, though the Spanish and Portuguese didn't seem to get out much. Mind you, the Belgians were a bit scruffy and the French stuck-up, but he liked the accents all the same. That's what made them attractive, the accents. Give a half-decent bird a European accent and he could feel his knob stirring before she'd finished the first sentence. He was turning over a new leaf on this trip and going back to square one. He was sticking with Carter the unstoppable sex machine, and picking up a few tips. Carter would be dabbling non-stop and Harry reasoned that if he followed the bloke like a shadow he could pick up the leftovers. He was the apprentice boy marching with the grand master. He'd learn from Carter and shag his way across Europe. The rest of the lads, Tom and Mark and that, they were more into the aggro side of things, but while Harry didn't mind that part of the national identity, he needed some sex. His bollocks were aching, down round his knees. If he stuck close to Carter he'd be alright. Holland and Germany wouldn't know what hit them and the girls had better be ready for the road show. He was looking forward to Europe, but London would always be his home.

Thinking of London, Harry felt the first tingle of homesickness. He couldn't believe it. They hadn't even set sail. Right now he'd be coming in from work, running the bath, putting the kettle on, sticking his kebab and chips in the oven, getting in the water and washing the paint and wallpaper paste off, out and dry, putting clean clothes on and stacking his work gear in the corner of his bedroom. Then with his mouth watering he'd be back in the kitchen buttering the bread and pouring boiling water into his Chelsea mug, covering the tea bag, adding milk and sugar and taking everything into the living room with the kebab and chips on a plate, using a knife to push the chilli sauce back over the meat and salad, sitting there all ready to go with his mouth watering and his arms feeling good from the roller, fucking starving after a long day grafting for West London Decoration, the kebab meat steaming with the chilli sauce and peppers, the chips piping hot, salt and vinegar on the tray ready to go, a beautiful mix of smells, sitting there ready to go and – FUCKING HELL – the remote was on the telly. So Harry would put everything aside and go for the remote control, hitting the On button and running through the channels till he found the news for some easy entertainment. He'd sit back at last and enjoy the full experience, getting stuck into the food with TV images of Protestants and Catholics in Belfast, Spanish fishermen nicking the English catch, and finally, just before the sport, news of a ferry sinking off the Philippines. Harry was digging into the kebab, sipping his tea, waiting for the football slot and a couple of minutes of gossip before the weather. The new weatherman was a weatherwoman with a nice pair of tits ruined by a BBC accent that promised a violent storm at sea. Ferries were sailing at their own risk. He almost choked on the kebab and swore. He should've guessed.

★ ★ ★

I catch up with Mark and he wants to know what Customs were on about. I tell him it's nothing personal. He wants to know if they've got me on record as part of some Dutch porno ring, dealing in kids and freaks. Rumanian orphans and drugged English teenyboppers. Limbless grannies and two-headed pygmies. I hate all that stuff and tell him he's a sick cunt. Tell him to fuck off. Child-molesters are the lowest brand of scum and I know Mark agrees, because when he was inside he gave this nonce a serious hiding. Wouldn't have cared if he'd killed the bloke. Long as he didn't get done for the murder. The telly says all the nonces are working overtime on their computers, hiding in Amsterdam wanking over the Internet. Dregs of Europe pulled to the magnet of a liberal society. Maybe the England boys will wreck the place as a taster and show the Dutch that it's worth maintaining standards. That it pays to fight back now and again. Stand up for what you believe in. An eye for an eye and a tooth for a tooth. There's no need to stand around trying to analyse scum like that.

Harris is already in Amsterdam and the word going round is that Berlin is going to be major. It's all there at the right time because you're not going to find many blokes on this trip who agree with the way England's being ripped apart by Europe. None of us wants to be ordered about by Berlin. That's what the last war was about. It's all big business and laws coming in through the back door. Not that I believe in our legal system being the best in the world, because that's bollocks. Anyone who's dealt with the English legal system knows it's run by the rich, for the rich. The only ones who believe that shit about being innocent till proven guilty are the people who never go outside their front door. Upbringing decides your fate. Commit the same crime and your accent says whether you get ten years or an apology. It's fucking mental thinking, though, that some cunt in another country can tell us what to do. It's bad enough having some jumped-up wanker telling you what to do in your own language, but who wants the lecture in German and French as well?

The politicians are all traitors. Keeping us in the dark, doing what they want. Just like they've always done. Berlin is pulling a lot of things in at the same time and when we get over to Europe nobody's telling us lot anything. We don't need an excuse for a riot. Don't need an excuse to go on a two-day bender in Amsterdam. We'll see if the Dutch can get a mob together. Don't know much about them to be honest, but Ajax have the F-Side and there's some Chelsea boys who've added Feyenoord to Glasgow Rangers as an extra interest. Widening their scope with things so tight in England these days.

Mind you, the idea of Amsterdam is more about sitting back and watching the world pass. It's not so much that the dope's legal, I mean that's common sense, but there's this atmosphere about the place that can calm you right down if you're not careful. Suppose we shouldn't stay around too long or we'll lose the edge. But that goes to show you what's wrong at home. Imagine us getting nicked for a bit of blow on a Sunday afternoon down the Great West Road when we're minding our own business, not hurting anyone. Thing is, the cunts in charge have got no bollocks. Those Crown Court duffers you can understand, because they live in another world – another fucking planet – with their livers burnt out on gin and tonic and their brains rotting from heavy-duty clap. Diseases they picked up in Asia and Africa during the days of the Empire. Filling all the hospital beds and demanding hanging for some fifteen-year-old kid flogging Es down the local youth club. Hang the boy and cut him down, then hang him again while the judge spurts off. All because the boy's selling some happiness that doesn't come in a bottle. Heavy drinking Empire administrators propped up in their hospital beds, packed in with heavy-smoking cancer victims. I mean, I don't care either way if they want to kill themselves, but it makes you think. It's all double standards. Let us drink twenty-four hours a day, take whatever other drugs we want, turn off the surveillance cameras, and England's the perfect place to raise kids. It's the best country in the world.

– What do you reckon on them over there, Mark asks, when we've caught up with the others. Look like West Ham to me.

I clock the blokes queueing for food. They look like West Ham well enough. Can spot them a mile off. The badge the tall one's wearing gives the game away. I know Mark holds a grudge when it comes to West Ham, his old man getting a slap outside Upton Park when he was a kid. They were fucking wankers doing that to a bloke taking his boy across London to watch a game of football.

– I've seen them at England games before. Outside The Globe before Holland during Euro 96.

Not that we spent much time down Baker Street. The place gets too packed and then everyone goes for the tube at the same time. The trains can't handle the crush and there's always some wanker who pulls the emergency lever, starts fucking about with the doors or mouthing off at the old bill. You're standing there waiting to move and the old bill aren't going to take any verbal off some pisshead when they've got the numbers and are on overtime. This is their big day out, so reinforcements are called in and they make everyone suffer for The Bad Old Days when the hooligans made their lives hell. No, we prefer drinking round St John's Wood and Kilburn. If we're playing someone fruity then we might even go down the ground and use one of the pubs there if the old bill are all over the trains. But the foreigners never bring a firm over. Where were the Dutch and Germans during Euro 96?

It's funny, though, because in the build-up the papers, radio and television were crying over the security situation, creaming themselves like the Customs and judges. Bunch of wankers the media. Mindless cunts saying how they couldn't understand the mentality of the men who were going to defend their country. They couldn't understand it, but fucking loved the idea all the same. Right-wing, left-wing and no-wing, every social commentator was earning a crust writing stupid articles and presenting self-righteous reports. Preaching double standards. Bleating through the airwaves while we were laughing at them, because everyone knew the Europeans wouldn't show. Just send their mums and dads and happy families over. Keep their own heads down. Makes you laugh sitting there reading the articles about the media's major love, Nazis. They can't leave it alone. The ignorance is unbelievable. And then you've got the old bill raring to go, because we don't want any nasty business, do we son? Everyone has to have an enemy.

– I fucking hate West Ham, Facelift says, nice and loud.

I look at the Dagenham cockneys again, but they don't react. Didn't hear or don't want to know. Too busy drinking in Barking and making plans in Gant's Hill, telling everyone how wonderful East London is now they're living in Essex. Chelsea always have a bit more class, tying up Kent, Surrey, Berks. Knowing the Happy Hammers, Facelift was out of range, because there's enough of them for a row. Fair enough. But Facelift has to realise the rules are different. You can't go away with England if you're kicking seven shades of shit out of each other the whole way. And another thing, we're on a ferry and you've got to behave when you're on a boat. If it kicks off on the ferry we'll be turning round and going straight back to Harwich. It's simple really. Doesn't take a lot of brains to work that one out. You're a sitting duck waiting for the Luftwaffe to blow you out of the water. Thing is, you get all these blokes who're ready to go, been looking forward to the trip for months, and they get on the boat and they can't fucking wait. Soon as they get on the train the cans come out and they're on the piss. We haven't even got out of the port yet and Facelift is acting the cunt. Could be a liability and I've never been sure about the bloke. You have to watch someone who glasses his own brother-in-law over a game of fucking snooker.

I can just see Customs and the old bill lining the pier ready to welcome us home after the ferry gets wrecked. The media circus tipped off for some special-edition moral outrage, running on about the English Disease and our rich history. Harping back to The Good Old Days when hooligans ruled the waves and sunk their ferries before they'd thought about getting off. That's the way those wankers see things anyway. You have to grin and carry on regardless. Work your way round things these days instead of going straight through the middle. I don't want to eat, so me and Mark piss off to the bar. Leave Facelift to make his own decisions.

– I'll have a word with Facelift, Mark says on the way. He's got to wait till we're in Holland before he starts anything.

I nod and we're thinking the same way. Great minds. We pass through the ranks of the brain dead. Guidebook tourists and confused travellers walking round in small circles. Hands on the shoulders of the zapped-out zombie in front. Worrying about their luggage. Bothered by the exchange rate and rip-off commission. They can't wait for the single currency to arrive so they can save a few pence changing their pounds to guilders, and then watch the price rocket on everything else. We have to skirt past these people and I wonder why they don't go and jump over the side. Hundreds of lemmings following the basket case in front all the way to the till. Follow the leader over the rails and into the deep blue sea.

– It's shut, Mark says. The fucking bar's shut.

The grille's pulled down and there's no sign of a barman. There's a few old boys standing around with light in their eyes and a hurt look on their faces. They need a drink after the coach down from Macclesfield.

– Let's go outside and have a wander.

– Like kids on a school outing, crossing the Channel and seeing the foreign port and supermarket, then coming straight back home again. Back in time for tea.

– I don't remember that.

– We never went on those trips, but that's what the kids get now. They get all the privileges.

We work our way through another herd of passengers moving at one mile an hour, out of their heads on Prozac, dumping our bags in the luggage store as we go. Squeezing through spotty teenagers and arguing couples. A baby starts crying. We push through the doors and get a face full of fresh sea breeze mixed in with what smells like oil. We pass along the side of the ferry and up some steps to a deck where we can see the port better. Pulling on the rails, feeling old rain on flaked paint. The Unity boys are there already and we go over. We drink in the same pub, and every time I'm in there these blokes are sitting by the window with their mates, on the piss. I know them from football so it's a double barrel. Fat Harry and Terry.

– I don't think those Brummies are going to get on, Harry says.

– Serves them right, Mark laughs, looking over to where a police van stands with its light rolling. You can't expect to arrive pissed like that and not attract some attention. Definitely not these days. It's up to them how they handle it, whether they behave and keep their mouths shut or start pissing about.

Harry laughs and nods. I like the bloke. He's alright. A big bastard with a heart. Terry too. Less heart, but sharper. They're a few years older and wiser. Terry's a bit of a Romeo as well and always on the pull. Listen to Harry and the others, and they reckon it's all dog meat, but I've seen him with some nice enough fanny through the years. Harry can drink any of us under the table and he's got the gut to prove it. He hasn't really been the same since his best mate got murdered. Another Chelsea boy from the pub. Head blown off by his old foreman. We went down to Balham and helped sort the cunt out several months before the killing. You never know where those things are going to end I suppose.

– It's manners, says Harry. It's the new way. Never mind, though, because it means there's more room for the rest of us. There'll be more Dutch birds going spare.

We see the Brummies being dragged along by the old bill. Another van arrives with its siren off so's not to upset the happy tourists. But it's hurrying all the same. Can just see the driver all pumped up at the thought of battering some football hooligans. The Brummies have probably got mouthy with the coppers and that's all the excuse the old bill need. It's honest in a way, telling the police to fuck off, but it only gets you in trouble. Where's the sense in that? There again, the old bill don't need an excuse. Strongbow is struggling like only a drunk struggles and he's got four coppers on him. They pull him into the van and crack his head on the door, the Bully boy bouncing back and the old bill trying again. A little harder this time. Head thumping metal panels and the body spilling into the van. All accidental of course, the fucking wankers.

– Fucking scum, says Terry. There's no need for that.

The back door slams shut and a tall copper thumps the side of the van. He's tall and thin and loves the power. The brown dirt cowboy at the controls puts his foot down and speeds off. It's pathetic. Thinks he's in The Bill or something. Things like that make you hate the cunts.

– Don't worry, we'll make up for all that when we get to Holland, says Mark.

Everyone nods. We all want the holiday and the chance to take out some frustration on the Europeans. We want the trip abroad. A nice break from the daily grind. Change as good as a rest.

Mark and Tom hung around for a while watching Harwich grind along, hung about till they got bored and said they were going inside to wait for the bar to open. Carter fancied a drink and went with them. There was nothing new to see on deck and he'd rather be watching the crumpet pass than a load of sweaty sailors. Harry was settled into his seat and enjoying the view. The others didn't understand, didn't appreciate the finer points. He wanted to stay where he was until they set sail. He wanted the full holiday experience and maximum value for money. There was some drizzle falling and the wind was picking up, but Harry liked the idea of sitting on deck till they got out to sea. It was good to be alone sometimes. He watched the lads walk away, heads turning for a girl in a short skirt and plastic mac. She was well dirty and Harry wondered if he was being clever letting the sex machine out of his sight.

Carter was probably off to pick up some sort and give her a portion in the luggage room, while the other two would get hold of one of the satellite town pearly kings in the canteen and set him on fire. They'd chuck the burning Iron over the side for the port authorities to fish out, killing time till the bar opened and they could have a decent drink, Carter in the top rack behind the bags of tea and I ♥ LONDON T-shirts servicing some Danish au pair who'd come to England and fallen in love with the bulldog breed. Fucked off with Copenhagen she'd gone to London looking for adventure. She was searching for the bulldog spirit, with Carter breeding in the top rack doing her doggy style, keeping their voices down so they didn't upset the other passengers. Imagine that. Mr and Mrs Rotterdam pulling a bag of dildos down and seeing a wide-eyed English hooligan shafting a Danish beauty queen. They probably wouldn't be all that bothered and take it in their stride, select a Dark Destroyer from the bag and disappear into the Ladies. The Dutch were a funny lot. Not like your Middle England couple who'd be narked they were missing out on the fun and call someone in a uniform to break things up. Pull those two apart steward and give them a good caning.

Harry turned and looked over the cars and lorries waiting to load, drivers held back by the barriers getting impatient, juggernauts narked they were losing precious time, all of them wanting to get on a free stretch of road and accelerate into the sunset. Funny how they called it Harwich International, like it was going to compete with Heathrow. He scanned dead grey buildings and oversized ships, passing through stacked containers and packed coaches. The containers were packed with rockets, and the coaches held rows of holiday-makers dreaming of Stockholm and Venice and Prague. Harry was glad of the break, but wouldn't really start enjoying himself till touch down in Holland. This was the worst part of the journey, crossing the English Channel, because Harry had a problem with ferries. He always got sick when he went to sea.

Joking apart, he was glad he wasn't in the Grimsby fleet or the Royal Navy. He wouldn't have lasted ten minutes. Those blokes in the old days who popped out for a pint and got lumbered with twenty years on the high seas definitely lived at the wrong time. The poor bastards put their coats on and went down the pub to meet their mates, and then when they're wandering home feeling good about life, glad to see the missus and check the kids, maybe get their leg over, then the fucking press-gang steams in and gives them a kicking, and next thing they're waking up on the way to Jamaica. That kind of thing was bang out of order and it made you think about how the men themselves felt. Wife and kids left to get on with things while Dad was forced into a life of rum, sodomy and the lash, but because it was so long ago it became some sort of joke. Nobody cared about the feelings of those men. You could put up gravestones and carve names and dates to last five hundred years, write books about the admirals even, but Joe Public was history as well. The difference was the unmarked grave. Another skeleton at the bottom of the ocean.

Harry had been a dreamer most of his life, rolling along and trying to work out the future, and it had taken the death of his mate Balti to bring home a few truths. It made him stop and look at the world. There was no place for dreams and soppy ideas. The bloke had been dead less than two years and already people were forgetting him. Not really forgetting him, it was more like he now belonged to some other story. The memory wasn't alive. That's what it was. The memory was stacked away with all the others. It was like it didn't make any difference whether Balti had ever lived. He was now known as that geezer from the pub who liked his drink, football and curries, and who'd got his head blown off by some mad old Paddy from South London. If that was all there was to show for all those years of life, then it was seriously fucking sad. It wasn't the drink, football and curries, because that was fair enough, but those were the things he did, not what he thought. Everyone said he was a good bloke, and that was important, but the memory had to stay alive. They'd forget he was a decent bloke and go back to the drink, football, curries line. That's what everyone did in the end.

Harry could hear the crew shouting to each other. The ferry was getting ready to leave and a lot of people were going to be left behind. They were impatient and angry because the system was failing them. The boat was full and the electronic board was passing on the message. Digital displays relayed the information in thin streaks of light. It was too bad. He watched the passengers around him, most of them leaning over the railings. They spoke different languages and this brought back his first thrill of going over the Channel. The boat was moving slowly and he realised the sheer size of the hull, looking back over the railyard and storage zones. Harwich did its job and nothing more. It was a gateway and didn't have time to sit still. The worker ants came and did their jobs, some of them getting to go to sea on the boats, while Customs looked out for drug smugglers and vans full of hardcore porn, checking the containers coming in from all over Europe and parts of the

Middle East, looking for that major heroin haul, the illegal guns and explosives, unwanted immigrants and asylum seekers.

There was no beauty in the place and Harry looked further along the coast, past half-hidden pubs and hotels, noticing the change of scene, the boat slow to move then gathering speed, the English coastline broadening fast as the people and buildings on the shore got smaller, shrinking as the view widened, the incredible shrinking nation, cities spilling into green fields, the ferry pushing out to sea until the first proper waves came through, deeper troughs that told you it was real, that the Channel was deep and dangerous, Harry hearing somewhere that the seas around Britain had claimed more than a million lives since records began. He tried to get his head round the figure. He wanted to make the most of this trip and had forgotten about being sick. He tried thinking of a million skeletons under the water without the headstone Balti's mum had put on her son's grave. The island race buried at sea.

Harry was looking forward and leaving Balti in the past, dead and at peace. He was crossing the Channel and when he came back it was going to be a fresh start. He wanted to get stuck into the birds in Amsterdam and hoped he could pull something nice, but if not he was straight down the red light and splashing out. With Carter at his side he was feeling lucky. He would watch and learn and try to repeat the bullshit the sex machine used. Everyone who ever went to Holland always came back with stories of the blow they'd smoked and the whores they'd fucked. It sounded good to Harry, because he hadn't got his leg over since Balti was killed. He'd been drinking more than usual and things were building up. He'd been getting so pissed when they went out that he couldn't speak halfway through the night, let alone chat up a woman. When he got to Amsterdam he'd get himself a right little cracker and fuck the arse off her. If it was a prossie he'd give her the best shag she'd get that night.

He started feeling better already. Mind you, he didn't really want to pay for the business. He'd prefer a nice Dutch bird who worked in a shop selling clothes rather than sex. Someone who wanted him for his personality – well, not his personality, but maybe a drink and a laugh. It didn't matter. He had to be realistic because the future was never going to be that rosy and he'd have to make sure he didn't get too pissed. He'd take a rubber along and remember to protect himself in the red light district. He didn't want to die young. He wanted to see what happened next. Get everything in order and see where things were leading.

Balti hadn't left a will, though in truth there wasn't much to leave. There were his clothes, and those went to the jumble, because no way was Harry walking about in a dead man's jeans and trainers. There were some odds and ends, a few records and CDs, a broken record player, a small pile of Chelsea programmes from when Balti was a kid. There wasn't a lot really, but then Balti hadn't had much, and towards the end he'd been skint and signing on. Just playing the lottery trying to get a lucky break, and imagine that . . . if he'd won and left Harry a fortune. He'd pocket the millions and buy himself the best whorehouse in Holland. He'd be Harry the Pimp and get himself a zoot suit and smoke Havana cigars, do his old mate proud. He was feeling positive. He used to dream at nights but now he was sleeping straight through. Death had blown everything away. What was the point of mights and maybes when you could die in the street in a pool of blood? He was going to live his life right and stick with Carter. Terry didn't bother thinking too much. He got on with the job and concentrated his attention on getting his end away.

There's different kinds of holidays. Different away days. Different ways to go. Following England is all about pride and history. Our place in the pecking order. For centuries we've been kicking shit out of the Europeans. They start something and we finish it. We're standing on the White Cliffs of Dover singing COME AND HAVE A GO IF YOU THINK YOU'RE HARD ENOUGH. Waiting for the Germans to get the bottle together and cross the Channel. Fifty English will run two hundred or more Europeans no problem. A thousand if you're talking Italians or Spanish. I'm proud to be English and proud to say so. This Germany game is a chance to escape the prison football at home and flex some muscle, because however hard the foreigners try to control us when we get on their soil they don't have a chance.

It's all in the head. In the genes. We've got this stubborn streak. We hang on and don't let go. They can't beat us. We know it and they know it as well, deep down inside. Where it hurts. We're winners. They can send in their riot squads and fire their tear gas and, if it's Luxembourg, they can even call out the army, but we just don't care. We're English, and if there's any slack then our drunks will walk through foreign borders with their jeans round their ankles, taking the piss. Flashing the forty-inch bust at the passport desk. The Europeans don't know how to handle us. They can do the mass arrests and that, try it on, corner someone in a back street and batter the fuck out of them. Try and crack your spine and open your skull. But still the English carry on, full steam ahead. That kind of pain's skin deep, though now and then they go overboard and you have to watch yourself. They take things too seriously and target someone. Try to cripple him. It comes with the landscape.

Thing is, they pull out all the stops, give it their best shot, and what happens? If they're waiting at the border we tread lightly because we're no mugs. We pick our spot and then when it goes off we keep coming back for more. The English have been rioting in Europe for well over twenty years, and that's just the football. Your Italian and Spanish old bill can't get their heads round it. They're used to dealing with the ultras of Juventus and Real Madrid. Holding seminars and printing scarves. That's why we won the war. No surrender. Get beaten to a pulp by a mob of spics and back you come before the wounds have healed. And because of what's happened you're worse than before. The mad dogs just get meaner.

If this game wasn't on I'd be spending my time somewhere else. In a Spanish or Greek resort taking things easy after the domestic season. On the pull shagging anything that moves. Cutting through the stereotypes servicing every brand of decent-looking English woman available. No-nonsense spunk-lovers from London and the Home Counties; the factory workers from Liverpool and barmaids from Newcastle; the officer girls from Leeds and johnny-sellers from Bristol; the shop assistants from Manchester and unemployed goths from Norwich. Then I'll be showing a healthy interest in foreign culture with the roving Morvern nutters of Scotland, the religious Orange Order girls of Northern Ireland and the Merthyr miners' daughters of Wales. Showing no prejudice and moving forward to the fish-slicers of Oslo and strippers of Munich and nurses of Vienna. Women are the best thing God invented. His greatest idea letting me sit on a Spanish beach watching the girls pass by during the afternoon, then slipping them a length at three in the morning. Now that's another kind of holiday.

It's an easy break where you don't have to do much work. Give it some bollocks and empty them inside the hour. Wander the clubs and bars putting up with the tinny music they play. Weaving in and out of the wankers lining the pavement talking through their arses. No need to go overboard. Taking things nice and steady. Keeping yourself together. Maintaining standards. Looking to get some bird on your knob by the end of the night. At first keeping a tab, but losing track when it gets boring. The same old words and the same old cunts. No challenge and no danger. Still, what else is there, because then you start looking forward to the mornings when you get up early and have a swim. The weather's fine and there's a buffet breakfast waiting, and you're having a laugh with Pedro the Barcelona fan. Tell him you know his brother Manuel. You do your duty and get your money's worth. Along to the pool for a couple of hours in the sun watching the bird you shagged last night up against the back wall of Del Boy's London Bar try and stroll past, too embarrassed to say hello. So you yell out alright Kim? She turns and goes red but seems keen. You give her the once over and she's not as fresh as last night. You've shot your wad up her so you let the small talk fade. She goes her way, you go yours. Straight in the pool. Have a swim. Mark and Rod awake now. Same old stories. Gets more boring day by day. Concrete blocks and formation palms. Chicken dinners and flat lager. Everyone pissing in the pool.

Then you've been there nearly a week and you're cranking up inside. You see the Munich boys in a bar across the road and start getting lairy. Feel the energy coming up. Keeping it back.

Taking your time. Those wankers across the road in their shitty megastore gear. You know it's going to kick off because you look at your mates standing around fucked off by the routine and they're feeling the same way. Want to take it easy, but need some excitement. The Munich boys aren't the real Munich. They're not your old-time Stretford Enders, just Premiership playboys. More into their club-sponsored clothes than a cold midweek game in Leeds. You have some respect for the Red Army, but these wankers make you laugh. Getting wound up looking at the slags giving it the big one with the women. Their own little world. Don't go to games half these cunts even though they've got all the gear and mouth.

But before you get anywhere there's a row on your own doorstep with some fucking yids at the bar. Can't believe it. Tottenham right next to you and you didn't even see the cunts. Taking the piss or what? Looking at the bloke two feet away with the side of his face sliced open, a neat cut from the bottle Mark's holding with blood spouting out of his face and you stand back looking at the fountain and, to be honest, it's not pretty. Bit naughty really. The Spurs holiday-makers come through and you don't have time to think about the ifs and buts, because you dodge back and smack some cunt in the head as he swings pissed and out of control on the old dodgems of life. Kick him in the top of the head twice and stroll away singing HE GOES TO THE BAR, TO BUY A LAGER, AND ONLY BUYS ONE FOR HIMSELF, leaving one cut, one twitching, and three more bruised and helping their mates. Nothing personal you fucking cunts, passing the Munich fashion dolls hiding now inside the bar. Cunts. Give us some Cockney Reds and we might even let them buy us a drink.

Different holidays for different things. Go to a resort and you're looking for a nice line of slappers flat on their backs. Leaning forward over the railings of the tenth floor balcony as you give that Nottingham bird with the tiny nipple-sized tits an oil change. Watching rockets explode, flashing orange and red sparks over the tourist tower blocks. Looking over the landscape of Cliff Richard's summer holiday nightmare. Cheap food and drink. Forget the music because it's shit and you take your own.

Play the cassettes in your room or by the pool. Wind the wankers up. That's the seaside in Spain, but go away with England and the whole thing's ten times better. Resorts are more sex and football's more violence. England away's sex and violence if you play your cards right, but the aggro comes first. Least that's how I see things, though Carter and Harry would list the birds first. Sex and violence are what we're good at. Right through England, from top to bottom, through the centuries, it's sex and violence all the way. The Cross of St George drenched in blood and spunk. Putting some bollocks in the Union Jack.

Look at your politicians and it's all there. It's the power trip. Sex gives them the power because they can pay some poor girl to do anything they want. They're in charge. Even the old cunts you read about who want to get whipped and tied up with barbed wire. They're still paying for the service, letting the tension run loose. It's their big treat. The violence, though, that's a bit different, because when they're mixing it up with the sex they can pay for that as well, but when there's no sex angle they don't fancy getting involved. Not personally anyway. They want the thrill but have to pay someone on their behalf, so fork out for their men in uniforms – the old bill, army, what have you. They want the control. Violence is allowed when they say so. Pass a law and it's on their terms, mixing in the power, while the trendy cunts want it in their films and documentaries. They want to sit in a circle discussing it through the night, throwing in their minority views and filling it with meaning, never going anywhere. Trying to settle their own grievances. Boring fuckers clogging the channels when you want a good horror film.

Sex and violence. Everyone loves it, because that's where the excitement comes. You don't have to confuse the two. It's what made us great. We move in on the women and they can't resist. We kick fuck out of anyone who has a go at us. The English are fair and square, and by English I mean your everyday bloke like me and Mark, and Rod as well if he wasn't a sad married cunt. People like Harry and Carter and Brighty and Facelift. Don't know about Facelift. We're hard but fair. That's the English. No pretence or pissing about, because what you see is what you get, standing outside the duty-free talking with a couple of Man City fans, old-time Kippax we know from before. They're eyeing up the rows of fags, spirits, choccies, wondering out loud whether there's any scousers on board, or maybe ICJ. Looking to fill their pockets. Mark tells them it's the yids who'd go for the instant thieving even though they're stuck on a ferry. Can't wait. We all laugh. Funny how it works.

We were in this bar in Paris one trip, making do paying over the odds drinking frog piss water, real shitty drink. Makes you wonder why all the Latin countries have piss for beer. They're all the same. I've been to Italy, Spain, France and all these cunts are the same, serving shit bottled lager. The more you pay the worse it is, and some of the England boys even end up drinking the local wine it's so bad. There's always one or two blokes who get stuck into the wine like it's lager. Drink gallons of the stuff and go mental. But in Paris there was over a hundred English from all over the country packed into this one bar doing their best to force the piss down. Lots of different clubs drinking and having a sing-song, making the most of life because the French were nowhere to be seen. Then out of nothing the bar starts singing SPURS ARE ON THEIR WAY TO AUSCHWITZ. We were cracking up laughing because it shows how everyone hates Spurs. Thing was, there was this big skinhead looking a bit embarrassed and the bloke's only a fucking yid. Well, not a yid as in Jew, but yid as in Tottenham. Harris was patting him on the head telling him not to worry, and the Stevenage skin was saying you've got it wrong, it's not all yiddos at White Hart Lane, I hate those Star of Davids like the rest of you, I'm an Anglo-Saxon. World turned upside down with nothing in its right place.

We go for a wander and catch up with Billy and Facelift. We spot some of the Pompey boys and have a chat. Old faces from England trips. Original 657 Crew with a few younger lads tagging along. Everything's mush and Millwall and scummers. Wonder who they hate most, Millwall or Southampton? They've got their ensign flag with them and it seems everyone's plotting the same route through Amsterdam. This is the early arrivals on the ferry, because give it a day or two and the boats will be packed with England. We're getting the march on the rest of the boys and it's going to be a good turn out. We head for the bar. At least the Dutch and Germans know how to brew decent lager.

Bill Farrell ordered a pint of bitter and walked over to his usual seat. He lowered himself into the chair and, once he was settled, took a mouthful of beer. He was drinking Directors and savoured the taste. Two or three pints was his limit these days. His legs were a little stiff, but apart from that he was fit for his age. His working life in a local park had served him well. He'd always drunk bitter and The Unity served a decent pint. He'd used the pub for the last three years since moving up the road from Hounslow to be nearer his daughter, and the beer was always good. He'd drunk in The Unity years ago, when visiting his brother who had lived locally. It was strange to think they'd drunk in this same pub as young men. He'd been coming in The Unity, on and off, for more than half a century. The secret of a good pint of bitter was clean pipes, and successive landlords had maintained standards.

He put the jug down, opened his paper and began reading. He was soon lost in one of the main features, only raising his head when Bob West entered the pub. The younger man nodded, checked Mr Farrell's glass, and went to the bar, ordering a pint of Tennent's from Denise. She smiled as she poured and asked Bob whether he wanted his usual plain crisps, or perhaps he fancied cheese and onion today. It was a joke they shared and Bob said he'd wait. He asked Denise if she'd like a drink and she said thanks, but it was okay. She knew he wasn't flush and appreciated the offer. She didn't normally drink when she was working anyway. Bob paid and went over to Farrell, asking if he could share the table.

– Of course you can, Farrell smiled. There's plenty of room.

Bill Farrell didn't mind the company one way or the other. He'd only become friendly with Bob West over the last few months. He'd known who Bob was, of course, and that the younger man had served as a pilot in the Gulf, but until recently they'd never spoken. He'd assumed Bob was keeping himself to himself, but the younger man had turned out to be a friendly enough character. He wasn't well, and it was only recently the Government had admitted there could possibly be something called Gulf War Syndrome. Bob had problems with his breathing and suffered from mood swings. He'd be down in the dumps and told Farrell he felt he was falling into a hole, where his part in the conflict no longer seemed real. His memory was becoming distorted and sometimes he imagined he was nothing more than one of the graphic air-force rangers flashing on the games machine in the corner of the pub. He had fought and most certainly killed, yet felt removed from the experience. He was imagining all sorts of things these days. His brain was running wild and he didn't enjoy the faces it was conjuring up. There was an initial excitement and blazing colour, but this soon vanished and was replaced by a prolonged, numbing horror. The faces were black and charred, the skulls clearly visible.

Coming back to London and signing on had been a huge culture shock for West. He'd dedicated his life to the RAF, thereby fulfilling his childhood dream and following in the footsteps of the Spitfire pilots who'd saved the country during the Battle of Britain. These men were his heroes and he'd tried to match their achievements. He passed the tests, trained hard and travelled the world. It had been a good life, disciplined and exciting, but now he'd come full circle and was back in London living three streets from where he was born. Every morning on his way to the cornershop for a carton of milk he passed the school he went to as a kid. He had been one of the élite and now he was a dole queue number. From the steak dinners and post-raid comradeship of Saudi to beans on toast and life in a lonely flat. He'd experienced the glory of the Gulf and come down with a thud. It seemed so unreal, part of someone else's life. His mood sank and then rushed back as he tried to recall the thrill he felt soaring over an Arab desert with his finger on the trigger and millions of pounds of precision technology at his command. He could wipe out entire streets with the press of a button and had felt like a god riding through the sky, dealing out death and destruction as he saw fit. Now he was powerless.

His moods were up and down. One minute he was a silver-screen hero with an orchestra roaring him on, the next he was sucked along with the missiles and forced to witness the aftermath.

Farrell had quickly become used to Bob West and let the younger man do the talking. If he was silent, Farrell concentrated on his paper or the street outside. Bob was sitting quietly now, so Farrell went with the bitter. He had time on his hands, drifting through the window to a wartime London of blackouts and air-raid shelters, where incendiaries set the streets burning and kids watched doodlebugs splutter to a halt, then fall silently to earth. Everyone waited for the explosion. It was high-tech warfare. The ranks of Nazi bombers, the V-1 buzzbombs and V-2 ballistic missiles. After the bombs and rockets, men and women scraped through charred rubble searching for survivors, full of hatred for the men in the clouds who killed and maimed while hiding in the darkness. Farrell remembered the bombing and thought of the time he'd spent billeted in camps waiting for the Allied invasion of Europe to begin, training and retraining. When the time came, they were ready and willing. There were a lot of debts to repay.

Farrell had played his part and was intensely proud of what he'd done. He'd gone across the Channel with the invasion force and helped defeat Hitler and the Nazis. Now he was back in the same old pubs. He didn't mind at all. He was happy to sit in The Unity. Very happy indeed. He liked the pub and he liked London. Many men never made it back. He was lucky to go full circle. He had survived and was proud to have got through the slaughter. Young people didn't appreciate just how precious continuity and community were. They wanted excitement and adventure, but you had to put things in perspective. He was thankful to drink a pint of Directors and enjoy the moment. Of course he had his memories, but the strongest memories were often the ones you never shared. The history of the English working class was buried in coffins and burnt in incinerators. From cradle to grave the details were often kept private, and if you did share the knowledge it was verbally, and this in turn meant that eventually it was lost. Nothing was written down. It was the English way. It some ways it gave you a dignity no-one could steal, but in another it was a cop out, letting the rich claim history along with everything else.

For a while after the war Farrell was withdrawn. Once demobbed, everything seemed trivial, and it was only the presence of his wife that stopped him becoming bitter. His wife had seen and experienced something far worse in the camp, and this in turn taught him humility. But he didn't like to remember those things. Before the war, he'd been a bit of a tearaway. It was part of growing up. After the war it had taken him time to adjust as he ran the pictures through and tried to make some sense of everything that had happened. Maybe that's what Bob was doing now, but he didn't think it was exactly the same. Farrell had seen the unimaginable, while from what Bob said it seemed he'd seen very little from the cockpit of his plane. Farrell didn't like to go back and remember the horror, but it was there and he'd kept the lid on things for over half a century. Bob had troubles Farrell didn't understand. Maybe it was weakness, because the younger man was from a different generation. There seemed to be more and more weak people around these days.

Perhaps it was the way West had fought or maybe it was this Gulf War Syndrome the papers were talking about. Perhaps — and this was just his own theory — perhaps it was the nature of the war itself. Maybe it was the justification for war that mattered more than anything else. War was a blend of excitement at what was to come and sickness when it arrived. The end had to justify the means. Farrell had thought about this a lot when he was younger. War was sold on glory and colour, while the fighting itself was repetitive and vicious. Farrell knew he was right fighting the Nazis, but wasn't so sure about Bob fighting Iraq on behalf of Kuwait and the oil industry. You had to feel justified in your actions, because there came a time when you had to think about these things. Bob was struggling with the reality. In the old days people put this off, and many managed to ignore such questions for the rest of their lives, but the younger generation was different. Farrell had done a good job keeping his memories in line. Most people didn't have the mental discipline and self-control. Bob West was back home on the dole with time to waste so his mind was bound to wander. Whatever the reason for his moods, the man was sick. His skin was patchy and his eyes glazed. There was sweat on West's forehead and the man didn't look well. Farrell sipped his drink. He didn't look well at all.

Harry leant over the railings and let the sickness go, his gut exploding as a full cooked breakfast roared back up at a hundred miles an hour, straight through his mouth in a hurricane twister. Gulls picked up the scent and turned their heads, rolling their eyes at the coming feast. There was a moment of calm, a freeze-frame second or so when the rolling green waves were solid rock and the motion of the ferry stuck, rudder jammed tight, a magic moment when Harry could blink and watch the sickness hover in front of him, a chance to understand the power of the sea. Then wallop. The video rushed away as he lost control, leaning over the railings and looking down. Bull's-eye.

He couldn't help laughing as the Spice Girl schoolkids on the deck below stopped their shrieking and realised the truth. There was another second of silence before the storm, when the waves rolled again and the ferry rocked, ducking and diving through the Channel, pushing against the elements dipping its bow into the wind. There was a second's pause on the video nasty and the thirteen-year-old girls looked at each other and understood what had happened. They understood that they'd just been soaked in a bacon-and-eggs English-breakfast £2.99 special, home delivered by the big fat bastard bent over the railings above looking down on them, laughing his head off. The head was square and shaved, and the man didn't care about their clothes and hair, everything ruined. There were bits in the sick as well. Pieces of what seemed liked bacon. It was horrible. The vomit and the man above who was laughing like something off The X Files. The mechanism clicked and the kids started howling.

Harry heard their screams rising through the thrashing of the wind, the flapping throb in his ears chopped away by teenage hysteria. A vicious cocktail of greasy cafe cooking and too much ketchup had ruined expensive haircuts and girl-power fashion. A mob of kids ran off crying their eyes out, all flashing lycra and long blonde curls trailing in the wind.

– Fucking slags, was all Harry could mumble, acid in his throat and tears in his eyes.

Harry pushed himself up on the rail, thinking of England and trying to keep his guts in. You had to see the funny side of things, though, because there was the future down below coated in the sick of the last two decades. The pretty young things that would shape the England to come soaked in the bile of the nutters who'd rampaged through the past. Well, not really the past, but someone twenty years older who should've known better. Together they represented the present, but the consumer kids were feeling the effects. No amount of ecstasy could save you when England mobbed up. Mind you, like the rest of the country he wouldn't have said no to a proper Spice Girl knocking on his door with a takeaway at three in the morning. It didn't have to be a Spice mind. He'd make do with some old slapper on her way home from Blues who fancied ten solid inches of BSE up her arse. But he couldn't be bothered with that sort of thinking right now because the wind was getting stronger and he had to sit down, moving away from the crime scene before Cracker appeared to go through his reasons, finding an empty bench where he could put his back to the wall and watch the English coastline disappear in the haze. Gulls followed the ferry the whole way, tracking the trawler from Grimsby with the press-ganged Harry on board, panicking fish thrashing on the deck, hungry gulls following Eric Cantona all the way back to Europe.

– You were sick all over those young girls, a voice said, appearing from nowhere.

Harry looked to his right and noticed the mini-skirt and mac sitting next to him. He hadn't seen the woman come over. She had to be a Scandinavian. A Danish beauty queen maybe. Someone to take along to the storage room and knob in the racks. No, she was Swedish. He was certain this bird was a Swede. A fucking lovely bit of skirt.

– It was not a nice thing to do, the woman said, laughing.

Harry felt awkward. It wasn't the ideal way to a bird's heart, puking on a bunch of school kids. He wasn't sure how to answer that one. What was he supposed to say? That it didn't matter?

– Can you understand me? You are English, aren't you?

– Yes, I'm English.

– Only an Englishman would do that to such young girls and then laugh. It is the English sense of humour I guess.

Harry was struggling now. Was she taking the piss? He didn't think so. Yes, the English sense of humour was alive and well and doing the business on the high seas. He wondered what Terry Thomas would do in this situation. Give it the sophisticated approach and use the old English gentleman routine, though Harry didn't think he could pull that off. But he was missing the point, because this bird had just seen him in action and she was still coming over for a chat. He was in, no fucking problem. They loved it, the Scandinavians, because their blokes were so fucking serious the girls flocked to any English cock going spare. The English knew how to enjoy themselves. That's what it was. They wanted a bit of that olde English magic. The blood, sweat and spunk of an English hooligan. Forget the wankers tucking into their health food and sipping low-alcohol lager, not wanting to lose control. The Swedish birds wanted some excitement. This girl was crying out for a night on the town, moving through the pubs of West London and filling up on a cheap Indian, then back to Harry's unmade bed for a quick shag, those ten pints of lager making sure his performance was up to the usual standard. It was the hooligan element making its mark, putting England on the map.

– My name is Ingrid, from Berlin, said the Swede.

– Harry. From London.

– Nice to meet you Harry.

– Likewise Ingrid.

The wind picked up and they were silent for half a minute or so. Harry was gagging for it and so was this bird. But he still had the taste of sick in his mouth and had to get his breath back. He needed a shag and was going to ask Ingrid what the chances were of climbing into that luggage rack when Carter had

35

finished servicing the Dane. They fucking loved it, the old fräuleins. Dirty slag had probably been shagging her way through all the London clubs, taking her pick of the ICF boys in Mile End and the Bushwhackers down in South London, the Gooners in North London, but missing out on the full experience. Shame he hadn't met her down Blues and given her the usual patter, shown her the local sites, but there again, reasoning the things through, she'd probably never got out of the West End, spending her time getting chased by trendy wankers and long queues of greasy Italians. What a waste.

– I have just spent two weeks in London. I enjoyed it very much. I am on holiday with my boyfriend.

Harry nodded.

Just his fucking luck. Nice-looking bird like that, with a mini-skirt and a plastic mac, sitting on deck flashing it about, and she's only travelling with some goose-stepping cunt who probably didn't realise what he was getting. Fucking gorgeous she was. Mind you, Ingrid was flirting and you never knew. Maybe the cunt she was knobbing worked part-time for the Gestapo and was bringing his work home. Handcuffing her to the bedposts and pulling out her fingernails. Ingrid had long, red nails that would pop out of her fingers easy enough. Poor old Ingrid shagging some Aryan superman in a full-length leather coat and jackboots. Pliers under the pillow and industrial voltage pulsing through the electric blanket. What she needed was a change of scene. She needed Harry to show her the way forward. Forget the Germans and kneel down for the England boys.

– I work in a bar called Bang in East Berlin, Ingrid said, handing Harry a card. You should visit me and bring your friends along.

Harry saw the boyfriend approach and Ingrid was up and running to some scruffy anarchist-communist cunt with one of those haircuts that stuck up like a bog brush on top of his head, small eyes shut away behind the regulation round glasses. Harry watched them go. First thing he was going to do in Amsterdam was get himself a bird. Ingrid was fucking lovely. He needed something like that and put the card in his pocket. You never knew. Stranger things happened.

Harry saw himself walking into Bang. He was looking good, with his head freshly shaved and a new Ben Sherman ironed by some bird at the luxury hotel. He'd been swimming in the hotel pool and then had a massage and blow job off a blonde number in silk stockings. She didn't even try to charge. He'd gone back to his room and eaten steak and chips and drunk a nice pint of lager delivered by an old boy who'd served in the war. He'd even given the man a tip. Now he was out and about, calling a taxi from reception, surrounded by wealthy American business-men, ten minutes later racing through the Berlin streets to Bang. He was walking into Ingrid's club with his head held high and straight into her arms, the Green cunt with the bog brush old news, Harry sitting at the bar enjoying the chat and flavour of the place. He would drink till closing and follow Ingrid upstairs for a night of non-stop sex.

– Who was that bird you were talking to? Billy Bright asked, sitting down next to Harry.

– She's German. Works in a bar in Berlin.

Harry showed Brighty the card.

– Sounds like a fucking queer bar, he said, sneering. What kind of name is Bang. Must be full of shirt-lifters. We'll wreck the place.

– Never thought of that. Suppose she looks a bit trendy.

– Nice arse on it.

– Bit flat-chested.

Billy laughed.

– It's probably alright. We should go down there and see if she's got any mates.

Harry didn't fancy Brighty coming along. He was planning a private party. He wanted to get out and about on his own. It was a killer that, going along hoping to get your leg over and taking a fucking mob as well. If Carter turned up, he'd be in there before Harry finished his first drink, and the rest of the boys would have a couple of lagers, rob the till and put all the windows through.

– I'll take some tapes along, Billy said. I spent last week

getting them together. Marching bands, Oi! and some modern stuff. A patriotic soundtrack for the trip. You know what these bars are like over in Europe. It's all poppy shit. You need some decent sounds to keep you happy.

Harry nodded. He looked at DJ Bright the bulldog mixmaster. It was a good idea. Billy opened the bag he was carrying and showed Harry the cassette player and ten or so tapes. It made sense, because you never got to listen to the music you wanted as the radio had its own ideas on what to play. The wind started pushing harder and Billy closed the bag quickly so the spitting rain didn't get in and ruin his music.

– Where have the others gone? he asked, looking around the empty deck.

– They're in the bar.

– I think I'll follow them. It's getting rough up here. You coming?

Harry was staying a bit longer. He'd always liked the rain; it was the rocking of the sea that did him in. DJ Bright looked at Harry as though he was mad and nodded, showing he understood.

It was still early, but with two pints of Director's in his belly it was the right time for Farrell to go home. He said goodnight to Bob and put his mug on the bar for Denise. She was a sweet girl and smiled at the pensioner. It was a fine summer's evening and he hoped Bob would be able to sort himself out, or if it was this Gulf War Syndrome then he hoped the Government would do its duty. He wasn't optimistic about the official angle, and it was odd how events constantly replayed. He thought of the mustard gas used on the Somme, the shell-shock and executions that were nothing short of murder, the madness of traumatised men brushed under the carpet and left to fester. He pushed this away. The memories had been coming back recently, rising more and more frequently. He thought he'd buried those things deep. He knew the reason of course. There was a decision to make, but it would have to wait for another day. Farrell wanted to enjoy the evening air. It was a strange world and one of the benefits of age was that you became more reflective and less angry. Life was unfair and it was cruel, but your moment passed and there was nothing more you could do.

Bill Farrell imagined life had been more innocent when he was young, but at the same time tougher, and once the bombing started people began living for the moment. There was little planning. You didn't know what was going to happen, whether you'd live or die. His time billeted in camps had been dull and repetitive and morale was low early in the war, with Doenitz's U-boats creating havoc in the Atlantic, the mass bombing, the defeats at Dunkirk and Dieppe. Conditions were basic in the camps and there was some bad feeling towards those in charge and resentment at the pay being so low. There'd been a class-consciousness among the men that didn't exist today, and the officers had to prove themselves. The Americanisation of English culture over the past thirty years had seen a crass materialism take hold, and this had allowed the establishment to sweeten the population without really giving them anything substantial in return. Farrell had watched this happen and it was the ease with which money had bought England's soul that he found most depressing.

The soldiers of the Second World War had learnt from the experience of those in the First. They'd been raised by men who'd served on the Western Front and seen hell on earth. There was a closeness between the two experiences, and Farrell was always amazed at the way the ordinary soldier was portrayed years after the event. In reality, they'd spoken their minds and not suffered fools gladly. The thousands of working-class men slaughtered on the Western Front due to the incompetence of upper-class officers hadn't been forgotten. Even now he felt the anger of his youth simmering, something that happened when he considered these things. He was disappointed that the gains made by his generation had been squandered by a superficial élite, but knew he had to let go. It didn't matter when you were old. He'd moved on and kept telling himself he didn't care until he almost believed it himself. He'd done his bit for England and there was little reward from the state. He'd learnt the hard way. But he hadn't fought for the politicians and businessmen, and the politicians and businessmen didn't think about old men living out their years in one-bedroom council flats. He remembered the VE Day celebrations and how the Tories had even wanted to march German troops through Central London. It really was unbelievable.

Farrell thought of the two pints he'd drunk and smiled. Two pints was a lot these days, and it wasn't just the price. In the old days he'd liked a drink, and so did his mates. It was his life and his culture and he'd had fun. The Unity always had a piano in those days, and there was one bloke who'd played boogie-woogie along with the more traditional London singalongs. He thought of his brother standing at the bar ordering all those years ago. The White Horse in Hounslow had been his local and they were bitter drinkers, though some of his mates drank mild. Beer was cheap and the pubs were packed. Lager didn't take over till years later. They'd had a few punch-ups too, though it wasn't something he ever talked about. It was foolish. They'd never used knives or bottles, just fists. It was good-natured and brief, caused by drink. The cuts and bruises healed and all that was left were vague memories doctored by time.

Farrell pulled himself up and knew he could remember if he really wanted, if he pushed himself. If he was completely honest with himself, age hadn't destroyed his memory. At least not yet. He thought about it some more and let his mind go back. It was hard to remember things how they were rather than how you wanted them to appear. This especially applied to the war. There were so many impressions and sights he'd pushed down, applying a gloss finish. It was the only way to survive such a thing. West had to learn this. It was the English way of dealing with things. Sometimes it worked, sometimes it failed. He thought he'd done okay. It was about self-discipline and control.

When he reached his flat, Farrell brewed a small pot of tea and went to sit by the window. He could see the buildings around him and the light was starting to dim. It was a nice time of day and the weather was fine. He liked hot weather and so had his wife. He looked at her picture on the wall. He saw her with the shaved head and broken ribs, raped and beaten and destined for the Nazi ovens. But he wouldn't think of that, because he preferred looking at the lights coming on outside and the peace of the evening. He'd left their old flat and started fresh. It was a good decision, though he'd been pushed by his daughter and would rather have stayed where he was. After all, the flat had been his home, but it was for the best. You had to leave things behind eventually. He could hear the thump of bass and the tinkle of people laughing. He felt happy with his lot.

There'd been some real tearaways in the old days, of course. He'd thought this last week when he heard about Johnny Bates dying. He was a hard case, old Johnny, always drunk and fighting with the police. There were unwritten rules and if you hit a copper then the biggest one in the station would pay you a visit in the cells. It was the way they kept order and most people went quietly. You never heard about men getting kicked to death like you did today. He wondered if it happened all those years ago, or whether the difference was that murder was more easily hidden. He couldn't imagine it happening. Today things were out in the open and that wasn't bad, it just depended how far it went, but England was a more violent place. There was greater freedom in many ways, but what they gave you with one hand they took back with the other.

Johnny Bates had lived in the next street to Farrell in Hounslow and they'd been close. Johnny was a few years older and Farrell admired him. He'd got Farrell interested in boxing and it was something the younger man kept up and developed in the army. Johnny's old man had fought in the Great War and some of the local boys said that the shells had damaged more than just his ears. They said his brain was scrambled by shrapnel, because there was a big scar across his temple and he often sat in his bedroom in the dark for hours on end with the curtains shut. Old man Bates was supposed to have a fancy woman in Chiswick, and this was while his wife was still alive, before the house was bombed out. People talked about Bates's madness and his mistress as if the two were linked. There was a lot of gossip before they invented television and there was even a story that Bates sat in the dark crying, proof enough that the Kaiser had driven him insane.

Maybe that's what made Johnny such a hard bastard. Maybe

he heard the talk and decided to put a stop to it. He didn't want to hear that sort of stuff about his dad, a brave soldier who'd fought for England and deserved better. Johnny loved a fight and Farrell reasoned it was more than the old man bruising his knuckles. Johnny used to tell Bill that he was a champion in waiting, teaching the big mouths some bare-knuckle manners. His nose was flat by the time he was fifteen. The two youths hung around together, but when Johnny joined the army they lost touch. After the war things weren't the same. Johnny was out every night living the life of Riley, while Farrell would go for a drink sometimes but spent most nights in with his new wife. They still saw each other, and it was Johnny who'd got Farrell to join the TA. Eventually they drifted apart. It was hard for Farrell's wife when she came to England, with everything that had happened, living in a strange city and dealing with her past. He'd done his best and had always treated her right. They'd had a good marriage. That was one thing he was certain about.

London was very different after the war. When he looked back he could remember so much, how things were, but this could turn a man inside out and he didn't want to end up like some ex-soldiers who thought everything today was rubbish and that the rest of the country was in their debt. Everyone wanted respect, and when you'd been through a war you wanted it even more than normal. It became a need. But things didn't work like that. It was impossible to ever get across the reality, and how could anyone know who wasn't there? So it was all buried and gaps appeared between people. He'd got along and his wife had helped. They'd never had much money but had made do and enjoyed life. Expectations were lower, and after the war it was enough to be alive. This was the important thing, and they realised how precious life was and this had given them a great sense of fulfilment.

A pint of beer had been an essential part of life and the pubs were happy places. There was music and laughter after the war ended, a massive sigh of relief. During the war it had been lively, but in a different, more frantic way. Farrell was young and grabbed his chances and it made the camps so boring because you felt you were missing out. Farrell looked at the young girls today and even though there was so much more money about and a lot more choice when it came to fashion, they couldn't compare with the girls of his day. There'd been some real beauties around. Farrell remembered that one Johnny had liked and somehow Farrell had ended up taking her to the pictures when he was on leave. Her name was Angie. Farrell was going right back now and found he could remember her with a clarity that was almost embarrassing. She really had been a beauty and she'd worn stockings that night as well. The back row was always full of couples because there wasn't the housing and most kids lived with their mums and dads. You had to get it where you could. It was only natural, after all.

If someone had gone into business recycling rubbers they could've made a fortune just going round the parks. That's where the young people went for sex. Once the war got going there was much more sex about. At least that was Farrell's impression, though he was a soldier so maybe it was just him and his mates and their time of life. It made sense, because the population was under threat and nature would take its own action. All he knew for sure was that he was on the job regularly. He'd had lots of sex in those days. He was careful and used a rubber. There was no pill and maybe men had a greater sense of responsibility. He knew that if he got a girl pregnant he'd most likely end up marrying her. You were both in on the thing together. Maybe they'd had greater respect for women, even if there was more chauvinism. It had been a good life in spite of everything. At least until he went to Europe and saw the other side of human nature. He hated the old Second World War films and the way they romanticised everything. They were propaganda really. Still, *Gone With The Wind* had been a good film to take a girl to see.

They'd gone for a drink afterwards. Come to think of it, Farrell probably took Angie to The Unity. He was amazed to remember this and wondered what they were doing away from Hounslow, remembering the film was showing in Hammersmith. What did Angie drink? He didn't have a clue. It was more than fifty years ago, but he could see them leaving the pub. They'd taken the bus and walked the last bit. The night had been much the same as now. The weather was warm and they'd gone to the park. He could feel the texture of Angie's stockings. It was so long ago, another world. For him at least. Because he was an old man and sex didn't matter. It did then, of course, and he'd peeled her knickers off and stuffed them in his pocket. He'd had her in the long grass by the hedge. He used a rubber and they'd had a fag afterwards and stayed there for ages talking. He'd seen Angie for a while after and they'd had a lot of sex before going their separate ways.

Drink and women were what counted when you were a young lad sowing your oats and he'd never thought badly of the girl. You didn't really consider the future. Now he was thinking about the past, something he normally tried to avoid.

We get ourselves a table and Billy hangs his Cross of St George over the windows behind. Nice little backdrop that says it all. The flag is England and the white letters Chelsea. His girlfriend cut up a sheet and did it special for the trip. It's a good-size flag as well, nicked from a five-star hotel in Victoria. Midnight job with a knife. Boot of the car and Billy's cruising home listening to his radio, tuned into a phone-in about law and order when he spies the old bill coming up behind. Lights flashing and siren screaming. He pulls over wondering about the bald tyres and out-of-date tax disc, the insurance he doesn't have and the Cross of St George tucked under the spare tyre. They keep going. Through a red light and on to something more exciting. After someone else. Says imagine that, they'll be putting electronic tags on our flag one day.

I can believe it as well. See, it's okay for the Spice Girls to wear Union Jack dresses and for magazines to put it on their covers, and for the knobs who go to the last night of the proms, but if it's us lot with the Union Jack or Cross of St George, then we're automatically Nazis. Imagine that. The fucking mentality of those media cunts. We're patriotic Englishmen and that's the truth. Some of the blokes on this ferry might not particularly like blacks and Pakis, but if you're white and working class then you're automatically labelled scum by the likes of the Anti-Nazi

League. Being patriotic doesn't mean we follow an Austrian. Our pride is in our history and culture. That's the way things are and one day the thought police will be tagging the flags and only selling them to pop stars and the upper classes. There's no politics here, but that doesn't mean we don't have views and opinions. Everyone's a patriot. How can there be anything wrong in loving your country? It doesn't make any sense at all.

Mark and Facelift come back from the bar carrying a tray each, balancing drinks, the ferry dipping suddenly so they spill some of the lager. Mark smiles but Facelift's face stiffens. The ferry evens itself and they're lining the glasses up on the table. Drop crisps in the middle of the glasses. They're some of the first ones to get served. I'm looking round the bar and it's starting to fill up, seeing what's what. A normal ferry mixture. Coachloads of pensioners off to see the sights, European students and travellers, English versions of the same thing, one or two half-decent birds, and quite a few youths and men who are probably on their way to Berlin. West Ham haven't turned up yet. Still having their tea. We're waiting for things to get going because the only way to get through the boredom of crossing to the Hook is to have a decent drink. That's what it's all about. A few lagers, a tasty bird or two, and you're set. The time flies when you're on the piss with some half-decent sort sitting across the way flashing her gash.

I look back round the table and Mark's going into one about how Rod couldn't come along, seeing as how he's a married man and has to behave himself. Facelift and Brighty lean back enjoying the lager and looking into space. Carter listens to Mark, nodding, with Bob Roberts nowhere to be seen. Harry Roberts everyone calls him. Nice one that. He's our friend, kills coppers. Carter and Roberts are blokes I remember looking up to when I was a kid. They're alright. Ready for a laugh, though they want the peaceful life most of the time. They're the kind who if something happens then they're ready and willing, but who don't go looking for trouble. Not these days anyway. England is different and they'll be up for it. Wouldn't be knocking about with us if they weren't. It's a special occasion, like getting Millwall in the Cup. I think back four years to that kicking I got down in South London. Everyone comes out of the woodwork for the big games, whether it's club or country. Then there's Biggs and High Street Ken, a couple of herberts from the pub back home, tagging along picking up scraps.

Have to laugh thinking about Biggs and High Street. You talk about scousers and how they're robbers and that, and the Mancs have their thieves as well, but fucking Biggs is the original tea-leaf. He's no juvenile and still loves nicking cars and running them through shop windows. He's a speed freak, fresh out of the nick. Did six months for thieving some drink. Imagine that. Six months for ramraiding a shop. It was the previous convictions that did him. Biggs and Ken are cousins and watch each other's backs. They're okay and they've been to football through the years. Not hundred-per-cent, but turn up for the big games. Now they're on their way to Berlin and that makes eight of us. We'll get to Amsterdam and meet up with Harris and the others. We're all Chelsea. All England. With the Cross of St George blocking out the night as the waves get deeper and the Channel heavier. We're on our way and it's going to be a good one. I finish my drink and push it towards Ken. His turn.

I watch High Street going over to the bar with the tray in his hand, Biggs following. It's getting deeper there as everyone starts crowding in, waiting their turn patiently because it's still early. Give it a couple of hours and the barmen will have to get their fingers out. We need our lager and we need it now. Have to keep the blood flowing at the right temperature and thickness. They're starting to earn their living and probably wish they were on another shift. I'm watching the men in their white shirts and black trousers, lager bubbling, taking those plastic scrapers and cutting off the head. It's a con because you end up with a glass that's a quarter froth. Fucking typical. Going metric and losing out in the translation. That's the power of the exchange rate mechanism for you. Forced to sit there like a mug for hours waiting for the fucking thing to sink down so you can have a sip of lager. It's like drinking candyfloss. Trying to drink candyfloss. You need a straw to fight your way through and taste the lager.

– This is the way to travel, says Mark, enjoying himself.
We all nod.
– No Eurostar bollocks for us.
We nod some more.
– Fuck me, talk about giving a drink some head. This is all fucking froth, the fucking Dutch cunts.
– You wouldn't get a bar like this on the train would you? Carter says, blowing the white top to the side.
I think about this. He's got a point.
– I tell you what, and Mark leans in, warming up. If those IRA cunts don't blow the tunnel up, then we should do it. I hate that fucking tunnel. We should get a squad together, have a whip round and buy some Semtex. The sea would soon flood it once we've opened a hole. You think of the money they wasted building it, and for what? So they can drive the ferry companies out of business and make us part of Europe. That's what they're trying to do. Fucking slags.

Mark's right. What's the point? Fuck knows what's going to go wrong with the tunnel in the future but, more important, it's symbolic. In truth, it should make long crossings like this unnecessary and one day you won't have to deal with every wanker who works for Customs, but it's missing the point. Thing is, we shouldn't have all that hassle in the first place. It's only small-minded cunts with the rule book jammed up their arses and let loose on the general population who cause the problems. Those people will just go and find a job somewhere else. They're not going to disappear.

Another thing with the Channel Tunnel is the rabies they're going to let in. You might as well put up a sign inviting all the diseased dogs of the East to come over and milk the benefits. Every other cunt is taking their share, and we're a nation of animal lovers. I know it's the future and they're not exactly going to turn round and fill it in, but it's unnatural. One day they'll probably build a bridge as well. Everyone will be forced to speak a new language and there'll be tunnels boring in from every angle. Even the Vikings will be at it, tunnelling in from Sweden and Norway. Taking the fast train through to the new shopping precincts of Central London. Looking for the excitement of football mobs, punk rockers and traditional London boozers. But all the Londoners will have been forced out to the new towns by then, the city overrun by Britain's yuppies and the world's rich tourists. You can't afford to buy a house where you grew up, so if you want to get ahead you have to move down the arterial roads. Maybe it's always been like that, but the way everyone sits back and lets the rich of Britain sell the silver to the rich of the world makes you wonder. They might as well not have bothered fighting the war, while our part in beating the Germans is dismissed by do-nothing intellectuals with no pride or culture of their own.

Even the East End is changing and that was a fucking bomb site not so long ago. Every time you pick up the paper there's some tale of rich-son-and-daughter artists in Hackney and Hoxton, or football-loving yuppies who've just discovered the game even though they're in their thirties. None of this reflects what you see around you day-in, day-out. There's no-one telling the truth, so you make do with the tabloid piss-take. By the time the Swedes get through there'll be nothing left but a maze of empty galleries, Jack The Ripper tours and coach trips out to the shires to view the natives. Europe is one more attempt to crush England. London run by some faceless wanker in Brussels banning bitter because it's a different colour to lager, insisting that everyone raises their metric measure at exactly the same time.

Europe's a plot by big business to centralise power and create a super-state with a super economy. Hitler had the same idea, though he was a nationalist who saw Germany at the heart of the union, controlling things from Berlin. Now the financiers are doing the same, but without the publicity. Everything is through the back door. Endless regulations piled on the already top-heavy stack of English laws. I just don't fancy some fat German or French businessman ramming Deutschmarks down my throat and telling me my vegetables are illegal because they haven't been genetically engineered by Dr Frankenstein. Fuck that for a game of soldiers. Could be worse I suppose. Could be the Spanish getting control. That would be a disaster. Least the Germans like their football and drink. None of your Real

Madrid, red wine bollocks. It's going to be a meeting of old enemies in Berlin. Time to put them in their place. They can have their penalty shoot-outs, because it's the fighting that counts. Someone starts singing TWO WORLD WARS AND ONE WORLD CUP at the bar and we all join in.

—You're an English tommy fighting the Nazis wondering what's coming next. You can feel the breath of the men surrounding you and the thump of the sea below. You're bobbing up and down on a waiting graveyard. The sea is cold and powerful and will pull you under if it gets the chance. Maybe there's a special smell, that's what they say, but you don't notice anything because you're struggling down the rigging and into the landing craft. The waves are big and you feel sick. You're scared because this is the real thing. You don't hear the breathing of your mates because you're too busy thinking of your mum, and if you're old enough or married young, then your wife and kids as well, making sure you don't lose your grip and fall into the sea. You don't look at the others because you're more concerned with keeping your dinner down. You don't want to get sick in front of the other lads, but you can feel the breathing inside your head and the landing craft keeps jumping in and out of the waves.

You're pressed in with everyone else and you keep quiet. You bide your time, not that there's much choice. Once you've been loaded onto the landing craft you start moving. The sea is rough and choppy and dangerous. There's thousands of men going the same way. Thousands of men are on the way to their deaths and everyone thinks about this. You don't say anything, of course, because that's how things are. You resist the fear and this makes you stronger. You want to fight and are a tiny part of a machine, but to you and yours the most important part. The years of waiting mean you're glad things are moving at last, but part of you wishes you could go home. Nobody wants to be one of the unlucky ones lost in the Channel. You keep your fingers crossed as the landing craft moves away from the ship and hope God will watch over you. Before going to Europe most men believed in God, but a lot were probably unsure after it was all over. One of the boys, a big man from the East End, passes some gum around and winks as the landing craft starts to plough through the waves. He's flash and makes you feel better, pulls everyone together with some hard cockney humour and disrespect for the sergeant.

We grew up around men who'd fought in the First World War and heard the stories. We were raised with the aftermath. Those men were part of our childhood and we saw the leftovers. They were treated badly and, what's more important in some ways, everyone knew what the upper class had done. It doesn't matter what anyone says now, because in the forties there was an impatience with the officers. They had to prove themselves and earn our respect. The mistakes of the trenches cost the ordinary man dear and the stupid games of the politicians were despised. We were fighting a different kind of war, but it wasn't until we got into Europe that we understood just *how* different. There was a spirit that said there was a job needed doing. We weren't blind and Kitchener's boys were pitied for their faith. We knew what was what. We got on with the job and made do. It wasn't like us to complain about things for the sake of it, but nobody was pushing us around. Once the landing craft started moving we were more of a unit, knowing we only had each other. Our minds were working fast, but we were strong and knew there was no turning back.

It's a terrible thing. The sergeant behind you with a machine gun pointing at your back and the Germans ahead waiting above the beaches with their guns trained on the Channel. If you don't go when the door opens the sergeant will shoot you and when you get on the sand the enemy will do their best to blow you to smithereens. There's no real choice when the moment comes, but at least you've finally got the chance to pay the bastards back for Dunkirk, the Blitz and the whole bloody war. It really is a terrible thing and you don't want to remember it too often. You want to keep the memories under control. You have to battle with time and your own mind if you want to find the reality. You don't want to make a fuss. That's not the English way.

★ ★ ★

It was time to move. The coast had vanished, the waves were rougher and the drizzle had turned to rain. Harry wasn't exactly soaked, and it wasn't a storm, but he was feeling left out, sitting there on his own with everyone inside having a laugh. He could fall over the side and no-one would notice. The rest of the lads wouldn't miss him till they arrived in Holland. Maybe they'd be so pissed it would be Amsterdam but, knowing that lot, it would probably be Berlin. They'd be enjoying a stein or two and Carter would suddenly look round all surprised and ask where the fat cunt was, looking left and right and then losing the thread as he focused on some Nordic tart strutting past in a G-string.

Harry had been miserable the last year, since Balti was killed, but this trip was going to put the past in its proper place. He felt better since he'd puked up over those girls. Fucking hell, he felt bad about that, and laughing didn't help, but there again, bollocks, those screaming teenage brats got right up his nose, with their repeat fashion and too-loud chatter, screaming so everyone could hear them, fucking and blinding their way through life. He didn't need to get sick in their hair, it wasn't nice, not really, but that's the way it was, and if a cooked breakfast was all they had to worry about in life then they were lucky. The same went for all of them, because you could moan about how the country was going to the dogs and everything, but you could also cross the wrong person and end up getting your fucking head blown off.

Harry hurried along the walkway. He opened the door and the light hit his eyes. It took a couple of seconds for him to adjust and take in the warmth and artificial smells of the ferry, the cheap carpet and blank faces. He could've murdered a pint an hour ago, but now he didn't fancy it. He turned left and walked through the passages, having a scout. He passed the canteen and the smells hit home, the counter doing a roaring trade in bangers and mash. One hour out of England and it was like everyone had to get in there and have a good feed, because they knew what was coming. The older ones were the worst, because for most of their lives they'd never had much choice in what they ate, making do, controlled by price and availability, so now they were faced with a couple of weeks eating foreign muck they were going to make a stand and go out with a bang. They were building up a supply of starch to see them through the coming ordeal. Harry smiled, because it was worse coming the other way.

When you got on a ferry from Calais to Dover, say, you could tell the English who'd been away for more than a few days – and it was the Scots and Welsh as well, he wasn't being prejudiced here. It was mental, because as soon as the boys and girls from Doncaster and Dorking and Derby were off the coaches and up the stairs it was a race to the canteen. Big queues formed and the kitchen had to work hard to keep up with the demand for pies, sausages, chips and bacon-eggs-beans, all the gourmet cuisine that made you what you were. Harry liked all that grub, who didn't, but he liked the other stuff as well. The paella in Spain and the fish dishes he'd had in Portugal. French food was shit, he had to be honest, unless you found an Arab cafe doing couscous. When everyone had had their feed and felt better, the strength back after starving for two weeks, they were straight in the bar looking for a pint of bitter or at least a decent pint of lager, sitting happy with their guts back to normal and the relaxing simmer of alcohol, feeling the sunburn ease as they looked forward to developing the holiday snaps.

Best of all was sitting on deck when the Dover cliffs appeared. He remembered one time and it was like a reverse of now, because he'd gone out when the sun was just coming up, the air cold and biting, and he'd sat there as the cliffs got bigger and whiter, sailing back to Kent really putting a lump in his throat. He'd been glad to get home. Even after a week away he couldn't believe how different everything seemed. The approach was the best bit, because back in England there was the slow grind of Customs, waiting for the coach to London, passing through the countryside, which was fair enough, but then you came into London, through Deptford and New Cross, Millwall territory, with the run-down estates and broken roads, the hustle and bustle which was fine if you were in the mood but shit when you were knackered and all you wanted to do was get back to Victoria and catch the tube home, have a bath and read the paper. A nice cup of tea and a wank over Page 3. Time to spill your beans over a pure English rose.

There he was again, missing home before he'd even made it to Holland. He was a right donut sometimes, but smart as well because there was a cinema on board and he didn't fancy getting pissed with the rest of the boys. There was enough time for that later. He didn't fancy meeting those girls again either, and at least in the dark he could keep his head down. It wasn't nice, but there you go, so he paid his money and went in, fumbling through the blackness to an aisle seat where he could stretch his legs out. The last advert was ending and he was ready for the main feature.

Harry had been raised on Second World War films, a wide-eyed kid taking in the dramatic music and exciting stories of bravery and self-sacrifice. The Second World War didn't get as much of a show now because the new enemies were vague and far away in the East, over the horizon where they couldn't be seen. There was a new agenda and nobody wanted to remember the bad times, for a variety of reasons. When he was a kid he'd got his history from *Battle of Britain* and *Dam Busters*. Everyone his age did. Ask any of the England boys on the ferry and they'd mention films like *The Longest Day*. He laughed when he thought of Nigger the dog. Fucking hell, you wouldn't get away with that now. Come here Nigger, there's a good boy. No Nigger, don't piss on Bomber's staff car. No fucking chance.

The stories were real as well, because you were surrounded by family and friends who'd grown up in London during the Blitz, people who'd had their houses burnt down and fought in Europe, Africa and the Far East. Civilians lost people overseas and suffered along with the soldiers. Most people were touched somehow. It was a simple thing to say, but to understand it was harder. The businessmen said it was better to sweep things under the carpet and not hold a grudge, because everyone wanted peace and prosperity, but maybe they went too far sometimes. You had to learn lessons. Even so, Harry liked Europe and counted England in with the Continent. True, the

English were different, but it was silly slaughtering each other like they'd done during the war. He preferred an easy life.

Harry was soon daydreaming his way through the film. It was the same old futuristic special effects for the sake of special effects. With the money and freedom these film cunts had you'd think they'd make something with a bit of soul. At least classic films had decent dialogue, even if the squaddies were generally thick as shit, either Alright-Me-Old-Cocker southerners or Ee-By-Gum northerners. The Scots were all red-haired little alkies called Jock who died early, and the Welsh had all been christened Taff and sang for their suppers, rolling dark eyes in the back of pixie heads. The stars were upper-crust and well-spoken, their superior accents naturally enough reflecting superior intelligence. The stereotypes were a load of bollocks, but Harry loved the heroes he saw on the screen, because everywhere you went there were people with stories to tell who didn't want to talk, keeping the details to themselves. It was how the English, the British, did things. Now they were dying as the years caught up, but that war experience was still deep inside everyone, young and old, whether first-, second-, or third-hand. Even the cunts who tried to walk all over the memories and laugh off the war years spirit did so because they knew how deep-rooted these things were. They couldn't get in and dictate like they did with everything else, so instead they sneered.

The Yanks often had big parts in the films because Hollywood was where the money was, and they said that if you went up Piccadilly during the war it was a knocking shop, with the GIs loaded and the English girls wanting a share. He found that hard to believe because there were higher standards in those days, but he didn't think too much about it because he was watching a battle between two semi-human machines firing off lasers and kicking each other in the head. He wondered what the soldiers thought, but nobody asked those sorts of questions. The officers wrote their memoirs and the squaddies signed on.

Harry was sitting there in the dark surrounded by strangers. Their fathers and grandfathers could've been the cunts in the pill boxes mowing down English tommies. It made you think, though you weren't supposed to think like that, because bygones were bygones, and that was right in its way, but Harry didn't feel guilty about the Empire and the slave traders because he wasn't even born then. Everyone had to get on, but he'd still like to see one of those old war films shown on the ferry, just for a laugh.

He'd like to sit back and watch *The Longest Day* and see what happened. He saw *Battle of Britain* at the pictures when it came out as a kid, and he'd loved the RAF dog-fights and the way Good had overcome superior odds and defeated Evil. What he remembered most was a bomber gunner getting his face shot up. The mask was splattered with blood and as a child it had hit Harry hard. It made him feel ill, the blood on the glass, and it had almost spoiled the film. The pomp and circumstance of the music soon took over and he was able to appreciate how a small number of brave men had saved the country. He thought of the burns many of them suffered and how one bloke's wife asked an officer what it was like to have a husband without a face. It stuck in his mind. A man without a face. Or was it another film? The details merged with time. All Harry had to do was drive down the Western Avenue a few miles and he could see the RAF bases at Northolt, Harefield and Uxbridge, right there, near enough on his doorstep.

It would be brilliant to sit in the cinema with all these Dutch and Germans and watch *Dam Busters*. He'd sit there with his popcorn and Coke and enjoy the show. The Dutch would cheer and the Germans would look embarrassed. The England boys in the bar would probably come along if *Dam Busters* was on. He loved the bit where they were using the bombs on the dams and they kept missing, then one of the fuckers got a bull's-eye. Those pilots had steel bollocks cruising through enemy flak. It wasn't going to happen in this particular cinema, so he made do with the bloodbath in front of him, except there wasn't any blood. The killing was clean and efficient and the semi-humans fought without thinking. There were no entry and exit points, and no mess. Everything was clear cut. It was an action-adventure and easy entertainment for the masses. Harry wasn't really taking it in, smiling as he imagined the trouble there'd be if they put on *Das Boot* and gave the passengers some U-boat action.

The bar's full and Bright Spark's got his cassette player out. Thinks he's on the World Service pumping out his own Radio Hooligan Roadshow as he places the machine on the table and starts fucking about with his tapes. He puts in this cassette of military music. The sort of songs the poor bastards played as they trooped off to the slaughter in the good old days. Red shirts so they couldn't see the blood and busbies so they couldn't feel their brains explode. The music's strong and patriotic and it must've helped the boys along. Play some loud music and you can't hear the guns up ahead and the pissed laughter of the generals miles behind. Beat the drum and stir the emotions. We have our own songs right here. Our own set of explanations. West Ham are on the other side of the bar drinking among themselves, looking over and smiling at the band. Music brings England together. There's a truce and everything's sweet. We do our thing and they do theirs. Same goes for the other clubs. We're not exactly going to start swapping stories with West Ham, but there's no need for aggravation, not here anyway.

There's a lot of England on board now that they're in the bar and we can see who's who. Strongbow and his mates are missing in action. Mugs are back in Harwich sobering up, the big man himself charged with something a bit more serious than drunk and disorderly. Looks likely seeing the way they were banging his head on the van door and the way he was trying to stop them. Something the old bill call resisting arrest. Stop us cracking your head open and we'll do you for that as well. There's other people in here, not just the England boys – middle-aged men and women in groups lining up the lager and shorts, a few made-up couples, solo travellers enjoying a bottle of lager and checking their passports. There's also three tasty birds nearby. Well nice in fact. Carter says he fancies a shag and might go and have a word, but I don't reckon he's got much chance on the ferry. Suppose he's got his reputation to consider.

I try to work out where they're from. Obviously not English.

Not tarty enough. That's the problem with English birds. They're a load of old brasses compared to some of the Europeans. Mind you, the Europeans are boring, even the dirty ones in their expensive designer jeans and sweaters. That's why the stuck-up birds at home like everything European, because they're thick and boring in one. Don't be fooled by the posh accent, because education doesn't mean intelligent. Your average English bird down the pub though, she's alright. Likes a laugh and doesn't waste her time posing. Best of all are the blondes, and then it doesn't matter where they come from. Everyone loves blondes. It's the Aryan ideal. Blondes have more fun and you can understand why. Every generation has its blonde pin-up on the screen doing the business.

There's more English coming in all the time, with one or two in colours, everyone else without. Can never get my head round grown men wearing replica shirts. There's a few flags and we get a couple of looks, but this is an easing-in period as everyone clocks everyone else, seeing if they recognise faces from previous trips. There's probably sixty or so English in the bar now, and there's another Chelsea crew who we know well enough. Doesn't take long for them to start singing ONE BOMBER HARRIS. All the English join in straight off because this is what it's all about. It winds up the Germans, and it upsets the trendy wankers and all that scum who are always trying to pick holes in everything to do with England and English pride. None of us is seriously laughing about Dresden, but why should Arthur take the blame? It was a fucking war and the Luftwaffe was flattening our cities, but there again the cunts slagging off Bomber Command are quick enough to laugh off the spirit of the Blitz. We sing deep in our throats. THERE'S ONLY ONE BOMBER HARRIS. It's a nice little ice-breaker and Billy turns the volume on the cassette down, then turns it off. Nice one Billy, showing respect for tradition.

I hate the musical accompaniment one or two clubs take along to football. Sheffield Wednesday have that brass band that plays some kind of lobotomy trance. It's some nothing Dutch tune and it goes on for hours. Like we don't have enough songs of our own. It kills the atmosphere. Don't know how Tango puts up with that whining in his ear game after game. The yids had a fucking drum last season at White Hart Lane as well, though the atmosphere there's fucked anyway. The drummer starts tapping out his rhythm and Chelsea fill in THE YIDS. It was like Euro 96 and all those years of football songs and humour were forgotten as the game was sold off to the corporations and you ended up with Fantasy Football supplying the soundtrack. That's what the businessmen are doing to football. The architects have made the grounds sterile and the seats have killed the atmosphere. They say yuppies have taken over football, but that's bollocks, because I never see them in the pubs where we drink, but they've mixed everyone in together and you're not going to be singing your songs if you're next to a granny or some bloke with his kids. It's in the media and business side of things that the trendies have cashed in. Football's expensive and most ordinary people spend the game recovering from the shagging they've just had at the turnstile. But Billy's songs are good. It's the humour and the situation. ONE BOMBER HARRIS.

I think of Dave Harris who's already in Amsterdam. Harris has been getting worse over the last few years and I hope he never gets sent down because I wouldn't want to share a cell with him. Nice enough bloke mind, but he's gone a bit mental recently. There's always respect for the big characters. You run through the main faces at Chelsea through the last thirty years and they've got massive respect. They're the ones everyone secretly wishes they could be, but know they just aren't that kind of material. It's the character that does the trick. Leadership qualities. These people are the real culture.

Everyone's loosening up in the bar and I can see the Red Hand of Ulster badge on Gary Davison's jacket as he raises his fist in the air and goes into No Surrender. Some of the younger element in their early twenties are catching on and beginning to see what's what, while the more peaceful people in the bar smile to themselves and pour extra alcohol down their throats. England games are interesting because there's always blokes who travel on their own. You get a lot of these characters. If you take the amount of men into football and then chop it down to those who go away with England, we're a fairly small percentage. It means that not everyone's going to have mates who want to go to the likes of Germany and Italy. These solo characters don't care about the reception committee. Just pack their bags and go. After the first trip they find out how easy it is to fit in. If you're sound then there's no problem. Sometimes you get a wanker or two, but that's life. The English can always sniff out a wanker. NO SURRENDER, NO SURRENDER, NO SURRENDER TO THE IRA.

I see the three birds a couple of tables away looking around and talking among themselves. As the drink eases in I start eyeing up the one with the shoulder length hair. Brown and pulled back from her face. She's wearing faded jeans and a thin top. Fucking beautiful. I'm trying to work out whether she's German, Dutch or something else. It's a game all the boys play. Her skin's too light to be an Italian or anything like that, and anyway, if she lived in Rome she'd be on a plane. No dirty ferry travel for the spaghetti princess. I'm putting my money on Dutch. Don't know why. Instinct probably. It's like working out where a firm comes from. You can usually suss them out by the clothes or faces. Same with the birds when you go overseas. I see her jump when Carter arrives, failing with the smooth approach. Sex machine leaning over the back of the seat. You have to laugh because the bloke's got more front than most people I could mention.

He's there for a while and the girls seem interested enough. Least they haven't blanked him. Three into one shouldn't really go, but you never know with Carter. He's going to have to share the catch with the rest of the boys. I'm watching him in action when I recognise an ugly mug from the past. A big geezer from Shropshire. Been watching England for donkey's years. Started in Spain in 1982 and has seen all the World Cups since. One of the original Man United boys who kept the club going before the Stretford End was sold off to the living dead. Have to feel sorry for them because the Stretford End was a major end and the Red Army a massive away support. Funny thing is, they still get huge crowds but the place is a morgue. They've still got a proper crew, but tucked out of sight. Old

Trafford's almost as bad as the Highbury Library. It's a load of bollocks what they've done to the game back in England and that's why getting over to Europe is a tonic. It's like clicking back to when you could do whatever the fuck you wanted.

– Alright bud? Kev asks, shaking hands, followed by a couple of other blokes I don't know who he introduces by name and says he met on the train down to London. Crewe and Bolton fans.

– Alright Munich?

Shouldn't really use the Munich tag, but he's okay long as I don't do it more than once. I know him well enough. Wouldn't want to try and take liberties. He still carries a scar down his face from when he steamed into a carriage-load of Brighton single-handed at Finchley Road, on his way to Wembley.

– Careful, he smiles. Or I'll have to do the helicopter.

Don't like that. Have to admit it gets right up my nose. When we played Forest some of them were doing chopper impressions, winding us up about Matthew Harding. Man U were doing it as well up at Old Trafford. Only a few of them, but I suppose we used to sing WHO'S THAT BURNING ON THE RUNWAY enough times. Chelsea sorted Forest out after the game. Can still see Facelift stamping on some cunt's face. Shouldn't take the piss though. Specially about something like that. Right out of order. Makes you wonder what's going on in the Midlands. Leicester is a grudge game, some kind of Baby Squad revival. Doesn't matter now. We're all England.

I start thinking about Matthew Harding, the respect the man had from everyone in football. Couldn't believe it when he died. Why did it have to be someone like that? It's always the good ones who die. If it wasn't for Harding then we'd still be scratching around in the dirt. Thing is, he was Chelsea right through, and even though he was a multi-millionaire he was still down The Imperial having a pint with your everyday fan. Real diamond. The sort who only comes along once a lifetime. That's why you get us singing MATTHEW HARDING'S BLUE AND WHITE ARMY. Matthew should've been there to see Wise go up to lift the FA Cup after all he'd done.

We were standing outside the old Beer Engine after the Cup Final and there was a line of knobs coming though in their cars. The kind of stuck-up cunts who've overrun the area around Stamford Bridge. The old bill had sent them down the wrong street. The younger element were jumping on the bonnets, roofs, right over the top, while further down the road everyone was enjoying themselves having a drink outside The Adelaide and Imperial. Don't know about The Palmerston. It was all good natured. Then the old bill come down the road with their riot horses and vans and a fucking helicopter with a spotlight. Ruining the fun. Saying four pubs had already been turned over. Wrecked and looted as Chelsea celebrated the Cup win in style. Everyone in a good mood because we've won the FA Cup at last.

Now it's England and we're still Chelsea but putting everything in its right place. It's all a game really. It's the same for soldiers, though they'd never admit as much, because they like to feel more important than they really are. They sign their name and do as they're told. There's none of that bollocks here, because we're a volunteer army with a set of rules that are basic common sense. It's a good laugh, based in the English way of life. We're here because we're here. Because we want to be.

Bill Farrell couldn't sleep. He got out of bed and went to the kitchen, where he made another cup of tea. There were two biscuits left so he polished those off. He had this decision to make and it was gnawing away, demanding an answer. He was an old man now and had his routine. The only time he'd been out of the country was in a uniform. He'd gone across the Channel, fought, killed and come back. Since then he'd never been outside England. Now his nephew wanted him to travel across the world for a holiday in Australia. It was a long way and he felt he was too old, but didn't want to let the boy down, especially when he'd supplied the ticket and Farrell's daughter had arranged the visa. The family told him to go, but he didn't want to leave. London was his life. What if he died over there? He didn't want to end up with his ashes floating around in a bloody billabong.

He'd always been close to his nephew. He didn't know why really. Farrell's dad had died when he was one, from TB. He'd never known him. He'd looked to his uncles instead. Everyone needed a role model. Maybe that's why him and Vince were so close, the boy bypassing a generation. Boys needed men to set an example. They pointed you in the direction you'd follow the rest of your life. He thought of his uncles and looked at the picture on the wall, a drawing of a nun with a lamp. He hadn't thought of his uncles for a long time. He sipped the tea and wished he had some more biscuits. He was glad he'd thought of them now.

He'd had three uncles on his mum's side and all had served in the Great War. They were in his mind as he approached Normandy and he'd told himself that nothing that was to come could possibly be as bad as what they had experienced. He remembered those thoughts clearly. But he'd had no idea what was ahead of him. It was the First World War but they called it Great because of the number of people killed and maimed. Men, women and children. Animals too, thousands of dead, rotting horses with maggots eating into their guts. It wasn't so great for those who signed up for this War To End All Wars. There were the words and the music of the recruiting sergeant and his band, urging the boys to take the King's shilling and kiss the book.

There must've been a lot of excitement when the army started recruiting, the Kaiser an evil monster on the horizon threatening the English way of life, a traditional Prussian enemy far off in the East. The sergeant would have smiled and slapped the English boys on the back, pushing the comradeship and unity in fighting a common enemy. He would've drawn on English history and exploited youth's love of adventure, the atmosphere of the time created by the men in control and a compliant media. Farrell guessed it sounded good, and his uncles had admitted as much. They were simple boys and knew nothing of the world.

Farrell's uncles were Stan, Gill and Nolan. They lived in Hounslow, but their mum, Farrell's gran, ran a pub in Great Bedwyn, a village in Wiltshire. When he was a boy he'd looked up to his uncles because they were grown men and he wanted to be like them. They were kind to him and even now he smiled when he thought about them, how they talked and acted. When he was older he got to know about the Great War. He found out Gill and Nolan had fought on the Somme, and Stan in German East Africa, though they never went into details about their experiences. They never talked about things much, and Farrell had to piece their histories together later. He was told stories by his aunts, and after he'd been away himself and come home, they answered some of his questions. He supposed he became like them, that they shared something. Much of it he never learnt, but at least some information was passed down. He never knew what they thought or really felt, just that the Somme had been hell on earth. Farrell knew some of the facts, the bones of their stories, but could never feel what they felt. He wished he could now, all these years later, and he had tried in the landing craft. At least it kept him quiet as they headed for Europe.

Stan was the Jack-the-Lad of the family. Farrell smiled thinking of the story his mum told him, that she was at school sitting in her classroom when there was a loud bang on the door. The teacher went to see who was there, but only found a rotten potato on the ground. She turned and looked at Farrell's mum and asked if her brother Stan was home. It was the first she knew of it, but it was him alright. He'd been away fighting in an African jungle and still threw potatoes at classroom doors.

Stan was a bit of a rebel, even though he was a career soldier. He was a Royal Marine who wanted to travel and see the world. It was a way to discover things, signing up and broadening horizons. But Stan caught malaria and was forced out. The illness affected Stan and made him very unhappy. He wasn't going to be defeated, though, because he wanted to cure himself of the malaria and get back in the Marines. He drank a bottle of quinine and spent two days in a coma. He swore he'd either die or make himself well again. When he came round, when he survived his do-or-die treatment, he was cured. Nobody could understand it. The doctors were amazed. Stan went back to the Marines and they agreed he was cured, but because he'd had malaria the regulations said he couldn't return. And because he didn't have malaria, he was no longer eligible for his disability pension.

All Farrell's three uncles were changed by the war, sitting in the mud with the rotting bodies of their mates, the rats chewing through dead skin, the blood, shit and mutilation of the trenches, or in Stan's case the hardship of fighting in the jungle. Thousands were blinded by chemical weapons. Every man who served was mentally scarred, and Farrell knew deep down that the same applied to him. When he was a boy they knew the men who had suffered most, men like Bates. Their minds must have been racked by the horror of what they'd seen and done.

Nolan was upset by the war and upset by the brothels. He believed in God and was a spiritualist, something Farrell's friend Albert Moss had practised before his death. The sight of the English soldiers queueing for the whorehouses stuck in Nolan's mind for the rest of his life. He thought of the women in the brothels on their backs with queues of laughing-drunk squaddies waiting their turn, reduced to production line, last-gasp sex before the German guns blew them to kingdom come, filling the girls with syphilis. He wouldn't have used the prostitutes. Nolan was a quiet man who loved the country and suggested Farrell tried for the parks after the war.

Nolan was accused of theft while in France and spent six months in the glasshouse. It would've been hard in a military prison and there weren't the same rights in those days. This was a time when the officers were having soldiers shot for shell shock and barely-proven offences. Legalised murder it was, and even today they wouldn't grant pardons. It was a disgrace and showed the contempt the establishment had for those doing its dirty work. Eventually someone else was found to be responsible. Nolan was released without any kind of apology. Six months in the glasshouse for something you didn't do and you were treated like that. Stan and Nolan always felt they were badly treated by the armed forces.

When their mum, Farrell's gran, died, they took her coffin to the cemetery on a hand cart and lined the grave with wildflowers. They didn't have money for a gravestone. Farrell wondered whether if someone dug the grave up they'd find the flowers. As a boy he'd tried to imagine the colours. Even now he wished he knew. It was in his head again, trying to picture the unmarked grave. A blanket of colour and the smell of wet earth. The vicar would've stood over the hole and said the right words, and there she'd stay unseen but remembered, till her children died and the generations went on, and one day she would be forgotten.

Gill drew a picture in 1915, shortly before he went to war. Now it was on the wall of Farrell's living room. The frame was cheap and coming apart, but the drawing stood out. The paper was yellow, yet the sharp pencil lines and foggy shaded areas made an impression. Gill had drawn a nun with her head bowed, a lantern in her hand. The head was covered by a hood and he'd drawn her from the side. It was a thoughtful, sad picture, and he signed his name and added the date. Farrell was sitting in his flat in the early hours suffering from insomnia, looking at the picture. He wondered whether it was drawn from memory or imagination. Maybe Gill saw his death and the figure was coming to lead him to the light, but it was more to do with survival. Gill didn't fall in the Great War.

Years later Gill did two paintings. They were watercolours and Farrell had them there next to the nun. Each painting was of a vase, and each of the vases was full of flowers. There were different shapes and colours, and the paintings were more childlike, more happy. Gill painted these in 1933, years after the war when peace had returned. Six years later, of course, there was another world war and his nephew was sent to fight the Germans again, the new enemy on the horizon coming from the same place. Farrell loved the nun and the flowers.

The next generation who went off to war were again fresh-faced youths such as Bill Farrell, again ready for adventure. They say nothing is learnt from history and he agreed, but the monster on the horizon really was a monster this time. The Second World War was different. When Farrell saw that concentration camp he knew it was different. His uncles sat in miles of trenches as the machine guns rattled and shells shattered human bodies. They would never forget and they'd never be able to share the feeling. Maybe that's why they never really tried. Farrell knew it was the way things were. He could never share what he felt. He could never make Bob West understand. That's why his wife had been special. One of the reasons anyway. She'd seen the horror and been through much worse than her husband. Both of them knew something. Even now, Farrell felt sorry for his uncles and the mates they'd lost. Maybe it was worse for them, because there was no real reason for the slaughter.

Stan had told Farrell he'd either be rich or hang. He said Farrell was a lot like him and Farrell's mum agreed. Farrell never got rich and he'd obviously never hung. He'd lived his life best he could. There were hard times, but mostly they were good.

He remembered the food and drink of the spread they'd done for him when he came back from Europe. It was a good time and he had to struggle to see the landing craft. It came back, the way the guns pounded the shore and the knowledge that the Beach Master would be in there first with the commandos who'd pave the way. They admired those men because they were brave enough to take the initial flak and would suffer the first losses. But they were all in the thing together. The troops rolling in were ready to fight. There were a lot of blokes who'd been evacuated from Dunkirk and their pride was at stake. They were going to give the Germans a going over.

Farrell didn't want the details, but they were there in his head. The sea was rough and there was a smell of shit. Farrell wasn't disgusted and it made him feel stronger because it wasn't him. The man behind him was praying quietly and he heard a couple of deep sobs from further back. Some of the rougher men were shouting and swearing and telling everyone what they were going to do to the Germans when they got hold of them. There was one they called Mangler, a villain who hung around the racetracks and was well known to the police, a bad man to know but worth having on your side. He wanted to kill and maim Germans, he told the lads he was looking forward to it, and despite what they put in the films there were men like that around. The films painted the English as naïve virgins, but they were men like other men.

There was sex and drink. There were fights and there were drugs. Mostly opium dens in the East End. It was in the background, and those interested kept their business to themselves. Around Piccadilly and into Soho there were prostitutes – painted dollies – and sex clubs. There were said to be sex parties with people twisted by the war. There were poofs, but they were looked down on and kept themselves to themselves. You just knew these things existed. There was no need to talk about it too much. It wasn't the English way.

Harry had forgotten the film and he'd only been out of the cinema for a few minutes. He wasn't thinking of vintage war films because they'd be arriving in the Hook soon enough and he was in the duty-free looking for a bargain. He caught sight of a couple of the Spice kids he'd showered with sick and moved behind a rack. They were washed and scrubbed and back to their giggling best, and didn't see him. It was the roll of the dice and he checked the Toblerone and Yorkie prices. His mouth watered as he considered the options, a heavy hand on his shoulder the hand of an arresting officer telling him he was nicked. He turned round fast and faced the wide boys themselves, the toy-shop gangland bosses thieving gin and vodka, thinking big and acting small. High Street and Biggs were helping themselves. Both were pissed and getting their money's worth.

– The bar's packed and there must be at least two hundred England in there, Biggs shouted. They're on the piss and there's going to be trouble before we get off this boat. I can see it boiling up.

– If this is the warm-up, what's the rest of the trip going to be like? Ken wanted to know. This ferry's full of headcases.

Before Harry had time to reply they were stumbling off round the aisles pushing each other back and forward, behaving like a couple of snotty-nosed juveniles. Harry decided to leave the chocolate till the return leg. He looked towards the woman on the till but she didn't seem bothered, yawning as she served a man with a stack of fag cartons and a hacking cough. The way High Street and Biggs were acting they were going to get themselves nicked. There were cameras and there'd probably be a security guard. Harry was sober and going down the bar. He wanted to get off the ferry and didn't fancy knocking about with a couple of shoplifters. He was bored as fuck. That film was shit. Why hadn't they put on the *The Cruel Sea* or something? Jack Hawkins doing the business in the North Atlantic. This was the worst bit, getting across the Channel without being torpedoed by a fucking U-boat, or sunk because the doors weren't shut properly.

The ferry was a mess of people and it smelt scabby. The flavours were all blending together now – sausages and bacon in the canteen, car fumes in the hold, drink from the bar, perfume from the duty-free, piss and sick from the bogs, plus the sweat of all these men and women packed in together. He clanked through the turnstyle and hurried towards the bar to find Carter and the others. It shouldn't take them too long to get to Amsterdam and they had a hotel lined up not far from the red light. Harry was looking forward to a couple of days sitting back having a good smoke, a chilled lager or two, with a nice Dutch model on the end of his knob. Not tonight though. He wanted to dump his bag in the hotel, find a bar and have a drink or two, then a few zeds.

WHO THE FUCK, WHO THE FUCK, WHO THE FUCKING HELL ARE YOU... WHO THE FUCKING HELL ARE YOU?

Harry could hear the singing right down the hall and noticed that a lot of passengers were looking nervous and going in the opposite direction. He'd seen the faces before. The shocked, stunned, half-disgusted faces of honest Middle Europeans coming face to face with the flower of English manhood. They'd caught a glimpse of the Expeditionary Force and didn't like what they saw. The invaders were drunk and noisy and turning nasty. The cropped hair, tattoos, jeans, jackets, broken glass, songs, Union Jacks and Crosses of St George made Franz Foreigner nervous. Harry had to laugh. Maybe it was just good humour, but the singing didn't sound too friendly, and he wondered who was asking who the question.

HELLO, HELLO, WE ARE THE PORTSMOUTH BOYS.

Harry had his answer.

HELLO, HELLO, WE ARE THE PORTSMOUTH BOYS.

He nodded.

AND IF YOU ARE A SOUTHAMPTON FAN, SURRENDER OR YOU'LL DIE, WE WILL FOLLOW THE PORTSMOUTH.

Portsmouth always travelled with England. If there was a Millwall or Southampton mob on board there was a very good chance the crossing would end in tears. He wondered if it would be Millwall or Southampton, heard the bells chime.

FUCK OFF POMPEY, POMPEY FUCK OFF.

Harry arrived as Southampton and Portsmouth met on the small area that acted as a temporary dancefloor. It was roughly ten a side and those non-football people still in the bar were running past him, getting out of the firing line. Several lager bottles landed behind the counter, lobbed by other drunk English further back simply enjoying the film, and the bartenders were pulling the shutters down. Another bottle hit a row of spirit bottles, drink and glass exploding with a hollow popping sound. He saw Gary Davison and a couple of his mob taking advantage and unloading the cash register, moving in from the side. In and out like scousers. Harry clocked all this in a second because walking in on the scene sober was mental, a laugh and a half seeing the funny side of life, even if Southampton and Pompey were going at each other full of the kind of hate that's personal and built on history and endless derby battles, bad blood frothing with the lager, spat out and kicked back twice as hard. He stood aside as one bloke went through a table and a couple of men started kicking him in the ribs and head, the man's mates piling in, tables and chairs cracking as some of the other English started wrecking a corner of the bar, building a splintered bonfire for Guy Fawkes and the Pope.

In the background Harry could see Billy Bright's flag with its CHELSEA headline and the man himself fucking about with his cassette player, laughing his head off trying to add a soundtrack, but he couldn't find what he wanted and gave up. When Harry looked left there were similar flags hanging over windows with SWINDON and ARSENAL and WEST BROM along the horizontal bar of the red crosses, a huge Union Jack with KENT LOYALISTS blaring out, Harry taking all this in fast as the battle spilled through the bar, the rest of the English drunk and backing off to let the South Coast rivals sort out their differences, harbour town clubs used to fighting at sea, more tables turned over and the sound of smashing glass mixing with the violence of the punches and kicks, a youth with short shiny hair and a stained leather jacket stumbling past with a wicked-looking cut along his cheek, blood all over the shop, standing there shocked as a couple of spectators gave him a hanky to stop the flood. Harry looked at the gash and shook his head.

Southampton and Pompey were taking no prisoners and there were enough cuts and bruises on the two sides, neither running the other, a stand-off as they battered the fuck out of each other, having a breather shouting insults, and then it kicked off with stewards coming in between the two sides trying to calm things down. The rest of the English hung about waiting to see what would happen next, knowing it was personal and daft somehow, because if you couldn't get it together for the battle in Europe you had no chance. They had to be united. Harry saw it clearly, that it was the stress and strain of crossing the water, and for a minute he wondered if the English would mob together and do the stewards, these men in white shirts, sinking the ferry for a laugh and swimming to shore. The moment passed and some kind of calm returned.

Tommy Johnson and the rest of the boys came over and Tom was laughing, telling them they'd better move down the boat otherwise they'd be there for hours in the Hook while the old bill tugged the sailors and anyone stupid enough to hang around watching. No fucking idea, he was saying to Harry, no fucking idea, and they started filtering down the ferry. Harry looked back and the bar was wrecked, the flags down and packed away. Tom was pulling a pissed Facelift back because he was eyeballing the West Ham boys and one of them was a Romford mirror of the Hayes man, pulled back by an Essex version of Tom.

Harry followed the rest of the lads. They were pulling into the Hook and the Dutch old bill would be waiting. They didn't need the grief. Holland might be a laid-back country, but not when it came to the old bill. They had enough hooligans of their own not to treat it like a circus, and they no longer thought of the English as good-natured eccentrics. You had to get across the Channel in one piece, but Harry understood. It was part of being an island race. The English Channel was built into everyone. It was a natural barrier that set Britain apart. If Hitler could've taken out the RAF he'd have crossed the Channel. The Luftwaffe couldn't do it and that bit of water kept England free. Harry had seen the films. There were no borders other than those with Scotland and Wales. No wonder the Europeans invented fascism, because they had to fight to preserve their identity the whole time inside man-made boundaries.

It was hard for the England boys going across the Channel, and naturally they needed a drink to ease things along, and naturally people could get out of hand, and naturally the continental lagers were that bit stronger and fucked your head up, but it didn't matter. Old rivalries came into the open and discipline was bound to go out the window. They were crossing the line and it was an emotional time, hanging on to the last link with home before they entered a strange, dangerous land, full of people who hated the English. Harry saw it differently, but then he liked Europe more than the others. He understood what the boys were going through and hoped they would relax in Amsterdam. Foreign travel helped broaden the mind and Harry couldn't wait.

—The English way of getting through something is to close our eyes and jump in at the deep end. When the front of the landing craft went down everything moved very fast. Our thoughts were confused as we approached the shore so I did my best to keep my mind on my uncles. For the first time in my life I was really trying to imagine how they felt. It was an impossible task, but it kept me calm. I breathed deep and it worked. I imagined I was the weak one, but I suppose most of the boys felt the same way. Being brave is being scared but conquering the fear. Even now, I find it hard to admit I was a scared young man. We did what had to be done. The noise was terrible and I tried to block it out. There was a man screaming, but he wasn't in our landing craft. I blocked this out as well, glancing at the pale white faces packed shoulder to shoulder. I didn't want to think about what had happened to him. I was trying to dig a hole in my head and bury myself. I wanted to be brave and I was going to be brave, bracing myself for the moment, because the front of the landing craft crashed down and there was a thud that snapped us into action. At that moment I was the most pointed I'd ever been in my life. The metal shield fell forward and we were faced with the reality, a beach crisscrossed with wire and barricades, explosions churning up great holes and the sea chopping about. We knew we had to get out of the landing craft fast and now I discovered that I actually wanted to get to the sand and feel my boots sink in. We were sitting ducks in the landing craft. We were exposed and the realisation was a massive electrical current through our bodies. One shell would wipe us out. The sergeant knew this better than anyone. We were angry now and wanted to kill. We wanted to wipe these Nazis off the face of the earth. Suddenly I wasn't scared because as we moved forward all our energy was centred on getting to the sand and from there fighting our way to the enemy. We wanted to kill these men and get the job done. I shouted and my hate made me hard. I was trained to channel this anger and my boxing helped. We surged forward and the feeling was incredible. It was the adrenalin that comes to save you when your life is threatened. There was an injection of the drug as a shell exploded in the water and rocked the craft. We stumbled and fought to stay standing. It's a chemical in the body that fights for your survival because surviving is everything, the survival of the individual and survival of the tribe. The sergeant didn't need his machine gun because we moved quickly as a unit, tramping through the water, and the next thing we knew we were knee deep in the sea. It must have felt good to touch the bottom, though I don't remember clearly. I was looking to my left and right briefly and the beach ahead was sandy and covered in obstacles, but the sea was packed with assault craft and the shapes of men battling against the water and the rattling of German guns, exploding mortars and shells creating havoc with the sea and sand. A shell whistled to my right and blew a man's head clean off his neck, blood pumping into the air and staining the Channel, and I could feel the bile in my mouth but somehow I swallowed it again, and for a couple of seconds I slowed up to look and try to understand what had happened. I was pushed forward by the man behind, my eyes locked to the body of the decapitated soldier which moved forward one or two steps before falling to the water and floating front down with the back hunched like a rock. I felt myself falling with the dead soldier. I stumbled towards the sea and my hands went out and under the water, a wave backing up from the shore and filling my mouth with salt, water flushing through my nose with the snot and covering my head. For a moment I thought the salt was the taste of blood and that I'd been hit by a bullet or shell. I was still and then pushed my head above the sea. I was choking on the water and the image of the soldier was confused in my head. I saw myself blown to bits before I'd even had a chance to fight the enemy and this made me angrier, thinking of my mum and family, the bombed out London streets and stories of Dunkirk, the suffering of my uncles fighting these Germans who were always stirring up trouble, Johnny Bates's old man alone in a dark room whimpering like a dog. I wasn't going to be one of the countless war dead filed on a church monument and forgotten. There was no way I was going to die in the Channel, sucked into the depths and left to rot. I had a life at home and I wanted to get back in one piece. I hauled myself up and someone gave me a hand. I was moving forward. The front of my uniform was soaked but I didn't feel the wetness, it was just the water made me heavier. I was determined and hurried to the beach. Getting to firm land reassured me. I was one of thousands of other men and just a name on a churchyard monument, but I was all I had right now and I wanted to see my mum again because she'd made me promise I'd come back. She didn't want to lose me to a stupid war. Why did this keep happening to her, because she'd spent years worrying about her brothers and I had to come back just as they'd done. Everything was precious on that beach, my memories kept me sharp. I was walking into a nightmare, but I had good mates with me. We were united together against a common enemy. All these boys would help me out. I wasn't really thinking this at the time, I just knew it was true, because if there is a hell on earth then this was near enough. The Germans were killing the English and it wasn't clean, bloodless bullet wounds. There were no rules. There was little mercy. It was bloody fighting and killing. Men were blown in half, their arms and legs torn in every direction. Teenagers took wounds in their guts and one boy saw his intestines spill into the sand, a mass of bloated worms. The blood was red and black. I was down on the sand and there was a man's arm under my chest. I moved forward quickly and we started working our way up the beach firing at the enemy. I couldn't see them but I could see what they were doing. Planes were screaming over as the RAF attacked the German fortifications, the boom of the big guns off-shore already established in our heads. The air force and the navy gave us hope because for the first time we really believed we were going to sort these bastards out. We were moving towards the enemy when Billy Walsh next to me took a round in his groin. It was in his balls, and he was leaning into me screaming blue murder. I could see the front of his uniform had turned black and the material was ripped. The Germans had blown his balls and dick off. There was nothing left. There was just gristle and I needed help. I called out but nobody came. There were wounded everywhere and I was cradling his head, because Billy was in shock and I didn't know if he was bleeding to death. I tried to stop the blood with my hands, but then someone with a cross took over. I held Billy's hand for a moment and I wondered what his life was going to be like, forced to live without his manhood. I wondered if he was better off dead and what I would do in his position. Maybe I should've smothered him there and then, put a bullet in his head, but there was no time to think with the sergeant yelling at us to go forward. I squeezed Billy's hand and let go. We shared the same name, but I was the lucky one, rubbing my bloody hands in the sand, bits sticking. He was screaming above the sound of the guns. We moved forward slowly and stopped. There was a long line of soldiers firing and I stayed for a while. I don't know how long, but I know my ears were numb from the sound. I might've pissed myself. I'm not sure. It could've been the sea. I hope I didn't piss myself. I'd never admit as much. Stopping wasn't good for you because it gave you time to think and look around at the mutilated bodies, the body parts cold and shapeless. There was a lot of blood where I was. I'll always remember that. The smell of blood is with me today. Sickly, rich, sweet and dead. I looked back and knew this was me gone now. I would never be the boy in the pub who liked a drink and a laugh. I wasn't made for this. None of us were made for this, but we were men and we conquered our fear and controlled ourselves, and then we were charging the enemy and working our way through defences opened up by professional, specialist commando units, the mob charging through shouting and swearing, a rabble of men tight and controlled somehow, pumping blood and ready for murder. I ripped my arm on the wire but felt nothing, kept moving with the rest of the boys.

I don't know how long we were fighting. It was slow and dirty. Eventually we were off the beach. There were German soldiers waiting for us, moving back from their burning pill-boxes as flames licked through the cracks incinerating their mates. I suppose they must've been more terrified than we were. They didn't scare me much individually. It was better hand-to-hand. Better than being picked off in the open. Hand-to-hand fighting suited me fine. I really wanted to fight now with the actual landing behind us and people I knew ripped apart. For years we'd been pinned down in our own country fearing invasion while Hitler killed our women and children, and now we were fresh from another assault with the chance to make amends. I felt brilliant. For the first time I felt great, though it wouldn't last long. I was concentrated and all my fury came through. This is what we'd been waiting for. Without uniforms the Germans would've looked like us, I suppose, but I didn't think of this at the time. There was an older German turning towards me and before he could fire I stuck him with my bayonet. The steel jammed into his heart and I had trouble pulling it out. He was a murdering kraut bastard and when the bayonet sprung out it was red and gleaming. His blood suited the steel and I enjoyed the kill. Not like a sadist, but like a soldier killing the enemy. It was me or him. It was us or them. I cut him across the neck and he dropped. I shot two Germans running towards me. One I killed and the other looked as though he was dying. Other Germans started to run and we followed. I was with Mangler and some others. There were fires everywhere and the burnt wrecks of cars and trucks. The smell was incredible and it was hard to breathe as we passed one burnt-out wreck. Mangler was shouting at the Germans and some other English soldiers cornered them. The Germans stopped and threw down their guns. They put up their hands. Mangler hit one in the face with his rifle butt and forced his bayonet against the man's balls, pushing him against a wall. He laughed in the German's face and said he was going to castrate him for Billy Walsh. The German was shaking. A sergeant intervened and, with some difficulty, pushed Mangler away. Maybe I wouldn't have cared if Mangler had done it at the time because I was mad. I don't know for sure. I think we were all a bit mad because you have to be mad to fight in a war. To kill people and see your friends butchered. Every normal value is forgotten. Afterwards they try and patch things up and apply a nice coat of paint, hand out some medals and compose tunes, but I know how I felt. I'm being honest with myself. We left the Germans and I suppose they were lucky. I like to think I would have stopped Mangler if he'd ripped the bloke's trousers and started cutting. I'm sure I would. Maybe he wouldn't have gone through with it and was trying to scare the man. That's what it was. It worked because the German started crying and his mates looked at him with disgust. We moved forward and the fighting continued. The killing went on. The German soldiers eventually surrendered. Men died and it became dull and repetitive as the killing on the beach was repeated, but more deliberately. Our senses were shattered. The noise and smell were sharp for a while, then disappeared. My ears were ringing and smoke made my eyes sting. I saw things I'd never forget, maybe because they were new, but the man having his head blown off and Billy Walsh losing his genitals, and shortly after, his life, stuck. The same things happened many times during my time in Europe and after a while I stopped feeling sick and there was a dull throb in my head that passed right through me. It was inside now and when we'd taken the beach we were able to stop for a while. Someone gave me a fag and even though I didn't smoke I took it and enjoyed the taste. It showed I was alive. I have to try and remember what I felt at that moment because it's over half a century away. Some things you never forget, and landing in Europe is one of them. I knew it was something I never wanted to experience again, but this was naïve. This was the beginning. I would see other things that would affect me, but this was where the liberation began. The men from Dunkirk had been through a lot already, but they seemed stunned. I sat there and smoked the cigarette and looked around for Mangler. I was glad now the sergeant had arrived and saved the German soldier. I wondered what Mangler was doing, because the sergeant had struggled to stop him. I thought of the beach and how the smell and colour of the blood had got inside my head. It's hard to be honest about those twenty or so minutes immediately after we knew we'd secured the bridge-head. I can't remember any of our mob cheering, and no-one seemed over happy. What did I do? How did I feel? Even though it would be unmanly, I'd like to say I shed a quiet tear or two. But I didn't. I think I just sat there and didn't feel anything at all.

NO-MAN'S LAND

It took Harry a few seconds to remember he was in an Amsterdam hotel and not back home in London. The room was dark, but a beam of light had broken under the curtains and created a spotlight effect on the floor. He looked at the clock on the bedside table, at the glowing digits swearing it was nine o'clock, and realised he felt fine after the ferry crossing. He hadn't slept long, but that childhood excitement of going on holiday was coming through with a vengeance. The sheets were crisp and the room airy, everything smelling clean and new. He definitely wasn't in London.

Once his eyes had adjusted he could see the shape of Carter under the duvet in the second bed, the sex machine snoring like a pig. The old hog-fucker was doing what pigs do best and he'd let the bloke sleep. The sex machine needed his energy for the girls running their way, and Harry would be spending enough time with him later when the action began. Once the lights went down and the birds started stirring, he'd stick closer than a shadow. He was learning some overdue lessons and could taste those red ruby lips already. He'd woken up with half a hard-on and thinking of the girls they'd be knobbing finished the job. He thought about banging off a quick one, but resisted the temptation. He wanted to be at his best. The lucky woman he was destined to meet later that day was going to get the back of her fucking head blown off.

Ten past and Harry was off down the hall for a shit, shower and shave. He stood under a full-throttle nozzle generous with the hot water, using a brand new Bic to remove the stubble on his face. He was impressed, because in England the hot water would've run out after five minutes they were so tight. People went on about Jocks and yiddos being mean, but the English even counted the peas on your plate to make sure you weren't getting one too many. He dabbed aftershave on his cheeks and checked himself in the mirror. He looked the part and went back down the hall with a towel around his waist, a middle-aged woman passing and not taking any notice. This was Holland and they didn't give a toss. Do that in a bed and breakfast in Bournemouth and they'd have the Tactical Support Group battering down your door.

Carter was still snoring and Harry got dressed quickly, selecting yesterday's Levi's, trainers and a crumpled shirt, running his hands over the material to try and get rid of the creases. He left Carter well alone, closing the door quietly and going down a narrow wooden staircase to the reception. He almost fell arse over tit it was so tight. Hank behind the counter was a middle-aged man with a balding head and a cup of coffee on the go. A typical Dutchman, he spoke perfect English.

– Did you sleep okay? he asked, radio low in the background and the smell of fresh coffee rising from the mug. You boys were tired when you got here and still you went out for a drink.

– Slept like a baby, Harry said.

He wanted to add that he'd done it without a nappy and hadn't wet the bed, but knew the joke would probably get lost in the translation. He didn't want Hank sniffing the sheets while he was out.

– Best night's rest I've had for a long time.

It was gone three by the time they arrived in Amsterdam. They'd had a few cans while they fucked about with the trains from the Hook, done the fifteen-minute walk from Centraal, dumped their gear, and then found a bar down the road. They'd lined the hotel up ahead of time, otherwise they'd have been fucking about all night banging on doors. Tom had stayed there before and got them a bulk discount.

The bar was quiet and they'd had a couple of lagers to wash away the dust before turning in for the night. Four in the morning and they were fucked. When they arrived in the Hook, the Dutch old bill had turned up in force decked out in riot helmets and backed up by dogs, and the Pompey and

Southampton boys were identified by members of the ferry crew. With a few whacks from the truncheons the seasiders were rounded up ready for deportation. They'd gone through the rest of the English and Facelift was sent home along with High Street and Biggs, both caught with their nicked gear. Facelift was pissed and mouthy and started sieg heiling the coppers. He was a thick cunt, because this didn't go down too well with the Dutch. They didn't fancy the Union Jack tattoos and the beer bottle in his hand, but worst of all the Gestapo routine wasn't too clever in a country where the Germans were hated for what they'd done during the war. Harry didn't know Facelift that well, he was Mark and Tom's mate, but though it got a laugh from the rest of the chaps, Facelift was a mug.

The rest of the lads kept quiet and did their boy scout routine, and Tom, Mark, Carter, Billy and Harry had got the train along with Gary Davison and his mob, plus Kevin and the lads from Crewe and Bolton, the rest of the English scattered through the carriages. There were probably a good twenty English kicked out for fighting, being pissed, thieving, or because the old bill just didn't like the look of them. The papers would have a field day back in England and there was bound to be some wanker on the boat ready to tip them off. Thank fuck that was over. Harry hated ferries.

– Breakfast is along the corridor, Hank said, shifting his head. It's not your traditional English food, but there is ham and cheese. The coffee is very good. It is an Italian blend I buy specially for my guests.

Harry went down the hall to a small room. He was the only one there and Mrs Hank brought him his food right away. The coffee smelt fucking brilliant, while the breakfast looked so-so. It was on the light side, and though he loved a good fry-up like the next man, there was more to England than greasy spoons. Harry started running through his favourites: jam donuts and bacon rolls from the baker's where Mango's sister worked, cod and chips from the chippy, chicken jalfrezi down Balti Heaven, spare ribs from the chinky, a double egg burger from the Istanbul Kebab House, patties and dumplings from the Jamaican, Heinz tomato soup and crusty rolls with a ton of butter in front of the telly. He could go on, but his mouth was watering and he wanted to forget London, that's why he was on holiday. Even the biggest food snob had to agree that England had its own fair share of decent grub. Or scran as Kevin would say when he came in and sat down.

– Alright bud? he asked.

– Not bad, Harry replied, feeling brilliant inside.

This was what it was all about. Going walkabout and seeing the world. Sitting in Holland with the sun shining through the window, stuffing cheese and ham inside his bread roll, eyeing up the croissant. He took a bite and had to admit it wasn't bad.

– That Hank who runs this place, Kevin said, once Mrs Hank had been and gone. He's a bit of a perv that one. You look behind the counter and he's got the wank mags piled right up for the nightshift. We probably interrupted him when we came in this morning. That's his on-duty reading by the looks of things. Big motorbike mamas with huge tits covered in tattoos, the dirty bastard.

– They're all like that over here, Harry reasoned. They don't care, do they? Anything goes in Amsterdam.

– You wouldn't want those women out on show if there were kids about, Kevin observed, looking at the thin ham and cheese with a worried expression. Not much chance of putting on any weight with this, is there?

– The coffee's alright.

– You take a young boy and he sees those monsters with fifty-inch tits and tattooed nipples, and it'll put him off birds for life. Could even turn him funny. I'm going to need a bit more than this to eat.

Harry had to agree with the northerner. He had a hole in his gut and the food was already gone. He polished off his drink and left Kev to eat his breakfast, asking Hank which way he should turn when he got outside. He tried to sneak a look and see the owner's magazines, but there only a couple of phone books and the register they'd signed last night. Hank was thinking hard and asked Harry what he was looking for, suggesting left, right, left for the busier areas.

Outside Harry was reborn. The ferry crossing hadn't been as

bad as he'd predicted. He laughed thinking about the school-kids and how he'd covered them in sick. It was all in the past now, a story to tell the rest of the boys over a few pints, and something the girls would learn to laugh about. It might take a few years, but they'd get there in the end. He was in Holland and determined to make the most of his time away from England. He wasn't thinking back any more. Looking at the buildings and the canal and the bikes on the railings, a clean sky above and happy people passing, Harry couldn't be bothered with the arguments against Europe. If this was Europe then he couldn't wait till England was fully signed up. All he got the whole time was propaganda shoved down his throat, but from now on he was going with what he saw. Imagine thinking of baked beans when there was a stall selling chips and mayonnaise. He went over and ordered his cone. He was served by a man with an Ajax badge on his shirt. The chips tasted good, the mayonnaise even better. This was the life. He'd crossed the Channel and left his sickness on the lower deck, in the curled hair of some Home Counties teenyboppers. It had done Harry the world of good. At night he was sticking with the sex machine on his hunting trips, but during the day he was off on his own.

The hotel was on a canal and Harry did as Hank suggested, turning left and strolling next to the slow-moving water, passing painted houseboats moored along tree-lined streets, cobbles clicking on the heels of pedestrians. He didn't fancy the dog shit he almost stepped in, but there was always someone acting the cunt. On the corners there were stacks of bikes locked together, the big windows at the top of the buildings beaming back leaves and clouds. The air was fresh for a city, the canal-side streets free from traffic. There weren't a lot of people around and that suited him fine, because it gave you space to breathe. It was a lot different to London, where everyone was packed in tight and the car fumes and traffic grinding along the high street stuck in your head.

Harry followed Hank's directions and after passing through a small square he ended up in a market stacked with flowers. It seemed right and he wandered along, turning back towards

Centraal. He spent the next three hours walking, looking at canals and dodging trams. His feet had started to ache, he needed a piss and he fancied a rest. He also fancied a drink and Rudi's Bar looked okay, so he went inside. There were twenty or so people scattered around, talking among themselves, a couple of birds at the bar, the barman fucking about with some glasses. He looked at the names chalked on a big blackboard and chose a Belgian beer made from wheat. He paid his guilders and shot off to the bog.

He stood over the toilet and the piss blew out of him. He was pissing for England and stopped to read the graffiti, a mixture of Ajax and Feyenoord football and drug-happy nursery rhymes. Something in his head made him think about adding his signature to the wall, but why bother? He was too old for graffiti. He could hear someone shitting in the cubicle and didn't hang around once he'd finished.

Harry went back to the bar and picked up his drink. It was a strange taste, a lot different to the lager he was used to drinking. You had to give these things a go, so he wasn't complaining. The two women next to him stopped to look when he made a face and he gave them his best smile. They nodded back and did what the Dutch do best, acting nice and friendly, asking him if he was English. Harry nodded and sat down on the bar stool. They were eating something that smelt of peanut sauce and looked like kebabs on skewers. He was hungry. The girls said they were satays and came from Indonesia. They said Indonesia had been a Dutch colony and this surprised Harry because he didn't know that the old clogs were into empires same as the English and Spanish. It was like the Indian food at home. The satays smelt good and Harry ordered some for himself, chatting with the girls as the Rolling Stones played quietly in the background and the barman boiled a plastic bag behind the counter.

This was living, finding a hideaway and chatting with a couple of nice-looking locals, a bit hippyish but more biker than smelly crusties, in their thirties with long hair and red and green trousers, but he wouldn't say no if they offered him a blow job, and their tits were a lot tighter than fifty inches. He could smell dope in the air, everyone in their own worlds.

– So why are you in Amsterdam? Hairy 1 asked.

– I'm just here for a couple of days, having a holiday, Harry said. I'm on my way to Berlin with a few friends.

– Have you been there before? Hairy 2 asked. Do you know people in Berlin?

Harry felt like he was on Mastermind, but without any light in his eyes. Either that or he'd been lined up by two undercover coppers sniffing for titbits. He was going to say he was off to a football match, but thought better of it, because the papers were the same wherever you went and they'd get the wrong idea. Long-hairs didn't understand these things. He didn't want to put them off, though he wasn't really looking to get his leg over right now. There was a time and place for everything. Maybe later.

– Not yet, but I think we're going to meet a lot of Germans when we get there.

A couple of greasers wandered in and sat down with the girls. They were big fuckers. Must've weighed twenty stone each. They weren't greasers either. More like Hell's Angels. Harry waited for the smell to hit him. He'd heard the Angels wore originals covered in the shit and piss of their mates. It was supposed to be some kind of initiation ceremony. It wasn't nice, but what did you expect from hairies? Maybe he was wrong about the shit and piss, because it sounded like something a bunch of queers would get up to, and the Angels definitely weren't bum bandits, no fucking way would he accuse these two of crimes against nature. He'd heard they were into gang-bangs as well, which he didn't fancy at all. He didn't know much about the Hell's Angels, just stories, and he knew from his time going to football that the way these things were written up was usually a load of bollocks. But they were big cunts, covered with tattoos and must've been forty if they were a day, and they even bought him a drink when they saw he was friendly with the girls.

Harry settled in for a couple of lagers and one of the Angels skinned up and passed him some blow. This was the life, but he had to laugh, because you wouldn't get this at home. If a couple of nutters walked in and found some bloke chatting with their girlfriends he'd get more than a drink and a smoke. The Dutch were classy people and Harry reckoned he could get used to this. Stroll on Europe.

We don't have to look far to find Harris because there he is at the end of the bar sitting on a stool, the wall behind him acting as a screen. There's a blonde bird worked into the lining of the plaster, flickering light showing off a nice pair of medium-sized tits and a cropped cunt. You can tell she's a good-looking girl and deserves better than the skinny ginger cock shooting spunk over her face. Ginger pumps a couple of gallons of mutant seed over an appreciative Blondie, somehow managing it in slow-motion. Talk about self-control. Blondie throws her head back and licks her lips as Ginger follows through with another better-placed spurt. I'm half expecting Andy Gray to start spouting a commentary, except this isn't something you'd get on satellite. There's no sound and the film drifts into shades of grey before bouncing back full-frontal. It's an early afternoon matinee with ten or so English sitting at the tables watching the show, Amstel and Heineken bottles in their right hands. One bloke isn't bothered. Head down on the table sleeping. Blondie's smearing spunk into her cheeks and taking it down to her tits. The camera moves closer so the whole bar can see her working the congealed mess into upright nipples. Ginger has disappeared and this other bird arrives with a massive black dildo strapped to her cunt. Apart from this and a pair of red stilettoes, she's naked. The dildo has a gold tip and is greased in a glistening cream. Blondie assumes the position. The camera moves in again and gives the punters a close-up of her fanny and then backs out so we can get a good look at this Black Dick Dyke moving in for the kill. The new girl doesn't hang about and we get to see Blondie's ecstasy as the creases of her moaning face crack the fast-hardening spunk. Mark's going fucking hell, you wouldn't get this down The Unity, looking at Carter in particular who's been poking Denise the barmaid and could well have been doing something similar in the cellar. Can't see any pub at home showing this sort of stuff, but now it seems the girl getting serviced by Black Dick isn't getting off so easy. Ginger's back for a second helping and this time he means business. He's back with a vengeance. The production crew's been busy behind the camera, sticking a needle in his knob and injecting some muscle. Ginger's frothing at the mouth and doing the stallion routine. Blondie opens her mouth and gets a genuine length rammed down her throat. The film settles and the cameraman moves back out for a long-shot of the happy threesome, probably having a wank himself. But the bird on the receiving is well nice and you have to wonder how much she's getting paid. It takes all of twenty seconds for Ginger to get bored with this oral pleasure, pull out and move aside for some Arab who's appeared out of thin air. A couple of the boys aren't too pleased about this, seeing a white slave girl getting abused by a camel-shagger. Ginger goes up behind Black Dick, moves her aside, greases Blondie's arse, and slips in, buried to the hilt. We get a close look at her face and she winces as Ginger enters. Now she shows her acting ability. The kind of talent that would go down a treat in Hollywood. Showing the boys in the bar she loves nothing more than a good six inches of ginger cock up the dirt box. The Dirty Arab is wide-eyed at the other end as he gets his first blow-job off a bird. A blonde as well. Can't believe his luck. Years spent in the desert humping young boys and geriatric camels and now he's getting stuck into the opposite sex.

– Move over Ginger, Carter laughs. It's my turn next.

There's an old grey-blonde woman sitting at a table with a glass of red wine. She's watching the film with a funny look on her face. Probably Blondie's mum. I wonder how she feels seeing her daughter on the silver screen, the wall of a bar.

– That bird's going to have trouble sitting down when Ginger's finished, Mark says, as we finally get to the bar. You wouldn't want to go in after Ginger. I reckon old Ginger's a bit ginger himself.

– He's not a shirt-lifter. He wouldn't be able to get it up, would he?

Harris turns round and has a look. Turns back.

– They had that one on last night, he says. There's worse to come.

Carter leans in and orders from the barman.

– This is Johan, Harris says, introducing the skinhead serving the drink. He lives in Amsterdam but supports Feyenoord.

Johan nods and pours the drinks. Says they're on the house.

– Did you read this? Harris asks, handing over an English paper. This should stir up a few people.

We have a look and run through the front-page story. The basic line is that the Germans have organised a truce between rival firms for what the paper is touting as the Hooligan Battle Of The Century. The Germans are supposed to be warning the English not to turn up because they're going to send us home in coffins. The paper doesn't know who to slag off, the Germans or the English, so goes for both sides. On the one hand they're warning of neo-Nazi English hooligans wrecking Berlin and terrorising innocent Germans, and on the other of neo-Nazi German hooligans killing innocent English football supporters. Don't know what they're talking about, basically, but in typical journalist tradition they're going to blame everything on Nazis. You have to laugh. They've been getting away with this for years. The word Nazi sells. Doesn't matter what kind of paper or magazine it is, Left or Right they all love the mysterious Nazi threat arriving from the shadows then vanishing again. To add some extra spice they've got a photo of a skinhead snarling at the camera. Except he's got a bonehead crop and isn't a skinhead. But they don't know the difference. Don't have a fucking clue. Surprised they haven't drawn a swastika on his forehead for good luck. It's mental the way they stick to stereotypes all the time. The tabloids set the agenda and everyone else in the media follows.

I've never been into politics because all the wankers in charge are the same. A bunch of cunts. None of them gives a toss about the ordinary man and woman struggling along. They'll all sell you down the drain. Berlin's the wannabe leader of the new Europe and this is going to add extra friction. It's got nothing to do with Nazis. Thing is, we've all done it, standing there singing No Surrender with a Union Jack behind us, right hand in the air, taking the piss. Or like that Dublin riot. They say it was just politics, but the situation in Ulster added an edge. Obviously nobody following England overseas is going to support the IRA, and naturally their sympathies are going to be with the Loyalists in Northern Ireland, and of course there was going to be some C18 doing the business, but it was more of a football mob making a point. To say it was one or two blokes stirring things up is nonsense, because it was a riot waiting to happen. England having their say.

I'm thinking about all this because there's enough old soldiers who say we fought on the wrong side during the war. That the Germans are just like us, brave fighters, and they're right. I mean, not that I want Hitler in Buckingham Palace instead of the Queen, but the Germans are okay. So are the Dutch come to think of it, because we're all Saxon blood. The Dutch and Germans are well into the English way of life. Look at Johan behind the bar with his Fred Perry and number one crop. He's got his Feyenoord pendant next to pictures of Judge Dread and Prince Buster. There's a big stack of CDs. The Cockney Rejects, 4-Skins, Business, Last Resort and various Oi! compilations. And then there's the ska of Madness and Bad Manners. Now that's the real skinhead there, plus some original Jamaican ska. They love our football and music and pubs and gear. The Dutch and Germans have their football mobs and they're going to have a go at us when we come over and take the piss. That's natural enough. Under the surface, though, we're similar. They have a lot of respect for the English. For our hooligan element.

It's the fucking spics and dagos most Englishmen really hate. Slimy cunts with their flick knives and expensive clothes. Always up for it when the odds are stacked in their favour, then run like shit when they're faced by an equal numbers mob of English. I've seen it enough times. Heard the stories. We hate them because they're cowards and flash. You watch a football game on the telly nowdays and every time the cameras look at the crowd they pin-point well-dressed women and kids. Or crying Newcastle fans in spanking new club shirts who never went near St James' Park when the club was struggling. The media ignores the real culture surrounding football because the cameras are part of the system that's squeezed the atmosphere from our grounds. When they show the Spanish and Italians it's all this Latin culture routine, dropping libero terms and playing opera, zooming in on their so-called ultras for some flavour. The media laps it up because these ultras are a nice little oddity, but look into our own crowds and they don't want to know. It's too near home and something they're not part of, so they pretend it doesn't exist. It's not just football. This comes across in everything. The media is controlled by class. They want everything to reflect themselves and forget the rest of us. Go to Italy and the England boys walk through the piazza with their underpants on their heads taking the piss while the locals stand around all confused.

Mind you, when I was at Wembley and Di Matteo went piling through the middle and smacked that ball past Roberts he was the greatest man on the planet. For a few seconds greater than Zola and Vialli, so there you go. What can you say? Zola's the best player I've ever seen in a Chelsea shirt and Vialli's the business with his shaved bonce, strolling along the touchline looking like Mussolini. Every Chelsea boy in the country, whether they were in the ground or down the pub in front of the telly, loved that Italian. So what does that say? Thing is, you have to have an enemy. There's no point spending good money and taking time off work just to go over to Europe and stand around shaking hands with the locals. What's the point of that? Where's the excitement? Playing happy families like a bunch of wankers. You have to have an edge. It makes things more fun. Football's a game so you need some opposition.

Like this time we played in Denmark and, truth be told, the Danes were friendly as well, though they knew what to expect. Every nutter in Denmark had made the pilgrimage to Copenhagen to see the English in action. First copper we come across walks up and asks when the fighting's going to start. Not long, pal. We were down this square in Copenhagen with shopping precincts running off from a market. The English were having a sing-song. The Danes were peaceful and you're not going to smack blokes who don't want to know. Then they have a couple of lagers and start taking the piss. You feel like a cunt letting them in. We piled into the cunts, and those who didn't leg it got a pasting. The whole thing turns because these wankers couldn't take their drink. England go on the rampage and everyone says how bad we are. We go through the shops and cafés smashing the place up, doing anyone who wants to have a go, the scousers tagging along on the side doing some shopping. It was ages before the old bill arrived and they didn't have a clue how to handle the situation. They were shitting it, trying to nick people who didn't want to get nicked. Trying to hush everything up. Calm it all down. Trying to get their heads round what was happening. We walked off as the riot vans arrived. Flagged down a couple of cabs and went straight to the ground.

The Scandinavians and Danes are too fucking honest. They're too nice. They don't realise what's happening and think we're all gentlemen with monocles and bowlers. That Gary Lineker rules the waves. So we just walk into their supermarkets and help ourselves. Go through the Tivoli Gardens and enjoy everything for free. Load up on cases of Elephant lager and lob bottles at shop windows for fun. We can drink in their bars then rob the till and smash the place up if we fancy it. We can do whatever we fucking well want because we're England and nothing can stop us. It's a massive beano. The Scandinavian old bill haven't got it worked out properly, though the Dutch and Belgians know what they're doing now, and the Germans don't fuck about. They've got the tradition. The Stasi and the Gestapo. When it comes to the Italians and Spanish, they hate the English and are straight in hammering anything that moves. The papers try and blame it on Heysel, but it was going on long before that. They fucking love it because they're scum. Look at Man U in Portugal. Women and kids trying to watch a football match and the old bill think they're on a firing range. We hate the Latins but they hate us more. Their police are always having a go at the English. Makes you laugh, seeing the reaction to Rome. The media gets a glimpse of the real world and doesn't have a clue what's going on.

It's great when you're in these northern countries though. Whistle at the girls and they love it. Big smiles on their faces giving us the nod. Suppose you feel bad for the decent people for a few minutes because you do get some English who go overboard, getting so pissed they don't know what they're doing. Feel sorry till you come round the corner and the local nutters have mobbed up. Trying to pick you off and do you through sheer weight of numbers. That's what it's all about. But eventually everyone learns and now when we go overseas the old bill are ready and waiting. It gives them the chance to batter a few Englishmen without any come back. The embassies don't want to know, because they hate us like all the rest. Bunch of cunts the lot of them.

– You have to smile, says Harris. The newspapers really wind things up. There's going to be enough soldiers going over to Berlin anyway, and now they're organising a recruitment drive for us.

None of us is bothered because the more English come over the better. It's a load of shit what these papers do though. They've probably given some unemployed kid from East Berlin fifty quid to spout off. During the build-up to Euro 96 they had this bloke from Derby boasting on the radio about how the Turks were going to get murdered. The media like stirring things up, and then when they've got people listening they deliver a lecture. I'm sitting there on the forklift at work listening to this radio programme and everyone's laughing because they've disguised the bloke's voice so he sounds like a poof.

– The Germans will give it a go with or without these stories, says Harris. Their papers will make sure of that. It'll be a fucking good laugh. It's going to be a classic in Berlin. It's been quiet here so far. We went down to Rotterdam and met up with some of the Feyenoord crew last night. There was a row in this club, but nothing major. How was the crossing?

We fill him in. How the seasiders went to war. He laughs and shakes his head.

– We'll see them again, Harris says. I know that Portsmouth mob and they'll be back. It's typical Facelift as well. He won't bother giving it another go. All you've got to do is go to a different port and the old bill are so fucking thick they won't get you a second time. I've done it before. They wouldn't let me go to Turkey one time. I had the ticket and they wouldn't let me out of Heathrow, so I got a coach to Gatwick and bought a standby and ended up having three days in Istanbul. That was mental. The Turks are dangerous. There's fucking thousands of the cunts and a lot of them are tooled-up. We did alright. You're in the Third World over there and there's none of these bars showing porn films. Istanbul's dirt poor. Shitty food and drink. At least over here you can have some fun. Decent food, drink, music and the women are sitting in the windows gagging for some English cock.

Harris has been following England for donkey's years. I've been at least fifteen times now and it's always been lively. Mark usually comes, and Rod's done a few.

– Yes, lads, Amsterdam is as good as it gets, Harris laughs. We're in the centre of the civilised world here. You can drink as much as you want, do some drugs, and then go and fight and fuck your way through the tourist attractions. This is European civilisation at its best.

Harry caught up with the others early evening. He found them easy enough because they were still in the bar where they'd planned to meet Harris at twelve. They started telling him about some film with a blonde bird and a William Hague lookalike who had a Rottweiler on a lead, but he didn't understand what they were on about. There was a big skinhead behind the bar playing a Madness tape. The sound was clear and he liked the bar, and he wouldn't have minded a drink, but the others were going for some food. Harris had been to a good place the night before and there were six of them following the leader. Harry could stay and have a beer or go with the rest of the boys. Harris said it was an Indonesian and the food was tasty and cheap. Harry thought of the satays and made up his mind.

The sunny weather had been replaced by a dark sky and it was spitting, but Harry was still in a good mood. His head was light but he was together. He had a bit of blow in his pocket from one of the girls in Rudi's Bar, a nice gesture making visitors welcome. It showed how it didn't pay to slag people off just because they had long hair. It worked both ways. He was going with popular opinion now and following Harris and Carter and Tom and Mark and a couple of other Chelsea boys he didn't know towards the Indonesian. The colours had changed from this morning, but the drizzle livened things up and made the streets smell fresh.

The man nearest the door didn't seem too pleased when seven half-cut Englishmen stumbled in, but then he recognised Harris and his face cracked into a grin. Suddenly he couldn't do enough for them, leading the lads to the best table in the house and getting the waiters to pull an extra table up so there was room for the customers to spread out.

– He likes you, Mark said. You could be in there.

– He's alright, Harris replied. Left Jakarta ten years ago after some problems with the government. Until two days ago I'd never had any Indonesian food. Knew fuck all about the place to be honest. I had a satay in Johan's and yesterday I came in here.

Harris joked with the owner and ordered seven bottles of lager. Harry was enjoying himself. There was a lot of bamboo and wood carvings were scattered around. It was great how it worked. Inside a day they'd set up in Hank's, had found themselves a local, and were sitting down for some cheap and tasty food. In each place they were in with the owners. They'd got their base sorted out and everything was ticking over nicely.

Mark seemed more pissed than the others and started going on about how Amsterdam was alright, but that didn't mean he wanted to be part of Europe. Tom joined in and Harry was listening to them going on about England and Europe and how it was all a load of bollocks, how they were going into the centre of the conspiracy and planning to wreck Berlin, that it was the master plan of big business and the financial institutions, and suddenly he was sitting there, minding his own business, and it was a line he went along with – most people did when you stopped and thought about it – but then he started thinking that they were talking shit. Sure, he'd come over and seen the Channel as the big barrier, those pirate crews from Southampton and Portsmouth feeling it more than most, but he was mellow after the blow and didn't really give a toss. That was the problem with blokes like Tom and Mark. They were too wound up, like they were on speed the whole time. There was too much of the geezer about them. They needed to calm down.

Harry had been in enough bother when he was young, but was a peaceful man at heart. You had to grow out of those things. If he got the chance he'd rather be a lover than a fighter. He didn't go looking for trouble like the others did. Thing was, now he was lost in the tangle of Amsterdam's canals and side streets he didn't give a fuck about all the usual nonsense. That's what the place did to you. It showed you there didn't have to be all that mental bulldog stuff, crunching his eyes to peer through the smoke, watching those two nutters across the table turning their heads and eyeing up the classy Dutch birds passing outside who smiled through the window but kept going, taking everything nice and easy, nice and mellow, Harry sipping his lager and thinking about his mate Will at home, a big influence with his outlook on life, and how he'd helped Balti through the bad times, signing on and everything.

– Those Germans won't know what's hit them, Mark said.

Maybe Europe wasn't such a bad idea after all. Look what you got in return – civilised drinking so you could go out any time you wanted and have a few sherbets; soft drugs legally available so you could sit back listening to old Stones songs playing in the background, taking things easy; and there were the birds as well. He was watching the two girls at the other end of the restaurant ordering, full of confidence. There were no small-minded wankers shouting for everyone to get a move on please, drink up gentlemen, get outside in the rain and piss off till tomorrow. There was none of the corruption and short-term thinking that turned your streets into traffic jams and meant you rarely got a say in what was going on around you. Look at the football. Everyone rated the Dutch. A small country like Holland had produced so much world–class talent over the last twenty years it was unbelievable. They played football for football's sake, and it was only the peso and lira that saw the talent leave. They were class, but couldn't compete with the finance of the Spanish and Italians. Now the English game was going the way of the Latins, with money dominating everything.

Harry wasn't bothered, because he had more interesting things running through his head than football. If he lived here he didn't think he'd ever see a game. What was the point when you could drop into a warm friendly bar and sit around with good people enjoying life, floating on a cloud like some zapped-out old hippy. That's what the herb had done to him. It had made Harry relaxed and happy. If this was Europe then it made perfect sense. Just lie back and let the world get on with things. The drug got rid of the need to fight back in a battle you were never going to win. If you didn't care what was going on outside the window, it didn't matter. The politicians and businessmen could do whatever they fucking well wanted, carve everything up between themselves, so Harry could see how it was better to have a smoke and let them get on with it.

– You remember that league we had? Carter asked, bringing Harry back out of Rudi's and into the Indonesian.

He had to think and didn't have a clue what the sex machine was on about.

– That Sex Division we had, Carter laughed. You haven't forgotten already, have you? It wasn't that long ago. I was playing total football, like the Dutch.

Harry remembered. He'd been relegated. But he didn't think of that any more because it tied in with Balti. He didn't want those kind of memories. Things had to be good. He just smiled.

– We had this league, Carter said. You got ten points for shitting in a bird's handbag.

Harry pictured Balti and wished Carter would leave it alone. It had been a bad time. Shortly after that Denise had married Slaughter and two weeks after they'd come back from the honeymoon someone told Slaughter that Carter had been servicing his blushing bride. Slaughter was a psycho, went mental and had gone after Carter with a machete. Denise was lucky, because she'd gone to Guildford for the night with her mum and dad. Carter had told Harry down The Unity soon after the event, hand shaking as he lifted his pint.

It was a Sunday morning and Carter was coming home after a hectic night with some half-decent tart from Blues. He was feeling pleased with himself because he'd been after this bird for a while. He'd got home and there was Slaughter standing in a doorway and the headcase had come and jammed the machete against his neck. Slaughter pushed Carter back against the wall and pushed hard on his jugular. It was sideways on but the blade was cutting his skin. Carter kept still. He saw his throat sliced open and the blood drained. He told Harry he'd been shitting it. Fucking shitting his load. He was about to die like a pig. Slaughter was crying and telling Carter he was going to kill him for fucking Denise. Did he understand that he was in love with the woman. The thought of you, you cunt, fucking my Denise makes me fucking sick. It makes me want to slit your throat and cut your bollocks off and that's what I'm going to do because they call you Carter and you think you're a sex machine but to me you're just a cunt, a fucking piece of shit who fucks up people's lives and you don't do that to me, you don't fuck me about you fucking slag, you don't take liberties and think you can walk away, you fucking cunt.

Carter was quick to think and said it wasn't true. It's not true. Someone's taking the piss. Who told you that? Someone's telling lies about me. I'm not that sort of bloke – yes I am, of course I am, Slaughter's a stupid cunt but he's not that stupid, he's never going to believe that – she's not that kind of girl. Denise isn't some old slapper is she? Do you really think Denise would do that to you? She fucking loves you. Denise would go out and top herself if she thought you had her down as a slag, just some whore who goes round fucking anything that moves. Do me a favour. Do Denise a favour. More than that, do yourself a favour Slaughter. Denise is a classy lady. It's just not true. I swear on my mother's life, there's nothing between me and Denise and there never has been (and even faced with having his throat cut Carter thought of the day after the newly weds came back from their honeymoon, and while Slaughter was at work he'd gone round the flat and Dirty Denise was up to her old tricks, fucking gagging for it, the dirty talk and everything).

People heard what they wanted to hear and that was the thing to remember. It worked in everyday life and it worked in the long term. That was why he was the sex machine and got the women. He told them what they wanted to hear and made them feel good about themselves. He was doing them a service talking shit. The shit made them feel good and he got his reward. The shit smelt good. Shit smelt like Chanel for these birds, and that's how he lived to shag again. He applied logic in a near death situation and simply treated Slaughter like a bird and told him what he wanted to hear, that his wife was a good, clean woman who was honest as the day was long. Carter told Harry he was standing there with that machete ready to cut his throat and Slaughter's face changed and he thought about what he was being told so Carter could almost hear the gears clanking. After a couple of minutes Slaughter told Carter he liked him, and that maybe he was wrong, jumping to conclusions.

Slaughter gave himself some more time to think about this and then he backed away and apologised. He even begged Carter not to say anything to Denise about what had happened. He felt really bad about all this now. What was he thinking of? It was the overtime he was doing. It was hard getting by sometimes. Everything was so expensive and they'd had the honeymoon in Greece. That hadn't been cheap. Sorry Terry. And Carter's first thought was to lay into the cunt and give him a kicking because the whole time he'd been thinking of Balti and how the poor cunt died on a Sunday morning in the street outside his home, and how it was all going to happen again. But he held back because he'd have to kill Slaughter and he wasn't going that far – don't worry Slaughter, just make sure you get the cunt telling lies about me, this wanker slagging off your wife, making out she's a slag.

Slaughter nodded and walked away. Next day Carter heard one of the regulars in The Unity had been found sitting at a bus stop with his face slashed. It had taken thirty stitches to sew the cunt back together. The bloke told the old bill he didn't recognise his attacker, even though the attack had happened during the day. Carter had a quiet word with Denise and she started shitting herself. She was happily married and didn't want to die. They knocked it on the head, at least for a while.

– Shitting in a bird's handbag? one of the blokes with Harris asked. Did anyone do it?

– This mate of ours managed it, Carter said, looking to Harry in apology. Did six of them. Lined them up and filled the lot.

– That's brave of him. He was lucky they didn't kill him. No bird likes getting shat on.

Harry thought of the kids on the boat, with sick in their hair and clothes. It could've been worse. He wished Carter hadn't brought all that up now, when he'd been on the puff and was feeling mellow.

– You can get all that kind of porn here, Harris said. You can get birds covered in the stuff like they're auditioning for some rap film. Birds getting golden showers, birds with midgets, birds with horses.

Everyone laughed and Harry relaxed again.

– You go round these sex shops and you wouldn't believe some of the stuff they've got here, Harris said. First time I came to Amsterdam was more than ten years ago and I went in one shop, picked up this magazine, and there was this fucking kid in there. Stark-bollock naked wrapped in barbed wire. Little boy of about nine. On the opposite page was a girl even younger. I couldn't believe it and had a go at the bloke behind the counter. I don't think they let that sort of stuff go any more. Makes you think though, the kind of scum there is in this world.

– Do you think they've really got rid of that stuff? Mark asked. Because if they haven't we should go and do the cunts selling it. Make it a righteous Christian crusade. You can be Richard the Lionheart.

– Must be underground now, Harris said. I don't know. Amsterdam's a good place and they're laid back, but you get the rubbish coming here and taking advantage. They know things are loose and they can get away with murder. Most of the nonces go to Asia, places like Thailand and the Philippines where they're poorer than in Europe. They can do what they want over there, but that'll change one day as well.

Harry didn't want to hear about all this. He was in a positive frame of mind and wished the others would ease up. He didn't want to think about nonces. You got enough of the child-killers, rapists and all that at home. When you were abroad you couldn't understand the language, so it was hear no evil, see no evil as far as he was concerned.

– That's the only thing wrong with Amsterdam, Harris said. The nonces and Ajax. They've got a good youth system and that's probably why the nonces come here in the first place.

– What's wrong with Ajax? Carter asked, coming awake.

After all, he believed in total football. In filling a bird any way you wanted. That's what it was all about. He thought Ajax were a respected outfit.

– They're a fucking yid team, Harris said. They're the Spurs of Holland.

– I thought Hitler gassed them all? Carter said.

– Doesn't seem like it. No, they're the yiddos of Holland. You wouldn't catch me going to see them play. It would be like going and spending your afternoons at White Hart Lane. You look the next time they're on the telly. They've got Stars of Davids on their flags. They're Tottenham alright.

Carter sat in silence for a while. That was a turn-up for the books. Ajax a yiddo team. As Chelsea boys they all had a natural hatred for Spurs that went back a good thirty years to the original skinhead era.

– So what are we having? Harry asked, studying the menu.

Harry had been talking with the hairies about the things to see in Amsterdam, and they told him about the Docker statue with its inscription: 'keep your filthy hands off our filthy Jews'. The Angels laughed and it showed a few things about the Dutch. One of the women said the Dutch starved under the Nazis and that there was still a lot of bitterness towards the Germans, which these days usually came out at football matches. Harry didn't want to think about that right now because he was starving as well, or at least hungry, and the owner was hovering in the background. They left Harris to order. They got seven more bottles of lager and waited for their food.

– Suppose this is like an Indian at home, Tom said, and Harry laughed. It was exactly what he was thinking.

– Funny how everywhere you go there's the same things. There's Ajax and Tottenham, and then there's Feyenoord and Chelsea, and there's this Indonesian same as a curry house. Mind you, walking into a bar and seeing Blondie getting one up the arse is different. You'd only get that at a serious sex club or on a stag night. You wouldn't get it on a screen down the pub before a game would you?

– I wouldn't mind a pint of Fosters, Carter pointed out.

– And a pack of English crisps, Mark added.

– A nice pint of Fosters in a pint glass.

Harry wondered sometimes. They'd just spent a bomb getting over here and Carter was moaning because he wanted a pint of Fosters. It was just lager and not exactly pure English heritage. Harris, now, he was a bit more together. He had a taste for Europe. The bloke had certain leadership qualities and needed room to manoeuvre, some extra living space. He was looking at bigger horizons and Harry wondered if he would stay in England all his life. No, he wouldn't be able to live without going to see Chelsea. After a while somewhere like Amsterdam would be too quiet. England was in his blood.

With some decent grub inside us, we're ready for a wander. The bill's cheap and we've done the place proud, paying and not doing a runner. Even leave a generous tip. Suppose the Dutch leg it often enough, but I remember when the yids played here a few years back and the Dutch were popping off shots at the English. Someone even got killed. Outside the rain's stopped and we walk slowly. Turn across another canal that could even be a river. There's not a lot of people about as we cross, and we turn a couple of corners. Dam Square's up ahead with a funfair buzzing away. Buildings tower over the commotion, all flashing lights and blaring music. Organ tunes and Abba pop favourites competing. We stand on the outside looking in. It's happy families and tourists, but I don't think any of us are interested in the rides. We're standing with the husbands and wives and kiddies having fun. Simple pleasures. We're just hanging about and seeing the sights. Not bothering anyone. I'm an ordinary bloke having a look and glad the kids are enjoying themselves. Laughing and screaming. Singing their heads off. I'm just standing around when this fucking cunt comes up to me and asks me if I want to buy some smack.

This pisses me off. First off, this is a family event. Second, he's a stroppy black bastard slurring his words with some wank street slang. Third, he's talking down like he's drug sussed and I'm shit. Fourth, and this is the one that gets right up my nose, the thing that does my fucking head in, is that he thinks I look like a fucking dosser. He's out of order and he's hit the chord. My hair's short and I wash my clothes. I shave my face and have a bath. I look like what I am. I don't look like a smackhead. I don't mind junkies, because that's their problem. Each to their own. But I work for my money. I pay my rent and get along. I work hard and keep my life in order. I don't like cunts I don't know coming along and telling me they think I'm a fucking loser.

This wanker stands there bouncing from foot to foot. I ask him if he's a Harlem Globetrotter. He looks at me half-sneering with this stroppy attitude that gets me where it hurts. I punch the cunt full in the face. He's not ready for this because he's used to dealing with scrawny wankers and hippy scum. I reckon I bust his nose. He stumbles back into a candyfloss stall. Luckily we're still on the outskirts of the fair and only the candyfloss man sees what's happening. The dealer goes inside his jacket, but before I can kick the cunt Harris pushes past and knifes him in the leg. He doesn't go deep but cuts the bastard and the cunt staggers sideways. Drops a razor. Harris goes to cut him down the back and rip his expensive top, but Mark clocks a couple of coppers and we move away. The old bill haven't seen us, and this wanker's not going to start screaming with his pockets full of a class A drug, or however they classify it over here. We filter towards a side street and disappear.

– What did you go and hit him for? Mark asks, as we go back over the river towards the red light and a drink. He only asked a question and you go straight into him.

– He wound me up, I say.

– He only asked. This is fucking Amsterdam. What do you expect?

Mark laughs.

– It's a fucking drugs town and they sell drugs. What's the matter with you, you silly cunt? You'll end up nicked with the old bill right there.

– Just didn't like the way he was muscling in. He was rude. I didn't see the coppers. It was bad manners. I didn't see the old bill.

– Neither did he, Harris says. He was a fucking wanker. Lucky for him they were around. Did you see the razor? I hate people who go round tooled-up like that.

Me and Mark look at each other and smile. Harris doesn't care. Old age is making him worse than ever. He's always been a nutter, but we're in the middle of Dam Square and he knifes someone. Mind you, I shouldn't have hit the bloke right there on stage. Lights shining in my eyes. I don't care now, but it was open and asking for trouble. It's the drink makes you careless. They've probably got video cameras like back home, but we're passing through so it doesn't really count. At least Harris didn't dig in like he could've done. He could've made the cunt scream. Thing is, you get the scent and now we're walking with a spring in our steps. Everything was nice and quiet and now it's turned round.

We keep moving and Mark says come on, let's go and have a look at the whores, we haven't seen the prossies yet. He's got a point. We all know about Amsterdam and the whores. I've seen them before but suppose we'll have to go and see them again. We follow the street back into the centre of the red light. The pavements are busy and we're away from Dam Square. A good percentage of the people who visit Amsterdam come down for a look, and you see enough Dutch as well. Always remember how bored the girls look, till you get near and they smell money. The sultry look comes out and they're better actresses than Blondie filling the wall of Johan's bar. Just keeps smiling as another queer junky actor corks her arse. A girl's got to work.

Amsterdam doesn't have things all its own way, because tourism and over-exposure destroys every good set-up in the end. We were on our way to Denmark that time when England played in Copenhagen, and we stopped in Hamburg for a night out. I'd never heard of the Reeperbahn but some of the older blokes who'd been that way before showed us where to go. There was England everywhere and the girls were legal. Logic is, it keeps them in order. There were girls on corners and in doorways, and there was this underground car park as well. It was fucking massive, with a big door and huge painted legs doing the splits. The girls were on little stages. Real crackers as well. Standing on platforms giving the shoppers a twirl. Mirrors in the background for an all over view. The England boys were on the prowl. When I think of it, most times I've been away with England we've ended up staying in or near the red light zones. Never really planned it that way, but it's true all the same. Maybe it's where the cheap accommodation is, but probably it shows how the English like to mingle and experience the local culture. Give us a choice of bars and drink, throw in some half-decent birds, and we're happy. And there's always going to be a punch-up somewhere along the line. Put all these things together and you've got the perfect package tour.

There was a bar in Hamburg where this big mob of English were drinking. We were watching these girls working from a doorway. There were three of them and none was a pig. Rod was eyeing up this blonde number. Couldn't have been more than twenty. Long hair down to her arse. Short white skirt. I can still see her. Rod was watching her for what must've been at least an hour. She was a German girl from the country who'd gone to the city to make her fortune. That's how we were telling the story. He kept saying he was going over but never did. Just stood there in the bar watching her approach passing men. Back and forward offering her services. Don't know why Rod didn't go and shag her. There weren't many punters around and none of the girls was getting anywhere. Rod was thinking big. Going over in a minute. Any minute now he was going to fuck the arse off her. Wrap that long blonde hair round his bollocks.

He started wondering why she was on the game. We gave him the fräulein story. Kept repeating it till he got bored. We were looking at Rod. He was going on and on about this blonde. What was she doing chatting to strangers in the street like that when he was ready and willing? We were pissing ourselves laughing. So was Rod after a while. Something stopped him going over. As soon as he finished his drink he was going over. He slammed his sixth or seventh bottle down and was on his way. This was it. He'd see us later. Big smile on his face. Hitching up his jeans. Except he had to stop and watch as the girl approached an old man. They started chatting. A sad old man in a saggy flea-bitten suit. Must've been at least sixty years old. The blonde's mate joined in. Licking her lips. There was some laughing and whispering, and then the two girls linked arms with the man and led him away. Down the street to a door and off inside. We told Rod that the girls were taking the old git to a big double bed and were going to give him the best heart attack he'd ever had. They'd give the man a line of coke and blow his brains out. Rod didn't know what to do or what to say. He'd missed out on a treat. He told us she was a fucking whore. A dirty old slag. A fucking scrubber. Couldn't we see she was a bad woman. We were all laughing. Me, Mark and Rod and a few others. He nodded his head all serious like a preacher and said she was a harlot. Rod was making the most of his missed opportunity. Taking the piss.

But we started rubbing it in. Telling him he'd taken too long and now he'd just have to make do with his imagination. Think of it, Rod, those two birds taking turns sucking that old codger's knob. First they'd have to clear away the cobwebs, and then they'd have to smooth out the wrinkles, but then he'd get the scent and be humping away for hours trying to dig up some fluid. Rod's bird would be leaning over the bed with that centurion behind her while her assistant offered encouragement. Trying to get a result. Rubbing his arse and those fossilised balls. And that dirty fucker would be beavering away for at least an hour with his dentures chattering and dribble falling on the girl's back. Heart racing and brain bulging. Finally reaching Go and giving her a bellyful just as the old ticker explodes. Could've been you Rod. But you missed out because you'd rather spend quality time with your mates. Rod just stood there. Stood there in silence before going back to the bar for another bottle of lager. Shaking his head.

I tell Harry this as we're walking along. He laughs.

– Maybe that's why he got married young. He wanted something more than tarts bending over a bed. Must be good if you fall in love with a decent woman, settle down and have some kids. It's hard to find anyone worthwhile. Most birds just want to grind you down, and if you haven't got money they don't want to know.

Don't know why he's getting all romantic. A fuck's a fuck as far as I can see.

– Married life's a life of misery, Mark says, overhearing Harry. You look at Rod, stuck at home with the wife. Mandy wants her cut and they've got bills to pay. He'd love to be in Berlin for the football. He'd love being in Amsterdam smoking some herb, but no, he's stuck at home like a fucking cunt. He's lucky as well, because he still gets out. Some blokes get married and you never see them again. I don't like Mandy much, because she nicked our mate, but she doesn't tell him what to do all the time like a lot of people I could mention.

Don't know what Harry's thinking. Must be age. He's a few years older than me and Mark. Suppose things change. Maybe that's what he wants. Some of that romantic nonsense. It's bollocks though, because there's plenty of birds around so why get stuck with one? It doesn't make any sense. Suppose it's in all of us, just depends on how much you're willing to change your life for a woman. Maybe it's his nature, though, because Carter's the same age and he's not exactly saving up for a white wedding.

I notice a shop that's still open. Selling all the usual tourist shit. There's a rack of cards and I stop to have a look. The others hang about waiting. The owner's standing there and I buy a card off him. He gives me the stamp. It's a scene from the red light district. Welcome to Amsterdam. There's black buildings and a row of lit windows. Girls behind plate glass in stockings and suspenders. Red neons glow. There's signs promising live sex. Live action. Promising the world. This one's for Rod and we'll think up a good message while we're pissed, and send it before we're sober. That'll wind the poor cunt up even more.

We turn down another street and look at the girls. Most are black. There's one or two Orientals and a few white girls. They look shagged out, and there's groups of wankers waving and making stupid jokes. Welcome to the show. We're spectators staring at the prostitutes lit up nice and pretty. There's this group of wankers nearby and they push a young lad forward. He goes to a black girl and has a word, then disappears inside. The men stand there not knowing what to do next. It's fucked them up, knowing he's in there getting his knob inspected. They move along quietly. The authorities are keeping it off the street and supplying an extra tourist attraction. Something to go with the art galleries and churches. Can't be bad. Might even splash out myself, but not with any of these.

– Anyone having a go? Harris asks.

We all shake our heads. Later on maybe.

– Come on then, let's have a drink. You can get a whore anywhere.

You can get a bottle of lager anywhere. But I know what he means.

Harry stayed with the girls in the windows. He watched Carter and the rest of the boys walking off, pissing about, and no-one even noticed he'd been left behind. It was the same as the ferry coming over, and if he'd fallen overboard they wouldn't have missed him till they got to Berlin, Carter sitting there in the room they were sharing talking to himself, but it gave him some space so he wasn't complaining. They'd been drinking all day and it was fair enough. They were starting to get edgy, with Tom and that wanker in the square, Harris doing his bit for Chelsea and England, but Harry wasn't interested in roaming the streets of Amsterdam looking for people to slap, not right now anyway. He was inspecting the girls on the meat racks and had to be honest and say there wasn't anything better than he'd find down Blues back in London. He didn't know whether to be glad or sad, so he headed in the opposite direction to the others, putting some extra distance between them in case Carter came back looking. Harry did some window shopping, checking the sex shop displays and sex club line-ups.

There was a big queue outside one club in particular and he couldn't help laughing how ordered and proper everyone was. He thought the English were the only ones who could be bothered queueing, but the hundred or so people outside were in a rigid two-by-two formation, gagging for a bed in the ark, handing their rubbers in at the door. They were people as well: men and women of all ages, shapes and sizes, and though he knew the clogs were open-minded he still didn't expect to see whole families chatting as they waited for the advertised live sex. It was mostly couples and small groups, but there were grey-haired parents with grown-up children, in-laws, cousins, all waiting patiently. He couldn't get his head round that at all. It was sick. Somehow perverted. It just wasn't right. He looked at the masked photos outside the club a bit closer and they were going to get some hardcore sex for their guilders.

Harry couldn't sit through something like that knowing he was surrounded by happy families. It was almost the same as incest. He turned away and passed a couple of smaller, dodgy-looking clip joints where the champagne was a hundred quid a bottle and the bouncers big bastards in tuxedos. He turned down a smaller side street lined with glass. This was more like it. There was a better mix of girls and the street's quieter atmosphere gave him confidence. He stood back and took his time because his balls were heavy and he wanted to make the right choice. There was a blonde who looked alright, with red stockings, suspenders and basque. She was a big girl with a healthy figure. Harry breathed deep and moved in for the kill. He was halfway there when he spotted a smaller brown girl. He stopped and looked her over. Now he'd spotted her, she stood out. She had short black hair and was dressed like a European tart, which didn't seem natural, a bit artificial somehow. The stockings and that looked right on white birds, but on black and brown girls it didn't work. He'd never find something like this down Blues. No fucking way.

He turned towards the girl and thought hard about what she saw coming. A big white man with a shaved head and drink on his breath, the smell of smoke on his clothes and half-stoned eyes, who in a few minutes would have his jeans on the floor and his knob racing in and out of her, his big white gut bouncing against her flat brown belly, arching his back as he finished in a pool of sweat. She probably saw one more pissed geezer from England swaggering towards her, on holiday looking for something dirty he couldn't get off the wife back home. Maybe she'd had a drink and was resting after that last wanker from France who'd given it three quick thrusts and finished, then started moaning about how he hadn't got his money's worth, causing trouble so she'd called her minder in to turf the ungrateful cunt out into the street, leaving a bad taste on both sides. Harry guessed it was something like that and hesitated, but then he was right in there talking to her and she was almost too friendly, inviting him inside after he'd agreed to her price. He didn't know what the going rate was, but went along with what the girl said. It was all about money in the end. He wasn't going to argue over a few guilders. He was Chelsea, not Tottenham.

The room was small and warm and the girl laughed a lot as she invited him to come and stand in front of her so she could have a look at his cock. She was professional, but friendly. She opened his jeans and did a quick check. There wasn't much of the Orient about her room and she put on a Sting CD for some flavour. He didn't like the music, but it was in the background and soon faded off. The girl had a way about her that put him at ease, but there she was handling his knob doing her clap-clinic routine and he was limp. He wasn't bothered because this was the preliminaries and she knew what she was doing. He started taking his trainers and jeans off and she was getting ready arranging the cushions, and to pass the time he asked her where she came from.

She said her name was Nicky and that she came from a Thai village near to the border with Laos. He stripped off his pants and she kept talking. She'd wanted to see the world and get away from Thailand, so she'd come to Amsterdam with a Dutchman she met in Pettaya. She was twenty at the time and he was in his forties. He'd treated her good for a couple of years and she'd got her residency, but then things changed. He started going with boys and wasn't interested in her any more. She didn't mind because he was old and she was young, and she wanted to be free. She'd been in Pettaya since she was sixteen and was determined to stay in Europe. All the girls dreamed of moving to Europe. Her village was poor and the resorts were full of Western men who paid good money, but she wanted to get ahead. European men usually treated the girls better than the Thais, and they had a lot more money.

She smiled this mental smile and Harry nodded not knowing what to say. She had a perfect body without any trace of fat, and she was still soft despite an adult life on the game. Nicky loved Amsterdam and hated Thailand with a vengeance he couldn't understand, because to him it sounded like a tropical paradise. Her Dutchman had given her enough money to keep going for a couple of months and then she'd had to find work. They'd had two years together and it had worked out okay, but now she was free and could have some fun. She'd done everything for him, and he'd looked after her. He'd bought her clothes and took her to restaurants. She'd never been in love with him, and he'd only loved her youth and body. Her life had improved.

Nicky made a good living and she liked white men, the colour of their skin. For Thais white skin was attractive. She hated Arabs. Harry liked the way she spoke and the way she moved. He couldn't help himself and asked how she'd ended up as a prostitute, even though he felt like a mug soon as the words came out of his mouth. He expected her to tell him to mind his own business and get on with it, because time was money, that stupid lines lifted from shit films would cost him extra, but she wasn't bothered and started going into one so he wished he'd kept his mouth shut. She was a fucking beauty and he wanted to get stuck in, to fuck the girl's brains out, to squeeze inside the tightest cunt on the planet and dump his load, but the way she started carrying on was killing his passion dead.

Because Nicky was telling him all about her village, set in the jungle but poorer than anything he would see in Europe, about the hunger and illness. She had three brothers and two sisters who'd survived infancy and the money she sent home helped the family survive. It didn't matter if she was a prostitute because she was getting along and helping other people. She wasn't just surviving either, she was enjoying herself in Amsterdam. She had clothes and went to clubs where she could take ecstasy and dance till early morning. She would never live in Thailand again. One day she would get married and settle down. Nobody really chose to have sex with people for money, it was something that was forced on you by karma, but she was lucky. She was glad to have a face and body that men desired, because otherwise she would be working in the paddy fields, and did he think she was pretty?

Harry nodded, because he did, but all this talk about brothers and sisters and extended families scratching around in the dirt and kids dying early was putting him right off. Everyone knew Thailand was a knocking shop. He'd made the mistake of treating her as a human being, but that was him all over, making mistakes Carter would never dream of making. Carter would've mumbled a few words and had the fucking slag over the bed inside thirty seconds, giving her one from behind as he planned his next move. More than that, he wouldn't bother with prostitutes in the first place. He didn't need to pay for sex. Bollocks, though, because Harry was his own man and he was riding the crest of a wave, seeing the world and meeting exotic tarts, getting wasted with hairies and on the piss with his mates.

Nicky pulled him to the bed but Harry was thinking about the girls in Rudi's and the blow, and his head was floating imagining a Thai village and a ready supply of poppy seed. He saw himself going from one opium den to another, surrounded by hippies and Siamese princesses, the prince in his harem spaced out on sex and drugs, no fucking rock-n-roll or even music as he turned off the CD. Nicky dimmed the lights and he was in this little palace somewhere in Bangkok, down by a river with the bustle of sticky-rice street vendors, while really he was in Amsterdam following the train of tourists shagging for their photo albums. He moved in on Nicky but when her hand went down to his knob he was sorry to say there was nothing there for her to get hold of. She looked at him and smiled, and started playing around, and then she pushed him back on the bed and went down and started using her mouth.

Harry laid back and thought of England. He thought of The Unity and Rod missing out, about the rest of the boys alive and well, his mate Balti dead and gone, a red ball of gristle at the top of his neck, brains seeping into the sewer. He stopped and tried to concentrate on Nicky. Here he was with the golden chance to shag a real cracker, even if she was a tart, and he was trying to will some steel into his cock but still nothing happened. The more he tried conjuring up a hard-on, the limper he got, shrinking from those Thai teeth as his brain drifted off again. He raised his head and could see this girl with small tits and a tight cunt, a suction pair of lips and perfect body, with years of training doing her best for her customer and not getting anywhere. Harry wished he'd stayed with the rest of the boys and given all this a miss. It was that fucking hippy smoke that had done him. Never trust a hippy. He had to admit there was no point going on, because the more he thought about what was happening the worse he got. He was thinking of England, but just couldn't get it up.

Harry moved away and started putting on his pants. He said sorry about that, bit too much drink, bit too much dope, and Nicky said it didn't matter, that he'd be surprised how often it happened. He told her to keep the money, that it was down to him, but he didn't look at the girl and she wasn't exactly going to hand it back. Fucking hell, if he couldn't shag something like that then he was in serious trouble. She had the rubber ready and everything. Nicky ran through a list of limp knobs, premature ejaculations and general rubbish sex that made him feel a bit better. She was trying to cheer him up and he supposed she didn't mind either way. It was probably better for her not having to lay down under yet another fat cunt. She was probably pleased.

She asked him where he was from and when he said England she asked if he liked the Queen. Everyone liked the Queen, and Nicky started going into one again as though nothing had happened, saying the Thais had a king who they loved as well. He sat down for a minute doing up his trainers and she was rambling on and offered him a drink, pouring two glasses of whisky. She had a small container of ice and for some reason she wasn't in a hurry to get rid of him. She asked him what London was like and what he did for a living and where he was going after Amsterdam. When he said Berlin she told him of a man she'd known in Thailand who came from Berlin. She'd stayed with him for two months on Ko Samui before he went home, leaving her pregnant when she was eighteen. She'd hoped he'd take her away from Thailand but he'd left suddenly and she'd found someone else. All the bar girls in Thailand wanted to get out, to go to Europe and America.

She said she was finished for the night. She'd been working hard and was tired. She aimed at ten men a night and Harry was number ten. He nodded and got up to leave and was surprised when she suggested he come with her for a drink. She pulled the hair on his arms and pinched his gut. Harry wasn't sure what she was doing. He wondered if it was a con, if she had an ambush lined up, but she said she had some whisky and hashish in her flat. She lived a couple of miles away in the flat her ex-friend had rented for her. He'd been good to her. She looked up at Harry and he could feel his knob stirring. He couldn't believe he'd paid good money and hadn't poked her, and though he was confused he thought why not, because what else was he going to do tonight?

They were soon walking out of the red light district, and once over the Amstel River everything seemed different. He was wondering where it was leading, but enjoying himself and this woman next to him. She had her arm through his and he had to remind himself she was a tart. She was fucking lovely, and it seemed unreal somehow. He felt like he was in a video. He remembered Mango saying how the girls in Thailand didn't see it so much as a shag as a possible introduction, but Harry was smart enough to know that Amsterdam would've changed some of that. He was looking for an angle and half-expected a couple of pimps to arrive and start slicing him up. But Nicky was talking about whisky and hashish and how she loved going out to buy clothes and music and how shit Thailand was, that he couldn't help wondering if Mango was right.

They took a cab the short journey to her flat. It was small but well done up and Harry sat down on the couch as Nicky brought out a bottle of Jack Daniels. She was asking about London and he found himself telling her about the pubs he used, about Blues and how he liked going to football. She rolled a chunky spliff and after a while he was even telling her about his mate Balti who'd been murdered in the street, her hand going to her mouth in shock. He told her how they'd grown up together and shared a flat, and how they'd been closer than brothers. Funny thing was, he didn't mind talking and didn't feel too bad about the memory. He couldn't smoke a lot and the hairies had already set him up, so maybe that was the reason, though it could've been because she was a stranger and, more than that, she was a whore who didn't really count.

That wasn't true, though, because Harry had to keep reminding himself that this woman sitting next to him was a prostitute. She had sex with ten men a night. Fuck knows what kind of diseases she was carrying. She was a fucking prostitute, and whores were supposed to turn their mouths away from you if you tried to kiss them, and they were supposed to be professional and blunt with their services, showing the punter who was in charge, and then if he was pissed he was going to get narked by this lack of respect and start having a go and fuck knows what could happen. No, Nicky was talking to him like he was a person rather than some sleazy cunt off the street. He found it hard remembering she was a pro, and with some of the old herb he soon forgot altogether.

Nicky got up and went for a piss as Harry poured himself another glass of whisky. He fancied a bottle of Heineken, but the Jack Daniels was fine for now, till she came back. He wondered what the rest of the boys were up to, but was happy enough here. It wasn't that late, and Nicky said she liked to finish early and avoid the worst of the drunks. He was in Amsterdam, but could've been anywhere in the world. This place was international, because you went for a simple shag with a whore and ended up sitting on a couch getting stoned with some Thai all the way from the Laos border. You didn't get this kind of thing down Blues.

Harry had never been outside Europe. One day he'd go to the States and, who knows, one day he might even go to the Far East. It would be hard, because the poverty would get you down, but there were a lot of places to see in the world. When England joined up with Europe they'd be getting all the influences and this would liven things up. Harry sipped his drink and put his feet on a stool. He looked up and saw Nicky walk into the room naked and this time he was ready.

We're standing by one of the humped-back bridges that arc over the canals enjoying the scenery, wondering where Harry's disappeared to. Little knots of English are scattered around. Sitting on cars and railings. A bottle lands in the water and ripples catch the sex club neons. The water's a burnt-out stretch of black in between brightly-lit buildings. There's clubs, restaurants and bars rubbing shoulders. Enough drink to keep us going and one or two shops still open selling stuff to the locals. We're outside two bars sitting side by side, having a drink and watching the show. It's after ten now and it's nice knowing the bars will be serving late. These two are packed. One with English and the other with a mixture of English and locals. Might not be local to the red light, but they're Dutch. The English bar is singing RULE BRITANNIA while the other has the music blaring out. Rule Britannia on one side and The Prodigy's Firestarter on the other. The songs mix together and somehow sound perfect.

– Did you see those sand niggers run? Carter asks, rocking back on the parked scooter he's sitting on. I've never seen men run that fast. I thought the Italians were nippy, but those blokes were greased lightning. Should sign those cunts up, give them passports and get them to run in the athletics team. You'd never get an Englishman moving like that.

Carter starts carving CFC and ENGLAND into the scooter with his keys, talking about the pimps we smacked on the way here.

– They knew their time was up, Mark says. Makes me sick seeing white girls getting used by those cunts. What were they? They weren't Turks, were they?

– Moroccans, Carter says. Moroccans, Tunisians, Algerians. Something like that. Fucking sand niggers. Fresh from the Sahara. You go down Bayswater and you'll find enough of them round there running the shops and kebab houses. They're not poor. How do you think they get out in the first place?

– Couldn't believe it when that cunt hit the girl in the gut like that, Mark says. Just punches her in the belly as if that's how we all behave. Fuck me, what kind of cunt is that? Still, I did him alright. Straight in the bollocks, and Tom slapped his mate. Couple of shitters.

I nod and agree. I mean prostitution's a natural enough business, but there's no need to hit the workers. I thought the Dutch had all this stuff sorted out. That's what they say. That's the impression you get back home. But they've only gone so far. It's the soft drugs that are legal and only so much in certain places. There's enough pushers around selling smack and what have you. As for the tarts, you'd think the shop windows would get rid of the pimps, but there they are. Scum always floats back. Suppose there's always going to be girls selling themselves, and that's the way it should be, because we live in a free-market economy. The girls get their money and the bloke gets his end away. Everyone's happy. Till some fucking sand nigger comes along and starts knocking them about. There's no excuse for those wankers. Pimps are fucking scum. They're always these fucking greaseballs as well. Either that or blacks That Turk or whatever he was won't be hitting anyone for a while. Never mind his sore bollocks, his hand's going to take some stitching after Harris slashed his knuckles. That's what those cunts believe in anyway. Chopping off hands. They treat their women like shit. An eye for an eye and a hand for a hand. Instant justice. Harris doing his good deed for the night.

– I had that bird down to ten guilders for a blow job when they turned up, Carter says. That's about three quid. Imagine a blow job for three quid. She wasn't bad was she? She wasn't Dutch though. Said she was from Russia. Blondie was well nice. Ten guilders for a blow job. I'm going to have to get in somewhere tonight.

118

– Don't look at me, Harris says, laughing, the old humour coming through again.

– I can't spend too much time thinking about that bird, Carter says. She had rubber lips as well. Ten fucking guilders. That's three quid.

– Fuck off, Mark says. She never said ten guilders.

– Straight up. Ten guilders. I gave her a line and she told me business is shit tonight because there's so many English about. Said the local news has been going on about the English hooligans drinking in the red light district. The office workers are too scared to come down here because they reckon there's going to be trouble. There seems to be enough punters around, but she said there's not a lot of work tonight. The girls are starving.

– You're telling me that bird was going to suck you off for ten guilders? You'd spend more than that on a round.

– Honest. Ten's better than nothing for a working girl. Thanks to that pimp I've got lover's balls. Just the thought of that old slag's doing my head in. If I don't pull anything later I'll go down and have one of those girls in the windows. Mind you, they're not going to be ten guilders. Maybe there was something wrong with those girls. Ten guilders. Fucking hell.

You have to laugh because it's pure justice seeing Carter getting let down. Thought he was supposed to be this big sex machine. It's early yet I suppose. Surprised he's going to pay for it though. A man of his talent and reputation should click his fingers and have the women come running.

The England bar starts up again. There's faces pressed against the glass, skulls coloured by red and blue light. There must be a hundred of them in there. Should move outside where they can breathe. The glass sweats and every now and then a hand comes through the bodies and wipes it clean. Big hand clearing a view of the street outside. I don't know about the punters being put off. There's tourists and that, but Dutch as well. Mind you, no middle-aged men in raincoats. The England boys by the windows watch Amsterdam pass in a pissed daze. Their eyes are glazed and they bang on the glass whenever something half-decent strolls past. It's funny watching the girls jump and look into that bar. Must be a horror show for the Dutch. Out for a walk looking in on a cave packed with drunk Englishmen. All tattoos and shaved heads, laughing and shouting faces, one or two wrapped in Union Jacks and Crosses of St George.

The window's almost popping, the multi-coloured lights opposite flashing on and off creating a strobe effect. Fucking mental how the skulls flash. The bar's singing NO SURRENDER and we all join in outside showing solidarity with the soldiers fighting for England. The window vibrates as that big love-and-hate hand comes through the crowd, banging out a Loyalist rhythm. There's England right outside and stretching down the road, and they all look round at the same moment in case the glass comes crashing down. The red hand disappears in the crowd and they go back to their singing.

– Why don't we go and find that bird? Mark says. She'll do us all for three quid after we saved them from the sand niggers. She'll do me for free because I kicked that bloke in the balls. St George riding across the desert saving white women from slavery.

– You're joking, aren't you? Carter asks. They'll be keeping their heads down because those cunts have been put in their place. They'll probably take it out on the girl and her mate once they've finished at the hospital.

– You think so?

– It's not like there's anyone around to stop them, is there? I don't suppose the old bill can be bothered because you're only talking about a couple of tarts, and you never know, they could be illegal immigrants or something.

– We should've cut that bloke's throat, Mark says.

I can see him getting wound up and tell him not to worry. She probably had broken teeth and would've ripped Carter's foreskin off. He laughs and Carter looks worried.

– We'll get something better later, Carter says. Blow jobs all round for five guilders. Don't worry, we'll get our legs over before we leave Amsterdam, and it won't be whores.

I look sideways to the music bar and there's enough England in there as well, mixed in with the locals having a laugh. There's a few birds, but nothing special from where I'm standing. The window in the England bar bounces again. The red hand of Ulster appears as the song ends and we're into ONE BOMBER HARRIS. I wait for the hand, but someone's had a word and the blokes outside can relax. THERE'S ONLY ONE BOMBER HARRIS, ONE BOMBER HARRIS. There's a few scousers, who you can always tell by the shape of their faces and style of dress, a small group of Leeds who look like Yorkshiremen, and I bet when they look at us they know we're from London. Probably know we're Chelsea as well.

Billy Bright comes outside and Harris goes over, and they start talking to the Pompey boys next door, the ones from the ferry who've arrived as Harris predicted. The scousers wander off taking their bottles with them, and then one of the Leeds mob starts chatting to Harris. Suppose he knows who he is and Harris starts laughing at something, and there you have Portsmouth, Chelsea and Leeds having a chat and that's something a lot of people who don't go away with England wouldn't understand or even believe.

That's what happens. A perfect example. Go back a few years and think of the rows we've had with Portsmouth and Leeds. But you get over here with England and all that filters away. Some things can never be smoothed out, and certain faces are remembered. Things can get personal. But with this lot it's okay. I see the scousers wandering back. I turn my head because Mark's banging me on the shoulder.

– Come on, it's your round, he says.

I nod and go towards the England bar, then think again and go in next door. It'll be easier to get served, and anyway, there's a few women in here. I lean over the counter and order three bottles. I look around the bar. There's not much on offer. Mostly small groups of boring-looking birds getting chatted up by pissed English. I go outside and talk with Harris and the others, but see Mark and Carter waiting for their drinks. I get to the bridge and hand the bottles over, turning to see a man with a Union Jack around his shoulders fall over in the street pissed. He's one of the Leeds lot and he stays there. A couple of blokes pull him over to a wall and leave him to sleep.

– Why don't we go to a club? Carter asks.

– You can see a sex show anywhere, Mark says.

– A proper club. Somewhere we can find some women. It's all tarts and tourists down here.

We look at each other and it makes sense. We're not going to meet any Dutch birds when there's hundreds of us hanging about, half the blokes pissed out of their heads. Move down the streets a bit and there's more English. We're everywhere. Harris and Brighty have gone inside the bar so we just leave. Halfway down the road I start wondering where we're going, but Carter says he sussed out a couple of places before leaving England.

It's a fair old hike so we stop a cab. Carter passes the address to the driver, a big friendly bloke who acts like he's known us all his life. He's a Norsk giant with a deep laugh. Says he knows the club and puts his foot down, cutting across tram lines. The air's hot inside the car and we roll down the windows. He tells us the climate's changing. It's June and there's rain. The air's turned muggy and we could do with another drink. Five minutes later he drops us off at the end of this pedestrian zone. We pay our money and we're lining up outside the club, but when we get to the door there's none of the hassle you get off the bouncers back in London. Blues is fine because we know the blokes on the door. I'm talking about the West End clubs. We're inside quick enough and there's a decent mixture of music. It's not really a club in the normal sense.

Carter doesn't waste any time and gets the drinks. Starts talking with these three birds at the bar. Piece of piss and we're straight in. Have to keep hold of things. Hanging about with a bunch of nutters all day can lead you astray. Have to be nice and polite. Luckily these girls are pissed as well so there's no chance of them storming off because they can't stand the drunk bollocks coming out of our mouths. They seem happy enough. Listening to everything from Block Rocking Beats to Babylon's Burning.

– It's my birthday tomorrow, this bird Monica says in my ear. I'm going to be thirty years old.

She looks younger but I'm not complaining.

– My friends are older. She smiles. How old do you think?

How the fuck should I know? Don't say it though. I have a guess and she laughs and whispers in their ears. They all laugh some more then piss off to dance around to Smack My Bitch Up. Nice one that. Mark nods and says those sand niggers must drink in here. I move over to the wall with Mark and Carter.

– No problem here lads, Carter says. We're all going back to Monica's. It's her birthday party and the girls are sleeping with her tonight. This is our night boys.

Carter is enjoying himself, doing what he does best.

– The blow jobs are on the house tonight, he shouts, trying to be heard. We owe those pimps a favour. Instead of these three we'd have been making do with those mangy old slappers down a back alley, throwing away good money.

I watch the dancefloor bouncing. I can see the girls dancing and looking over. They keep going through Nirvana, Oasis and Black Grape. When they come back Monica's leaning in heavy, asking if I want some ecstasy or speed? I go for the whizz with Mark and Carter. It gives me a pick-up and the strength returns. I have that dedicated feeling now. Dedicated to getting this bird's G-string off and in my pocket. Fuck the arse off this bird. Give her the perfect birthday present. She's full of life and it's a couple of hours later when we get around to leaving.

There's six of us walking near empty streets. The girls are singing a song in Dutch that sounds like shit. Some languages fit music, others don't. English is the perfect example where it works. French the worst. The song they're singing means nothing to us. It's a short walk and we climb these cold stone stairs to Monica's flat. It's a big place, and one of her mates goes and takes out a punk compilation. There's old stuff from Stiff Little Fingers, X-Ray Spex and the Pistols, and newer material from the likes of Leatherface, Fugazi and the Blaggers. She puts the CD on and music fills the flat, Monica going over and turning it down. In the light they look dirtier than down the club. Their make-up's blurred and Monica just stands there and takes off her black jeans. She laughs and says it's too hot, one of the girls opening a window. I want to get stuck in right away but hang on, because they're acting coy with Monica half-naked.

One of the girls brings in a pack of lager. It's nice and cold. Monica puts a lamp on and turns the main light off. Carter laughs and says Harry will be angry he missed out. Probably got lost and is back in the hotel right now fast asleep. I have a long swig of lager and my mind is racing trying to keep up with my tongue. I'm going on about Blues back home and talking about the Dutch-German border for some reason. Fuck knows what I'm on about. I stop talking and sit listening. Can still hear my voice somewhere.

Don't know how much longer it is but Carter and one of the girls has gone. The sex machine is doing his duty. I look at the chair opposite and Mark's got this bird on his lap. Her top's up and her tits are out. They're kissing and so am I, but it's not Monica. She must be with Carter. Or maybe she's with Mark. Fuck knows and who cares, because I'm up and following this bird to a small box room. We go inside and I'm thinking of that film in Johan's bar. Blondie getting serviced by Ginger. This isn't Blondie, but it's a blonde bird. I don't follow what's happening but I know what has to be done. I can't come for ages and this gives the girl the kind of sex she wants. Eventually I finish and lie there next to her. She promises me a blow job first thing in the morning. Starts snoring. I spend the next hour trying to shut down and get to sleep. I hope she keeps her word.

Nicky was down between Harry's legs when he woke, and it took him a couple of seconds to realise where he was and what was going on. It wasn't London and if it had been the hotel with Carter he'd have topped himself. When he realised where he was Harry was king of the castle. He looked down and saw the Thai dealing with a serious hard-on. This was the life, leaning back and admiring the wonders of the East, and it wasn't long till he filled her mouth with some fine English seed. He shut his eyes and rested with Nicky's head against his shoulder and next thing he knew he was waking up with a cup of coffee next to the bed and Nicky parading a dress she'd just bought. It was bright yellow and showed off her brown skin. She showed him a pair of matching open shoes and he didn't really know what to say, telling her they were very nice. This did the trick and she seemed pleased. She laughed and skipped across the room and Harry wondered what the fuck was going on.

Last night his brain had been working overtime as he drifted in and out of sleep. He was walking into a Saigon hotel and falling down on the bed, playing a star role in *Apocalypse Now*. Then he was in *The Deer Hunter*, falling from a helicopter. From being a cocky bastard firing into ancient rainforest, he was a scared little man on his own, hated by the people he was helping to slaughter. When Harry was a kid Vietnam had been on the telly more than the war in Northern Ireland. He remembered the images – the man getting shot at point blank range and the girl running down a road, back burnt by napalm. The Vietnamese didn't count because the coverage was all about the number of American soldiers getting killed by Ho Chi Minh.

– This is my son, Nicky said, stripping off the dress and shoes and getting in bed next to Harry.

She propped a picture album on his lap.

– This is my son. He lives with the monks in a monastery outside Surat Thani in Southern Thailand. There is a school near the monastery and that is where he lives. The nuns and monks teach him.

Harry looked at the first picture. A short-haired boy of four or five stood by two cross-legged Buddhist monks. He was wearing brown shorts and a white shirt. The monks wore orange robes. It was the brightest orange he'd ever seen. Their heads were shaved in number one crops, and Nicky laughed, ran her hand over Harry's head and said their skinheads were even better. Harry said he wasn't a skinhead, but it didn't matter. He got the joke. The kid was smiling and Harry wondered if he thought about his mum. One of the monks had tattoos around his neck and on his arms, and when he asked what they meant Nicky said there was a tradition of tattooing in many Thai monasteries. The necklace was for protection and the monks did the tattoos themselves, using swords. She hoped that one day her son would come and live with her in Europe. One day in the future when she had enough money.

Nicky was sitting close with her legs drawn up to her chest.

Her tits were perfect, pressed against scar-free knees. Small but perfect. He left it alone and went back to the photos. She was keen and wanted to show them off. There were pictures of the school and the monastery. Some were slightly blurred and showed two golden Buddhas, various buildings, a collection of monks and nuns and kids, some ordinary Thais, and a forest of tightly-packed trees and big shiny plants. There were lots of photos of the boy and Harry looked sideways at Nicky's face. She seemed proud of her son and he imagined it must be hard being separated.

Harry felt like a cunt sitting there. What did she expect from him? What did she think about her son growing up in an orphanage thousands of miles away? How often did she get to see him? Thing was, you never thought about prostitutes making mistakes. He imagined they just had abortions if anything went wrong, but maybe things were different in Asia. Maybe they didn't have the same birth control and hospital treatment. He wasn't looking for answers. He wanted a good time and should skim the photos and piss off, but he couldn't brush it away. He tried to think what the rest of the boys would do. Fuck off and never think about her again. He was just like Balti. They were too fat and slow. They didn't work things out ahead of time, so hung about and got lumbered with photo albums and sob stories.

He sipped his coffee and the caffeine helped. Nicky jumped out of bed and went to skin up. She was quick and efficient, struck a match and inhaled. Harry didn't know how she did it first thing in the morning. The coffee gave him a kick because he was slow and tired, but she was jumping around and trying to slow herself down. Fuck knows what else she was on, because when he forgot about her laughter and smiles it had to be a fucking hard life. She had to have something to get her through. She came back to the bed and sucked smoke down her lungs, not caring about her nakedness as she leant over Harry and pointed him back to the photos.

– This is Marc, she said.

Harry thought he looked like any other everyday European. There was nothing to say he hung around massage parlours and go-go bars in Pettaya worrying young girls, and then ended up turning his attention to blokes. He just seemed ordinary.

– This is when we stayed at Chaweng on Ko Samui, Nicky said, running through various beaches and temples.

She looked happy in the pictures. She was wearing sunglasses and her skin was a shade darker. He pointed this out.

– In Thailand it is better to have white skin. The lighter my skin, the better I am considered by Thai people. Western men like dark-skinned girls. Europeans want to sit in the sun and turn brown, Thais want to stay indoors and become white. We both want what the other has.

Harry laughed at this because it was true. People were like that wherever you went, always wanting what the other person had but didn't value. It was the same in the old days. Dark skin in England showed you were a peasant, while pale skin belonged to the rich who didn't have to work outdoors. Things had changed, but it was interesting what Nicky said about Thailand, and he supposed it was the same in other countries as well. She was dark in the photo from her time on the beach behaving like a Westerner. Other Thais would've looked down on her skin colour, but in the photos she was happy and almost cocky, walking with the European and not caring what the small-minded cunts thought. It wasn't because he was European, but because he had money, and money was important for both the peasants and rich snobs. They fucking hated it when someone they considered below them came racing through the ranks. He thought of Mango, who'd gone for the shilling and done himself proud, but there was always going to be jealousy from those he worked with who had a massive head start yet found themselves trailing behind.

Harry respected Nicky for the photos, because her pride was obvious as she showed off her victories. Life had been a struggle, but she hadn't given up. She pointed to a picture that showed her sitting in a posh restaurant.

– This is in Bangkok, before we came to Holland.

She looked happy and sad in the photo, but was making her mark and he laughed at the light-skinned waiters forced to serve this whore and treat her with respect. Harry saw it clearly. She was coming through from a poor village, coming up from the go-go bars of Bangkok and the two-on-one massage parlours of Pettaya, walking tall after years of getting the white man's spunk drilled into her belly. Nicky was getting out on the last helicopter gunship, leaving the entrepreneurs behind to cut each other's throats. The pimps and hustlers couldn't touch her sitting in the Bangkok Continental. She was eating tom yum soup that cost more than she usually got for sucking off a dirty old slob who wanted to stick three fingers up her arse while she worked. She'd surrendered everything physical and come through the other side. He thought of Vietnam and the ability of the Viet Cong to take everything the Yanks could drop on them and still come back for more. Peasants in tiny villages brought down B52s with vintage rifles. All the high-tech killing power of the industrialised world failed. He'd seen it so many times on the television and now he was seeing it played back here. Nicky was fighting her own war and she'd survived. The restaurant was her medal.

Nicky was fighting back against the foreigners taking advantage of her poverty, but more than that against the traitors who kept her poor and sold her to the highest bidder. Harry was getting a bit emotional. There was no respect, but she had used the system to escape. He saw this but what could anyone do? Thailand was a good friend of the West because its politicians accepted the new imperialism, and while the men in suits didn't bend over personally, they were quite happy for others to do so on their behalf. Funny thing was, Harry understood what was going on, but as a kid he'd always wanted to be the gunner in one of those helicopters, the man with the machinery at his command. It was natural, really, because everyone wanted the glory and none of the mess. But you had to look on the bright side. At least she'd had the chance to work her passage out.

– Here is our home in Amsterdam, Nicky said, pointing out the rooms of a three-bedroomed flat.

She went through the apartment in detail, like she was shopping for furniture. She was house proud, but Harry wasn't interested. He had to move on and fancied something to eat. He listened but didn't hear what she was saying, and when she finished he asked if she had any food. Nicky jumped up again and put on a T-shirt. She went to the kitchen and fucked about in the fridge, coming back with some cheese and bread. He ate this and then went for a shower. He fancied a shag but Nicky was dressed now and he couldn't insist. It wasn't like he was the punter any more. He didn't know whether to leg it or go down this bar she was talking about. Harry dressed quickly and had some coffee. If he went back he'd just be hanging about with the others, so he might as well see some of Amsterdam with the girl. It didn't mean anything. She'd be off to work in a few hours and that would be that. She was skinning up again and he noticed a glass of Jack Daniels. It was eleven o'clock. He sat down and had a puff. He felt okay. He was seeing the world and wondered if they'd make it outside as Nicky came and sat next to him on the couch, coming close, fishing the rubbers out of his pocket and dropping them in his lap.

The tour boat chugs along and gives us a different view of the city. It's one of those things that's shit, but you end up doing it anyway. An hour and a half to see the sights. I've left the others behind and paid my money. Taken a chance on the hostess pointing to bricks and mortar. Telling us about Amsterdam's rich history. It's the same as taking a train is some ways. On a train you pass through the back of a city and see the place with its trousers down. There's no development-zone plastic coating. Pass through on a train and you get empty warehouses and rusted railway sidings. Terraced houses spilling into overgrown nettles. Stacked rubbish and burnt-out sheds. Derelict factories and steaming wasteland. It's the best way to travel, though I suppose this boat's not going to major on that sort of thing. But it's interesting going through the back door. Don't care what anyone says. Playing tourists.

There's a couple of stuck-up English in front talking down their noses about the Van Gogh Museum. I remember seeing the film on telly. The silly cunt wanted to be with the poor. Wanted to do something to help the peasants but his old man told him to get a career. He lived with a prostitute and cut off his ear. He was a fucking nutter who did his own thing, but now he's dead the sort of scum who made his life hell when he was alive come back and claim the glory. It's all fame and fortune and who can pay the most for his paintings.

We pass the warehouse where Anne Frank lived. The tour guide fills us in. Gently rocking on the canal. Fat tourists with cameras and travel books. On holiday, having fun. Tickling emotions. The woman tells us Anne Frank was a Jewish girl who lived in the back of the warehouse, in what they called the back annexe, for two years with her family and friends, hiding from the Gestapo. They were helped by non-Jewish friends and survived for two years. Their spirits were getting better because the Allies were starting to win the war. Then they were betrayed by a collaborator. The families were discovered and the eight people there were shipped off to the concentration camps. Otto Frank, Anne Frank's dad, was the only one to survive. Anne Frank and her sister died from typhus one week before the Germans surrendered.

I remember that film as well. It was hard to watch and made me sad. The tour guide is silent for a few seconds.

I wonder what happened to Otto Frank. What would you think after going through that? Must be millions of people alive still in the same situation. More than that, I wonder about the collaborator. The wanker who grassed them up. Out of Amsterdam's 80,000 Jews, 75,000 were killed. The tour guide says there's a statue erected to mark the spot where, in 1941, 400 Jewish men were shipped off to Mauthausen concentration camp after a Nazi sympathiser was killed following fights between members of the Jewish Resistance and the Dutch Nazi party. Didn't know the Dutch had a Nazi party. They were killed in retaliation for the Nazi's death. Following this there was a strike led by the dockers and transport workers. She says it was arranged by the communist party, illegal at the time. It lasted two days before it was broken. She says it was unusual in Holland, where people did little to protest against the treatment of Jews. An old Dutch couple tut and shake their heads. The guide says that most European countries under German rule did little to save the Jews.

I wonder what England would've done. Would people have stood up and tried to save the women and children? Can't imagine the English standing aside. We're just not like that. I know we call Spurs yids and that, but it's different. There's no real feeling because we're not religious. No, the English don't kill women and kids. We're hard, but fair.

The boat picks up speed and we move to more cheerful subjects. Snips of information are fed through the microphone. Anne Frank is forgotten as the water parts and tourists click their cameras. There's camcorders recording life. Picking up on moving boats and still buildings. Eventually the tour ends and we troop off. I see Kevin and catch him up. Tap him on the shoulder.

– Didn't see you there, he says. Were you on the boat as well? Bit boring wasn't it? Do you fancy a bevvy?

We walk for a few minutes and I sit at an outdoor table while he goes inside for a piss. When he comes back we order a couple of draught lagers.

– The only interesting thing was that girl dying one week before she was going to be free, Kevin says, emptying half the glass in one swig. Imagine being so close to freedom. They were wankers the Germans. Fucking scum of the earth. A bunch of child-molesting poofs.

Don't know about that, but no-one's going to agree with killing kids. Imagine what her old man must've felt like when he found out what had happened. It seems unreal somehow. You can't imagine that sort of thing actually happening.

– I went to Dachau, Kevin says, finishing his drink and ordering another.

He looks at my glass because it's still two-thirds full. For some reason I finish it in one go so he can't take the piss and call me a soft southern wanker. It's hot now and knocking about in Amsterdam is thirsty work. He's a big bastard and takes his shirt off. The waiter minces back and looks at the Man U crest on his arm. Takes the money and pisses off. Kevin has another swig and leans forward to continue his story. Just as he's about to fill me in on Dachau this executive-type cunt leans over and asks

Kevin to put his shirt back on because he's causing offence. He says this is a decent bar.

– Fuck off, Kevin says.

The executive is with a couple of other wankers and doesn't move, so Kevin pulls him by his collar and topples him half off the chair. He brings his fist up and holds it in front of the bloke's face.

– Fuck off bud. I'm trying to have a conversation I come in peace. Understand?

He lets go and the businessman goes inside with his chums looking shaken. Kevin finishes his beer and tells me to come on, we'll go round the corner in case the cunt calls the old bill. You never know with these Europeans, there might be a law against taking your shirt off. He says there was this time in Oslo when some of them were sitting in the park having a drink and the old bill pulled up in a van.

– They were a bunch of wankers, he says. They stood there and poured our cans away. It was illegal to drink in a public place. They even said they were being generous, because if they wanted they could put us in the cells. They're mad about their laws in Europe.

He leads the way to another bar and we go inside. We get our drinks and sit in among a mixture of office workers, labourers and one or two tourists. It's a clean bar but without the petty attitude of the last place.

– I was in Munich for the beer festival, he continues, and we got the train out to Dachau. I was expecting something like you see on the telly, something like Auschwitz with the wire and hair and glasses. All the buildings where the prisoners were kept had been knocked down and there was this big, flat space. We went to the furnaces but it was hard to imagine that people were killed in them. The thing that made the biggest impression was the museum.

He leans forward.

– There were these pictures of experiments. Altitude experiments and things like that. Outside was where these things happened, but I couldn't feel anything. Inside it was a museum and it showed you what went on. Thing was, there were all these German kids on school trips and they just looked bored. A few of them were laughing and the teachers had to tell them off. There we all were in this place where they killed political prisoners and Jews and anyone else they wanted to get rid of, and it wasn't what we'd expected. It was like we were let down. We couldn't imagine what had happened. You just couldn't get a feeling. We took the train back and that night we were on the piss surrounded by big German women singing along with this small cunt dressed in shorts and squeezing an accordion. It was as though nothing had happened. We knew it had, but it didn't feel like it. I suppose you had to be there.

Harry said goodbye to Nicky and she kissed him on the mouth. He even thought he saw a small tear in her eye as they went their separate ways. He turned his head briefly and saw her disappear down a side street, a frail little thing in among the beating neon and dead corners. She kept going and he admired her, because she'd been through a lot and was positive. It had been a good day, and he'd promised to see her on his way back from Berlin. He meant it when he said it but now, walking towards Johan's bar, he knew he was acting soft. He probably wouldn't bother. He was asking for trouble getting involved and feeling sorry for her. She was nice enough, and had a fit body, and she knew how to look after him, but she was a fucking whore, he had to remember that she was a prostitute who sucked blokes dry for the price of a four-star meal. Nothing more and nothing less, and he had to apply standards. He'd keep it quiet because he remembered the story of Rod in the Reeperbahn, when they were in Hamburg, and he didn't want everyone taking the piss out of him.

Harry turned his head for another look, but Nicky was gone, off to sit in a window for the tourists cruising the streets adding some spice to their holidays. Nicky was off to service her ten men, sucking and shagging her way to rest and recreation, an inflatable doll for a troop of drunks and dirty old men. She was a tart and he had to look after himself. He was over here to enjoy himself without any hassle and now he was getting wound up about a whore. She'd done an E before leaving the flat and would be feeling good.

He could stop for a shag on his way back, but shouldn't look for anything else. He felt sorry for her when she didn't feel sorry for herself. It was the photo album. Leaving the crowd ogling the fanny and walking over to the pin-ups, then making conversation, was dangerous. You were better off in the crowd. He had to pull on a human-size condom and protect himself. Start fucking about with birds like that and it would bring you down. It was all a game and he had to think what Carter would do in the same situation, but then Carter had got himself in enough bother sniffing round that nutter Denise. They were leaving for Berlin tomorrow morning and tonight he was going to get pissed. You were better off sticking with the rest of the boys and having a good old-fashioned punch-up.

Entering the bar Harry felt like he was walking into a major convention, where the dope had been replaced by lager and the Eastern magic of a Buddhist peasant by the solid Christian realism of a select football firm. He moved through the faces – some familiar, others new – and tapped Carter on the shoulder. The sex machine turned with a drunk grin and Tom moved aside to let him through. They didn't ask any questions, which was how things should be, and Harry looked around and saw that a good mob was already forming – Tom and Mark, Billy Bright and Dave Harris, Martin Howe, Gary Davison and his mates, plus some older faces who showed up for the high-profile games, preferring European travel to domestic games. Don Wright and some of the Slough mob were there, along with small firms from Feltham, Battersea and Camberley. There was an assortment of other English picked up along the way, but it was mostly London and the Home Counties in the bar, which was fair enough, and of those it was mainly Chelsea. Harry settled down with a bottle of lager, picking up on the conversation at the table.

– It's Garry Bushell, said Billy. He was the bloke who gave Oi! a chance when he was at *Sounds*. He was the one who ignored the middle-class wankers in the music press and gave working-class punk its chance.

Harry asked Carter what they were on about, and the sex machine said they were arguing over who was the greatest ever Englishman.

– I thought he wrote a television column, Mark said.

– He does, but before that he was into music. Bands saying what nobody was allowed to say, that it was alright to be white and working class, and that it didn't make you a fascist if you carried the Union Jack. The bands were saying that because you were proud to be English didn't mean you hated blacks.

– Everyone knows that, Mark said.

– We do, but he was standing up for what normal people think against the media.

– Those cunts aren't real anyway, Harris laughed. Who cares what they think.

– But the thing was, he took stick for what he did and it was a brave thing to do.

– Maybe it was, but it doesn't make him the greatest ever Englishman, does it? Harris said. It's just because you like the music. Do us a favour. No, it's got to be someone from history. Richard the Lionheart or Oliver Cromwell. They gave the Arabs and the Irish a good slap, didn't they?

A few of the lads laughed at that one. Harris might've been going a bit over the top recently, but he still had his sense of humour intact. There was a short silence then, because suddenly nobody knew if he was serious or not. Richard the Lionheart and Cromwell were going right back.

– What about Churchill? Harry asked. He has to be one of the top boys.

– You can't have a politician, can you? Tom said. I mean, he did the job and that, but you want someone like Montgomery.

– Winston did alright, Billy said, but I know what you mean. He was safe at home when they were going through Europe. How about Bomber Harris?

A few people nodded. The stick Bomber Harris had been getting off the trendy press gave him added attraction. It always worked like that.

– What about Maggie Thatcher? She did the Falklands.

– Politician again. Anyway, look what she did to football. All the undercover operations and the all–seater grounds. No football fan can vote for Thatcher.

Harry sipped his drink and looked around. People were moving away from the conversation. It was losing its humour.

– It has to be someone with a sense of humour, he said. That's what makes the greatest Englishman.

– Charlie Chaplin?

– Too far back.

– What about Black Adder?

They thought about this one for a while. He was funny and Harry thought Rowan Atkinson was the choice. He was fucking brilliant in the First World War sketches, the way he took the piss out of the generals and everything. All those series were good, getting under the skin.

– We're not a bunch of comedians, Harris said, putting his foot down. It was Churchill, whatever Tom says. Churchill was the main man. It doesn't matter if he was a politician. He was an exception.

They didn't want to argue with Harris and he had a point. They all agreed that Churchill had been there in the country's hour of need, and that he represented all the soldiers who'd died. Harry could handle the choice, because he wanted a drink and a laugh and didn't care about titles.

To be honest, his head was a bit spaced out from the blow. He couldn't smoke a lot of the stuff, and it seemed like Amsterdam grew some strong weed. He supposed it helped Nicky get through life. There he went again, being all paranoid and making her out to be unhappy. It suited him to see her as carefree and loving her work. The ecstasy helped. He didn't know, his brain slipping in with the humour of those around him. He looked at the faces and Tom and Carter and Mark were all laughing at something. For a moment he thought it was him, that they were taking the piss, but it was something else. They were happy and the feeling spread to Harry.

The bar was a good place to be and Tom leant over and said Johan had put that film they'd told him about on again, you'd think he'd get another one the tight cunt. Harry looked through the mass of faces packed in and there, playing on the wall where

Brighty's Cross of St George hung, was some blonde bint on the go with this weedy-looking bloke. Harry didn't watch much of the film but he got the idea. He was feeling sick suddenly and got up to go outside. He struggled through the crowd and went over by the railings lining the canal. He leant over the water and saw a vague reflection, then threw up into the water. He could see the schoolkids from the ferry and he could see this kid sent from a Thai village to Sex City. Fucking hell, he should've left the dope to Nicky and stuck to the drink. It was doing his head in and he could feel the ground heaving.

— You alright? Carter asked, standing next to him.

Harry stood up, the sickness finished.

— Just felt sick, that's all. Had a hard night.

— So how come you ended up with this bird then? Carter asked. You said on the phone it was a whore you'd knobbed.

Harry wasn't going to admit he couldn't get it up. Specially not when he'd paid good money. He'd phoned Carter earlier at the hotel to check where they'd be.

— Suppose she enjoyed what she got and wanted some more. She was knocking off for the night and just fancied having a drink and a chat. She had this blow and it's done my head in. I'm fucked.

— You stayed with her all day then?

— We went out and had something to eat at a café and then a couple of beers. We went back to her place. Fucking hell, Carter, that girl gives the best blow job I've ever had. She's fucking beautiful as well.

Carter looked at Harry in a strange way.

— She's a tart though. That's her job. She's probably shagged ten thousand blokes and had ten gallons of the stuff down her throat. I hope you were careful. You know what those girls get up to.

— I know all that.

— Long as you do.

— I was careful. She said she was clean anyway, but I made sure I used a rubber. So did she. I mean, she doesn't know where I've been either, does she? It works both ways.

Carter laughed.

– You haven't been anywhere recently. No, that's a result getting a whore for nothing. Shows you stood out from the rest of the blokes standing in line. If she was good-looking, all the better. Some of those prossies are right old boilers. I was surprised there's so many ugly ones sitting in the windows all banged out and full of the clap and Aids. Suppose they get worn down before their time. Cunts like concrete.

Harry nodded, trying to imagine Nicky as some wrinkled peasant woman sitting in the jungle with an opium pipe and a handful of sticky rice, watching the patrols burn her village and kill the pigs. His head was fucked. He was sweet as a nut on his own, but this stuff was getting him confused. He had to sort himself out and told Carter he was going back to the hotel.

– See you later on, Carter said, slapping him on the shoulder. Mind how you go and leave those girls alone.

Harry laughed and headed towards the hotel, but instead of turning into the street he kept going, working his way through the clubs and bars to the street where Nicky worked. He found a doorway and stood there for an hour before sitting down in the shadows with his back against the wood. He stayed for another hour and a half. People came with roars of laughter. There was every kind of male and a lot of females just having a laugh. He saw a few pervs and a lot of drunk men in small gangs, but most were just decent citizens. They came and stared and pointed. These were the little people. Men and women who wouldn't say boo to a goose. They came and looked at the spectacle, leaving their living rooms and filling up on sleaze. They were window-shopping for memories and tales to tell their mates. A lot of them laughed and some pushed men forward.

Harry could see Nicky in her window. He counted five men who disappeared inside before reappearing after varying lengths of time. There were two drunk tourists, an older man, a business type and a couple. Strangely, he didn't think about what was happening on the other side of the curtain. He was simply counting. After five he saw the light shut off and he imagined she must've done five before he got there. For the first time he thought of the reality. He saw her taking a mouthful of spunk and tying up a succession of condoms. He saw the gel by the side of the bed next to the mouthwash and could smell the sweat of the men and the perfume of the girl. He could taste the lager on the men's breath and the sweetness of Nicky's mouth. He remembered Nicky saying how she didn't like Arabs because they always wanted to give her one up the bum and he laughed at that, because she always said no. The Thai girls got pissed off at the Arabs because they only wanted the girls up the arse. Them and the boys. Then it was all gone and it was numbers and meant nothing, the rubbers putting up a barrier and her kisses something private.

He stood up and moved down the road. He waited for Nicky to come outside. She closed the side door behind her and she was alone. Harry thought she would be because he'd been counting properly, but he wanted to see it with his own eyes. He saw Nicky hurry down the street, a jungle spirit nipping through the city, so small she passed inside the cracks. He followed her a short way, feelings of being a spy replaced by those of a bodyguard. He saw her cross the Amstel River and jump in a taxi. She was home and dry. Harry turned and aimed for the hotel, his head a little clearer now. He'd seen her alright. More than that, he'd seen her leave work on her own. For some reason that was important.

When he got back to the hotel Hank was sitting at the night desk reading a magazine. He made no attempt to hide it away and it was like Kev had said, full of big flabby mamas with big flabby tits. Hank winked and remarked that Harry hadn't been home last night. He had a flask and offered his guest a cup of coffee. Harry said no thanks and hauled himself up the stairs. He was tired but happy. Sheets had never felt better and a minute after hitting the pillow he was asleep.

More English have arrived in Amsterdam and everyone's got together in a small square on the edge of the red light district. It's getting late and things are starting to liven up. If the Dutch are going to have a go then now's the time, because tomorrow we're on our way to Germany. Word's gone round that there's a mob of Dutch by Centraal Station. They know where we are, but shouldn't leave it too late. We're in the middle of Amsterdam taking the piss and it's up to them to approach us. This isn't going to be about pimps and drug dealers, but a mixture of Ajax and other local hooligans. Probably some travelling football fans from Rotterdam, the Hague and Utrecht. Who knows and who cares where they come from. Give us a few hundred punch-bags and we'll batter the fuck out of them.

There must be at least three hundred English drinking around the square and there's a buzz going because this could be the start, the Charity Shield warm-up for the big kick-off in Berlin. Up till now it's all been nice and quiet. The Dutch have got to make an appearance otherwise they're going to look like shit. They've had snippets on the local news. The Dutch have to know there's a big English presence in Amsterdam so it's up to them to make an appearance. We're standing in the middle of the city, ready and willing, waiting for the cunts to live up to this reputation we're always hearing so much about. They've got to show sooner or later.

There's blokes from all over England mobbed up in the square. There's all the firms you'd normally expect and it's amazing what a cross-section you get. There's a new enemy and the club stuff is frozen. It's all a game. It's a game with something extra to get the adrenalin going. That's how I feel now seeing all the England together with three riot vans parked down the road. The old bill obviously know there's got to be a riot of some kind before we move on. Just depends how bad it gets and whether they can get a handle on things.

There's some Bolton lads who have been drinking all day and they go into NO SURRENDER, pissed out of their heads, and everyone else joins in. We're hanging about seeing the numbers grow as different English find out where everyone is, and though it's not hard to guess we'll be down the red light district where all the whores and bars are, they still have to find the main England mob. Now they know because you can't miss this square full of Englishmen waiting for something to happen. It's only a matter of time, because with this many men knocking about some kind of disturbance is guaranteed. In a way I'm surprised the old bill haven't moved in already and closed the bars. The bomb's packed and the detonator's ticking. We're having a drink behaving ourselves. If the Dutch come down looking for trouble then naturally enough we'll respond. Nothing more than self-defence. We're minding our own business. Keeping our noses clean. Conducting ourselves with dignity and restraint. Working hard to please our masters at home. We're doing the decent thing. Turning the other cheek. Promising we'll walk away from provocation. Making the most of the local culture. Doing our best to avoid aggravation. And when the Dutch appear at the other end of the street a massive hit of patriotism swamps everything else. The energy comes through and this is what we're here for.

We're off and running up the street towards the Dutch who are lobbing bottles and a couple of firebombs. We're all united now steaming into the battle and you know you're with some of the most dedicated here. Everything is forgotten. The drink and drugs and whores vanish. Any lingering club grudges disappear. We're England, united, we'll never be defeated. We're England and run towards the Dutch who've pulled a decent mob together and are raining bottles and bricks at us, hitting a couple of blokes who slow down with cut heads, but the rest of us keep going and the Dutch manage to stand firm and we go straight through them like a fucking rocket. They do their best but it's more or less equal numbers and we kick the fuck out of them. There's some hard cunts but they don't have a chance. They haven't got the history. We run them over the canal and do a few of the big boys brave enough to stand and proud enough to take a hiding for Holland. There's a few stragglers paying the penalty, but the main mob are back down the road.

The old bill are the ones to worry about because there's a good hundred of the cunts appearing from a couple of side streets. They're the business this lot, decked out in the height of riot control fashion, like machines off another planet with their body suits and air-force helmets. It's the same at home and probably right through Europe now, with coppers everywhere looking the same and sharing their information down the computer lines. They go for the high-tech paramilitary look these days and it's a long way from those seventies riots in Lewisham and Southall and all the other inner cities that used to burn in the summer, because in those days the coppers were defending themselves with fucking dustbin lids. That's how it should be. Coppers digging around in bins looking for scraps. Not these days. They spend a fucking fortune on the right gear and weapons. They've got everything they need to fight a war. The old bill are all over the nearest people and doing whoever they can get their hands on. They go straight towards the bars where we were drinking and start laying into the English fans still there, the tiny number who weren't interested in steaming the Dutch. Not many have stayed behind and they don't have a chance.

All that wishy-washy liberalism is forgotten by the Dutch as their police force fights back. They've had their hands tied behind their backs by faggot politicians who've flooded their country with immigrants and drugs and perverts, so when they get the chance they want to make up for lost time. A few blokes get battered, and once the old bill have finished there they start moving our way.

We're already on the move ourselves, smashing every bit of glass we can see. Wouldn't bother with this sort of vandalism normally, but for some reason it's different when England go away. Takes you back. There's Dutch tourists and workers standing back watching the spectacle and none of the English bothers them. The police come so far and then stop as the bottles rain in. We start rocking a car and turn it on its roof. A couple of youths stuff a ripped T-shirt into a Renault's petrol tank and set it alight. Everyone moves out of the way and the fucker explodes. White and red fire shatters the darkness and it starts to burn. A column of flame rises and the old bill back off as more bottles are lobbed their way. The faces in the glow are sort of mesmerised by the flames, and the same blokes start doing a Saab. We back off again and after a delay that explodes as well. The old bill don't move, using some kind of tactic they haven't told us about. There's a mob wrecking the shops and a couple of Dutch blokes get a slap for protesting, and then Harris is over by this big sex shop with vibrators and bodies in the window, and there's this scouse lad saying that the cunt who runs it was selling kiddie porn when they were looking at the merchandise earlier in the day. There's a load of England boys gathered round and they smash the windows. There's a mixture of shoppers and hiding Dutch inside and they filter out, the dodgy ones getting a kick and punch, and then the fucking owner comes out with a baseball bat.

Harris takes him out and the English pile in because the bloke's a cunt doing the paedophile stuff and he's getting done badly like he deserves. The scouser and a few other lads run in the shop and they must be after the till. The police have moved forward and we all walk back a bit further leaving the nonce on the ground unconscious in a small pool of blood. We stand there along two streets and on a bridge going over one of the canals. Brighty's flag is out on show hanging over the rails and I can see a couple of flash bulbs popping behind the old bill. A few of the lads have cameras and take their own pictures. There's another car, a Volkswagen, and we rock this over. Ten or so English sit on the upside-down car and have their photos taken against a line of coppers in the distance. It's easy this and it's a show with a mob of three hundred English standing here in the middle of Amsterdam fronting up the old bill who've got all the paramilitary gear in the world, and even they're keeping their distance.

We're singing ONE BOMBER HARRIS, THERE'S ONLY ONE BOMBER HARRIS, ONE BOMBER HARRIS as the Volkswagen explodes, singing as the cars burn bright and the flames light up the splintered glass lining the street. There's a bar with the windows done and everyone's helping themselves to bottles of spirits inside, having a drink and a laugh, and it's a mad scene and I don't understand why the old bill don't charge. There's a lot of England around so that must be the reason, but I start thinking, then look inside and there's Kev pouring drinks and a load of blokes ordering draught lager. Outside the bottles are still flying at the police. We're getting our money's worth. Nice stretch of the muscles. The riot police are behind their shields and they've got to get stuck in soon. They must be gagging for a row with the commander playing his own game. The English old bill would be straight over the space between the two sides, but maybe the Dutch are that bit more intelligent.

We're into RULE BRITANNIA and GOD SAVE THE QUEEN when Harris comes round and says we should shift, because the old bill will be closing the area off right now and we shouldn't get cocky. They're not standing there for their health. This clicks home and the Chelsea boys get together and start moving in the same direction as the Dutch mob because they're not just going to disappear. Most of the English follow. It's a stroll this one with a few windows getting kicked in as we go and the English split up gradually, smaller mobs patrolling the streets. A sort of search-and-destroy operation that happens without anything being said. The streets are smaller and darker and we've already made our mark. I look back as we leave the canal, see the burning cars and the wreckage. It's like a bomb's gone off. It's fucking brilliant and a taster for Berlin. Getting everyone in the mood. Now it's a case of working through the streets looking for the Dutch, but the area will be mobbed soon with old bill, like Harris says, so we've got to watch our step.

The riot police have started moving forward. There's dogs barking and we move further away from the lights. We've made our point. I see the riot police pass over the sex shop owner lying there in the street. They don't even look at the cunt. The coppers take back the main street. Leave him face down in his own blood, a piece of scum in the mud of no-man's land.

GATES OF THE WEST

THE TELEVISION SET in The Unity was showing video footage from Holland. There were three cars burning in the middle of the screen and a thick line of riot police dodging a hail of bottles thrown by a big group of English football fans. The film had been shot the night before and rushed to various news studios around the country. It had also been sold abroad. The camera was steady and the black silhouettes of the rioters contrasted with the vivid colours of the burning cars. The soundtrack mixed human voices, barking dogs, smashing glass and the well-chosen clichés of a disgusted reporter. There was also an alarm ringing. When a car exploded there was a loud cheer from the English.

Bill Farrell and Bob West watched the images and heard the outraged moralising of a politician demanding instant cat-o'-nine-tails retribution. National Service was mentioned. The politician's message was followed by the ecstatic self-congratulation of a social commentator. Farrell wasn't exactly impressed, but his nephew Vince had gone to football when he was younger so he knew something of what happened. West, though, was shocked and angry at the behaviour of the thugs. They were nothing more than a lawless bunch of vandals dragging the good name of England through the mud.

The barmaid Denise was talking with her husband, a local man with a reputation for extreme violence, and didn't seem too upset by the burning cars, looted shops and flying bottles. The man was known as Slaughter and was encouraging the rioters. He was telling them to 'do the old bill' and 'kill the fucking cunts', while his wife shushed him and tried to pick out the faces of people they knew. Another man, who they called

Rod, was moaning about how he was missing all the fun stuck at home with the wife. He wished he was over in Europe with the rest of the boys and bet they were having the time of their lives. Just to wind up Denise he said Carter would be chasing everything that moved. He'd be doing two or three girls a night down the red light, not to mention the ones he didn't have to pay for in the bars and clubs.

Slaughter laughed and Rod told him that Tom, Mark and the rest of the English would be running the Dutch mobs ragged. Rod had heard that Carter had been servicing Denise behind her husband's back and threw the red light comment in for fun, acting ignorant. Slaughter said it wouldn't just be Carter, because all the lads would be shagging and rioting right through to Berlin. Rod nodded, because he was never going to live this down. He noticed Denise making herself busy washing glasses and he was sure her cheeks were red.

West was starting to seethe, hearing the men at the bar and seeing the hooligans on the screen. Moral disgust at the disturbances swamped his own uncertainties. He was surprised at Denise. She was a nice, decent girl and he expected her to show some shock at this stain on the country's reputation. Instead she was looking for people she knew as though it was a game of I-spy.

Farrell finished his pint and said his goodbyes as the presenter shook her head sadly and bemoaned the state of the nation before moving on to the happier news that an English firm had secured a multi-million pound contract to help build a new state-of-the-art prison in the Middle East. There was a short discussion about the gallows the company was going to include, with a civil servant pointing out that this was a question of democracy rather than morality. With a dismissive laugh he said that just because the gallows were built for executions didn't mean they would necessarily be used. Anyway, it wasn't the manufacturer's responsibility what went on in another country. The report faded inconclusively and the programme continued.

Farrell put his empty glass on the bar and Denise told him to have a nice time. She was a sweet girl and said Farrell looked smart in his jacket and tie. She'd forgotten Terry and was glowing with the knowledge she only had another week behind the bar before she was off on holiday – a two-week last-minute package in Greece. Denise was looking forward to some sun, sand and sangria. Her husband and the other man smiled and nodded, and Farrell left the pub as the midday news moved to a story of bravery in the Solent, a teenager saving a young boy from drowning just off Hirst Castle. The shaky hand-held film showed a skinhead with a red rose tattoo on his arm and a surfing towel around his shoulders explaining what had happened. The youth was shivering but happy he'd saved a life, while the presenter had adopted a condescending tone in the voice-over as the event was relegated to an amusing happy ending.

With a double whisky inside him Farrell felt confident. He was glad to leave the pub and the news behind. He could see West boiling up inside and didn't know why he got so upset. Maybe he was trying to shift his own feelings of blame, clutching at the righteous citizen angle. Farrell knew West had to sink or swim by himself. There was nothing anyone could do for him in his situation. He had to sort things out himself.

Farrell was leaving West behind and going into the unknown. It was all a game with the reassuring Teacher's warming his blood and giving him courage. There was a nice breeze and he felt good about his decision. He turned right and walked towards the station, passing through shoppers and skiving children, past the amusement arcade with its napalm graphics and man-animal-machine super-heroes, on to the dirty chimes of London Underground. He heard the rattling of a train but didn't rush. He was early and too old to run for the tube. There'd be another one along soon enough. He bought his ticket and went through the barrier, down the steps to the platform. He sat on a bench and waited. The man explaining the gallows situation came into his head. It was hard to understand his logic.

I stick my head in the next compartment and Kev passes over a bottle of vodka. I have a swig and hand it back. It's cheap and tastes like shit but washes away the dryness. You have to be friendly. There's eight Northerners packed in playing cards and laughing about last night – Kevin, Crewe, Bolton, three Blackburn lads and two younger boys from Birmingham. They're having a sociable drink and playing for guilders as we hurry towards Berlin and our meeting with the Hun. The train is packed with every kind of Englishman, with a few rivals naturally enough keeping their distance – Man U and Leeds, the two Bristol clubs.

– I wonder how that nonce's head is today, Kevin wonders. It was the scousers who pointed him out. I hope we got the right bloke. You never know with scousers. I fucking hate scallies.

Man U and Liverpool is another war zone and I can't imagine Burnley and Blackburn sharing the same cards. I continue along the carriage and go back to my seat, squeezing past this long-haired Arsenal man who's already been nicknamed Student because it's rumoured he did a night course in engineering. The long hair seals his fate.

We've got this old boy in the middle of our compartment. Fuck knows where he turned up from, but he must be fifty if he's a day. This bloke's glad to be travelling overseas and experiencing foreign cultures. He works on a sewage plant somewhere outside Swindon and keeps reminding us that it's only the condoms that survive. Says it gives a man like him confidence knowing the rubber he buys in the pub can stand the toughest battering. He could tell us a few stories about the married women of Swindon and the surrounding countryside. He's a tall man with bottle-top glasses. Drinks from a duty-free bottle of Gordon's. He's told us five times now that he deals in shit. That he hasn't slept since he left Swindon for Paddington. And that last night he was stuck in a carriage full of Dutch who were so fucking boring he had to take some kind of action.

He smiles and says there wasn't any room to stretch out and they were so clean-living and healthy he decided on some chemical warfare. He was silent but effective. He laughs and tells us younger lads that nothing upsets the Europeans more than being stuck in a confined space with someone who's got rotten guts. Says they hate it when the smell starts leaking out. But these health-food nutters weren't to know he dealt in shit. Yes, he deals in shit. Sixth time. We should've seen their faces when he shifted his arse and eased another one out. At first they tried to ignore his bombing runs, but fifth raid in they were struggling. Naturally they looked his way, because he was the outsider and the English are barbarians in their eyes, but he acted innocent and continued with the assault. We laugh and look at him in a different way.

Mr Shit says that a couple of minutes after he started farting the compartment was clear of foreigners. He was scorching the earth and clearing the land. The Dutch went and stood in the corridor muttering to themselves, so he shrugged his shoulders and tried to look hurt. He told this woman there must be something wrong with the bog, but winks and says that really it was the baked beans on the ferry. That beans means Heinz and the krauts wouldn't even have noticed. You'd need a vindaloo for those Germans. The woman didn't believe him, but with space to stretch out he was able to relax and take his shoes off. Still couldn't get to sleep he was that excited about seeing England play. He loves upsetting foreigners and says you have to do it the right way. Says he stopped in Amsterdam for a few hours. Just enough time to have a drink and a meal, then knob this big black girl in the red light district. He paid her well and got her to lick his arse. He deals in shit. Mark calls him a dirty cunt, half with humour and half fed up listening to the bumpkin voice. Tells him that if he does his baked beans routine in here he'll be doing a flying header off the train. Mr Shit nods and smiles back, but a few minutes later he goes into the corridor himself and starts talking with Student. Then when Student eventually blanks him he fucks off to another carriage.

– Thank fuck that cunt's gone, Mark says. He was doing my head in. I haven't come over here to spend my time listening to some mangy old fucker going on about his guts.

– I wonder how much he paid that whore to lick his arse, Harry slurs.

– You'd do it for half the price, wouldn't you? Carter says.

We all laugh and Harry tells him to fuck off. He just wondered, that's all.

I open a bottle of lager and have a drink, washing away the vodka. Look outside and watch a village flash past. Small column of Nissans and Volkswagens waiting for the train to pass. The Japanese and German industries did well out of the war. Lose against the Yanks and they'll rebuild your economy for you in return for some fast-food outlets. These decent German citizens are living well and not bothered by the contents of the carriages heading East. Not bothered by the glazed eyes of Fat Harry looking their way, getting stuck into the drink like there's no tomorrow. I look at him as he asks us to imagine a poor little prostitute having that lanky Swindon cunt standing there in his birthday suit, making her kneel down and tickle his bum. We nod, but what does he expect? That's what they do for a living. It's their role in life. Paid to service the menfolk and keep them happy. Mr Shit gets to play the big hard master for fifteen minutes. She only has to say no and keep her tongue clean.

Harry nods and moves on. Starts winding Carter up asking the sex machine why he's only got his leg over once so far. Has his big end gone or is it just the rust? Carter the rust bucket runaround clanking to a halt on the Great West Road. Carter ignores this best he can, but Harry's in one of those moods. He's pissed as a cunt and I watch Carter steer him away from sex and onto something a bit more healthy.

– Remember that time we were coming back from Bristol and the coach broke down at the services, he says. Don't know if the big end had gone, but we were stuck outside Swindon. Do you remember, fat boy?

– What were we doing in Bristol? Harry asks.

– Coming back from that Cup game against City. We were at the services and that Tottenham coach arrived and we were going to kick them off and hijack the driver.

– The time when Chelsea did that pub and you got bitten by some farmer with rabies.

Carter goes red. It must be the one. I ask Carter what happened.

– There was this pub full of City and Chelsea steamed in, Harry says. We were fighting them out in the back of the pub in a car park and this scrawny little cunt jumped on Carter and bit his arm. The bloke dug in and wouldn't let go. Must've held on for at least a minute. We thought he had rabies. He was a fucking wild man. Nobody went near the cunt after he let go. He was spitting and dribbling and walked through us. He was a fucking dangerous man. He's probably still around, in a farm-worker's cottage baying at the moon then going along to Bristol to see City play. I wouldn't want to be a Rovers fan with that loony around.

– Forget the fucking Wolf Man, Carter says. I was thinking about that Spurs coach right behind us. Remember we all piled off and queued up waiting for the yids to come and get it, but they wouldn't get off. They were sitting there shitting themselves. We wanted their transport but they wouldn't open the fucking door.

– That's right, they wouldn't get off, Harry laughs. They were dying for a piss and some bagels and then they finally get to a kosher services blessed by the rabbi and there's this mob of Chelsea in the middle of Wiltshire waiting for them, eating bacon rolls. Balti put a bottle through the back window and Martin Howe was trying to open the emergency door when the yiddo driving said enough's enough and went back on the M4.

– The best bit was these younger lads on the coach nicked all the ice-creams from the shop and the old bill turned up. The silly cunts got done for robbing lollies.

– The services usually got robbed of something, Harry says, getting all nostalgic. There used to be a lot of trouble at the motorway stops. You wouldn't get away with it now.

– You can't get away with anything today, Mark sighs.

– We always had a good time in the West Country, Carter tells Tom. There was this stampede years ago when we played Reading in the League Cup. All these Reading wankers were down the side of the ground behind their fence mouthing off and there was this steward or something fucking about with a gate.

– I remember that, Harry says. Chelsea jumped him. The gate swung open and they piled through.

– Never seen anything like it. It was the same as one of those wildlife documentaries studying buffalo on the plains of Africa. There was probably fifty Chelsea who got through the gate and the whole of the Reading side started running. It was like they were bouncing in the air. It was fucking brilliant. The Chelsea end was pissing themselves.

– It was the same at Burnley when we lost 3–0. There'd always be a crew who left the ground ten minutes from the end and tried to get in with the home fans. The old bill were busy changing positions preparing for crowd control outside and in they'd go. It was seeing so many run from so few that made you laugh.

Go back ten or so years and a mob went in the Stretford End at the end of a midweek game. The United crew down the side were going mental seeing Chelsea doing damage in the home end. We were kept in and filled the ground with WHAT'S IT LIKE TO RUN AT HOME? Shift forward through the years and Kevin could've been a kid as well in the streets around Old Trafford trying to do the cockneys, while there could even be a Reading fan on the train. None of that matters right now and the memories don't include faces, just shapes. Everyone gets lost in the crowd. Travelling through Holland and Germany we see the features and name tags. Picking up speed and getting tighter as Germany closes in.

The train was racing and they'd crossed the border into Germany an hour before, a Doctor Mengele ticket inspector coming along and sneering at the English until Mark asked him what the problem was, do you think you're Goering you German cunt, and because Mark was on his feet Mengele backed away and bottled it, then pissed off down the carriage. Harry took a long drink from his bottle of lager and laughed. Mark and Tom didn't stand for any nonsense, and it was a good job the death-camp doctor had decided to fuck off. Nobody liked people who experimented on children. The Angel of Death was a fucking nonce. Harry would've let it go with some verbal because, after all, the world was full of cunts in uniform searching for a plum position where they could unload their frustration and tell every other cunt what to do, tie them down and start experimenting, sharpening the scalpel and playing God with mice and rabbits and dogs, playing Frankenstein with Jews, pikeys, queers – doing the vivisection routine with whatever came off the conveyor belt. Now they got rabbits and pigs. This week's special offer on items that nobody cared about. But Mark and Tom, they didn't fuck about and Harry could see Mengele joining the sewers cunt on the road running along next to the railway track.

Harry made his point and Tom was agreeing, forgetting his story of Chelsea and Leicester's Baby Squad to tell the boys that the world was full of wankers, and how much he hated small-minded cunts trying to tell you what to do all the time, and did they see that wanker at Harwich, the Customs cunt questioning him about his drug use? He couldn't fucking believe the bloke. Only Mark remembered and he didn't seem to care, and as far as Harry could make out it was a small incident not worth its weight, just part of the everyday routine. The old bill, ticket wardens, security guards, bouncers, all of them only obeying orders. Tom said he'd been on the verge of nutting that wanker at Customs and had to use all his self-discipline, and Harry had to admit that was a bit over the top because after all, they may have been small-minded little cunts – the world, like Tom said, was full of small-minded little cunts; in fact when you really stopped and thought about it, being a small-minded cunt had to be one of the main qualifications for getting a job in politics, the police, whatever; all you had to be was be a small-minded, petty little fucking cunt – but every cunt had a job to do. Fucking hell, how many bottles had he drunk, because he was well pissed and they were still a few hours from Berlin.

Harry sat back and listened to the others laughing and joking and enjoying the journey, Carter punching him playfully on the shoulder and saying remember that time when we played Sunderland in the League Cup semi-final, the game when Dale Jasper thought it was a basketball tournament and gave away two penalties. That was a mad night and did he remember how that copper had come up to Balti and smacked him in the bollocks with his truncheon. Stroppy little cunt hit him right in the balls and somehow Balti had done the iron nuts routine and stood there and told the wanker to come on, let's see how fucking hard you are. He never showed the pain, and it had hurt, but he wasn't giving the copper the satisfaction. Carter laughed and explained to the rest of them that this small-minded little cunt looked at this nutter in front of him who could take a truncheon in the bollocks and feel no pain, and he'd just bottled out and legged it. There was no way the old bill could deal with that. They'd nicknamed Balti Iron Bollocks for a while, but eventually he'd got a new name because of the amount of Indian he was eating.

Then Carter was telling Tom and Mark and Gary, and Billy Bright and Harris and a few others who were hanging around the door, how after the game when everything was kicking off and Chelsea were fighting the old bill and Sunderland, how Harry had walked right up to this copper and nutted him, then disappeared into the darkness. Tom said nice one and Harry could tell they were impressed, because the way Carter explained it the head butt was perfect and the copper went straight down. But it was a long time ago and Harry didn't think of those days very often, had forgotten a lot of what went on and saw himself in a different light to the person Carter was describing. Carter asked Harris if he remembered that night, and Bomber said of course he did. Sunderland had their coaches done with baseball bats back at the Bridge, the benches had come out as Chelsea went on the pitch, and then they'd had a go at the old bill outside. Harry was listening and wondered if there were any Sunderland on board and Tom must've been on the same wavelength because he was saying how funny it was being on this train with all these different clubs who Chelsea had probably done at some point over the past ten years.

Harry stood and opened the window, pulled the sheet of glass right down and lobbed his empty bottle onto the road, aiming at a shiny red Porsche with some wanker in a cravat breaking the English speed limit, credit cards to burn, the bottle just missing the Porsche and smashing on the tarmac. The driver fought for control as he veered away and back again, shitting himself and slowing down like a good little cunt. Harry laughed and his right hand trembled in a wanker sign as he pushed his head through the gap. That would teach Jurgen a lesson for taking the piss. The train pulled away from the Porsche which had decided to keep its distance, the carriages fluttering Union Jacks and Crosses of St George, the red, white and blue of the Crusaders steaming towards the German heartland with Harry Roberts feeling the rush of air against his skull and the warm beer in his blood.

Bill Farrell had been abroad once in his life, to Europe during the war. More than half a century later he was considering a second trip, this time to Australia. His nephew Vince had saved his money and gone off to see the world. He'd returned to England for a short time, but then emigrated to Australia. Now he was settled in New South Wales and had bought a small farm.

Vince had a house and a hundred acres of land. His plot was in a valley, with aboriginal rock drawings in the caves on one side, and a forest on the other. There was a billabong and rows of fast-growing Japanese trees Vince was raising and selling to farmers, who in turn used them as shade for their cattle. He also had a woman, a Sydney girl whose family went back to the prison ships sent over from Mother England. There was a small caravan under a tarpaulin cover for visitors and a garden where they grew food. When Farrell thought about it, Vince sounded like a hippy, but knew his nephew would have been upset by the term. He was a farmer pure and simple, working the land and waiting for the rains to come.

Every Saturday night Vince drove to the nearest town and had a drink. Some traditions never changed. It was a small place with wooden buildings and a population of under a thousand. It was a twenty-mile drive and the people were mostly descended from the English. There was a Chinese restaurant and a Greek shop. Vince promised his granddad he'd take him as well, the pub like something from the lager commercials, the difference being the Chelsea team photograph behind the bar. There was a pendant and another photo of Ruud Gullit and the FA Cup winners on the pitch at Wembley. Vince had flown back for the final and paid three hundred quid for a ticket. On the other side of the world there was a little outpost that would forever be Chelsea and England. He said it was a decent pub with lots of things that reminded him of home. The lad had always liked his football and Farrell flashed back to Vince as a child, excited by life and the world around him. Farrell was pleased he'd done something different, even if it meant he was a long way from his family.

Farrell had thought about going to Australia when he was young. He'd had a mate from the army who went over and wanted Farrell to go as well. It was as though Vince was doing it on his behalf. Vince knew his granddad was reluctant to accept what he saw as charity, so he'd bought the ticket and sent it over, while his mum had arranged the visa.

Farrell was weighing it all up in his head. He would sleep in the caravan and have to get used to the spiders. Vince wrote regularly and said they were big and silent, with long legs and small bodies, but most weren't poisonous. Farrell thought of Albert Moss, who'd fought in Asia and been stuck with these things for years. Farrell had lived in London all his life and was used to the hustle and bustle of ten million people arguing and treading on each other's toes. London was in his head and his memories of travelling abroad weren't good. On his return, he'd jumped back into everything English for protection. He was in two minds about Australia, unable to make a decision.

Vince had written about the Anzac Day celebrations he'd seen in Sydney. Even in the scorching heat they marched and remembered. There was a platform at the end of the parade with various dignitaries giving speeches as a small group of Aborigines stood silently on the margins, ragged men, women and kids transported to a city of shining towers and tarmac paths. The dignitaries spoke about Gallipoli and how the slaughter of Australians had helped put the country on the map. It had gained them respect in the eyes of the English. They sang God Save The Queen and Waltzing Matilda.

The country was big and Vince felt free. The sheer size of the place put things in perspective. In England everyone was on top of everyone else, and events seemed more important than they were. He'd always liked the sun and found things to do away from the endless work ethic. He'd slowed right down. At first he thought it was the heat and the slow pace of life, but after a while he realised it was the lack of pressure. At home everything was pumped up the whole time. It wasn't the people so much as the establishment urging them on. There was a constant bombardment, whether it was from the media, politicians or advertisers. Everything had to keep expanding for them to feel content. The media, politicians and advertisers eventually blurred in together until people couldn't tell the difference. There was little difference in reality, because all three were run for personal advancement. Principles didn't matter any more, though the ordinary man and woman in the street was still basically decent, trying to scratch a living against the odds. Coming back for the Cup Final, Vince was amazed by the pace of everything.

He kept on at his granddad that they'd go to the Great Barrier Reef. The old man could come for as long as his visa allowed. The Reef was fantastic, something you'd never know existed unless you dipped your head under the water. The Pacific had always seemed dangerous to Farrell. From the photos it looked like a beautiful place, but the war there had been violent and bloody. The sharks knew that a bang in the water meant food, a drowning pilot or a ship's human cargo. It made him sick thinking of hundreds of men struggling in the water thousands of miles from home. He thought of the water thick with blood as sharks pulled the men below the surface and ripped them to threads. Vince had reminded him of the time they spent in Kew Gardens after Albert's funeral, about the pictures they'd seen. Anyone could travel, you just needed the will. Farrell thought of the Pacific and how for him the name conjured up dark images.

Farrell saw the colour of the Barrier Reef. It really was fantastic in the photos. That was what a holiday was about and he was lucky to have the chance, but it could only ever be a holiday. He was English and his home was in London. Vince had gone away, but he was the exception. The boy had the spark to do something different with his life. Not that Farrell was complaining. Everyone did their own thing and he'd been blessed. His wife was a fantastic woman. She was the only woman he'd ever loved and even though she'd been gone all these years, there wasn't a day went by when he didn't think about her. She'd never wanted to go back to Hungary. She hated the place and became more English than her husband in some ways. Like a lot of refugees who settled in England after the war, she adopted the country without reservations. She saw things differently to the cynics. What she went through was terrible, yet she survived with so much strength she'd put him to shame.

Farrell was on the platform waiting for his train to pull in. It was the middle of the day and quiet. He heard a couple of Australian voices and thought of Vince again, except this time he imagined that Anzac Day parade. The temperature was way up and the marchers kept in time along the road, their collars done up and shirts smart. They were sweating, but despite their English skin they'd lived with the climate all their lives and adapted. Australia was their country, yet they had a sense of belonging to England. They couldn't shake it off. Farrell laughed at how the Aussies called the English poms, Prisoners of Mother England. That's what he was, a Prisoner of Mother England. He nodded his head and smiled.

The tube arrived and Farrell found a seat. There was an American couple at the other end of the carriage with three suitcases, travelling up from Heathrow to see Big Ben and the Tower of London. Farrell imagined the man as a young boy in the Philippines. Maybe he'd been one of the Marines taking Manila or under the ridge at Iwo Jima, held down by Japanese guns. The Yanks had suffered at Utah beach during the D-Day landings and had a worse time of things than the British and Canadians at Sword, Juno and Gold, which had been bad enough. That bloke at the end of the carriage would've been making the most of London in the forties, hanging around Piccadilly where the prostitutes helped themselves to the GI pay-packets. But there were plenty of other girls interested and Soho offered a lot of life. Funny how everything went around, but when he looked more closely the man wasn't old enough for the war.

The tube started moving and Farrell forgot the tourists. He looked at the black and brown faces around him reflecting the Commonwealth troops who'd fought and died for Britain. He felt that the Commonwealth had been sold out as multinationals pushed for European union. If some of these kids today saw the troops gathered in the south of England for the D-Day invasion they'd be surprised. When they saw a Polish name did they understand what had happened in Poland, how the Free Poles had fought and died? Did they know Bomber Command was forty per cent non-British? In his own lifetime he'd seen history rewritten so many times. They didn't even have the decency to wait till you were dead.

It was a line of thought Farrell couldn't resist, because sitting in The Unity he'd heard one of the men at the bar laughing about the newsflash from Holland, saying how the English would be marching back into Berlin again. That they'd be taking it for a second time and rubbing salt in the wound. Farrell was amazed this man didn't know it was the Red Army who'd captured Berlin. It was incredible they didn't get taught these things in school. It wasn't that long ago either. Not really.

Of course, the Allies went in later, but it was the Russians who fought their way through the city, street by street, with the loss of 100,000 men. Not that it was solely men, because women fought with the Soviets and it was a woman who'd lifted the flag over the Reich Chancellory. It made him smile when pop shows talked about girl power. Was that all it had become? Maybe it was part of Hitler's downfall, because Stalin had his women working next to the men and fighting for victory, while Hitler saw women as there to mother children and build a super-race.

Farrell had met some Russian soldiers in Germany. They couldn't really talk, of course, but they'd toasted each other. They were allies. The Germans and Russians called each other fascists and communists, but in England it was different. When Stalin and Hitler fell out after the invasion of Poland, and when Hitler went on to attack the Soviet Union, the people in London had looked to the Russians and admired their bravery. This comradeship had been promoted by the Government. It would be hard for people raised in the post-war years to believe, but Stalin was Uncle Joe and the Russians brave allies much admired by ordinary English people. Politics didn't come into it. The Russians were allies and their resistance gave Farrell and the people around him hope. Many people forgot this under a post-war propaganda offensive, while Stalin closed up shop and tried to crush the people of Eastern Europe.

When Vince was a child Farrell had played soldiers with him. He only did it when his wife wasn't around, because it seemed wrong. But he played because boys were interested in these things, and the Action Men were either English, American or German. He didn't remember any Russian uniforms. But the kids today, their soldiers were different. The enemy was distant and imaginary and the weapons more complicated. Animals and machines merged with men. Now the boys preferred Power Rangers to Action Man. He supposed it was a good thing, but imagined they'd learn little about, and from, the Second World War. His own uncles, men he admired as a young boy, were already lost in the distant past. If the memories faded so quickly, why had they bothered? He knew the answer, but it was always a battle, and one many people his age lost. People's moods swung this way and that. For years after the war the Russians had been promoted as cruel tyrants who wanted to turn England into a dour communist slave state, while now they were confused criminals and drunks who craved Western-style democracy.

Farrell's memory was clear as the train rolled along. The Russians had suffered like nobody else. Twenty million had died. When the Germans attacked it was a blitzkreig, but the Russians destroyed everything as they retreated. Farrell knew what the Germans were capable of, having seen a concentration camp first hand. During the war five million Soviet soldiers were taken prisoner, but less than two million survived. That left over three million who had died. The Germans treated the Russians like scum and it was no surprise that a couple of years later, following the seige of Leningrad, when the Russians had recovered and were ready to attack, they wanted to wipe the Germans off the face of the earth. The soldiers who survived would never forget and would pass the hatred on. It was the same on both sides.

Bill Farrell was on his way to a meeting of old soldiers. He didn't usually go in for this sort of thing. He had never been that interested in ceremonies and reunions, but today he was sitting on the tube with a clear head. It didn't seem to matter now. Before, when his wife had been alive, it was enough to live with her and enjoy their time together. His own experiences were insignificant after what she'd been through. He never thought too hard about this, but following her death he'd started trawling through the past. The more time passed the more he went back. He didn't see anything glorious in the war. He tried to forget but it was impossible. Fifty-five million people had died in the Second World War. Whenever a politician came on the television screen and said the old days were less violent he knew they were insane. It was like the newsflash about the football. Three cars exploded and these reporters were describing it as a war zone. It really was ridiculous and Bob West shouldn't have got upset. There was no perspective, just sensationalism and hypocrisy.

Farrell's sip of whisky had put him in a positive frame of mind but had loosened his self-control. He looked at the other passengers and wondered how many knew what things had been like, how many even guessed or cared. Even now, all these years after the war had ended, everyday life could seem very trivial. He tried not to think this, but it was inevitable really. It had been much worse after he'd returned from Europe, but he'd fought back and won the mental battle. When Farrell watched these idiots on the television and read their editorials in the papers he couldn't take them seriously. The war had made him immune. It was a strength, he thought, as his stop arrived.

—After the landing we started moving forward. Once we were on shore and off the beach, we had to consolidate our positions and begin fighting our way out of the bridgehead. We did this, but it was a slow, bitter advance. Neither side was going to give up. I don't believe in the all-comrades-under-the-uniform view because the Germans caused a great deal of pain and were killers, but they were brave men. The same is true of the Russians, British, Poles, Canadians and Americans. In fact, anyone you care to mention. We all believed in what we were doing and fought to the death. Once we were through the initial defences things changed. It was the expectation and build-up to the landing that was hard to handle, but once we were through that and had killed it was different. It's a hard thing to admit but we had more confidence. We were closer with our mates and we were harder now than the Germans. We were going to win. We were afraid we'd die when we were in the landing crafts because we had too much time to think, but now we believed we were going to come through the fighting. The idea that an Englishman couldn't be beaten was built into us from an early age, and when the killing started we found this belief made us tough enough for the job. We had this confidence, which when the waiting was over made us strong. We had the determination to win and went forward. The Germans would fight us all the way and there was a lot of killing. It was terrible seeing the bodies, and Billy Walsh and the soldier with his head blown off were right there in our heads. We didn't think we could see worse. Death became common. The Mulberrys did their job and troops and tanks were pouring into France. The countryside was tight with hedges so we had to move slowly. It was all very much within our group and our space. The speeches of Monty were nice but didn't really mean anything. We saw what was in front of us and watched each other's backs. Mangler was nearby and a bloke from Bolton called Charlie Williams. He was a smiling lad with red hair who'd worked in a textile factory before the war. He was married with a baby and carried a picture of his wife and son in his wallet. Billy Walsh was dead, but this North London lad Tiny Dodds was a good mate and of course Jeff Morrison from Hounslow. We were on the move now, getting stronger all the time. We knew each other from training and the camps, but now there was a stronger feeling. We needed the unity as we faced the enemy. You never have friends in quite the same way because all the little prejudices and stereotypes vanish and it's basic survival. There's a link with men who've lived the same life, something that goes unsaid and lasts through the years. It doesn't matter how old you are, it never fades.

Harry kicks my trainers as he goes for a piss, slamming the compartment door open and stumbling into the corridor. Surprised he didn't break the glass. Stops to say sorry then fucks off. Born in a barn that cunt. There's some English singing CAN I TELL YOU THE STORY OF A POOR BOY. Must be scousers. Their history goes back to the Boer War and the Battle of Spion Kop, the old Anfield terrace named in memory of the men who died there. Wonder what Kev makes of it. Quietly impressed because it was Englishmen fighting for England. Mark leans over and pulls the door shut, turning down the volume. He gives me a fresh bottle. Hands lager to Harris, Billy and Carter. Gary Davison and Martin Howe are looking down the corridor, talking to some other English. The train keeps moving. The lager's getting warmer, but it's still cold enough to drink. Passing the time.

Chelsea and England go together. We've always supplied a good chunk of the England away support. We fly the flag no matter how many foreigners the club pulls in. It changes nothing, because we're the ones paying their wages. The Europeans work for us. We pay for their expensive apartments and designer gear. You need the class foreigners, but English football doesn't get the credit it deserves. In Rome it was another story, the English pulling together a big mob in a dangerous city. England will always do the Italians. It's been going on for years. It's in the blood.

Germany is a blur through the window with none of us taking much notice of the towns, villages and countryside. I sit back listening to Harris talking about Berlin and the Germans. I lean my head on the rest. It's a great feeling being on the move with something to look forward to at the end of the journey. That trouble in Amsterdam firmed up the travelling English. People talk about the trouble and that, but it's the whole thing that makes following England worthwhile. Going overseas is another step on from club football. It's more exciting, especially these days with the cameras and everything.

It feels like my eyes have just closed when I bang forward. At first I think it's Harry back from the bog, but then I see him in the far corner. The others are looking around and I realise the train isn't moving. Harris is up and opening the door, looking for a reason for the delay. We go into the corridor and someone says the emergency chord has been pulled. Mengele's coming along with a couple of SS guards, and he has to squeeze through the English. He's a lot more polite now and doesn't look Mark in the eye, but he's got the same attitude. Cunt in a uniform who thinks he's the fucking business. We want to know what's happening, stopping in the middle of nowhere. Maybe the train's been set on fire by juvenile delinquents, or the engine blown apart by that dirty old Swindon geezer. Can't see him anywhere. Gary leans through the window and starts laughing. We try to get a view of what's happening. The Hooligan Express is at a standstill and if he's not careful Mengele's going to have to deal with several hundred unhappy customers. The least these German cunts can do is make sure the fucking trains run on time.

Then we see this figure running from the train. Someone says it's a scouser bunking the fare, but Gary says no, he's a Geordie. A northern voice says it's a cockney. Could be anyone, but the youth is young and fit and heading for some nearby woods. He's got a head start on the guards trying to keep up. Big fat krauts tempting a heart attack. The English start cheering and banging on the side of the train, and the bloke keeps running, increasing his lead over the Gestapo. Something's gone wrong. Bunking the train without a passport. Fuck knows. But he's getting nearer the trees and finally turns and raises his fist towards the train, gives the guards a wanker sign, then disappears into the woods. When the Germans get there they lean forward with their hands on their knees, knackered. They peer into the trees, shrug their shoulders and walk back to the train, the English packing the corridors, hanging out of the windows and putting their hands around their eyes in imitation RAF goggles, humming the tune from *Dam Busters*. Don't know if the Germans understand, but they must know we're taking the piss. They don't look happy.

After a short delay the train starts moving again and we settle down. Don't know where the bloke's gone, but it shouldn't be too hard for him to find his way to Berlin. Mind you, stuck in the German countryside, who knows. Bailing out behind enemy lines. I suppose we'll find him in a Berlin bar sooner or later, and if he's smart he'll live off the story for the rest of the trip. Everyone has a story to tell. The train picks up speed and we have another drink.

Bill Farrell stood outside Sloane Square tube waiting for the traffic lights to change colour. He was in another world now, surrounded by expensive shops and wealthy people. The faces were different from those of working-class London. They were tanned and manicured, and even the features seemed different. He smiled at all these stern men and women who'd probably never done a hard day's graft in their lives. There was nothing new under the sun, and the English squaddie wasn't looking for a revolution after the war, just something better. Demobbed soldiers wanted work and a future, and he couldn't remember any of his mates being interested in party politics or ideology.

The northern lads were different because they had a strong union and industrial tradition, though a lot of East Londoners knew all about Jack Dash and the London dockers. Ulster had its own thing going on, but London and the South were different again. He'd never known any Northerners before the war threw everyone together, and they were good people like anyone else, a long way from the stereotypes. They had their own view of Londoners as well. They thought Londoners were all cockney wide boys and flash harrys, spivs and cosh boys with a soft belly. Cheeky chappies, barrow boys and racetrack wheeler-dealers. But the barriers were ripped down during the war and they'd all got on fine. The same went for the Welsh and Scots, while Farrell had never realised there were so many Catholics fighting for England in the Irish Guards. It was a mixed up world where nothing was ever what it seemed. And anyone who had trouble adapting soon sorted themselves out when the bullets started to fly.

People wanted something better after VE Day and Churchill

wasn't re-elected despite his role as a wartime leader. They were looking for peace and stability and social change. The soldiers had self-respect and wanted the understanding of those at home. Beveridge made his famous report and if the country got anything out of the Second World War it had been a welfare state. As a young man fighting in Europe, Farrell wanted the things that had been denied his uncles. He knew how they felt about the war and its aftermath, and had expected better. At least Farrell's generation got the NHS and a welfare system, but it had suffered badly under the Tories, while New Labour saw socialism as a dirty word. Farrell tried not to get angry, but it was unbelievable. Even during the war there'd been a few strikes, and Churchill had respected Bevin enough to give him a role in the cabinet. People seemed to have no long-term memory of where their benefits began. Either they forgot or reinvented the past to fit in with what they were told. The young ones weren't even told.

When the lights changed he crossed and started down the King's Road. He was on his way to a TA meeting in the Duke of York's HQ. He'd joined the Territorials after the war, when it had consisted of old soldiers, and had made some good friends. He'd lost track of them, just like the boys he'd actually fought with in Europe, those that survived, but had met up with Ted at Johnny Bates's funeral and been persuaded to come along today. It was just a chat and a drink and a cheap meal. Farrell had never gone in for these things, but Ted was enthusiastic and he didn't see why not. With his wife dead maybe it was time to look back and find some comradeship. It was something he'd only get from a shared experience. She'd always wanted him to go along and show off his medals at the Cenotaph because she'd been proud of him, but it had seemed pointless somehow. He was a man and she was a woman, and she'd been raped and brutalised by the scum of Europe while he'd killed German boys like himself who had no choice whether they fought. He wanted to forget, but you could never forget. At least he didn't want to forget the reality. Anyway, the bar was subsidised and he'd have a laugh with some of his old mates.

Farrell passed the gates of the Duke of York's HQ and found the pub they were meeting in beforehand. He took a deep breath and went inside. It was one o'clock and fairly busy, but Ted said they'd meet on the left as he went in and Farrell spotted him straight away. He was sitting with Eddie Wicks and Barry James They jumped up and pumped his hand and almost fell over themselves offering to buy him a pint. Farrell was embarrassed by the attention, but Ted was already doing the honours so he sat at the table in the corner with the others. He'd seen Eddie and Barry at Johnny Bates's cremation and they'd exchanged a few words, but it had been very brief. Now the circumstances were different and it was okay to show some pleasure at meeting again They were good lads and Ted put a pint of London Pride in front of Farrell. Eddie had been a corporal in the Paras and had jumped at Arnhem and swum the Rhine to escape capture. The Germans fired at him as he went but Eddie made it to safety and went back to fight again. He'd also been at Dunkirk and was a big man with a handlebar moustache who immediately took control. He got the others to raise their glasses and drink to Johnny Bates.

– You came along then, Billy boy, Ted said, slapping Farrell on the back after he'd tasted the Pride We wondered if you'd make it. Not that we doubted your word, but things crop up when you get older.

– I'm glad you came, Barry said These things are much less formal than you'd think. The bar's subsidised and the food's good. A fiver for as much as you can eat NAAFI conditions, but there's chicken curry today.

Farrell had another sip of the Pride and savoured the taste. The pub wasn't as professional as The Unity, but that was often the case with high-street boozers Those pubs tucked down back streets had to satisfy the locals while pubs like this could pull in enough passers-by to keep ticking over no matter what. Not that Farrell was complaining, because he liked a pint of London Pride. Chiswick was another decent West London beer. The whisky had got him through the journey and now he was sitting in this pub he had no second thoughts. Eddie was 'a big character and they'd had a good few sessions when they were in the TA. Eddie and Farrell had both fought in Europe, while Barry had been a merchant seaman and Ted had served in North Africa. They all had their stories but never said much. There were things that filtered through as the years passed so it was possible to build a picture. When they'd been in the TA and drinking they tended to open up and tell individual stories. Afterwards life continued as normal.

– Not a bad pint for Chelsea, Eddie said. You pay extra, but it can't be helped. Have to keep the blood flowing.

Eddie had done well after the war. He'd stayed in the army before eventually leaving and running a pub. He'd served in Palestine and seen members of his regiment killed by the Jewish resistance, which had turned him against Israel. He knew Mrs Farrell's history, but separated Judaism and Zionism. Eddie was a strong royalist and felt England had been betrayed, that socialism had eaten away at the backbone of the country. Bill and Eddie had different views and once, when they were young and drunk, had even come to blows. But it was in the past, and time and old age had blurred the edges of Eddie's resentment. Like a lot of people, though, he felt let down.

Eddie had run a drinker's pub in Brentford and done okay. He could always handle himself and wasn't someone to muck about. He'd pulled in a lot of the local hardcases, and they liked a pint or ten. Civvy street had treated him well and he had five sons, all of them following in his footsteps. He was big on army tradition and loved the comradeship. He was a good man, and in some ways a pussy cat. Farrell remembered the time he'd taken his wife to Eddie's pub and she'd been treated like a queen. He used to talk rubbish sometimes when he was pissed, but it was just talk. Eddie respected Bill and his views and the fact that he'd married a woman from a concentration camp and helped her recover. Eddie's right-wing sympathies didn't extend to genocide. Farrell was a hard man, in some ways harder than Eddie, but he had a softer shell. Eddie was the reverse. Farrell had put Eddie on his arse when they argued all those years ago, and Eddie had got up and done the same to Farrell. He was a soldier to the bone and respected a good fighter. Add Farrell's dignity and convictions and he considered the man a class apart.

– Look at the arse on that, Ted said, indicating a well-dressed executive-type woman at the bar.

– She's too old for you, Eddie laughed. She must be all of forty-five.

– Do you think she's that old? Ted asked. Oh well, not to worry. She's still young enough to be my daughter.

– You want something nearer your own age, Bill remarked.

– You must be joking, Ted said. What do I want with a horrible old granny. All dried up and wrinkled with soggy gums. Give me a youngster any day. A nice forty-five-year-old will do me fine. Look at those legs and arse. She can sit on my lap and rustle up some life any time she wants.

– She'd have to work hard to get any life out of you, Eddie said.

Ted was a confirmed bachelor. He'd never married and always been one for the women. Farrell remembered him as a young man with slicked back hair and more than his share of charm. He'd served in North Africa with the Western Desert Force and fought Rommel and the Afrika Korps. Before that he'd been one of the 30,000 who took 200,000 Italians prisoner. He'd been under the command of O'Connor and later Montgomery, and been involved in Operation Lightfoot and the battle at El Alamein. Farrell recalled how much Tobruk and El Alamein had raised his and the country's spirits.

Ted preferred talking about the time he'd spent on leave in Cairo than the dysentery, flies and bully beef of the desert. The fighting had been bloody when the British finally pushed Rommel back. He always said victory in war owed more to nature than strategy. England had survived because of the Channel, the Russians had defeated the Germans because their winters were so harsh, while the victory at El Alamein owed a massive debt to the Qattara Depression. The salt marshes and quicksand of the Depression had prevented the Germans using the usual desert tactic of outflanking the enemy. His favourite line about the desert was that both the English and Germans sung along to Lili Marlene. They were fighting and killing each other, but both sides fancied the woman in the lamplight. It was odd, but proved music had always crossed borders. At least they'd had their leave in Cairo, and those Egyptian girls were special. The English didn't appreciate the fine features of Arab women.

– I can still get it up, don't you worry about that, Ted said. She could do worse than come and sit on my knee. There's life in the old codger yet. There's nothing better than a fine pair of stockings and she's wearing some sheer heaven.

– Calm down, Eddie laughed. You'll give yourself a stroke.

– I'm younger than I look, Ted replied, indignantly. When I got to sixty-five I started going backwards. I'm getting younger year by year. I've turned time on its head. It's the after effects of serving in the desert and spending your time with Egyptian girls.

– You might be getting younger, but I'm feeling the years, Barry said, moaning. If the desert made you younger then the sea aged me. It's my foot giving me gip.

– You've got a bad foot because you were pissed and fell off the pavement, Eddie pointed out. You never could drink. Four pints and you're falling down in the street.

Farrell thought of Bob West soaring over the Iraqi desert. Ted had told him there was no place to hide in the desert. Air superiority was vital because any movement stirred up clouds of dust and gave the game away. Nothing could move on the ground that wasn't seen in the air. The same would've happened in the Gulf, though West had also attacked cities. They said the war in North Africa was the last war where chivalry survived and maybe it was true to a certain extent, but Ted insisted it was brutal. It was always brutal, whether there were rules or not. There was no such thing as humane killing. In the Gulf the scale had been massive and West was paying the penalty. Farrell would rather have died in the desert than at sea.

Even though Barry had been a merchant seaman, Farrell wouldn't have wanted his job for anything in the world. Barry had helped keep England alive sailing back and forward across the Atlantic bringing food and supplies from North America. Crossing the Channel for the invasion had been bad enough, but to be torpedoed in the ice-cold mountains of the Atlantic would've been terrible. Barry had been sunk twice during the war. He hated Doenitz and his Wolf Pack U-boat crews. The second time he'd been sunk a U-boat had come up close and the sailors had laughed at the English in their lifeboat hundreds of miles from land. They just laughed and left them to die.

Farrell remembered Barry telling him about the U-boat, more than thirty years ago in a pub in Salisbury when they were away training with the TA. He'd got really angry about it, but Farrell understood. To be left to die was bad enough, but the Germans laughing made it worse somehow. Barry could never forgive that. It was personal. The U-boats' silhouettes were low and the hunters killed tens of thousands of merchant seamen. Without the merchant navy the country would have starved. Barry was an unsung hero in many ways, but Bill, Eddie and Ted recognised his value. He was a good man, but liked a moan, which when you'd been sunk once and then gone back for more, then been sunk again and still returned, was maybe something to which you were entitled.

– I'd had five pints when I went off the kerb, Barry insisted. I can still manage six.

– No you can't, Eddie roared. What do you think, Bill?

Farrell was thinking of the U-boats and how it had taken the idiots in Whitehall time to sort out a common policy to deal with the problem. He wondered how many seamen had died because the RAF and navy commanders were playing games with each other. These things were brushed away and you ended up convincing yourself they didn't matter, because otherwise you'd go mad with the injustice of it all. Nobody else cared, so why should an old man at the end of his life? It was something Farrell could never mention to Barry because, especially in his case, maybe it really was better to forget.

– What's that? Bill asked.

– Wake up boy, Eddie said. You've only just got here and you're nodding off. I was asking how many pints you think Barry can drink before he falls down drunk in the street.

– Five or six, Bill ventured. Four's enough for me these days.

– You're having more than that today, Eddie insisted. You're out of practice, that's all. You're a soldier and you'll do better than four bloody pints today, mate. You can't let the squad down.

Bill smiled. Eddie hadn't changed a bit and his light-hearted bully boy routine never failed. Eddie would always be the corporal and take charge. He pointed you in the right direction and made sure you didn't stray. There was no time to feel sorry for yourself when this man was sitting there with a pint in his hand. They were all in their seventies and Eddie was still doing the I-can-drink-more-than-you routine. Thing was, he knew he was doing it and loved winding Barry up, because the old sea dog took life too seriously. Eddie was acting like a young man because behind the wrinkles that's what he was.

Bill nodded and knew he was on for a session. He didn't mind. It would do him good to get pissed and forget the cost for once. Even though he hadn't served with these blokes during the war he felt a strong bond he couldn't get from someone who'd never been involved. He felt no link with Bob West, despite the fact that he'd met Spitfire pilots and Lancaster crew men in the past and felt a connection. They'd flown nailed-together buckets, while West was part of a minimal-risk machine. He'd told Farrell about the controllers urging him on, telling him to kill the Iraqis. Farrell remembered the song the RAF sang in the Second World War – 'the controller said how can you miss them, and I heed you to guess what I said, bring back, bring back, oh bring back my bomber and me, and me, bring back, bring back, bring back my bomber and me'. Farrell hummed it in his head. Same old story. And Eddie still drank more than his fair share.

– We've got to make the most of these pint glasses while we can, Eddie said, snorting now. Before you know it those wankers in Brussels will be replacing them with some metric rubbish. Then you'll end up with even less for your money.

– It makes you sick what they're doing, Barry moaned. They're giving England up without a fight. Put one of those politicians in the front line and they'd run a mile before the shooting starts.

– Nobody wants this Union, Eddie said, warming up. The German banks want to control Europe but the people themselves don't care. Even the French don't want to be part of the Union while the Scandinavians are showing some national pride for once. If every country admitted to their patriotism we wouldn't have to worry. They want to crush our identity. They couldn't do it during the war.

– It's the right-wing businessmen, Barry said.

– It's the fucking communists and socialists, Eddie insisted. They can't stand us having an identity. All through the seventies they were trying to run down the economy, the unions going on strike over nothing. The Russians always had their eye on England. They knew that if they could get in and subvert us they could take over Europe. It's the Bolshevik plan. International communism.

Farrell doubted the Soviets had been that concerned with England. They had other problems and were busy crushing their own people, but it was true that the atmosphere in England had been very heavy during the seventies. That was how Thatcher managed to get a foothold. She'd promised the good old days and the chance for working people to better themselves, but at the same time had sold them short. She adopted policies which owed everything to rampant capitalism and nothing to the more casual, traditional approach. Farrell believed in a mixed economy. The Tories had set out to dismantle everything and sell it off to the highest bidder, thinking short term. He let Eddie go on, because although they disagreed on certain things, it was only talk. At least they both recognised the dangers of the EU.

The end feeling was the same, and while he agreed with Eddie that there was an attempt to eradicate individual cultures and replace them with a bland shopping-mall-type society, he felt the biggest danger was the centralising of power. At the moment unelected bureaucrats were easing themselves into well-paid positions of power with smooth-talking liberal policies, but if the structure was in place that allowed this to happen then what was to stop the extreme right taking advantage? But he wasn't going to get drawn into the argument. He had his views and that was enough.

– The best sex I ever had was with a Japanese woman, Ted pointed out, blocking Eddie's rant. I was sixty at the time and I met her at the car showroom. She was under fifty and well preserved. Bloody brilliant it was. I wonder what happened to her?

Eddie stopped and looked at the Desert Rat.

– Great, isn't it? he said, laughing. Ted never changes. You try and get the boy thinking about how England is being destroyed from within and he's rambling on about a Jap he had sex with a thousand years ago. He'll die with a hard-on. There's too many people thinking about women and having fun when they should be thinking about England. Come on Ted, it's your round.

– You're the only one who's finished.

– Well hurry up then. We've still got time.

– Alright, Eddie. I don't know how you managed five children the amount you drink. You must have been pissed the whole time.

Eddie frowned, wondering if Ted was taking the piss.

– Every one's a winner.

– They're good kids, Ted said. You did well there, Eddie.

Farrell liked Ted. He was a decent man and had always been a sharp dresser. Farrell could see why women fell for his charm. He was like Leslie Phillips or Terry Thomas, but without the accent. He'd made money selling cars right after the war before running through a variety of vague jobs, eventually returning to cars. It was money in his pocket, but his big love was music. He loved jazz and spent his cash at Ronnie Scott's and various other London clubs. He'd knocked around Eel Pie Island in the old days with Eddie. He could name all the jazz masters and knew a lot of London musicians. Alexis Korner was someone he admired. Ted was a smooth talker. He was wearing well and didn't want any problems. He had no interest in politics. He said the sun in North Africa had burnt all that out of him. It was a time and a place and he'd answer any question thrown at him about Monty and Rommel. He lived in Shepherd's Bush now and had developed an interest in pool. He played regularly in his local and earnt a few pounds extra from the kids hanging around the tables. Ted knew how to handle Eddie.

– Come on, Eddie. Let's get going. We're paying too much

in here. We should be drinking cheaply, at the army's expense. They'll serve a better pint in the club.

Eddie nodded and the others saw their chance and drank up. You couldn't argue with reasoning like that. Ted had a point. The army would do the business.

Everything's quiet now, heading east, the youth in the woods forgotten. Probably flagging down a tractor at this very moment. I see these blokes from Blackburn pass and go back a few years to the time we had a go at this club up there. We were travelling by train and after a brief row by the station the old bill made sure we got on the service back to London. Thing was, the train stopped ten minutes later, so we jumped off, had a drink, and caught another one straight back. It was easy enough to filter off and mob up in this pub. A shitty boozer with ten or so brain-dead punters dribbling into their bitter. They soon fucked off. The landlord didn't care if he was serving cockneys or Pakis, because this was pay day and he wasn't about to phone the old bill and complain about the tenners filling his till. He didn't give a fuck and we drank in peace and quiet, then headed to this club Harris knew about. There were fifty of us and it was early for a club, but we knew there'd be some chaps there as this was supposed to be where this particular firm drank.

We didn't bother paying. Facelift took out one bouncer, and a combination of Harris and Black John did the other. The rest of the lads smashed the big glass windows, nodded to the girl taking money, asking how much for a blow job love, and we were straight down the corridor and onto the dancefloor. We slapped anyone who didn't shift and it didn't take long for Blackburn to sort themselves out. It was a disco with fairy lights, but was playing the same fire-alarm techno all these places run on. Don't imagine there was much ecstasy in this place though. These Blackburn were game enough and it was more or less equal numbers. Thing was, we didn't want to stay too late because we still had a train to catch and we were making the most of our surprise visit. Harris checked his watch and was running things like it was a commando raid. Don't think they could believe their eyes. They've relaxed and kicked back, and suddenly there's a Chelsea mob in their front garden. We had to work fast and get back to the station for the London service.

It was fucking great because the drumbeats kept going and the lights continued flashing, and after working through the nearest blokes and announcing our presence we went into the bar where all these fat cunts were getting pissed. They were worse off than Chelsea and though they gave it a go they didn't have a chance. We'd kept our heads and were acting sober. Turned over the bar, robbed the till, and Harris even let off some tear gas as we made our withdrawal. It was a clean operation and looked like a good result, but things don't always run to plan. When we went back to the station there was a pub full of locals and the snotty-nosed kids begging crisps outside filled them in. The drinkers inside piled out and there was this battle through to the station. There were a few black eyes and cuts on the platform, but nothing too serious, because this was Saturday night on the piss and just like any other Saturday night punch-up. The old bill had turned up by now and everything quietened down as BR pulled in and took us home in comfort.

Every club tells a story. Like that time at Southampton before the grounds were all-seater. There were nine or ten nutters who went in the Southampton end and just piled in five minutes before kick-off. Knew they were going to get battered but didn't give a fuck. Went in the home end, stood nice and quiet, then bang. Just went mental. Now those blokes were hard as nails, and it's always stuck in my mind. Never knew who they were, but that's Casualty behaviour. Knowing you're going to get done. Zero life expectancy. Southampton were nothing special, but doing something like that right against the odds shows how serious some blokes can be. It takes a lot of courage. The old bill waded in and these Chelsea boys trotted back down the middle of the pitch to a standing ovation from the four thousand Chelsea at the opposite end.

Back in the sixties and seventies the main aim was to take the home end, but it died out in the eighties with better policing and the nineties has seen the whole thing shift again. Those blokes were left to jog down the middle of the pitch whereas today they'd be filmed and indexed and banged up for six months. Every paper in the country would run their pictures and every wanker with a column or slot on the telly would be coining it on their behalf. We were young hooligans singing LOYAL SUPPORTERS while down the side there was what passed for a Southampton crew, and these Chelsea boys saw them, ran over and piled in. This set the main mob of Chelsea trying to get over the fences, but the old bill were ready. Somehow those blokes came out alive and it set the tone for the day.

After the game Chelsea went for the old bill. One of the funniest things I ever saw was this copper getting a kicking and this bonehead went over and pulled a plank from the remains of a wooden fence that Chelsea had demolished and been using for ammunition. He worked the plank out and checked the weight. Made sure it felt right. Ran over to the copper who was alone now and trying to get up, and broke it over his head. Real silent movie routine with a Keystone Cop getting his skull bruised. The bloke got ready for a second swing but this woman in a club scarf ran over and slapped him. Told him to fuck off and leave the policeman alone. The bonehead shrugged and walked back into the main Chelsea mob which was busy throwing everything they could at the line of coppers behind the copper on the ground. Chelsea were mad that day and the old bill couldn't cope. It must've gone on for half an hour before we moved towards the town centre.

I think about the carriage and the people travelling with England. There's so many stories to tell. The major rows, small-time vandalism and peaceful Saturday afternoon football. It all merges together eventually. But that's domestic. This is England on tour and the English know how to enjoy themselves. We're living in the moment, rooted in the past. A volunteer army marching into the sunset.

Eddie lined the boys up and did a quick head count. One, two, three, four. All present and correct and no-one forgotten in the pub bogs. When the traffic stalled he led them across the road. Eddie believed in leading from the front and Ted pointed out that this was the route Charles II took when he rode down to ride Nell Gwyn. The rest of the troops laughed as he pointed out that royalty knew how to have a good time with the nags. They were all enjoying themselves, and that included Barry. Once safely across the street, Eddie peeled away towards the Duke of York's. Bill had the others line up behind Eddie and get in step with their leader. The men were marching in a column now – left, right, left, right – with the corporal at the front unaware of the battalion behind. All he needed was a Union Jack or some bagpipes to pipe the boys through the gate.

Eddie was leading the lads to the Battle of the Bulge, with his bulging beer gut out in front doing the job of the sappers. He was defeating the last great German offensive – the war of attrition lager was waging against the great English pint – with a jug of best bitter. Eddie gave his full support to the Ulstermen resisting union with the Papists, and fully believed that the Apprentice Boys should be allowed to march whenever and wherever they wished, but in the war against lager he was even prepared to stretch to a Fenian pint, whether it was Guinness or Murphy's. He didn't care about religion and had mates who were Catholic, but where there was a Union Jack flying Eddie would stand shoulder to shoulder with its defenders. They were all patriots, but Eddie wore his flag on his sleeve. As they approached the Duke of York's he looked behind and saw the boys mucking about. He fell in with the joke and told them to break rank and prepare for some well-deserved leave. Ted would organise the Egyptian girls.

The police at the gate checked their names and let the four ex-soldiers through, and when they turned left in the car park the noise of the King's Road faded away. It was a short walk over an empty square to their destination. There were some cars and a couple of army jeeps, but otherwise the runway was clear. Eddie pointed out his old Rover and carried on. The rest of the boys were impressed by the way the car had been maintained, and were mindful of the fact that they'd arrived by public transport. Eddie had the officer mentality and it was only his working-class origins that had stopped him progressing through the ranks.

Farrell knew Eddie would laugh such a remark off. He

believed in the status quo and the honesty of the establishment. There was no point arguing with Eddie, trying to tell him that if it hadn't been for blatant class prejudice he could have become a major, or better. What was the point anyway? Eddie was happy and had no sense of injustice. He accepted his place in the pecking order and was content.

– Hurry up, you lazy buggers, a voice boomed. The bar's almost dry.

Farrell looked up and saw a grey head leaning out of a second floor window. Sunlight caught the glass and lit the skin, the man's hair turning white. The head looked as though it was glistening and for some reason Bill contrasted it with a youthful Barry struggling in the Atlantic, hanging onto a mast in an oil slick, skin peeled from his back, the oil burning. He thought of Barry's legs dangling under the surface and saw the Great Barrier Reef, Vince reassuring his granddad that the sharks wouldn't come across the coral. No wonder Barry was miserable, torpedoed and left in the sea thousands of miles from home. The thing was, he'd gone back. Then Farrell saw Bob West and imagined him leaving The Unity and returning home. He saw the RAF pilot rigging up a noose and standing there thinking the thing through. Cold and methodical he kicked the chair away. His legs started to jerk. Piss ran down his skin as he struggled, limbs under the water, eventually sucked through space and into some kind of nightmare. Farrell saw West in limbo, Christian and Muslim war dead manoeuvring for space reinventing themselves to fit in with the new order. But West was young and had so much to live for once he sorted himself out. Farrell knew you had no control over other people. He could listen and offer an opinion, but everyone went their own way in the end.

– That's the bar, Ted told him. They'll all be in there, making their pensions stretch and enjoying the company. That's one of the best things about these get-togethers. When you're younger everyone else is young as well, but now we're on our own. Get inside that bar and the outside world vanishes. It's like going home in a way. That's the bar for you.

– And that's Dave Horning, Barry said. He's probably drunk

already. He can't drink as much as Eddie, but he can hold his beer. Me, I can't keep up any more. I spend too much time recovering. It's not like the old days. When you don't know whether the next day's your last you want to make sure you feel your best if you wake up in the morning.

– Shut up, you bloody misery, Ted said. You're the same as you were when I met you. You've always been old.

Barry smiled because he knew Ted had a point, whereas Ted had always been young. Farrell smiled as well, but was thinking hard because he recognised Horning from somewhere. He looked again and saw the grey head disappear inside, window swinging back against the brick and losing the sun. The name came back suddenly and it was a shock that slowed him down. They'd called Horning something else all those years ago. His name was Mangler then. It was a turn up for the books, and Farrell felt uneasy.

He flashed back to Mangler charging across the sand calling the men facing them every name under the sun. They'd lived and fought together for a long time, but Mangler had always been separate from the others. He thought about the bayonet and the German prisoner Mangler had threatened to castrate. It was so long ago now and Farrell had to push his memory to remember the look on the German's face. He could see the scene but for a few seconds the face was blank, then it returned, full of terror. Somehow mutilation and torture seemed worse than death. Poor old Billy Walsh. The worst thing that could happen to a man was to have his balls blown off, or taken by a bayonet. War was a sickness and Farrell had to remind himself he was here for the drink, food and company. He hadn't seen Mangler since they'd been demobbed. No, he told a lie. He'd seen him once.

It was the only get-together Farrell had ever been to and he'd hated every minute of the evening. Farrell had a wife at home trying to recover from the chicken-farmer Himmler's Final Solution, and he found himself sitting at a table with chicken bones on his plate and three idiots moaning about the communists and how England had fought on the wrong side. He almost blushed remembering how he'd argued with one of the men and pulled him outside and into the car park. Everyone at the event was drunk and they were on their own, left to sort out their differences. Farrell might have been drinking, but his boxing moves came through and he dumped Donald Smith on his arse, then kicked him several times to make sure he didn't get up in a hurry.

Farrell went back inside as everyone raised their glasses for a toast. Smith was outside propped against a wall, his nose full of blood and two of his teeth on the ground. Half an hour later, Farrell went back out and pulled him to his feet. He dusted him down and apologised. They went into the toilets and Smith washed up. They were drunk and disorderly. Farrell felt he shouldn't have really done that, but idle talk cost lives. Maybe he'd over-reacted, because Smith was mirroring a growing hatred for communism. Farrell explained things and the man was embarrassed and ashamed. He told Farrell he'd been right to stand up for his wife and knock him down. Smith said he'd forgotten what had happened a few years before. He felt like a fool because he'd seen the same things as Farrell. It ended with a handshake and they went back to their table. Next morning Farrell had a hangover and his wife took him his breakfast in bed. He never went to an army dinner again.

Farrell wondered if Mangler would recognise him. They were so much older now. Rock-n-roll had come and gone and they were still plodding along. Mangler would look at him and see an old man, not the young squaddie fighting his way through Europe. It had been a mad time. He wouldn't know what to say to Mangler. There was nothing needed saying. None of them could ever experience life in the same way again. What did the chaplain say? In life we are in death. Something like that.

– Come on, no slacking, Eddie called, and Ted, Barry and Bill caught up, entering the building and going up the stairs.

– Left, right, left, right, Ted said, taking the piss.

He'd always been the comedian, making fun of the tradition and regimentation, a thorn in Eddie's side.

– I hate stairs, Eddie confided. It does something to my right knee. I'm a fucking para, not a mountain climber. I'm used to dropping straight in among the enemy and getting stuck in.

There was the hum of voices coming from the bar to their left, and a couple of men at the entrance to a small museum on their right. Bill looked in and saw various pictures, the first one showing English soldiers sitting on a jeep in the Sahara. Further back there were several tunics. It was a funny thing, but he still had his Uncle Stan's tunic at home. It was a small red Royal Marine jacket that he'd kept all these years. He would get it out again when he went home. There were some medals as well, and he thought of his own decorations, but he'd leave them in the drawer. He remembered how his wife had loved his medals. It was silly really, but he'd just kept quiet. He didn't want to upset her too.

The bar was busy with eighty or so men standing in small groups talking. Several welcomed Eddie, and Farrell looked around for Mangler but couldn't see him. He went to the bar and ordered, pleasantly surprised by the price. It was another kind of working-man's club, with a central location and framed pictures on the walls. It was nothing particularly grand, but there was a sense of history and a friendly atmosphere. The men in the bar were mainly around his own age, give or take a few years, and he had to admit that it was a nice feeling. He felt at ease. This surprised him as well, because he'd expected something different. He couldn't really put his finger on what he'd expected. The woman pouring was very nice and handed him his change as she took another order. A couple of men next to him were a lot younger than the rest and probably serving soldiers. They moved and nodded as he passed the drinks back.

He stood next to Ted and Barry and looked around. There were several well-padded armchairs and a couch, some tables with newspapers, and a club feel to the place. It wasn't posh at all, but felt right somehow. He sipped his pint. Farrell stood with Ted and Barry because Eddie was a big, sociable character and had gone over to talk with some grey-haired men in blazers.

— Not bad, Ted said. Not bad at all. Certainly gets the blood flowing.

Farrell thought he was referring to the pint, but saw that Ted's eyes were focused on the middle-aged woman behind the bar. She was opening a bottle of light ale and Ted was admiring her action. Farrell supposed she wasn't bad-looking and had made the effort with her clothes and make-up. He had no desire in that direction, though he of course appreciated beauty, but Ted would always have an eye for the women.

– She's sagging a bit around the jaw, Barry said. She's showing her age I'm afraid, and you're showing yours as well Ted, just by fancying her.

Farrell looked at this man in his seventies and there was no hint of self-mockery. Men were like that. Even when they were old and grey, they still judged women as though they were in the prime of life.

– I hear she speaks highly of you, Ted replied.

Barry nodded and understood.

– So how's your new place, Bill? Ted asked. You're nearer me now. You should jump on a bus and come round. It's nice meeting old mates after so long.

– It's fine, Farrell replied. I'm nearer the family and I know people locally. It's okay. It was good to move really. It's a new start and I cleared through a lot of stuff. It was a new beginning. Not that I was unhappy before, I wasn't. It's good to have a change, even when you're old.

– I've lived in the same place since the beginning of time, Barry moaned.

Ted spluttered in his pint.

– You miserable old git, he said. You were there in the Garden of Eden spying on Eve. You're like one of those vampires lurking in the ivy of the churchyard looking for victims. Barry Dracula all the way from Transylvania.

Bill laughed and Barry nodded, shrugging his shoulders, playing along with his image.

– Come on boys, Ted continued. There's a world of women waiting for blokes like us. There's a cheap bar as well.

Farrell spotted Mangler. He looked smaller and less dangerous than he remembered. He watched him through the crowd, talking with another man. Mangler was Dave Horning. He wondered what he'd been doing all these years, but wasn't drunk enough to go and find out. What if Mangler didn't recognise him? Worse than that, what if he started talking about D-Day and the advance through Europe? What if he talked about the killing? Farrell tried to remember where Mangler was and when. His head was fuzzy. He knew Mangler wasn't there when he killed the boy. But he'd had to do it, there was no choice. It was him or the German soldier. He was nervous suddenly, because if he had a view and memory of Mangler then it followed that the same was true for both of them. Farrell saw his medals. The clean ribbons and shining surfaces. The King's head gleaming. Blood on the ribbons and sweat on his hands. Farrell lifted his pint and took a long drink. He asked Barry how his wife was doing.

– Very well thanks, Bill, Barry said, reviving. We're going down to Selsey this summer for a couple of weeks in a caravan. We always took the boys to the caravans when they were young. We've been going there for years and know people locally now. It's a lot of fun, and Dick and Bernie are coming down with the kids for a few days.

– How many grandchildren have you got?

– Nine now, Barry said, smiling. Three kids of my own and nine grandchildren. Five boys and four girls.

– Sounds like your kids take after Eddie, Ted noted.

– I don't mind. The more the merrier, and at least I don't have to put food in their mouths.

Farrell nodded and wondered what it was like for Ted not having kids. It made all the difference, but he knew Ted liked the ladies too much to settle down. He'd always had his wits about him, ducking and diving and listening to jazz. When they'd been in the TA together there'd been stories about Ted, told in jest but with an undercurrent of truth. Stories about gun-running and semi-precious stones, and something about a gambling ring. Farrell didn't remember exactly, but if Eddie was the up-front English patriot with the bluster, and Barry the moaning family man, then Ted was the slicked back wide boy with a deep soul. Farrell had to admit they were all a bit special somehow.

– I had a child, Ted said, lowering his voice. I was living with this woman for a while and we had a boy. Lovely little thing he was. It didn't last between us and she took him with her when she left. I found out later that she gave him away.

There was silence and Farrell could see the sadness in Ted's face.

– What happened to him? Barry asked. Did you ever find out?

Ted's face brightened again.

– He looked me up a few years ago. I searched for both of them and then when I found out he'd been adopted I put my name down so I was there if he ever wanted to contact me. He's a great lad. We see each other every couple of weeks. Funny thing is, he was taken in by this family in Neasden and was never very far from me. I didn't think too much about it at first, because I knew he was with his mum, and I was out and about. It was a time of life when I wasn't thinking about anyone else but myself. She had problems later with drink and even went on the game for a while. I could've done a lot more and she did what she thought was best I suppose. She was always highly-strung, a boozer. My son ended up with a good family, and his new mum and dad loved kids. Those sort of people love children for what they are, not just because they're related by blood. It worked out in the end.

There was another silence and Farrell didn't know what to say.

– What happened to his mum? Barry asked.

– She's dead. Her life got better as she got older. She married a man who looked after her better than the other blokes she'd known. He treated her with respect. She had another twenty-five years until she died of cancer. I haven't told the boy that his mum was a drunk who went on the game, because it's a long time ago and it just doesn't matter. I've known working girls through the years and they love and suffer like anyone else. It's funny, because you look back and think of all the problems you've had, and you wonder what all the fuss was about. Whatever I say about her is his truth. Why give the boy sad memories?

187

Ted stopped and looked at the others. He was a chatty, funny man and didn't usually open up like this. It was the mention of his son, his pride and joy, that had made him break the carefree image.

– Me and the boy get on a treat. He's like a mate really. We go and get drunk together and have a meal. He likes the women. Just like his dad. So I'm not the lonely old sod you think.

They laughed now and Eddie came back through the crowd at just the right moment, showing his officer potential. He took charge again and told the boys to drink up. Were they turning into a bunch of poofs? Ted was standing like a fucking teapot. He went straight to the bar and even now he was a big man with a big presence. He ordered and swapped a joke with the barmaid, then started talking to the squaddies nearby. He was exchanging stories and Farrell could see that the soldiers appreciated this former para, one of the Arnhem mob. Eddie was living history. He was a living, drinking, fighting man who'd gone into enemy territory and fought against the odds. Eddie was a one-off and wouldn't let the sentimentality of old age get a foothold.

– Come on, Eddie, Ted shouted.

Eddie nodded and the younger men laughed.

– We're dying of thirst over here.

There was a lot of genuine affection among these men that Farrell hadn't expected. They were all drinking a lot and Barry said they'd be going in soon for the meeting. It was routine stuff and didn't last too long. Farrell needed a piss and Barry gave him directions to the Gents. He went into a big room, split between a changing area with showers and pegs, and the actual toilets. He saw himself in the mirror and knew he looked a great deal different to how he felt. The years might have passed, but with these blokes he felt like a young man again. It was being with people your own age, who had all the same reference points, just like Ted said. He walked across the empty room, his shoes echoing.

Farrell was almost finished when another man came in. Farrell shook, zipped up and went to wash his hands, then filled the sink and splashed his face with cold water. He was happy and looking forward to the curry, drying himself on a green paper towel. The other man started humming to himself and Farrell looked at him in the mirror. He started at the grey head and knew immediately that it was Mangler. Farrell had kept away from Mangler, knowing that he was safe in the crowd. He looked so different now that if Mangler did look his way he was unlikely to be recognised. Farrell briefly thought about saying hello, but then what, and anyway, he didn't want to talk about the old days. He hurried out of the Gents. He didn't want to get involved in all that right now. Maybe after the meeting and the food. Maybe later on he'd sit down with Mangler and have a chat, but he felt uneasy. Maybe another time.

It would be a rough trip through memories that were more than half a century old, the two men shadow-boxing, knowing they could say more. Farrell didn't want Mangler pulling things apart, didn't even like him. Mangler was always spoiling for a fight, stirring up trouble, and Farrell didn't want his ability to remember his own life questioned. With Eddie, Ted and Barry it was okay. He was secure with them. Mangler was different. He was too close.

– Where have you been? Eddie frowned, holding Farrell's pint.

– I went for a jimmy, Farrell said, taking the glass. Did you want to come as well and shake it dry?

– You haven't turned queer on us as well, have you? Eddie asked. If you've turned funny you'd better give us a warning.

– Eddie needs to know, Ted laughed. Don't you, Eddie?

– You behave yourself, the corporal growled. We don't want any poofs around here, do we?

– Barry might, Ted replied.

– Fuck off, Barry said. I'm happily married with children. I reckon Ted's the one you've got to watch.

Ted smiled and blew Barry a kiss. Bill and Eddie laughed as Barry threw a pretend punch at Ted, who made to grab Barry's balls. Eddie came between them and said no punching below the belt, and at that moment everyone was called to the meeting, Eddie leading his rioting troops towards the hall.

★ ★ ★

Sitting in the corner listening to the rest of the lads pissing about, Harry wasn't feeling too clever. He was sitting quiet as a mouse letting the rest of the boys babble away about nothing in particular, leaning his head against the window thinking of that Porsche and the flash cunt driving, about the autobahns of Germany and how Mussolini got the Italian trains to run on time. The countryside outside was green and starting to blur as he nodded his head. He was tired, drifting, thinking about Nicky. He was on a train heading east and she was stuck in Amsterdam listening to her CDs. It was the afternoon and she'd be getting ready to go to work.

It sounded strange putting it like that, Nicky on her way to the checkout. Yesterday he wasn't too bothered, because she was a prossie and that was her business, and even though she was nice enough he had to meet the lads later on, but now he had the chance to think, killing time. He saw Nicky sitting in her flat alone, with a cup of coffee and a slice of cake, while outside the bars and cafés and markets bustled with life. She was sitting there on the side of her bed stretching those beautiful legs and getting dressed. She'd go outside into the rain and wait for a tram to take her to work, getting off and crossing the river and taking her place with the rank and file. Maybe she'd go and have a drink first, sipping whisky with the other prostitutes, knocking back a double with the greasers and junkies and all the rest of Amsterdam society. She liked her ecstasy and he thought of the Buddha he'd done in Blackpool.

Nicky had a Buddha statue in the corner of her bedroom and a little shrine for the house spirits. She said it was a Thai tradition. The Buddha was sitting pretty, the gold paint on one of his ears chipped and revealing plastic. Harry saw the coffee and CDs and the bed where he'd sat like another, fatter Buddha. She said she liked big men. She told Harry he was a baby sumo wrestler, except he had hair on his body. She laughed and said she loved his hair. Thai men were hairless. She pulled at his arms and his chest. Nicky was natural and unscarred even though she'd been on the game for years. He'd heard about Thailand and Pettaya, and Pat Pong in Bangkok. He thought of Nicky as a teenager leaving her village and taking the bus south, working in the bars of boom-town Bangkok before moving down to the coast.

Harry was half asleep, with images playing in his head. Nicky was sitting on the lap of a sixty-year-old pharmaceutical executive enjoying a holiday from the wife and family, his pockets full of pills. A fatter bastard than Harry with a deep wallet and some unnatural things on his mind. This man was rich and liberated away from England, running his hands over Nicky's arse and rubbing her cunt in front of a gang of other men gathered from the civilised West, these decent gentlemen from London, Berlin, Paris, Rome, Vienna, Copenhagen, Washington DC rubbing shoulders with the more obvious nonces. Men from every corner of the civilised world in light cotton shirts and flip-flops watching the straining young boys and girls on stage fucking each other in time to elevator mood music more suited to the Hilton and Holiday Inn. Their crisp twenty-dollar bills were putting a nice commercial gloss on the oldest profession in the world. They were giving generously as the collection tray was passed from left to right. It was another kind of war and Harry was mixing his sex and violence, seeing Nicky as a casualty of war. It was a battle to survive, the East taking everything the West could fire its way. His head jolted and he heard Tom laugh and tell the others that Harry was sleeping like a baby, but then he was gone and Harry was alone with the pictures. He was sitting in a multiplex watching re-run Vietnam films, riding with Jesus Saves painted on his computerised helmet.

Along with Second World War stories, Harry and his generation were raised on Vietnam, the images big and exotic with hills burning in the distance, soldiers picking their way through tropical rainforests. They saw the scale of the bombing and the freedom of Hollywood gunships. It added something to *Dam Busters* and *The Longest Day*. It was better than Northern Ireland because that was bitter city street-fighting through British housing estates, and every now and then you heard about someone's older brother or cousin who'd been killed or wounded, almost every day a name announced on the news, blokes you didn't know personally but understood were a bit too near you and yours for comfort. Northern Ireland was grim and miserable, while Vietnam was the other side of the world, the enemy small and unseen, the news footage of childhood blending into the films of their youth. The squaddies listed on the news were young and white, their heads shaved and the faces familiar. They looked like you'd look when you grew up. They were English and counted. In the Far East it was jungles burning, not people. It seemed unreal, the difference between the Gulf and the Falklands.

It was the Yanks who'd turned Thailand into a knocking shop. Harry's mate Mango had been to Pettaya and said a lot of bars were run by former servicemen who'd gone back and set up in business. During the Vietnam War they were flown into Pettaya for some rest and recreation, and afterwards the place kept going. Tourists came to join the Gulf workers and soldiers. When the Gulf War ended Pettaya suffered what they called the mother of all hangovers. Along with the bombing raids went sex missions. Mango said it was a mental place, going on about the go-go bars, sex clubs, blow-job bars and so on. Harry imagined kids forced to work hard for their bowl of rice and felt sorry for Nicky.

He jolted when he wondered how she'd managed to avoid Aids. She said she was clean and he believed her, but had been careful anyway. It was chemical warfare, poison in the blood stream. You didn't have to bother with invasions and air strikes any more, just send over the rich holiday-makers and fat nonces to fuck the poor and the thin up the arse. Make them squeal and get girls like Nicky to lick the sewer clean. Harry sat up and had another drink. He had to get that woman out of his head. He was here to enjoy himself. What was the matter with him? He was part of the Expeditionary Force and they weren't taking any prisoners.

—I sit in the meeting but don't really listen to what's being said. I think of Europe and the way the English behaved. I believe we did what had to be done and compared to the Germans and the Russians we were decent and honest. I sit between Eddie and Barry. These two and Ted are good, decent men. They all have their experiences and their lives after the war. It is the same for me and for Dave Horning. I think of the men I killed now because I have it all laid out in some kind of formation. I have thought about what we did and it makes sense. Dave Horning is Mangler and he was with me in Normandy. He was in the same landing craft and he would have smelt the same shit and heard the same sobs. I don't know if he will remember things in the same way. I have my version of events and one thing I have learnt and observed through the years is how history is reinvented. It isn't just the people who make a living from the subject, because in some ways it is the people who were there as well. I hope I haven't done this myself. The thing is, sometimes I wonder. I have done my best to keep my mind clear and remember things clearly, but try as you will you can never fully escape your surroundings. Little things start to niggle. I think of the boy, the last German I killed. I shot him in the head. He was crawling away through the rubble but there was a gun in his hand. The village was a ruin and there were many corpses. I didn't want to come this far and die. It was more than that, because maybe I could have kicked the gun away. Would it have made a difference? I find it hard to know after all this time and I wonder how Mangler would see things. I remember him with his bayonet threatening to castrate a man. I remember other things I don't want to remember. It was war and you can do anything. I know what Mangler did in that village. I saw the woman with her dress up around her hips and the bloody cuts along her legs. His eyes were wild and he was mad. I wonder if he's mad now. There was more gunfire from the enemy. The woman could be alive today, but she'd be ancient. We were numb and I swore at him and asked him what he'd done. I could have turned my gun on him but there was another enemy. We fought on. I wonder if he saw me kill the boy, but I know he didn't. There's always a possibility. Mangler was elsewhere doing other things to other people. I think of the woman and I think of my wife who was raped in the concentration camp. I hate rapists. I don't want the bitterness and the anger, but I hate Mangler. I didn't see him rape the woman, but this is what I believe happened. I am not certain. I don't want to be a moral Christian because there's no God that would let these things happen. I prayed in the landing craft, but how can you trust God? It is bad enough that Mangler could have raped the woman, but I don't want him to think about the boy. Germany was in ruins, like the rest of Europe. We were monsters roaming the earth. There's music and flags and medals to cover the madness and make sure the means justify the ends. I think of the boy and the doubt goes. It was me or him, a battle for survival. A clean shot to kill an enemy soldier.

Bill Farrell found himself squeezed between Eddie and another man Ted introduced as Rai. The meal put on by the kitchen wasn't bad at all and Farrell was tucking into the curry, rice, bread and salad. The others said it was like being back in the army, but he'd never had all this when he was a soldier. The others were joking about something or other, but Farrell was concentrating on the food. He was hungry and had to agree with Rai when he said that it was well worth the fiver they'd paid. The meeting had been alright, but he wasn't involved in the running of the place so wasn't too concerned, his thoughts elsewhere. It was only when he'd cleared his plate and Rai mentioned something about Burma that Farrell started taking notice of his surroundings.

– I had a mate who was in Asia, Farrell said, wiping his mouth. His name was Albert Moss. He fought in Burma. He's dead now, but he never forgot what the Japs did. He wasn't a prisoner of war there, but he saw some of what they left behind.

– It was a hard place to fight, Rai nodded. Everywhere is hard in its own way. A lot of Indian boys died under the Japanese. I went back to see the graves in Thailand one year. The War Graves Commission looks after the cemeteries very well. There's a lot of respect from the local people.

Farrell knew the Commonwealth had fought with the British, and this was one of the things wrong about the European Union. He was no colonialist, but believed the Commonwealth had evolved into something positive. A lot of people felt this, and you only had to look at the young for confirmation. It was a union based on something other than race and geography. This was forgotten by the vested interests. He knew the Thailand–Burma Railway had been built from both ends, with the British dying at the Thai end of the route. Albert had seen the living skeletons and heard about the Japanese torturers. There was the malaria and the snakes and the tropical conditions Englishmen found hard to handle. Even more men died at the other end of the railway line, Asians who were largely forgotten.

Albert had been a good friend. He carried a dislike of the Japanese to the grave, however hard he tried to forgive and forget. It was something that didn't happen so much with the Germans. Farrell knew it was down to personal experience. Compared to the Russians, British POWs had been well-treated, while the Germans and Russians left millions of the other side's men to starve. The same happened with the Japs. It was personal, and Albert didn't like the Japanese selling their cars in England or their politicians shaking hands with the British. It was the same as Eddie and Palestine. It was natural enough.

– Are you having some more? Rai asked, looking at Farrell's plate.

Farrell was and so was Rai, so they went along the counter again, and then to a table for the bread and salad.

– I've got an allotment, Rai said. I grow a lot of this stuff so it's funny eating it when it's not my own. I'm still digging for victory.

Farrell laughed and said he'd worked in the parks. He missed grafting outdoors, but his years working manually with plants and the earth had given him good health.

– I've been there for thirty years now, and I've never felt better, Rai said. You get all sorts of people. There's no class or prejudice there. Mostly it's the retired people who keep their allotments up to scratch, but there's others. We've got a punk who can't be more than twenty-five. It's a haven.

It sounded good and Rai told Farrell about the vegetables he was growing. About the way the soil had to be looked after and allowed to develop. He told him about roots, brassicas and others, and about the bulbs he planted. He had some frogs who lived there and helped keep down the slug population. He was growing everything from potatoes and spinach to pumpkins and corn. He had a good crop of chillis coming up and this year his tomatoes were already flourishing.

– You watch that bastard, Eddie said, leaning over Farrell and jabbing his fork at Rai when they returned to the table.

– You bloody watch him, Billy boy. He'll have you down that allotment of his tomorrow working your bollocks off while he sits in his deckchair brewing tea. It's the tea that never brews. The teabags that never were. Just watch your step or he'll have you breaking your back for him.

– That's not true, Rai said. The tea just took a bit of time.

– A bit of time? Eddie roared, so Ted and Barry stopped and listened. It took hours. Am I lying, Ted?

– It was a nice cuppa though, Ted said. You've got to admit that, haven't you, Eddie?

– And Rai bought us all a pint afterwards as well.

– True, Eddie admitted, feeling better.

– I bought you two pints each, Rai insisted. Don't listen to them, Bill.

Farrell couldn't help but listen as Ted explained how Rai had been ill a few months back and needed to get his soil turned over. Eddie had assembled a crack commando unit and organised an assault plan. Farrell snuck a glance and saw Eddie settle back to enjoy the tale. Ted explained how they'd had to meet at Eddie's and then gone down in the Centurion, picked up Rai in Roehampton and continued to Putney Vale. The allotment was in a perfect site, on a slight hill but right at the top next to Wimbledon Common. Looking down you couldn't even see the M3, just trees and allotments on one side, and the woods of Richmond on the other. They'd gone four days in one week and suddenly Rai was back in business. His groin-strain had healed and everything was fine.

Eddie nodded and Farrell could imagine the big man bullying the others into action. He was all front, but would do anything for anyone. That's what made him special, and Bill thought about telling him, but it would sound soft and only be embarrassing.

– I've got some new potatoes for you all later, Rai said. They're in a bag behind the couch in the bar. Shall we have another drink? I need something to cool my mouth down after the curry. The English never learn, do they? They love their chillies too much. English curries are too bloody hot.

They went through to the bar, and as they were the first ones in they got the couch. It was a nice position. Farrell sat in a chair that could have been made for him. It was so comfortable he'd gladly have taken it home. Eddie had the other chair, while Ted, Barry and Rai sat on the couch. There were five pint jugs on the table. Four contained bitter and the other lager. Eddie was telling Rai off for drinking a girl's drink, but when he pointed out that the lager was chilled and that it was a hot day and they'd eaten hot food, the corporal graciously conceded defeat. He warned the others there could be no surrender. Exceptions could be made about everything, but in the end they had to maintain standards.

– I always maintain standards with the ladies, Ted pointed out.

– There must be standards when it comes to the fairer sex, Rai agreed. Men must guard themselves at all times against the power of the flesh.

The others laughed and explained to Farrell that Rai was a charmer from the same mould as Ted. The difference was that Rai was married, but had what he termed a modern relationship. He was a man of romance and thought rather than action, and had never been unfaithful to his wife. Farrell wondered if Ted was still having sex, or whether he'd also chosen love and romance without the physical side. Farrell hadn't had an erection for years and didn't think about women much these days. It was funny how it was so important when you were young and you spent so much time chasing the girls. He thought of Mary Peacock suddenly. He remembered having her when she was young, after a drink in The White Horse. Now that was a rough pub. He'd had his share of fights in the old days. Funny, because that had gone as well. No more sex and no more violence. It made life a lot less complicated.

★ ★ ★

Corporal Wicks led his squad to the staff car. Privates Farrell, James and Miller were pissed as newts. The corporal was drunk as well, but with a stripe on his arm had to set a good example. He was in charge of the transport and made sure the front-seat passenger was strapped in before starting the engine. Bill was next to Eddie and acting as navigator. He had his wits about him and was already looking for the enemy. Bill also had seven pints of bitter, a double whisky and a large brandy sharpening his senses. He was alert and invincible as he watched Rai stumble through the gates to a waiting mini-cab. Bill rolled down the window and shouted that he'd see him the day after tomorrow when they would blitz the nettles. Rai turned and waved and fell into the cab.

Bill could hear Ted and Barry laughing in the back telling Bill that they wanted to head west, not east. They were part of the West London Brigade and didn't want to die on the Mile End Road. Like the Germans, they wanted to be taken prisoner in the West. Ted and Barry were paralytic. He was the only one keeping up with Eddie. The corporal started crunching gears. It took him a couple of goes to find reverse, but he reassured Ted he was in total control. It was after eleven and they were the last to leave. He reversed and stalled. Eddie hit the brake hard to stop the car rolling and Ted and Barry swore. He turned the key and inched backwards.

– Fucking piece of shit, Eddie mumbled. I learnt to drive in the army, in lorries. You know where you are in a lorry. I wouldn't mind driving a tank right now. That would be fun.

Bill nodded and wondered if this was a good idea, but he was as pissed as Eddie and the alternative was trying to find a night bus or a tube. Corporal Wicks had always been the British bulldog at its best and nothing had changed in later life. He would see this operation through and clicked into action.

– Keep looking straight ahead, Eddie ordered, as they rolled towards the gate. We don't want the SS coming over and smelling our breath. Getting through the gates has to be perfect. We could dig a tunnel and crawl out like rats, but I'm going through the front door. If those wankers get a smell we're dead. We've got to stay calm. They'll smell the drink on our breath.

– We should've drunk lager so they thought we were Nazis, Ted pointed out. We've had it now, boys.

– Don't panic, Barry shouted.

– Come on Captain Mainwaring, Ted said. Sort it out, chief.

– They don't like it up them, Barry laughed, almost pissing himself. The fuzzy wuzzies don't like the cold steel of a bayonet up the jacksie. Who can blame them?

– Stupid boy, Eddie muttered, looking in the mirror at the drunks behind him. You lot can't hold your beer. No English now lads, we've got to be German for a couple of minutes to get past the guards.

The barrier was lifted without a problem and they were on the move. They all agreed that the King's Road was a funny old place. It wasn't really part of London at all. It was a strip of Occupied Europe transported to London, with Mussolini fashion, Vichy food and the kind of prices only a Swede could afford. The people were young as well and Bill honestly wondered how they ended up so wealthy. It didn't matter of course, and he advised turning right towards Earl's Court, but Eddie had his own plan, and carried on till they were passing Stamford Bridge. Ted had watched Chelsea play when he was a young man. He'd been been born in Fulham, but moved to Notting Hill in the fifties, before the teddy boy riots. In the sixties he'd gone to Shepherd's Bush and stayed there ever since. Fulham had changed since he was a boy and now the streets around the football ground were empty of life.

Ted got Eddie to slow down so they could look at the new stadium. The hotel was huge. Funny thing was, Ted had been a big football fan in his youth. He'd watched the club win the League in 1955 and gone on the pitch at the end to celebrate. He'd spent his pennies on Drake's Ducklings and Docherty's Diamonds, and had even been to Wembley and Old Trafford to watch the Cup Final games against Leeds in 1970. He remembered the mods and skinheads in the sixties and the time when Manchester United had gone into The Shed and there'd been a lot of trouble. He'd been to the League Cup defeat against Stoke City in 1972 and the FA Cup Final against Spurs in 1967. When they sold Osgood and Hudson he stopped going. Selling those two was unforgivable, and their loss plus his age meant he'd never been since. The wages some of these players were paid now was ridiculous and the football methodical and system-based. It was all money-motivated. He had lost interest, but was curious to have a look. He remembered the streets and the crowds of people. There'd been some rough pubs in the area, but it was the sixties when he remembered the first real hooliganism. It was annoying, but if you watched yourself you were okay. There were skinheads everywhere in those days. It was another era and he didn't care any more. There were better things in life than football.

Eddie veered right at Fulham Broadway and headed for Shepherd's Bush, planning to drop Ted off first. The corporal had worked out the best route back to Feltham, the boys bailing out on the way. Shepherd's Bush, Hammersmith, Isleworth and home. He was in control and soon on North End Road with its market litter and wandering drunks, on through the tower block estates at the back of Earl's Court. Two miles from the wine bars of Chelsea and the population could've been from a different planet. Farrell felt Eddie was taking an unnecessarily complicated route that invited the attentions of police patrols, but kept quiet. He knew his rank and Eddie wouldn't stand for insubordination. He was a brawler and used to getting his way. It was his car and the punishment for mutiny was a long walk home.

At a set of traffic lights Eddie reached over and pulled out a small box of tapes. There always had to be music when the troops marched into battle. He inserted one and punched the button on the cassette player. Bill was expecting a Royal Tournament collection, Vera Lynn or some old paratrooper sing-along, but instead there was a blast of sentimental ballad. He didn't have a clue who the singer was, but it wasn't anyone he'd heard before. Bill looked at the corporal, who was glaring straight ahead.

– What's all this shit then? Barry slurred from the back. Sounds like country-and-western to me.

– It's the Rolling Stones, Eddie said. An early track.

– Didn't take you for a Stones man, Barry remarked. I thought you'd prefer something off the parade ground.

– I saw the Stones years back, before they were famous, when they were starting off. I've always liked their music. Local lads as well. Ted knows my musical tastes.

Eddie pulled away from the lights and before long they were on a search-and-destroy mission through Shepherd's Bush with the music picking up and Sympathy For The Devil coming through the speakers. Bill Farrell had never listened to the Rolling Stones much but found himself pulled in by the rhythm. The words were good as well, talking about the Devil and how evil cropped up through the centuries, all over the planet at important moments in history. It was part of the human condition and no-one escaped. It was depressing but at the same time he felt uplifted. It made him understand the Lucifer mythology and the need for some kind of belief. He was drunk. He was an atheist.

– Turn it up will you, Ted called from the back. Do the next right, Eddie. It's quicker that way.

As they drove around W12, Farrell marvelled at how for years he'd avoided these drink-ups because he didn't want to sit around listening to old soldiers rambling on about the war all night. For some reason he thought it was going to be an endless post-mortem, both of their own actions and the aftermath, but today had been nothing like that at all. He hadn't laughed so much for ages. He knew these people from way back and it was easy company. It was a good laugh, like tapping into his youth. There was nothing to say about death and destruction, because they'd seen enough first hand. The thing they all appreciated was the comradeship they'd felt at the time. It was still there, and Farrell never thought he'd admit something like that. He supposed whatever side you fought on and whatever the battle it was the same. People needed to feel that unity. It was just a shame it took something like a war to make it happen.

The details of their army lives were buried below the surface and that's why he'd avoided Mangler. The man had been a few feet away, but Farrell had kept quiet. All that mattered in the bar was the funny stories and piss-taking that made the bloodshed somehow ridiculous. Fine details were bound to be blurred. They'd all stood their ground and that's what counted. How could any of them explain the war? They just wanted another pint and the chance to take the piss out of each other like they did when they were young. The drink made them forever young, not words on a headstone.

– Right here, Eddie, Ted said. Turn the music down will you, because the ravers across the road need their beauty sleep.

Ted jumped out and banged on the roof. Eddie pulled away with a screech of rubber, showing off, then slowed down when Bill reminded him that if they were stopped the corporal would face a ban.

– You sound like one of my sons, Eddie said, but he took notice. The old bill would have a fight trying to take me. You mark my words Bill, you too Barry if you're alive back there, I can still fight like a young man. I might not use this dragon between my legs much these days, but I can take anyone, young or old. I'll fight to the death and die in the carnage. Feel that muscle, Bill.

– What muscle?

– His prick, that's what he wants, Barry laughed from the back.

– The muscle in my arm, you cunt.

Private Farrell did as Corporal Wicks ordered.

– What do you think of that then? Eddie beamed.

– Police up ahead, Barry said.

Eddie concentrated on the driving. There was a patrol car coming the other way, moving slowly.

– Don't panic, Barry whispered in Eddie's ear, pretending to nibble the lobe.

– Fuck off will you, Eddie hissed. You'll make me swerve and then we'll have the SS after us.

The police car kept going and Eddie checked it in the mirror.

– That was lucky. You have to watch out for patrols when you're on a mission behind enemy lines, trying to get that miserable cunt Barry back to England in one piece. That's the most important thing. It doesn't matter what you do overseas as long as we all get home in one piece. You're next Bill, then Barry. Not far to go now.

– Put another tape on will you, Barry said, but Eddie just grinned.

It didn't take long before Eddie was dropping Farrell off in front of his flat. He staggered out of the car after they'd said their goodbyes, with the promise of a trip to Rai's on nettle detail and a drink. Farrell slammed the door hard and was soon indoors. He turned on the lights and put the kettle on. He was pissed, but didn't feel sick. He hadn't drunk this much for years. He kissed the picture of his wife and went to the bathroom for a piss, returning to the kitchen and making his cuppa. He stirred the brew and went into the living room, sitting in his favourite chair by the window. Farrell waited for the tea to cool, the stillness and silence calming him. He looked at the picture of the nun with the lantern, a council glow outside, the fuzz of a summer night taking over. He saw the nun calling him forward and the name of his Uncle Gill scribbled on yellow paper, a scared boy off to the trenches wondering if he'd ever see England again.

—I walk down the gangplank and look into an ocean of faces. There's a band playing and my head feels woolly. I can hear the drums and brass but can't name the tune. It could be God Save The King or a funeral march. I'm grateful I haven't been killed during the last few days of fighting and listed as missing in action, presumed dead. It was only a question of time before the Germans surrendered. We had them beat. I can't imagine how families feel when they discover their boy fell on the last day of war. To go through so much and die needlessly causes the sort of bitterness that gnaws at the mind for ever. A lot of people will never recover. The person who'd feel my death most is Mum. She'd never survive the shock. To carry a child and raise it, then see him shipped off and buried hundreds of miles from home would destroy any woman. To carry your child on the trains and have it ripped from your hands is beyond belief. Many men will never recover, but my mum brought me up after Dad died so I'm extra special to her. I'm a special boy and that's what she told me when I was a nipper. I'm glad for myself but glad for her. She prays for me every night, begging God to watch over me and make sure I keep my head down. She says her prayers and will do whatever it takes to keep her boy alive. Nothing else matters when it comes to survival. Sailing back to England and walking down the gangplank is my biggest triumph. This is the real victory, coming back to English soil. If I drop dead now I'll be buried at home. That's important. I don't mind dying here. Flags don't matter in this new world. Coming home alive shows I'm a man and can look after myself. I'm happy and drunk, but I'm drifting. Coffins draped in Union Jacks belong somewhere else. The faces blend together in a vague pattern. The music is slurred and there's mist on the Channel. The sea is calm and I can hear it lapping against the dock, the voices of the other men fading into the background so I suddenly feel very alone. I know it's not true. There's thousands of faces out there waiting for the boys to come home. There's so many people waiting I hope there'll be someone for me. Nobody can live alone, shutting everything out. I can't see anyone in the crowd and slump forward. The surface under my feet is uneven. When I steady myself and finally set foot on firm ground again I walk slowly, floating in the clouds with sunlight beating against the mist, the lights ahead bright in my eyes. Suddenly I see them, even though the faces are still merged. They're small balls of white, but I can guess the rest. My mum is here. I see Stan and Gill and Nolan. For a minute I think I see my dad, but he's dead. He died when I was a baby. I see others behind them and know everyone is here. These are the first ones and they'll guide me home. I'm drifting and following the pattern. My uncles fought and sailed home more than a quarter of a century before me. They're pleased to see Billy breathing fresh air. London's at the end of the line. I have to remind myself where I am. My uncles are a surprise, but even now, so many years later as an old man myself, I can feel the pride I felt all those years before. I admired my uncles more than I knew. I wanted to be like them. I was the same blood. Pride swamps the relief, drowns the shock. I'm running through my life and the dates are lost. I'm going home. I see that clearly. I'm on my way and what's done is done. There's no turning back the clock. I dig my heels in and refuse to surrender. I'm a survivor and the survivors have more pride than the murderers and rapists. All my choices were right. I wouldn't be here if I'd done wrong. The spirits see everything. I made the right decisions.

Farrell shook off the ghosts and sat up straight. He'd never been the same since he left England and never been abroad since. He wouldn't admit it, but he was scared to leave. England was safe while the rest of the world represented danger. He'd seen enough. There was pain even now. Maybe his time had come and this was the heart attack that would kill him once and for all, but no, he was okay. It had been a fantastic feeling returning after the war. At first he was tired, but the nearer the ship got to England the stronger he became. He was excited and contrasted it to the fear of the invasion, but once they landed he forgot everything as his mum pushed through the crowd with a swagger and pulled him close. Everything went in a circle and he'd been right round.

He had a biscuit and sipped his tea. He felt good about his day out. He couldn't believe he'd drunk so much. He understood now why old soldiers kept in touch. It made sense. He felt at ease with Eddie, Barry, Ted and Rai. It would do him good to see them again. He'd renew these friendships and have some fun. He let himself go back.

He supposed Germany did well in the post-war years. It was rebuilt and the Western half of the country got democracy. The US became a true world power. Other countries regained their freedom. In some ways England had missed out. It was near enough in ruins and had to start again. Of course, the same old problems returned with the rich coming along to claim victory for themselves. Nobody took much notice and that was a problem, because it gave them a clear run. The ordinary man and woman in the street had something much more important. For that period following Germany's invasion of France, when Stalin still had his pact with Hitler and the Americans didn't want to get involved, Britain was the only one standing up to the Nazis. Farrell passionately believed this was something to be proud of, even if the view was often dismissed. Even now it made him proud and meant nothing could touch him, no matter what the Government did to his pension, heating allowance and health care. Farrell had the moral victory to go with the medals he never wore.

At first it had been pure relief to be back in England. They'd taken the train to London and the family had laid out a spread. Farrell got quite drunk and his uncles treated him differently. They were sensible men and Farrell had talked about the concentration camps. He told them what he'd seen but they found it hard to comprehend. The boy was a grown man and had seen something they could never know or understand. It was the same hearing about the First World War. They spoke of their experiences more now, though never fully opened up. They were English. They couldn't understand torture and experiments. Farrell remembered Gill saying that if he'd been a German standing in a queue and someone said they were making soap out of Jews, he'd think they were mad.

Farrell's uncles drank more than he'd ever seen them drink and everyone was happy. He'd wondered how Billy Walsh's wife and boy were feeling. Mrs Walsh would never see her husband again. She'd never see his body and would have to make do with a war grave. A part of France forever English. Her son would grow with a memory for a dad. The old man would be a hero figure, shaping his life from the grave. The boy would be bitter and pass the feeling on. There were millions of people in the same situation. Farrell had felt lucky at the time and he still did today. There were millions worse off. He'd prayed in the landing craft but couldn't say God had helped. How could he know?

He felt he was fortunate to have a roof over his head and be able to dunk biscuits in a cup of tea. It was a luxury he tried to make sure he always appreciated. The bitter, whisky and brandy was making him tired and emotional. Drink made him sentimental and he had to struggle to push his wife's face into the photos, holding back the nun coming with her lantern. For decades he had held out but now the past was right in front of his eyes. There were clips of stories fitted together and Farrell had to keep them in order. They said that when you died your whole life flashed in front of your eyes. They said you ran through every experience without any idea of time. He'd always heard it happened fast. Suddenly you were sitting on the bus and then you slumped sideways, and in the time it took to hit the window your life had raced past.

The rational world Farrell had created was fraying. He thought of Mangler, but told himself he was mistaken. He thought of his wife, but the memory was too sad. He thought of the bodies, and the boy returned. The last person he killed kept coming back into his head. The order was crumbling and new pictures appeared. He knew he must be dying, but the flashbacks were slow and cruel. He was being tortured slowly now, forced to fight harder to justify his actions. Farrell could see the lights through his window. The memories were too strong and he saw the faces. They'd say he was sleeping because it sounded better than death. He was in the ruins but fighting back, the earth black from a plague that had risen from the soil and destroyed civilisation. The buildings had been bombed and torched. Smoke hung over the earth. The English were fighting house to house, young men moving through towns and villages, flushing out the last remaining resistance. The ruins had no name. It was a German village crushed and burnt. Farrell had sworn he'd find out the name of the village one day, but he never did. The memory was pushed back, festered, rose up, and was pushed back again. There was the smell of burnt bodies and the reek of gasoline, flame-throwers turning men into screaming fireballs.

Farrell was tired and his head throbbed. He was dirty and hungry, but the strongest he'd ever been, charging through what was left of people's homes, possessions scattered and ruined by rain and mud and fire. The stink of death was in his nostrils and his skin coated in scum. He was moving automatically. German snipers were popping off shots and the soldier next to him was hit in the head. Farrell felt the tears as he looked at the man and saw a black hollow where his left eye should have been. Half a century later it was coming back, a dirty rush of horror. The smell was strong. The fear and hatred worked its way under his skin and pulsed through the lining. The only direction was forward, more slowly now, with every ounce of concentration focused on survival. The war had sent Farrell back to the wild as the English fought for their lives, knowing a mistake meant death. He didn't want to die overseas. He didn't want to end up in a foreign grave, buried poor like his gran, buried in a place where there were no wildflowers and no family.

Leaning forward in his chair Farrell thought of his mum. With the shock of bullets splintering bone he saw the woman crying when they came to break the news that her boy was dead. She'd heard enough stories from the first war to know that death was ugly and without honour. Despite this she would ask for a quick death, a painless death for a brave boy, a special boy, a small boy forever young in the photographs, a young man crawling on his belly seeing a nun with a lantern. It was better that way. She didn't need to know the details.

BLITZKRIEG

THERE'S THIS OLD dear sitting next to me bending my ear, really going into one. It's late morning in West Berlin and the English are starting to gather along the main street around the corner from the hotel where we're staying. Must be sixty or so here at the moment. We're drinking outside a small row of bars, in among white metal tables set out on a wide pavement. The sun is shining through a clear blue sky and we're settling in nicely. The journey's over and we're enjoying the scenery. Doing our own special sightseeing. The woman's got a good head of strong blonde hair, but reminds me of a witch. Don't know why, but there's something about her. The eyes are clear and blue, and she seems sane enough, but then she goes and mentions guardian angels. Maybe she's religious with some serious contacts. Better treat her right. She says that she's a decent German and knew nothing about the concentration camps. Says she was a child during the war but will never forget the horror that followed the German army's retreat from the Eastern Front.

Childhood shapes the rest of your life. Her life has been miserable, yet she was one of the lucky ones. Can I understand that? There were many Germans of her age who did not survive the war. Do I understand what she is saying? The point she is trying to make? That she was helped and looked after and cherished because she was young and innocent and destined to live. I nod and look towards the rest of the lads. They aren't taking much notice. They're enjoying their drink and keeping away from the loony. Avoiding the mad old girl sitting with Tom giving him a headache. I've done it myself enough times. Let some other cunt deal with the nutter wandering round tapping people for attention. They all want someone to talk to.

Someone to listen and understand. They just want to have their say.

I look at her powerful blue eyes and wonder. The strong bones and straight shoulders. She leans in close and I can smell the schnapps on her breath. It's hard but sweetened with fruit. Could be strawberry flavour. I wonder if those white teeth are her own. She asks me if I know what the Russians did to the Germans? I shake my head. Probably kicked fuck out of them, but I'll let her explain. Her eyes water as she starts telling me how thousands of German civilians were left behind by the army's retreat, the countryside around her village swamped by the communists. She says the Bolsheviks were worse than animals. Her voice trembles. They showed no mercy, raping the women and, when they'd finished, killing them along with their children. There were massacres everywhere as the Russians looted houses and exterminated innocent people, ransacking and burning whole villages. The land was thick with blood. It wasn't fair, because they were simple folk and none of the people she knew were members of the Nazi party. They were being made to pay a debt according to their nationality. So much for communist ideals. The communists were less than human. She hates communists and is glad the Soviet Union has collapsed.

She lowers her head and I feel bad for her, an old woman lost in a big city like Berlin. She raises her head and tells me she's a peasant forced to hide among cold towers. That she wanders through heartless office blocks watching strangers. Her father was a peasant forced to fight in the East when all he wanted to do was stay in his village and grow vegetables. He was a gentle man who died somewhere outside Stalingrad. Before she became a refugee and was forced towards Berlin, life was uncomplicated. The village would still be her home today and she would have married a local boy if it wasn't for the Soviets. They'd have had children. Lots of children with blond hair and blue eyes like their mother and father. But everything was destroyed by the communists and her life was never the same, her father frozen in ice and left for the wolves.

She holds her gaze steady and says she was very friendly with the British, French and American soldiers. She worked hard to survive and refused to give in. There's a swelling pride in her classic face and the water has cleared from eyes that stare into mine. I can imagine she was a good-looking woman when she was young. She puts her hand on my leg and smiles for the first time. The blue eyes sparkle and there's a hard, piss-taking humour. She runs her hand towards my bollocks but stops short. I don't know what to do and this old dear has put me in my place. Her eyes never leave mine and she's got the power of a woman who knows what's what. Her fingers are inches from my balls and she squeezes. Digging her nails in. She holds it for a few seconds then softens and starts stroking my leg. The worst thing that could happen now would be if I got a hard-on. Sitting in the street in front of the troops. It's a fucking nightmare and I shrug my shoulders. She nods and moves her hand back to the table – I was a good girl for you British boys and you've all forgotten me now my skin is wrinkled.

The woman is sad and serious, switching back and forward. She lowers her voice and turns her head quickly to the Englishmen nearby, making sure I'm the only one listening. She says that the people were running from the communist murderers gripped by a panic someone like me can never believe. It was an extermination of innocents, a holocaust. Stalin was a monster. She knows Hitler was a monster, everyone knows that now, but do they understand about Stalin? They were both monsters who never lived in her village and never knew she even existed, yet together they destroyed everything she held precious. The Soviets were out of control – hard, bitter men with no kindness in their hearts for German civilians. There were women too, fighting for the communists. Imagine that, tough peasant women matching the men. The Nazis started everything and then hid, buried in their bunkers. They left the ordinary people to pay the party's debt. Hitler didn't even evacuate her family. She was lucky to get out of her village before the Bolsheviks arrived.

She lowers her voice further. She seems uncertain for a moment and then tells her story. There were angels. She is telling the truth about this. There were angels who came at night to help the German people. Many Germans know about these angels. They were mysterious figures who appeared in areas invaded by the Soviets. Angels led the people back through enemy lines to safe German territory. She went through the woods as a child, heading for the magic city of Berlin where they hoped they would be safe. Where were the men when they were needed? The angels helped her reach Berlin and she stayed for the rest of her life. Her mother and brother died in the shelling. Their bodies were burnt in a street near where we're sitting now, drinking lager and feeling the sun, their corpses bruised and distorted. Everything was destroyed. God was on her side though, and she wants me to understand that God was with her because she was young and innocent.

She saw the Berlin Wall go up and she saw the Berlin Wall come down. Nature made her beautiful so she could work and survive. What happened to the ugly people? Did I ever think what happened to the ugly women with scarred faces and missing limbs? Who would care for these women? She grew quickly and was working when she was thirteen. She had been lucky because the soldiers liked blonde hair and blue eyes, and they liked her breasts and some of them liked her behind. She laughs.

– Yes, some of them liked my behind as well as the other places. Mostly it was the French boys who liked that kind of love. I was beautiful and they wanted my body. They paid and I saved and one day I bought an apartment. I worked hard and built a new life. My brother was nine when he died. My mother was twenty-eight and my father thirty-one. I was the only one left to continue.

Tears trickle down her face. I feel like shit and don't know what to say. I nod my head. I can see Carter behind the old woman with a bottle of lager in his mouth. Raising his eyes to the sky and laughing through the drink because I've got the nutter. Tom's got the fucking headcase. The mad old granny pissed on meths, schnapps, whatever. Brain rotting with the clap and dementia taking a grip. Mark shakes his head, glad it's not him. You can't tell old people to fuck off and leave you alone.

Doesn't matter where they come from and how bad they make you feel. You can't tell the old folk to fuck off and die.

Carter and Mark turn away and go back to their conversation, the England boys drinking and enjoying the day. Not a care in the world. Probably don't see anything in the old girl except decay and weakness. We're young and hard as nails. We don't care about anything except ourselves. Don't let the disease in. Stand together and have the dignity to fade away when your time's up instead of causing trouble for people with the sadness of age. It'll happen to all of us eventually. The ones who last that long. There's no story the young want to hear from this old dear. But I'm interested. Trying to imagine the panic of war. Must be a fucking nightmare for the women and kids. The weak left defenceless. Left to pay the tab for their men's behaviour. Mothers watching their kids bayoneted in the street. Young boys and girls seeing their mum gang-raped by Russians, Germans, whoever. Never the English. Suppose there's always someone left to pay in the end and it doesn't matter if it's your fault or not. All that bollocks about the meek inheriting the earth. The woman takes out a hanky and dabs her eyes. Focuses on the table. Lost in her memories.

I look down the main street and feel the rush of being in Berlin. Have to shut this old girl out and stop thinking. Don't know what it is, but Berlin is the place to be. Maybe it's the history lodged in our heads. All those pictures fed to you as a kid. It was the centre of the Cold War and a focus between East and West. Now we've got it off the communists, but the memory of the Wall is still fresh.

This woman is old and battered but has her pride. Maybe she's a nutter, I don't know. I'm not a fucking doctor. But she's glad she lived to tell the tale. One day she'll die and it'll be sooner rather than later. In some ways she's already gone because the financiers are rebuilding Berlin and the young girl sweating under a column of Allied soldiers doesn't count. As long as the boys pay in hard currency everyone's happy. There's no need for pride in the multinational equation. This might be Germany but the ordinary Germans in their run-down estates and rural hovels don't count either. None of these banker cunts know the name of a kid's village swallowed up by the Soviets. It's the new dictators who'll piss all over her and say she's better off – the bankers and industrialists, and every kind of cunt you can imagine. They're looking our way next, England in their sights.

The prossies in Amsterdam must've made a killing from the England boys and one day those girls will be touching up young men when their looks have gone, their blood riddled with tropical disease. But the latest wave of English hooligans don't give a fuck. I don't give a fuck about all that bollocks. You can't do anything about what happened half a century ago. At least we won the war and didn't do what the Red Army did. We've moved on and now we're on the piss in the middle of the same city the RAF bombed. It's sinking in. Where we are and what we're doing. Sitting in Berlin hearing an echo of a miserable past who'll piss off in a minute. Life is for the living.

Mark comes over to help out and tells me to forget the old grannies and feel sorry for all those sad wankers at home stuck in front of the box. Or if Rod's lucky he'll be wandering round Blockbuster trying to make the right choice. Keep the missus sweet. Rod trying to get the CD player to stop jumping. Mandy's disco compilation skipping while his mates are in Germany with some extra-strong Deutschelager in their hands. We're centre of the world. Maybe not the world, but the wannabe leader of a brave new reich. Berlin is a place you hear so much about as a kid that you form this strong image.

The Berlin Wall was right there as kids and we were raised on Cold War politics and the threat of nuclear disaster. We're packed full of anti-Soviet images, our papers matching KGB sadists to the trendy cunts on the council, all those pro-queer, pro-black, anti-white cunts chipping away at England. We've been taught to hate the scum in the East and the rubbish selling our culture down the drain. Listening to the woman brings it back. It's the real story and I can't imagine the English acting like the Russians in a war. Maybe if you've lost twenty million people you just don't care any more, but that's not the English way. We're not mass murderers like some of these cunts. We fight because we have to and have our honour. That's why the

Germans wanted to surrender to the English. That and the fact they'd killed so many Russians.

The woman looks at Mark and nods. She understands more than I think and I feel small. I've seen nothing compared to her. He's cut across her and the tears have stopped. Her pride is there for everyone to see, except I'm the only one looking. She says she has to go to the shops and stands up, and though part of me wants to hear her stories another part wants her to fuck off and leave me alone. Let me enjoy myself without all this misery. She has to be a headcase anyway. Talking about angels like that. Fucking nutters everywhere these days.

Football is serious, but it's still a game. We're doing our own thing without anyone shouting orders. I don't want to start thinking about women and kids getting butchered. It makes you sick, don't care who it is. So when the woman leaves I bury her in my head. It all becomes unreal again, something for the film-makers and soundtrack writers. I don't know. Her time has come and gone, I suppose, just like the pensioners who fought for us in the war. We respect them, of course we do, but respect doesn't pay the bills. The Government doesn't give a fuck, whether it's the Conservatives or Labour. It's all money to Parliament. People's names are just more statistics.

The old woman walks through this mob of English hooligans. Blonde teenager getting fucked rigid by the troops of the great democratic experiment. The boys move aside and let an old woman pass. A shadow filtering through the years. Tiny pin-prick face on the horizon waiting for the strategic missile to pass by and destroy the munitions dump. Designer explosives directing shrapnel in the opposite direction. I wonder if she's making it up about the angels. I try to imagine these figures in the wood. All I can think of is fat cherubs with wings, but know that's not what she means. I suddenly wonder if she ever got married and had kids. I wish I'd asked. A happy ending makes you feel better about things.

– What was she on about? Mark asks, sitting down, looking at my face and laughing. What's the matter you miserable cunt? Cheer up, you slag, you look like you've seen a ghost. She was a bit pale I suppose, but just another nutter like you get back home. They've all got the same story.

– She was talking about how the Russians killed the people in her village and how she escaped to Berlin through the woods.

– Couldn't have been much fun, Mark nods. Still, they did enough themselves didn't they, the old Germans and that. They slaughtered the Russians and Jews and anyone else they could get hold of without any problem, so what do they expect? Hitler didn't think about all that when he was bombing London did he? They killed enough of our boys. Bet she wasn't out there protesting when the bombers left for London or the yids were being hauled out of their homes. There were enough kids ripped from their parents then.

– She was a child. So it wasn't her fault, was it? I mean, how was she to know what was going on? It wasn't down to her personally.

Mark thinks for a moment and looks for the woman. She's gone.

– Suppose not. Don't worry about it anyway. It's all in the past.

– Those Russians were fucking scum, says Brighty, coming over. I heard what that granny said and she's right. Communists are the fucking scum of the earth. There's enough of the cunts over in East Berlin. Me and Harris are going over there later to have a look. There's some Germans he knows coming in from Leipzig. They're from the East, know what they're talking about because they had to grow up under the cunts. They know where to go. You want to come along. We should have a tidy firm together. There's a few card carriers, but they're mostly along for the ride. They're not into the football.

Football and politics are separate as far as I'm concerned. That's the way I see it anyway. Still, it's an excuse for a row I suppose and these things are always played up. Long as it's not against some hostel for women and kids. Harris comes over and a few other blokes seem game enough. The majority keep clear. Harris tells Billy he doesn't reckon it'll be up to much, because the area of East Berlin they're talking about is full of wankers. They're students and squatters, people like that, a few cracked hippies, white dreads and such-like. But we'll visit some of the sights because we're staying in West Berlin. A cheap hotel behind these bars and restaurants. Might as well see the rest of the town.

We were lucky getting the place when we arrived. We get off the train expecting a reception committee but the locals are sleeping. Ends up a few of us turn down this street where there's a flashing sign. Harris leads the Expeditionary Force into Reception. There's this old Turk sitting behind the desk reading his papers. He's finished the Arabic and is studying the German version. Looks tired and lifts his head. He's got the muddy remains of his Turkish coffee. I think of Hank in Amsterdam. A night-shift brotherhood hooked on caffeine. Abdul's peering through his glasses. Harris asks if there's any rooms going and the bloke can't be bothered. He's tired and probably doesn't fancy the look of the clientele. Men stinking of drink and a railway journey. Short hair, tattoos, jeans, trainers, small bags, a Cross of St George around the shoulders of the man with the missing hand. Can't say I blame him. Abdul says the place is full. Harris stares hard for a moment, then shrugs and turns. We head back to the door.

Suddenly something clicks. The caffeine kick-starts Abdul's brain.

– Hey, he says. You English?

Harris turns back again and nods. He's not impressed.

– That's right mate, we're English. You got a problem with that?

The man's face opens and his manner changes.

– You, he stammers. You hooligans?

There's a second's pause and we start laughing. Abdul seems excited for some reason.

– We've come for the football, Harris says.

Abdul frowns.

– But, you hooligan?

Harris shakes his head.

– We're good boys. We won't wreck the place if that's what you're worried about. We're the Society For Better Anglo-Kraut Relations.

The man doesn't get the joke and hurries around the front of the desk. He's short and chubby. He peers at Harris, then points to the Chelsea tattoo and Cross of St George. Points to the rest of the boys waiting to see what happens.

– No, he insists, you boys are hooligans.

– Is he taking the piss? Mark asks.

– You hooligans, the man half shouts. Come and sit down boys. I have rooms for hooligans.

Nobody knows what the fuck the bloke's on about, but he's obviously been reading his papers. We sit down and he starts rabbiting on about the English hooligans and how there's going to be a lot of fighting with the Germans. We go through the routine of signing the book and this takes ages, but Abdul's the owner and his hooligan prices are low. He calls some help for the bags. The bloke's suddenly a character instead of a grumpy old cunt. He's running around and can't do enough for us. It's a mad world. It's worked out well. The hotel's handy and cheap, and now we're pointing new arrivals in Abdul's direction.

– Tell your friends, he insisted when we went out this morning. Tell them that hooligans are welcome at the Hotel Kasbah.

I go over to a table where Carter and Harry are sitting with three Millwall boys. I sit down and listen to the conversation, running through names and dates and a Chelsea-Millwall connection. The South London blood ties of certain characters. Harry knows them through some contract West London Decoration was doing. One comes from Tooting and knows someone else and before you know what's happening there's marriage and mates arriving from every direction. Funny how it works. Wouldn't get that with West Ham, because they're miles out down the Commercial Road. As for Arsenal and Tottenham, you won't get any mixed blood there. No fucking chance.

We hang around enjoying the atmosphere, and when I get hungry I order some food off a poofy cunt in a white jacket and black dickie bow. He minces off and comes back with a plate of cold sausage and Hitler only knows what other type of spiced meat. I take a bite and it's not bad. Continental shit, but it'll do for now. The poof opens another bottle of lager and hands it over. Pisses off. This is the life, in the heart of the fatherland whistling at the reich-birds hurrying past. Bottle of ice-cold lager in my hand. I lean back and look around. There's more English drinking here now, with small groups coming along the street and seeing what's what and who's who. Popping in for a quiet drink. Being nice and sociable. Ticking over nicely.

The old stone church stood against a background of new developments. It was similar to the ones you got back in England and somehow it had come through the Allied bombing. Glass towers had replaced burnt-out homes, businesses rising from the devastation. Harry remembered a picture he'd seen of St Paul's in London, the dome rising through a wall of flames. Somehow St Paul's had survived the German bombs. Everyone said it was a miracle, and he bet the people of the time had taken it as a sign that God had a soft spot for the English. It was good to have God on your side, and it must be true whoever you were, whether it was the Muslims waging holy war against Allied infidels, or God-fearing Born Again pilots strafing unbelievers in the Iraqi desert. Everyone was always right, and as a kid that photo of St Paul's stuck in Harry's mind, proving that in England's and London's case, it really was true.

Here he was all these years later in the middle of Berlin seeing a mirror image. It was smaller because St Paul's was fucking massive, but he stood and stared at this Berlin church all the same. The only time he'd been to St Paul's was as a kid, but when you went overseas you looked at these things.

There was a square further forward, but Harry turned the other way and walked under the shelter of a jutting roof that shielded a selection of small food outlets and several amusement arcades. The fast-food places smelt like their equivalents in London, the grease and fried onions not making much of an impression after the satay sauce of Holland. He looked in the arcades and saw a familiar collection of kids and youths, with older men and women thrown into the war zone. He spotted a gang of boys standing around Smart Bomb Parade, screens everywhere flashing cartoon characters and brightly-lit graphics. Good was fighting Evil all over the arcade, but Smart Bomb had caught the punters' imagination. They'd had it in The Unity for a few months now. It was taking over. Whoever had the idea must be coining it, living a great life somewhere, straight down the travel agent's for a one-way flight to the Philippines, leaving the wife and kids to fend for themselves as the genius inventor prepared to enjoy the spoils of war.

Harry saw Nicky, her small frame popping up again, sitting on the edge of her bed with a cup of coffee and the photo album, running through the pictures one more time. He saw Nicky working in the Philippines with the not-so-good Catholic girls left behind by the Spanish, working the Manila go-go bars. Harry was pleased, though, because that was Christian Manila and Nicky was from Buddhist Thailand, and Smart Bomb wasn't bothered with Asian trading zones. The people were hard workers and had the right attitude. They grafted and wanted to get ahead, so accepted low wages and saved hard. No, Smart Bomb Parade was focused on the East but somewhere a little nearer home, pinpointing the wicked General Mahmet, leader of a deviant oil-stealing regime, concentrating on another kind of warfare. It was an exciting game, matching moral justification with high kill ratios and negligible personal risk.

Harry left the Germans to their war games and stopped at a pizza shop. He bought a big slice of ham and cheese from a skinny punk and went over to a bench, sitting in the sunshine feeding his gut and working on yesterday's hangover, wondering where to go next. He wasn't far from the Hotel Kasbah, and he smiled thinking of last night and this morning, the owner a fucking nutter doing everything he could to make the English invasion force feel at home. Berlin was a lot different to Amsterdam. It seemed more controlled in a lot of ways, but then you came across someone like Abdul at the reception desk, a reminder that Berlin was supposed to be a mad city. A big chunk of the Nazi party came from southern Germany and considered Berlin a centre of Mahmet-style deviance, so maybe he'd scout out something similar, but where did you start? He wasn't looking for whores, because he'd had enough of that for right now. He was happy and didn't want any hassle.

– Alright? Billy Bright said, coming and sitting next to Harry.
What are you doing?

Harry had to think about that one. What the fuck was he
doing? He was in Berlin and he'd read something about the
place before leaving, about the music and clubs, investment
pouring into a city busy building for a brighter future. It
sounded good. But he wasn't doing much except thinking.

– Just having something to eat, Harry answered. What about
you?

– I'm going to see the bunker where Hitler committed
suicide.

Harry nodded and took a big bite of pizza. The cheese was
thick and stringy, and a big blob dropped on his jeans.

– Fucking hell.

Billy sat down and Harry offered him a bite. Billy shook his
head.

– The bunker's not marked because they don't want people
finding out where it is in case it becomes a shrine. They're shit
scared because they know there's still interest, specially among
the East Germans who were pissed on for years by the reds.
They had to deal with the Stasi their whole lives so swung to
the right. They wanted to have some pride so they looked
around. All they found was the neo-Nazis. That's why you get
things like Rostock. People struggling to get by don't want
millions of Turks turning up and nicking their jobs. They want
to get on with life and have some pride.

– That Turk at the hotel's alright, Harry said.

– It's not the Turks I'm talking about, Billy said. It's people
wanting to have some pride in their country and fighting back.

Harry nodded again because he knew Berlin could be an
extreme place. He didn't want to get into a discussion about
poverty-stricken, harshly-treated locals. He hadn't been here
long, but Amsterdam was more his sort of place. He was
probably one of the exceptions, because the others would like
the energy extremes brought. Now he was here, he wanted to
get into the future instead of the past. Berlin was the future of a
united Europe. There was no point fighting the inevitable.
Harry was going to enjoy his holiday no matter what.

Everywhere had its own atmosphere. He believed in these things, because when he looked at someone nine times out of ten he sussed them right off. He could tell a lot about people by how they looked. If someone had mean eyes they generally turned out to be a cunt, and if someone was friendly they were usually generous and honest. Harry went with the feeling. People were prejudiced, but that was because they stuck with what they were told to see. You had to work things out for yourself. He thought about Nicky and knew it could be hard getting through the wrapper.

– Eva Braun stood by Adolf right to the end. Imagine being stuck in the bunker with your woman and dog, with the Red Army getting closer and closer. They did the right thing and were dead before the scum arrived.

Berlin wasn't going to be easy. Harry understood that now, sitting on the bench with the smell of kebabs and the exploding rockets of the amusement arcade, and with Billy Bright doing a Nuremburg on him. No, Berlin was different, another planet to Amsterdam. The people had to deal with the same problems but Amsterdam was a melting pot, where the ideas blended together. Berlin, he didn't really know, but could guess. The buildings seemed so clean, yet under the roof behind him there was dirt and grease. England was halfway between the two countries, trying to con itself everything was running efficiently, the same as in Germany, while those in charge were fucking useless.

He saw Billy Bright sitting there like he was expecting something. Harry wondered what he wanted. The bloke was alright in his way, but went on a bit. Everyone had their views, but Billy's weren't the same as Harry's. He didn't give a toss about all that nonsense, just wanted an easy life, finishing the pizza and throwing the paper plate at a bin, missing and leaving it in the gutter. What the fuck was the bloke waiting for?

Billy was a Barnardo's boy and had never really got over the fact that his mum and dad had given him away. Harry had heard the story second-hand and never asked him what it was all about, because it wasn't the sort of thing you brought up over a pint. Even if he'd been a close mate he would've found it hard dealing with something so personal.

He saw Billy sitting there with his short hair and frowning face and thought of Nicky's kid and how the little boy must feel stuck in an orphanage, with his mum on the other side of the world, on the game. He wouldn't know about all that sex stuff, and so it wouldn't matter, but he must miss his mum. Maybe he saw other kids and they had mums and dads and he wondered what made him special. In the picture the kid had light brown skin and Oriental features. He didn't really stand out from the crowd and that was a good thing. It was better to blend in, keep your head down and not make too many waves.

The monks didn't look dodgy like some of the vicars you got in England, and the boy had a smile on his face. At least the kid was better off in a tropical paradise than a grey European city where it rained for months on end and the cold got right inside your bones. In Europe he'd go to a hard city school with none of the sun and calm he had in Thailand. Harry convinced himself the boy was happy and Harry felt good about that. Maybe one day Nicky would send for him and he'd go and live in Holland, the kid's old girl sitting pretty in a smart apartment, or maybe she'd get a one-way ticket to Bangkok and take the train south, settle on one of the islands and live happy ever after.

Harry thought about Balti and how he said he'd like to live in a tropical paradise one day, usually after a curry. Harry had dreamt about the tropics and wondered if it meant something, but it would be hard to give up everything because England was a difficult place to leave, with all the history and tradition nobody really knew about in any specific detail still strong enough to keep you tied down. Even though he moaned, England was home and the best country in the world, and that didn't stop him wanting the best Europe had to offer as well. Harry stopped himself because soon he'd be standing in the square singing God Save The Queen with Billy Bright.

According to the story he'd heard, Billy had spent the first ten years of his life in care before an elderly couple took him in. They were good people, but were old and the husband died when Billy was fifteen. He still lived near his foster mum and they were close. He'd been lucky, Harry supposed, because he could've gone through life without ever getting a chance. When the old girl got mugged one day coming back with her pension Billy went off his head. The attackers were black and the old bill never found them. She was knocked over and kicked in the face, and from that day on Billy was different. Harry didn't hate blacks but there was nothing he could say to Billy. He didn't necessarily want to change his mind, because he didn't care one way or the other, but because a couple of blokes were scum didn't mean everyone else was the same.

When Harry thought about it, the Nazis wouldn't have been too impressed with Billy. They wanted the same perfection as the modern corporations, and loved the sick experiments just like today's scientists. Look at the experiments and it was going on right now. It was round the back door. But Billy didn't give a toss about genetic engineering and artificial insemination, or whether the valves of a pig's heart would mould with human flesh. Harry saw Billy celebrating victory against the evil forces of international Jewry and communism, having helped clean the scum from the pond, standing in front of the Leader who was focusing on a new element, taking another step towards perfection with the erasing of physical deformities. Billy would expect better.

– Do you want to go and see the bunker? Billy asked.

– What bunker?

– The bunker where Hitler killed himself. We could get a taxi there if you want.

– I thought you said it was buried away so nobody could see it, so it won't become a shrine.

– It's just hidden, Billy said, thinking. I asked some of the others but none of them were interested. Said they'd rather have a drink. We're going to East Berlin tonight and meeting up with these blokes from Leipzig. See if we can have a row with some anarchists or reds, anyone who's up for it really.

Harry shook his head and said he wasn't interested either. He was going walkabout and tonight he was going to get a decent fräulein to suck his knob. Billy was obviously disappointed, then said what about Bang, they could all go there, take a big firm along and have a good night out. Harry had forgotten about the bar and the card that trendy bird gave him on the ferry. It was worth thinking about. She was well tasty and the boyfriend looked like a cunt. One of those sincere wankers who gave it the big one all the time but when it came down to everyday politeness was a slag. That's the way Harry preferred to see things. It meant he might have a chance. She was a cracker no matter what anyone said, and he had to be honest that Nicky had been cropping up a bit too often. It wasn't healthy and not something you read in the Carter training manual. Deliver your load and turn for home. It was the only way, but sometimes you had to be honest, and if Harry was totally honest what he needed was a good shag here in Berlin to burn away the memory of that Thai slag.

Billy was going on about Adolf and Eva again, and how it must've been hard to shoot the dog, and Harry agreed but said he had to get back to the hotel. He didn't have anything against the bloke, but he wanted to have a walk around on his own and go to that bar later, early evening maybe, after he'd seen some of Berlin. He was on a roll and didn't have time for all that political shit.

Three o'clock in the afternoon and the bars are packed. I'm fucked before we've even moved. It's kick-off time and I'm feeling the ten bottles of lager. That poof cunt of a waiter has stopped coming outside because there's hundreds of English on the pavement singing RULE BRITANNIA. Maybe his shift's finished and the timing's right. Let off the hook with some of his customers calling him a fucking German queer. We have to go inside for our drink, but at least there's more staff behind the counter now. The owner's smiling, everyone on the piss and enjoying themselves.

I'm in the bar starting another bottle and spot this familiar ginger head. I blink and make sure. Standing there a few feet away. Haven't seen the bloke for years. It's this nutter from Derby I met years back watching England. I start to move towards him but suddenly remember an incident between Chelsea and Derby. It worked out alright and I'm pissed, so I tap him on the shoulder and after a couple of seconds he smiles. We shake hands laughing, running through what we've been doing and all the usual bollocks. The years vanish. He's a good bloke. Running through Derby's end-of-season rows while I think of the incident. It was at night and he slashed Facelift. Right across the arse. I should've said something but kept quiet. It worked out okay with the old bill coming along at the right time. Didn't feel good about it and I'm glad Facelift's not here. I almost start laughing, thinking of him with his arse slashed, stabbed in the gut. Mark and Harris are nearby and they don't know Derby from Adam. It's fucking mental and doing my head in.

We have a couple of drinks together, but I'm fucked. Tell him I'll find him later on. Down the same bar. I go back to the hotel for the speed Harris has brought along from Amsterdam. That's what he says – skunk in Holland and whizz in Germany. Must be the train journey or sitting in the sun for hours doing me in. The streets are baking and it just means you drink more. I follow Harris, Mark and Carter to the Kasbah.

Harry was having a break in a bar, somewhere in East Berlin, because his feet were aching and he'd hoped for a repeat of that Amsterdam effort, where the girls were friendly and passed the dutchie, and where their Angel boyfriends were polite and bought you a bottle of lager. He'd struck lucky there, but this place was well quiet. He got himself a drink and sat by the window. His shirt was soaked from the walking. He must've done miles, and it had to be at least eighty degrees outside.

He'd been for a wander around Zoo station, and then caught the train from West to East. It passed over a stretch of land where he guessed the Berlin Wall had been. There was a big tent on some wasteland, a circus or rave venue maybe, everything moving on with new freaks and new sounds. One minute the Wall was there and the next it was gone in a puff of dust and the thud of pickaxes, East and West united. The English press said there was a new German superstate in the making and some hinted that the old Prussian spirit was stirring, except it hadn't really worked out like that, because instead of the goose-stepping they got love parades and techno drilling through the brick torture chambers, skinheads and punks eyeballing each other for the leftovers. He enjoyed the ride, getting off when his stop arrived.

The first thing Harry saw as he came out of the station was a sex shop and some dodgy cunt selling burgers, a few rancid boilers pushing snotty-nosed kids in pushchairs. There were a couple of cartoon drug dealers leaning against a fence doing their best to look like drug dealers, with dark shades and greased-back hair. He was in the shade of the station, with dirt ground into the stone and the ticket hall dark and dingy, smelling of piss. The sex shop was small and seedier than normal, the sort of business that only ever survived showing the hardest porn, something you'd be hard pressed to find in Soho. A man came out in the regulation mac, looked up and down the street and shot off, examining the pavement. It was June and the temperature was in the eighties and this wanker was going round like he didn't know the school holidays had started. Maybe they hadn't, but if the England boys found out they'd probably do him like they did that cunt in Amsterdam. The English had standards to maintain. Even Harry knew that.

The burgers were greasy and smelt like shit, and he didn't need that on a nice day like today. They were worse than the dog food you found outside football grounds. They reeked and even Carter wouldn't have touched them. The slags pushing the pushchairs had stopped to argue with the drug dealers and the snotty-nosed kids were looking on bored because they'd seen it all before. There was an argument and some bloke rolled over the street. A big fucker with tattoos up his arms and a long scar from cheek to chin, pissed and jabbering, having his say, and then suddenly they all strolled off in three separate directions as though nothing had happened.

Harry moved out of the shadows and into the sun, crossing a bridge and passing several small, busy cafés. There were decent Germans here sipping small glasses of spirit and watching the world. Harry kept going along wide roads lined by run-down, empty buildings. The cars were spewing out fumes and he was sweating, but finally found the street he was looking for. There were a lot of bars and a quieter atmosphere, but he didn't stop, taking notice of the bars as he'd be back. At the other end of the street he turned and found some grand buildings, a big church and the oversized communist architecture of Alexanderplatz. He looked at the church or cathedral or whatever the fuck it was for a couple of minutes, but he was fed up with religion and headed for Alexanderplatz itself.

Harry stood in the square and looked around. The buildings were major. There was a row of flats and the kind of building he'd only ever seen on the telly, big and grey and communist, most of all impressive. It reminded him of the photos of Hitler's buildings. These dictators knew how to build big and he supposed that when you could do whatever the fuck you wanted you tended to think big. He doubted whether Stalin or Hitler had to answer to an accountant when they went on a spree. He sat down on a bench and looked around. Alexander-platz wasn't bad and it felt different from West Berlin, less commercial. When the Wall was still standing it would've been different again, one side free and packed with adverts, the other confined and advert-free, but despite the misery there had to be a strong belief in what they were doing. Maybe not, he didn't know. It was better to have everyone in together.

Harry drank his lager and watched the people pass outside. Alexanderplatz was something he'd never seen before and he preferred it to West Berlin. He was getting into the feel of the place now, having a cold drink in this small corner of the city wondering what time things livened up. He looked at his watch and it was almost six. A couple of women wandered in and sat at the bar, and the barman put some hip-hop or trip-hop or whatever on, but at least he kept the volume down. Harry tapped his foot and sipped his lager, relaxed and calm, Nicky in her right place and at peace with the world, getting into the European state of mind, loving every minute of his time on the Continent without any kind of media propaganda, doing his own thing, loving everything he saw. The tang of cold German lager tickling the back of his throat as he took things nice and slow.

★ ★ ★

Must be Millwall going into NO-ONE LIKES US substituting English lions for the lions of New Cross, the sound drifting down the street, and I'm walking back from the Kasbah after a shower and then some whizz with the rest of the boys, and we get back to the bar where there's more English than before and a couple of police vans parked across the road now that the evening's coming and the English are pissed up singing TWO WORLD WARS AND ONE WORLD CUP pointing at the old bill, trying to wind them up, and then moving straight into ONE BOMBER HARRIS and I wonder if the old bill know that we're taking the piss trying to wind them up about Dresden, Bomber doing Stalin a favour there, wonder if the cunts can understand English humour, but we're peaceful enough and this speed is good blowing my head off and I'm feeling fucking brilliant now looking at the lights, slowly clocking the street and for a few seconds I imagine we're in Hong Kong or somewhere, before the Chinese took the place back, typical English honesty that, keeping to agreements but suppose it had more to do with the Chinese army and a million men in uniform, but who cares about a chinky outpost because it's only money and the lights go on as the sun starts sinking and the cheers go up as a bird across the road blushes with hundreds of Englishmen singing DO YOU TAKE IT, DO YOU TAKE IT . . . a thin girl in her twenties with a short skirt and nicely tanned legs . . . DO YOU TAKE IT UP THE ARSE? and she understands what's being said and her face is red through the bronze skin but she waves and shakes her head, so the England boys give her a big cheer and she waves back, and everything's funny again because it's an old football favourite, and I'm thinking of the Charity Shield when David Beckham came down to the end where 30 or 40,000 Chelsea were sitting and started warming up and suddenly this mass of supposedly New Football Fans – the megastore, club-shirted, middle-class family support – suddenly 30,000 people (mostly working-class men – thirty-year-old men – men with short hair – those men – men like us – men like me), 30,000 geezers are taking the piss out of the bloke singing SHE'S A WHORE because lucky David's going out with a Spice Girl, and he holds his hand to his ear and asks for something better seeing if the Chelsea boys are still up to scratch and within seconds there's 30 or 40,000 Chelsea singing DOES SHE TAKE IT UP THE ARSE? again and again until the stewards come over and off Beckham goes. It makes you laugh. Makes you grin. Makes you want to go over to that fräulein and give her one. Even the bird four rows down was singing at Wembley, my head racing ahead to the next game at Coventry and at half-time they bring on this troupe of thirteen- or fourteen-year-old girls in skirts and pom poms, get them doing the cheer-leader routine, a few harmless movements dancing about playing at baby pop stars, the way the media does, lowering the age of consent all the time, spreading fashion further down the scale just making a living, but the PA is turned up full crank and one or two blokes remember the David Beckham incident and try to get something going but nobody joins in because these kids are too young, knowing the boundaries, and then they come over and line up in front of 4,000 Chelsea, who are mainly half-cut blokes in their thirties sweating in the sun, and the girls do their routine and Chelsea give them a chorus of IF SHE DON'T COME I'LL TICKLE HER BUM WITH A LUMP OF CELERY, and I'm standing in Berlin and this comes in with the rush seeing that bird across the street, having another drink with the boys and there's a mob who were following England in the early eighties, someone says the Salonika 7 are there, and they start something the others pick up on, a golden oldie, singing OLD TED CROKER SAID, WHAT IS HAPPENING, WHAT IS HAPPENING, WHAT IS HAPPENING, OLD TED CROKER SAID, WHAT IS HAPPENING, AND THIS IS WHAT WE SAID, OH, THE ENGLAND BOYS ARE ON THE PISS AGAIN, ON THE PISS AGAIN, ON THE PISS AGAIN, THE ENGLAND BOYS ARE ON THE PISS AGAIN, THIS IS WHAT WE SAID, and I hold my bottle and half drain the lager and I suppose we've been making life hard for the FA for decades now, wherever they go the England mob are already there, shagging the local women and giving the local hooligans a slap, ready and waiting, spoiling the FA's foreign travel, and I'm feeling fucking great, feeling fucking brilliant, and I know it's going to be a good night as a few of us walk away following Harris, leaving the main mob of English behind – they're behaving themselves and not looking for trouble, minding their Ps and Qs, acting like gentlemen with none of those bad German swear words, ambassadors for Tony Blair and the suits at home, the G&T fossils in the British Embassy – walking away and turning down a side street to a taxi office.

We order two cabs driven by Nigerians – big old boys who've escaped their government and the oil industry – eight of us off to meet the Germans – do something for international relations – Billy says neo-Nazis from the East – distant tower blocks covered in football graffiti – no jobs and too much time – fed on hatred for their old controllers – bitter memories – and I sit by the window with the sun down – can't believe the time's gone – maybe the clocks are wrong – whizzing by the window – head on glass speeding through the present day – driver piling along – playing some classical stuff on the radio – friendly enough geezer – doesn't know who he's got on board – travelling with a Billy Boy Gruff – how serious does he take the right-wing stuff? – grown-up and bad tempered – the driver saying how his mum and dad and brothers died and he came to Europe to earn a crust – talking loud about tribal wars and how bad these things are – booming voice fills my ears – then the sound dips down – watching the cars and buses and people strolling along – suddenly look up and see the Reichstag – fucking hell, it's the Reichstag and Brandenburg Gate – seeing the sights but keeping it to myself – flashes of colour – drank too much and did the speed – gone a bit overboard if I'm honest – an Anglo-Saxon who likes his lager – but bollocks – it feels good and I fancy some more – dead silence inside the car – the music's gone and I wonder what's happened – the cab's stopped and I don't want to look – I mean, Brighty says he hates niggers and Harris likes cutting people – not enough to kill a man – not enough for Harris to lean over from the back seat and pull the driver's head back – hold it firm – the Nigerian trying to struggle and get loose – doesn't want to die like the rest of the family – doesn't want to die like the German kids in their villages – just wants the angels to come and spare his life – wants to live to fight another day – Harris holding him firm so Reich-Bright can do his Aryan Brotherhood routine – pull out a razor and laugh in the face of the black man – lean over and cut the pulsing throat – lean in close with his face distorted – watching the blood pump in a slaughterhouse massacre – tribesmen shagging blue monkeys – greasing the primate's arse and slipping in – buried to the hilt – only girl monkeys because there's nothing the tribes hate more than queers – and I suppose the old monkey doesn't have much choice – caught in a trap and brought into the village for some slap and tickle – slapping its face and tickling its bum – with celery – Reich-Bright leaning in close so the black man can smell the lager on his breath and the powder on his gums – leaning in close but saying fuck all – this deathly silence that does my fucking head in – knowing this is shit – fucking shit – just something Bright says for a laugh and I don't want to see anyone die – tiredness and the sun and drink and speed taking advantage – burning everything as it races forward – brain bulging – the blood pumping from a severed jugular and hitting the roof of this beat-up car – thought the Germans built quality cars and empires to last a thousand years – rust on the doors and the smell of petrol – stink of blood hitting the roof and hitting my face – eyes buried on the dark tarmac outside – hard jungle red – the tinkle of green as I raise my right hand to wipe away the blood – get rid of the sweat – red turning to green so the car starts moving again and I hear the band strike up with DJ Bright the man at the controls . . . the Expeditionary Force moving ahead – the driver laughing and saying he likes the music – where did you get the tape? – and Brighty must be fucked as well because he starts asking this bloke all these questions like where did your family die and how old were you and it's hard being an orphan and you better stop round the corner because the place we're going might not be too friendly – says good luck mate as we shut the door and I stumble on the pavement – the second cab stopping behind – eight of us crossing the road and heading for a bar near some place Harris calls Alexanderplatz.

I stand in the shadows, tapping Harris for a top-up, and he's ready enough. Hasn't been drinking like me because he's the leader of our team. Has to keep his head straight. Standing in the shadows knowing my head's fucked. Left myself wide open. Don't give a toss, because I make the effort and get the concentration pointing in the right direction here in some dark corner of East Berlin following the leader into this bar with the tinted windows, carved German words in the glass, walking in on a mini Nuremburg and a bar stuffed with fifty or so blokes, most of them in black combat jackets and DMs, feel like I've gone back a few years here though it's a German style they've picked up along the way and changed from the original just like the style English skinheads picked up from Jamaica and changed, shedding some skin and some weight, marching straight in, and a few of the Germans turn their heads at these eight England boys strolling in without a care in the world and I'm glad to see Harris spot the blokes he knows. We're soon sitting at the bar and the Germans are lining up the lager with a big selection of white noise sounding out, all Screwdriver and Skullhead and Blood & Honour tunes brought along by their own resident gruppen-DJ, keeping the reich-sounds going, settling in and taking a look at the bar, sipping lager with the whizz shifting my head forward a gear and cruising, because once you sit down and look at things more clearly they pan out, clocking the big reich-geezers, obviously the hardcore, and a mix of other blokes who look like they're along for the night out, Harris introducing us to several of these Germans whose names I don't understand, expecting them to launch into one and start going on about the Turks and asylum-seekers and the coming new world order, but they're very formal asking us what we think of Berlin, and one bloke who you'd never guess was an animal-lover asks Mark if he's been to the zoo. Mark obviously thinks it's a trick question and pauses, that the zoo's some inner-city ghetto full of Pakis, but the bloke's straight up because there's a panda on loan that they're trying to mate with this other panda who's also on loan as well but neither seems interested in sex, preferring the bamboo. We're sitting in Nuremburg with Ian Stuart belting out a song and we're in a conversation about pandas with this modern-day storm-trooper. Maybe the bloke's speeding as well, maybe there's a glut of the stuff and they're giving it away with the frankfurters in the train station. Another zoo. Laughing now with these fucking nutters talking about how the pandas can't be bothered having a shag because it's too much effort and they'd rather sit in the bar and have a few beers and then piss off for a bamboo special with water chestnuts, and we say we know a lot of geezers like that back home in London, like old Harry Roberts who's a good bloke but a pisshead who can't be bothered half the time, him and a hundred other blokes just the same, and this German is almost pissing himself, almost crying with laughter because he says he knows these people, he knows these men dedicated to another kind of life, the bierkeller and burger men. There's enough of them in Leipzig and every other German city. I say they're everywhere because they just can't be bothered with all that sex stuff when they can sit in front of the telly and have a wank over some skin flick of a bird getting serviced on their behalf. The old medical condition, Blow Job By Proxy, but then I go and spoil it all by saying that's the fucking chinks for you, been smoking too much opium.

– Yes, this bloke says, it is a problem in Germany. The immigrants are taking over with their drug dealers and pimps. There are four million Turks in Germany and millions of Germans unemployed.

I nod and have another drink and let Brighty and Harris lead the conversation, looking round at the men drinking and laughing, and there's quite a few with their hair grown out and a couple with flat-tops, and there's this little geezer, a real wide boy with a jack-in-the-box manner, explaining to Mark how the Europeans look at the English hooligans, that whatever they say and do to us, deep down they respect England for the trouble we've caused through the years. Whatever happens, England is the role model for football hooligans. They can't get over these mobs of barbarians who come over and raid their cities, pillaging but not raping, smashing up their shopping centres and causing havoc against the odds. Doesn't matter whether they come from London, Birmingham, Leeds, Newcastle, whatever, they're on a different scale that frightens the shit out of the Continentals. He says the English are rebels. Not in their politics but in their young men, the working class who drink and riot, it's part of the Saxon nature to get pissed and have a laugh, and if anyone starts on them give them a kicking.

Have to admit this bloke knows what he's on about and he's not saying this like he's trying to lick anyone's arse. Has a feel about him that tells you he's dangerous. He knows we're Chelsea and says Chelsea have a cult support, a rebel following, and that the fans have made the club famous through the years. That the Europeans always talk about Chelsea with respect, whether it's Scandinavia, Germany, Croatia. He doesn't know about the Italians and Spanish because they're another set of people, fucking subhumans, and he starts going on about how Western Europe is split between the Saxons and the Latins, that the Germans and English share the same blood and that it was a tragedy how we fought each other during the war. With the English fighting next to the Germans, the Russians would have been annihilated, the Slavs working as slaves for their masters in the West. France wants to be Latin, but they can't pull it off, though there's no way you can connect the French and English or the French and Germans. Everyone does the French.

I think of that game in Paris and the French riot police were firing tear gas as the English gave a mob of French skinheads the run-around. I laugh out loud remembering Rod trying to piss on the eternal flame and wipe out their memories before he was nicked. Mark and the nutter look at me and another German leans in and says his grandfather died fighting the English. I don't know if he wants to have a go or what, but then he says it's stupid this was allowed to happen – friends fighting among themselves when there are better enemies to join forces against. We all nod because there's logic in that, what's the point of killing each other, and I'm off thinking of Vince Matthews and the stories he told us once about the World Cup in 1982 and how the Spanish riot police were always after the English, the police and local fascists both thinking along similar lines, cornering small groups of English when they had the numbers, and how the English were always up for it. The Spanish went for the race connection because we'd given the Argies a good kicking in the Falklands, and when England played Argentina in

Mexico a few years later, when Maradona punched the ball over Shilton, the England boys mobbed up outside waiting for the Argies who bottled out, but even so, I don't know about the English and Germans joining up because I hate the idea of European union. We have to keep ourselves separate, have a drink but go our own ways. I want to tell Hans or whatever the bloke's called that the English don't kill women and kids in concentration camps, no fucking way. It's an essential difference. I know it's not a good idea right now but I can feel the words forming, wondering if I should mention the bombing of London and the plans the Nazis had at the end of the war to execute English prisoners of war, and if that had happened I doubt we'd be sitting here now. But I know it's not the time or place and I have to fight back against laughing, so I look over and concentrate on these birds in the corner, focus on their tits and forget about the heavy stuff. There's three of them and they're fucking beautiful with the speed getting me in that mean-sex frame of mind so I want to go over and drag them in the bogs and fuck the arse off them one by one, humming under my breath THE GERMANS COME IN ONE BY ONE, AND ONE BY ONE THEY ALL GOT DONE to the tune of When Johnny Comes Marching Home, adapting an old Chelsea song from West Ham to Germany, looking at the man next to me and fighting the urge to nut the cunt, what's he fucking looking at, shifting back to the women.

I keep an eye on what they're up to and concentrate on the one with peroxide hair who looks more punk than skin, but it's not the hair I'm bothered about, concentrating on her tits. I'm not that bad yet that I don't show a bit of modesty and slowly look away when she turns her head. Keep her guessing. No need to stir up a bar full of krauts. I can imagine her in the old jackboots. Nothing else except a mouthful of English. I try to push this out of my head and get back in the conversation but the bar suddenly seems hot and stuffy and the white noise fuzzy, everything harder than before. I want to move and get some air and it seems the rest of the bar feels the same way, because we're up and moving, banging through the doors and out into the street, Harris saying how he met these blokes a few years back when he was on holiday in Majorca – imagine that, taking the kids away for a holiday and one night he gets talking with these Germans at the bar and there you go – and Billy met them when they were over in London for the weekend one time. He says they give it the big right-wing thing but most of them are normal aggro merchants. They're not the real thing, whatever they like to think, and I remember that old woman earlier today and how the Nazis stitched her up, how the Allies followed through and fucked her as well but paid for the privilege, and she was just a kid at the time and sees one thing, and there were the Russians getting shafted by the Germans and I suppose the bad blood goes back and forward with the tide. I think about the bombed-out English cities and all the English people the Germans killed. By rights we should be steaming this little lot instead of drinking with them. Fair enough, if it was neutral territory then we could have a laugh, but this seems wrong somehow. Our job is to come into Berlin and do the cunts. I don't know. It's all getting confused.

We walk for a while and come to a street with bars at fairly regular intervals. A lot of them are trendy, and looking through the windows of one or two they're full of wankers. The music's shit and the people look a bit too pleased with themselves and not too happy to see this mob turning up. When a bottle breaks a window our hosts pile in. They wreck the place and give some of the wankers inside a slap. It's no real battle. This one gruppen-geezer, suppose he's the main boy, says this is the easy place, now we're going to do some real communists. People with real politics who'll stand up and fight back and we'd better be ready, because they're more anarchists than reds, and I can almost feel some hidden respect in with the hate. The mob goes along the street sieg-heiling with me and Mark tagging along at the side, Harris and the others a bit further ahead. It's fucking mental because in my head there's films of rallies and I'm thinking how it was all ordered and controlled and now there's these blokes flowing along with the power as the people in the bars try to hide, a few bottles breaking glass, unreal somehow.

I look through a window that doesn't get the treatment and see this face looking back, watching the show, and I tell Mark to look as well because there's the man himself, Fat Harry, with a bottle in his hand and a smile on his face, some tasty-looking bird on his arm.

I slow down and the bar looks good enough, and it seems like it's stacked with crumpet. I'm thinking about peeling off when I hear the sirens. That does it for me and I pull Mark back because my head's fucked and I'm not into all this because we're England and it's all distorted. I call to the others but they're turning down a side street and we take our chance . . . dipping into the bar and giving Harry the surprise of his life . . . fucking hell Harry, you kept her quiet . . . speeding up and slowing down, taking things easy now . . . and Harry looked at Tom and Mark and knew they were pissed and speeding – he'd been enjoying the show outside and suddenly these two had appeared from nowhere. The German crew had disappeared off the main street, but even with the music going Harry could hear the smash of glass. But now he had to think about Tom and Mark and he could see problems ahead, his night ending in tears, because they were stumbling through to the bar and Ingrid was looking at them and asking who they were, and she laughed when he told her they were mates of his from London and said they seemed very happy to see him.

Harry was feeling good about life in general and this bird in particular. He'd been in the bar for a couple of hours when Ingrid turned up. It was down to chance whether she came in or not, but he didn't mind being on his own, and maybe she wouldn't even remember him, or if she did, then think he was a stalker. He was just the bloke by the window sitting alone, and it didn't matter if you were somewhere foreign because it was a different set of circumstances. It wasn't like back home, where if you sat in some club-type bar on your own you looked like a right old wanker, a sad case without any mates left to sniff bar stools.

Everything was a bit new in Bang, but the people coming in were nothing special. There was a theme to the bar, something from a tropical island. The people were laid back and friendly enough, but there wasn't the same warmth as Amsterdam, and it wasn't Harry's sort of place. Here he was in East Berlin and this line of bars and clubs wasn't what he'd expected. The other streets were how he'd imagined this part of the city to look, run down and with a harder edge. He could imagine the secret police giving you grief and border guards shooting runaways making a break for the West, but this bar could've been anywhere. He didn't mind, especially when Ingrid walked in.

– Hello, she said, spotting him straight off.

She didn't seem surprised and this made Harry feel better.

– So you found the bar, she said, sitting right next to him.

Harry didn't want to look but couldn't help it. She had another mini-skirt on shorter than the one she'd been wearing on the ferry. It hitched even further up her legs when she sat down and he knew he had to get a look at the white pants peeping out. She was a fucking raver and much too good for a fat cunt like him, but you never knew, stranger things happened in life, but those legs were doing his head in. He started imagining her peeling off her panties and lying back on the bed, and it was the bed in Nicky's flat for some reason with a closed photo album and open-eyed statue; no, he shifted the scene somewhere else. It didn't matter where the fucking bed was because Ingrid was doing a strip, but Harry put himself in a Sunday dinner-time boozer with a plump old slapper on stage doing her routine, except Ingrid was a hundred times better-looking and stripping for fun. Then she was on Nicky's bed again and Harry was just about to get stuck in when he pulled back and went to buy her a drink.

– It is not my bar, Ingrid said, when he returned. I work here, but today I have the day off. I still come for a drink because the music is good. It is a nice place.

Harry was trying to think of something to say but was getting sidetracked. Whenever Ingrid moved on her stool the mini-skirt rode further up her arse. It wasn't fair, because she was doing his head in and didn't seem to realise. A lot of birds were like that, not knowing the power they had over a bloke's cock and acting like sex didn't exist, wandering around half-dressed flashing their tits and fanny, Ingrid sitting there on the stool with her panties on show, and all he could think about was pulling them off and knobbing her. It had to be the heat because he couldn't get his mind off her legs, and when she shifted a bit she even brushed against his knee, very faintly but still a touch, and he tried to ignore it because he didn't want to end up with a hard-on in the middle of the fucking bar. Funny thing was, Nicky was a cracker as well, but even though she was on the game and shagging ten blokes a night, with the smell of rubber between her legs and spunk in her mouth, this German bird was more dirty somehow. It didn't make much sense because Nicky was a professional, but she was different. He reckoned this Ingrid was a nympho, she had to be dressed like that, he bet she fucking loved it, the dirty cow. But even if she was a sex maniac he had to speak because she'd think he was dumb or thick. With a big effort he looked at her face.

– It's alright here, Harry said. A lot different to the bars in Amsterdam, but I suppose that's because the place is new. There's a lot of pictures on the wall. Where's it supposed to be?

– Hat Rin in Thailand, Ingrid said. It is a place a lot of travellers go, people who want to sit around and take drugs and go raving. I have been there a couple of times. It is not really Thailand, but it is somewhere you can live for a long time on not very much money.

Harry thought of Nicky again and wondered if she'd been to Hat Rin. He didn't think so, because the places she'd talked about were for men content to listen to disco covers and drink imported lager, and from what he could make out they didn't seem short of a few bob. He saw Nicky as a kid sent down from the north to service men two or three times her age and knew it was a different scene. Funny thing was, she told him a few stories about her time there in a matter-of-fact kind of way, and they didn't do anything for him. Watching wank videos he liked birds getting done at both ends or a couple of birds doing a bloke, or best of all two birds doing each other, but when she told him about exactly the same things in real life his cock didn't even flicker. Knowing her took something away and it was a mistake Carter wouldn't make, and thinking of Carter he realised he was on his own and out of the sex machine's shadow. Harry was doing very well for himself, without any help from the professional.

This cheered Harry up because maybe the shag man was losing his touch. There was no more total football from the flash cunt, just Sunday league leftovers, watching some tart trying to get her sagging tits to spin tassels, cheering with the rest of the lads. Harry had to laugh, the pictures on the wall a different world to the go-go bars and blow-job parlours of Nicky's life.

– The first time was best, Ingrid said. The second time I saw it differently, all these bums wandering around who weren't really bums at all. They weren't poor, and certainly not poor like the Thais, and the people who make the money from the businesses are often outsiders. They are from Bangkok. I won't go back to Hat Rin because there is a lack of respect for the local people.

Harry waited for her to light a fag. In Holland it would be dope, but here the drugs were designer rather than natural.

– A lot of the people who go to these places, Hat Rin and Goa and similar areas, don't care about the people who live there. They take but give nothing. The Thais are very traditional people, whatever the West says about them. They don't like to see Westerners naked on the beach and taking drugs. Why should they be pushed aside so the businessmen can build cabins and the travellers fill their beaches with bottles?

Ingrid smiled and shifted again, but Harry kept looking straight ahead, resisting the temptation.

– No, I will not go there again, but I think the bar is okay because it has the original spirit of places like Hat Rin. There is a world culture now of theme bars, techno, ecstasy, world music. All the cultures are blending together so soon there will be no more individual identities.

Harry nodded, but didn't believe all the cultures would disappear, whatever happened, though he wasn't going to argue. He wasn't going to rock the boat and tell her he didn't mind having the extended drinking and relaxed laws on drugs, but knew that his mates weren't going to suddenly start wearing berets and switching from lager to red wine, preferring Bernard's Bistro to Balti Heaven. They finished their drinks at the same time and Ingrid went to the bar and stayed there talking to the bloke serving, while he watched the night get going and more people come in. Ingrid returned and sat down, and Harry was both relieved and disappointed to see her pull her skirt towards her knees. He moved up her body and snuck a look at a nice pair of tits pushing through a thin shirt, nipples visible, moving up to her head. Very nice.

– I don't want to keep you here if you've got somewhere to go, he said, playing the gentleman, kind and considerate.

– I just came in for one drink, but now I have had two. It is not a problem. Do you remember on the boat from England, when you were sick on the heads of those English schoolgirls?

She smiled.

– They were very upset and you laughed. That was very funny. For me at least it was funny, but not for you or the girls.

Harry hoped he wasn't going red because it wasn't the kind of thing you wanted a woman to have in her head when you were looking to get your leg over. He remembered that time when Chelsea played Sheffield Wednesday. They'd gone to Northampton after for a night out and he'd pulled this bird in a club, and though she was nothing special she was game enough. He'd gone back with her and one thing led to another, and there he was pissed out of his fucking skull if he was honest, and this old tart was gagging for it and he wasn't going to disappoint her, but a couple of seconds after he'd got in and started giving it the big one he was sick on her face. He was so pissed he couldn't help himself. He didn't like to think about it too much because she'd gone off her trolley. At first she didn't get what had happened and he was willing himself to come before she found out, but then she worked out what the mess on her face was and she pushed him off and started hitting him. She'd punched him a couple of times then ran off to the bog to wash. He sat down in a chair and pulled his shirt on, but he was pissed and not thinking, giving her time to get clean, and then the fucking door opened and the light went on and she was standing there with a baseball bat. She'd gone for him big time and he had to leg it. Thinking back it was funny because it must've looked like something from Benny Hill, Harry getting chased by this bird who was screaming her head off, and Balti was servicing some sort next door and Carter was downstairs on the couch with another one of her mates. This bird bashed Harry on the head and chased him onto the landing. He was pissed but couldn't hit her, couldn't do anything, and he legged it down the stairs and into the living room where Carter was standing behind this other bird giving her one, and the old sex machine kept going while this psycho chased Harry around the room and out through the back door. He'd done a runner and looked back towards the room where Carter was carrying on regardless, imagining the scene inside, the happy couple half-lit by street lights.

Harry had hid in bushes across the road and waited. At about six he went back to the house and tapped on the window. He only had his shirt on and his balls were frozen, a bad hangover made worse by the baseball bat. He had a lump on the side of his head and one of his eyes was half shut. She'd done him good and proper, but luckily Carter was sleeping on the couch and he passed Harry's clothes out, smiled, then went back to his pillow and blanket. Harry walked to the train station and waited on the platform feeling like shit, carrying Carter's smug grin in his head, the sex machine well pleased. Harry couldn't blame the woman he supposed, but she was a fucking old slag all the same going spastic like that just because he'd puked in her face. He didn't see the others till he got back to London, and his balls were aching so much from the interrupted sex he'd had to go in and have a wank in the train bogs. That was the worst life could get – attacked by a bird and left to wank in a smelly BR bog early on Sunday morning. What a life. Still, you moved on and things were definitely looking better now.

– I didn't mean to get sick, he said, weakly. It's the sea that does it. I've always been like that. Wasn't the best introduction, was it?

– I don't know, Ingrid said, for the first time showing this might be more than a friendly chat about nothing in particular. Sometimes it is not what people do but how they react. I liked the way you laughed because it showed you did not care. German men are too serious. Even the ones who hate being

German and want to escape the mentality can't because it is inside them. They want to relax and laugh, but they can't.

– The Germans have always seemed friendly enough to me.

– But you didn't care. You didn't care what the other people saw. Maybe they saw this man with short hair doing something disgusting, but you didn't care if they thought you were an idiot.

Harry thought she should go easy there. He wasn't an idiot and he never thought anyone else thought so, the fucking tart. Just because she had a nice pair of legs that went right up the crack of her arse, and probably had a perfect cunt to go with them, didn't mean she could take the piss.

– They might think you are an idiot because you were sick but you aren't, and you didn't care. Do you understand?

Harry wasn't sure. He nodded all the same because he didn't see why she'd want to make fun of him. It must be the language barrier.

– Anyway, I thought you were attractive so it was a good excuse to talk to you.

Harry felt his knob flutter, because that's what he wanted to hear. The green light was beaming and boyfriend or not he was in. Maybe she was kinky or something, getting turned on by the bulldog emptying his guts over young girls, but as long as she didn't expect a repeat performance he was happy enough, because he was the lover boy on tour and didn't need to splash out on prostitutes tonight. She was a fucking nympho this one, he could feel it in his bones and he could feel it in his bollocks. She was moving around on the stool and he could see the skirt shifting up her legs again, and this time he was less careful whether she noticed him having a peep. She did notice and smiled, and told him to look out of the window, and when Harry did as he was told he saw a strange sight. Two prostitutes in stockings and suspenders were walking down the street with a Turkish-looking bloke who must've been the pimp. They were well-built girls but not ugly. It was like something off a stage and he couldn't believe they were patrolling this street with its line of new bars. It was like in France where the girls waited for truck drivers by the side of the motorways dressed up to the nines in full view of everyone. It was a lot different to England where they were driven down side streets and kept away from the light, operating in shadows, and it was another European tradition he wouldn't mind England absorbing into everyday life.

– They walk up and down every night, Ingrid said. Do you think they are attractive?

Harry said they were okay, but nothing special. He watched them pass and turn the corner. He didn't care about prostitutes because he had something better and cheaper lined up. The windows in Amsterdam were strange, but seeing a couple of girls walking down the road in stockings was mental. You wouldn't get that round his way and it was a shame, it added a lot of spice. He knew The Unity would be packed to the ceiling twenty-four hours a day with crumpet like that marching past.

– Look at this, Ingrid said, pointing outside.

Harry followed her finger and saw this mob coming down the street, heading their way but stopping and steaming into another place. He could hear the glass going and when he leant forward he could've sworn Harris was in there somewhere, but knew they were Germans by the way they dressed. Fuck, there was another bloke who looked like Billy Bright, and it just went to show how international the English look had become, because now they were copying the fucking faces. Either that or Ingrid had been putting something in his drink.

The mob started moving again and passed the bar, and they were making a lot of noise, but Harry couldn't work out what they were doing down here when most of the English were over in West Berlin. Maybe it was too early and they were having a warm-up before they tried to take on England. He watched them go and was thinking he'd have to tell the rest of the lads about this and, fucking hell, he was seeing things because right there on the other side of the glass was Tom pointing his way. Mark came over and they were moving away from the others and heading for the bar. Maybe it was an English firm, but he didn't think so, didn't understand what was going on, realising it was too late to duck his head and avoid unwanted company.

– Shall we go somewhere else? Ingrid asked. There's a good club down the road if you would like to see some other places.

Harry thought it was a good idea but they were too late, Tom and Mark coming in and introducing themselves, then pissing off to the bar. They couldn't just walk out now and, anyway, Ingrid was looking at them and asking who they were, and she laughed when he said they were mates of his from London, and she said they seemed very happy to see him.

This was all he fucking needed and it was typical, because here he was out on the pull and doing well when these two turn up out of nowhere. They were either pissed or on something the way they were acting, the way they looked, and it was like he would never be able to escape his mates and their influence. Looking away from Ingrid he saw Billy Bright and Harris coming into the bar. Maybe someone was selling tickets. He wondered where Carter was.

– I thought I recognised the name, Brighty said.

– Hello darling, Harris said, leaning over and introducing himself to Ingrid.

Billy was standing next to Ingrid and staring at her legs.

– Very nice, he said, swaying.

When they went over to the bar Harry asked Ingrid if she wanted to go somewhere else. The others wouldn't mind and there was enough of them not to miss him.

– No, she said, your friends seem very nice. We can all have fun together.

Harry groaned. He didn't need this and knew the kind of fun the rest of the boys would enjoy. He looked over and saw Mark hanging over the bar saying something to the barman, who shrugged his shoulders.

– Why's this place called Bang? Billy asked, back from the bar. It sounds like a fucking queer place, but I can't see any poofs. A lot of wankers, but no obvious shirt-lifters.

– It is just a sound, Ingrid said. I don't know why they chose it.

– Do you want a drink? Billy asked. That's what I've come back for. We had to jump in here because the old bill have started nicking Nazis, suppressing free speech. Some blokes Harris knows. I'll tell you later.

Harry watched Billy push through to Harris and noticed the others chatting up some girls. This was his big chance to get out before he was lumbered. They were pissed and he could see trouble brewing. Fuck knows what they were doing with those Germans. Maybe he was getting things confused but he thought it was a football match coming up and that the English were the enemy. He'd got hold of something worthwhile here and wasn't going to let the rest of the lads fuck it up, because the same thing had happened enough times in the past. He could see the rest of the night and how it would develop with Ingrid either storming off or, worse than that, pulling one of the others. They were in better shape, but there again he was a sick bastard and Ingrid liked her men sick.

– Why don't you want to stay with your friends? She asked as they walked down the road. I don't mind if you want to talk with them.

– Just fancy going to that club you mentioned, Harry said, wondering where the fuck they were going to end up.

To be honest, Bang had started getting on his nerves. He'd come to Germany to see something German and instead he was in a fucking theme bar. It was like the rich cunts buying into certain areas of London who couldn't make do with the local boozers and had to have them ripped apart and rebuilt, killing the character. You could be anywhere. No, he fancied a few beers in a German bar, but Ingrid had other ideas.

She stopped a cab and he was sitting in the back while Ingrid did the honours, telling the driver where to go. They were driving along and then they were snogging in the back and Harry started to think that the driver was probably watching them in the mirror, the dirty cunt, but he didn't want to let the girl down. She broke off and said something else to the driver and he swore and did a big U-turn, making sure he burnt lots of rubber, the fucking slag. Harry didn't ask what she'd said and sat back watching the streets flash past. He was playing things easy now because he was in and didn't have any more work to do. He felt bad about walking out like that, but none of the others would notice or care. He knew tonight could well end in tears, and there were going to be murders tomorrow, the day of the game.

They were going on a long drive and Harry sat in silence listening to the radio. He got into the sound of the woman speaking and thought how German was a nice language. He knew people said it was hard and ugly, but Harry liked it. Then the woman stopped speaking and classical music filled the car. There was something grand about Berlin at night, with the street lights and music, a feeling Amsterdam didn't have. It probably depended on your mood, but driving through Berlin with this soundtrack was perfect. He leant back in the seat wondering if he'd fuck things up trying to get Ingrid to give him a blow job in the taxi, dismissing the idea and concentrating on the passing city. This was something he'd always remember.

They drove by the Reichstag and Harry thought long and hard, remembering the building from old war footage. He could also see images of Russian soldiers raising the red flag over a burning Berlin, and wondered if it was the same place. Where were the English when this was happening? He started recognising streets and eventually saw these West Berlin bars packed with drinking and singing Englishmen. There were police vans nearby but no German mob in sight. He didn't know if there'd been any trouble yet, imagining that most of the English would either be here or wandering around nearby, enjoying the nightlife. Tomorrow was D-Day. There must've been at least a thousand English milling around, with more tucked down side streets, mobbing the bars. Harris reckoned there'd be seven or eight thousand English attending the game, but you never could tell exactly.

The cab had to slow down and looking out of the window Harry tried to spot Carter, but there were too many people. They were cheering something or other and the old bill were looking nervous, and there were a lot of coppers as well. Someone had hung a big SCARBOROUGH Union Jack over a bar window and there was a couple of Crosses of St George with CHARLTON and CARLISLE on either side. The bars were jammed and everyone was having a laugh. Part of Harry wanted to jump out and go and join in the fun, leave this bird alone and get pissed, but there was time enough for that tomorrow and he couldn't let Ingrid down. He had to do his duty for England and keep the girl happy, because she said her flat was only five minutes away and did he mind listening to some music there instead of in a noisy club, because then they could be alone?

– That's alright with me.

– There's a lot of England supporters here, Ingrid said. They look very dangerous, don't they? I wouldn't like to be a German hooligan fighting with the English, but the police are very strict here and will stop anything that happens.

The England boys were singing GOD SAVE THE QUEEN as they passed and Harry couldn't help feeling proud that he was English and proud of the country's hooligan element. It was the feeling of power you could only get from everyone mobbing together. Sex gave you something, but the threat and use of violence was something else. It let you play God for a while, like you could do whatever the fuck you wanted and nothing could touch you and make you pay a price. He put his hand on Ingrid's leg and agreed that the police would know what to do with the hooligans.

It's one of those miracles that come round a couple of times in your life. Because I'm lying here thinking of last night. It's a bit after ten and I'm a lazy cunt, stuck in bed. Pulling the different strands apart. Fuck knows what time we got in but Abdul was awake and drinking coffee. Listening to the night-time sounds with a hotel full of pissed English sleeping off the drink. Last thing I remember is walking back from that street with the bars. Looked down this alley and there's two tarts in stockings. The alley's pitch black with an open door letting out a beam of light. They're standing around having a fag. On their tea break maybe. Real old grinders. I couldn't handle it and thought it was some kind of bad trip. Fat old girls with beer guts. Fuck that. I didn't tell the others and we kept on walking. Next thing we're by this bunker.

Couldn't believe it was right there beside us, that those things were still standing. You'd think the communists would've bulldozed the bunkers right away. It still had bullet and rocket dents in the brickwork and the entrance was made from this carved wood. Same as the porch of a Norman church in an English village. The others had disappeared round the corner and me and Mark were left standing there looking at this thing.

We were down a small street and the place was deserted. Mark goes up to the door and tries to open it, but it was locked with a padlock and thick chains. The links were old but strong. We backed off and just stood there for five minutes looking at this square block with tiny windows. I was slowing down. Finding this relic was clearing my head. Thinking of what the torturers got up to inside those walls. You wouldn't have a chance if the Gestapo got you in there. I'm standing in the middle of this fucking street lost in Berlin thinking about torture chambers and medical instruments. Mad cunts in white coats stripping the skin from men's legs while some nonce in a black leather coat asks where it's going off tomorrow. Where the England boys are mobbing up. Eventually we left the bunker because we had a long journey home and I didn't have a clue where we were going. We were looking for the Nigerians, but they were long gone, so we waved down a passing cab and the driver brought us back here.

The miracle is I don't have a hangover. Maybe it's the excitement of the game coming through and washing away the drink and chemicals, because the build-up starts here. There's this wave that comes from somewhere. I know it's going to be a great day out. I'm a kid in a way, even though I'm into my thirties now, because this is how I felt when I was a boy just thinking about going to see Chelsea play football. Now there's the other side. The chance to go on the rampage. See what the Germans can do. It's all bottled and ready to go and most of the England boys will be feeling the same way. All the preliminaries are over. Everyone will get in tight and target the enemy. Give it another ten minutes and I'll get up, because last night was mental and that part-time Nazi effort was a dream really, mixing drink and drugs and fucking up the newspaper headlines.

Today will be different. Time to be on our guard. Thinking

of that meeting makes me laugh. Fuck knows what it was all
about. There's going to be some bigger boys over here with
better connections. First the Nazis, then the bar and those birds
we were chatting up. Then the trek back here after they blew us
out. Must've been something we said. Or Billy grabbing that
bird's arse. Right up the crack. I think we even saw Harry in a
bar with some decent bird. But that's got to be another dream,
because one minute he's there and the next he's gone. The bird
I thought I saw him with was too good for a fat cunt like that.

— What time is it? Mark asks.

His voice sounds rough as fuck. I tell him ten.

— That's alright. It's still early.

There's silence. I stretch.

— Do you remember that bunker? he asks. We tried to get
inside.

Mark tried to break the chain but it was a heavy duty effort.
No chance. I tell him we were lucky the sound didn't wake the
dead. Worse than that the living. They wouldn't have liked us
breaking into the vaults because most Germans want to forget
the past. Don't want to hear us singing about two World Wars
and one World Cup.

— You think what it would've been like in there, Mark says.
The Russians must've gone through the place and closed it, left
everything how it was. It's funny they never got around to
knocking it down.

— Probably left it as a reminder. Or maybe they didn't have
the time or money for the bulldozers. You look round this area
here and there's not a lot to remind you of the Third Reich, is
there?

— That's because we bombed fuck out of the cunts. No-one's
ever going to forget with that fucking bunker right there. It was
built to last. There were other buildings I saw in East Berlin that
had bullet holes in them. All those years and they've still got the
scars.

He stops talking and is quiet for a while. Then the cunt's out
of bed and opening the curtains, telling me to get up, and don't
I feel like shit? He starts going on about how I was mouthing off
with those birds and that's why they fucked off, but I say it was

Bright Spark squeezing that bird's arse and cunt, and Mark nods. Do I remember walking in and seeing Fat Harry with the Page 3 girl? We wonder what happened to them, but you have to fear the worst. The bloke's been sniffing around ever since we got to Europe and all the time I thought Carter was supposed to be the sex machine. Maybe it's to do with his mate getting topped. Sometimes blokes take that kind of thing out on women. Not hurting them, but getting in there and shagging them silly. It's like in a war, where all that death makes you want to make babies. Maybe he's gone soft in his old age, because by rights he should be hanging about with the rest of the boys a bit more.

It's another half-hour before we're across the road having some breakfast. Carter's sitting there with a cooked meal and an English paper he's dug up from somewhere. There's scare stories about the trouble that's coming to Berlin. Comments from various upright establishment figures. Rent-a-quote, do-nothing cunts trotting out the same old bollocks their mums and dads were using twenty years ago.

– You missed a good night, Carter said. We were out till gone two when the old bill started closing the bars. It was all going alright, just good clean fun and that, but they have to come along and start winding everyone up. They soon realised the English were up for it and backed off.

He cuts into a chunky-looking sausage and suddenly I'm starving hungry. This is better than the shit we were getting in Holland. More like English cooking. Something that'll give you energy. Good old-fashioned grease and gristle. Kevin's sitting at the next table with Crewe and they give us a nod. Ask where we got to last night. Laugh when Mark mentions the bunker.

– Have you seen Harry? Carter asks. He didn't come home last night.

– He was in this bar in East Berlin, Mark says, sitting down and pulling a couple of pages out from the middle of the paper. We saw him with some bird. She was fucking beautiful as well. I don't think you need to worry about him, because they seemed happy enough. She had this fucking mini-skirt on and the smallest pair of knickers you've ever seen.

Carter stops eating. Doesn't look too impressed.

– I don't know what's happened to the bloke, he says, with some moral distaste in his voice. How the fuck did he end up over there? One minute he's here, the next he's on the other side of the city. That's not Harry's style. Normally he's at the bar the whole time getting pissed.

From what I've seen and heard about Carter in the past he's the one who's usually sniffing, so I don't know what he's wound up about.

– At home he never bothers. I don't know what he's up to. He should get his priorities sorted out. His mates should come first.

We order some food and have a feed. Other England start coming over. Harris and Brighty roll in with a load of Chelsea and a mix of strays. I look twice and Facelift is standing there with High Street and Biggs. They shake our hands and I can see Facelift is buzzing. Says they got a flight over and beat the system. That they weren't going to miss today for anything. Everyone's steaming. Excited as kids, knowing there's going to be a major row in a few hours' time.

After our breakfast we walk ten minutes to this bar tucked down a side street, away from the main bars. We line up the lager and kick back, killing time. We're trying to be relaxed about things but there's this feeling in the air. It's always like this when it's going to go off against some tasty opposition. Everyone's trying to act calm, but inside they're boiling away. The excitement is there because it's what you live for. It's international level this, another step along. I can feel the buzz sitting with Dave Harris and this Chelsea crew tucked out of the way in Berlin while the rest of the English gather on the main street. I can feel the pride come through and it's starting to replace everything else. It's like Chelsea, but with a bonus track. Today is all about England, and our place in the pecking order is obvious. The patriotism comes through and it's a case of keeping everything under control. Maintaining discipline. All the other bollocks goes out the window and you stop thinking about all the ifs and buts. We strip it all down. That's what patriotism is really, stripping the machine down and getting rid of the accessories. This is the stripped-down England coming through, putting all the soft options on hold. We're England, united, we'll never be defeated.

We kill time in the bar swapping stories and rumours, then move back to the bigger bars filling with English. Fuck knows how many are down here now. Seems like thousands. It's going to be a big one. A rerun of the war. Tapping into the spirit of the Blitz. Firming up as the spirit takes over. Some of the England boys are knocking back the drink, others staying sober, most blokes somewhere in the middle. Depends who you are and what your angle is.

There's this bloke with a telephoto camera across the road and he snaps off a couple of shots. The England boys start cheering. He thinks this is the go-ahead and comes nearer inviting some sieg-heils. Bottles fly his way and one hits him on the head. There isn't any blood but it does the job. He staggers back rubbing his skull. Looks dazed. Two men leg it across the road and get hold of the wanker's camera. He tries to struggle so one of them smacks him. Down the photographer goes. Flat out on the pavement. The other bloke holds the camera in the air and exposes the film. Smashes the camera on the pavement. Everyone cheers louder than before, and as the photographer starts to haul himself up the same man kicks him in the face. Tells him he's a slimy paparazzi slag, that this one's for Diana. Everyone hates the press, and everyone cheers again.

– I didn't tell you, Carter says. There were these two journalists hanging about last night trying to be friendly. We got talking and that and they invited us for a drink round the corner. Wanted to know what was going on. Me, Gary and some others. We went to this bar for half an hour and the main one, David Morgan he said his name was, gave us five hundred marks, so Gary fed them this line about the leader of the English being this geezer Cromwell from Chelsea. Said there was a paramilitary mob called the New Model Army and that Cromwell had his boys tooled-up and was going to do the Germans on the steps of the Reichstag. He said Cromwell has links with the Loyalists. Then he says there's another firm called

The Dam Busters, who were going to steam in first, to soften the Germans up.

We're all pissing ourselves thinking of the journalists feeding the names through to London, because usually they get all that stuff wrong, but a name like Cromwell is going to stick in even the smallest brain. I try to imagine Gary Davison's face as he tells the cunts what they want to hear, Carter and the others trying not to laugh in their faces.

– Should've seen the cunts lapping it up, Gary says, sitting down. Almost as good as that story about Emu and the Kamikaze Kids. Talk about a wind up. I'm surprised they didn't work it out, but when you think about it Cromwell's a good name for a general. It's in the paper this morning, all over the front page, three extra pages inside.

Facelift passes the paper round and it's hard to believe those cunts are so dopey. It's a classic moment. One to remember.

– There was another journalist trying to get English skinheads to do sieg-heils and there was this trendy wanker from a radio station who asked us to make some threats in his microphone, Gary continues. You know, playground stuff. They're a bunch of wankers desperate for a story. They've got no souls. They weren't offering to pay either. I'd have done a sieg-heil for twenty quid, if the cunt had asked nicely. Would've sung the Red Flag for forty.

– Kevin poured his lager down the microphone, Carter says. The radio wanker was almost crying.

– It was nothing to do with me, Kev insists. It was Cromwell.

Everyone's cracking up. We start singing CROMWELL WHERE ARE YOU? and enough of the English already know the story and join in. The press will be over in big mobs for this game. Enjoying the expenses and pissing it up the wall. Shagging the bell boys and turning in some primary school essays. The blokes last night and that one today are the cunts who bother to come out of their four-star hotels. Usually they make it up, while there's always enough slags at home ready to claim some column inches. Makes you laugh. Gary says it's a shame more of them don't get out and about because it's easy money, good publicity and a chance to take the piss. They're a bunch of hypocrites and everyone here knows the score.

Funny thing is, when we're at home we're thinking about the surveillance cameras the whole time. The way the old bill have got things now you have to be smart. The tougher the police get the further underground it goes. Here in Europe we just don't give a fuck. We know the European old bill aren't going to bother tracking us down. Unless you do something major they'll just move the problem on. If you get nicked you'll probably get deported. So people like Gary Davison don't care if they're in the papers back home posing for the cameras. He's younger and coming through the ranks. None of us give a toss. It's all a laugh and this kind of publicity is a joke. A lot of the blokes love the attention and the media wankers get some action in their dull little lives. It's another collection of holiday snapshots. We're living without laws. We can do what we want. We haven't had respect for foreigners drilled into us. The way football is at home, Europe gives us more freedom, especially for those blokes who face long sentences if they get done again back in England.

The time's passing quickly and there's still no old bill around. Probably tucked down a street somewhere keeping out of sight so as not to stir things up. Small mobs of England are walking around having a look, but everything's sweet. The old bill will have their plan and the paper reckons all police leave has been cancelled. There's flags draped along the bars and enough noise, so they're not going to have any trouble finding us. It's not as hot as yesterday, but nice and sunny. A good proportion of the Expeditionary Force are having a drink, people like Harris making do with fizzy water. The army did the same thing. Gave the boys a drink before they went over the top. Poor cunts wiped out by the officer class then executed if the nerve gas and shell-shock got too much. Fucking wankers, and there's no officer core here, just a few blokes who earn respect and people follow, but overall we're bad-tempered Englishmen who do our own thing most of the time then come together when the occasion demands. Doesn't matter now if we're from London or Liverpool or anywhere else in between, because there's a common enemy and England's bigger than all the local rivalries.

It's moving on from family. You start with family and that's the core. Family is blood and you stick together. Nobody takes liberties with family. The closer the better. Your mum and dad and brothers and sisters, then cousins and aunts and uncles and all that. Your mates are next up. Close mates leading down to acquaintances. Then I suppose it's the area you grow up in with football fitting in somehow, and then the city and the country and so on. Probably gets into race or the bigger tribe, whatever you want to call it. That's what was wrong about last night. It was too far down the road. For a start me and Mark didn't have much interest, but bigger than that it felt wrong because today the Germans are going to get a kicking. Nice people who you can have a drink with any other time, but today it's different.

The singing dips and we drink up. Start moving. Chelsea and the London mobs start strolling. So do the Northerners and Midlanders and everyone else. It happens without much talk. The time's come and we cross the road and take a smaller side street. We move comfortably and silently. There's no old bill to be seen, which is suspicious. We take a few turns following the leaders, a mile or so from our meet with the Germans. We turn another corner and keep going. A missile cruising towards its target. Silent and controlled. Going back to silent films. Wanting to move faster but keeping ourselves together.

We turn a corner and it looks like the old bill are holding a fucking rally. They're waiting for us in full riot gear with a line of vans behind the ranks. It had to be expected somewhere because no way can this many blokes move without being seen. We stall with the surprise and several of the English start throwing bottles. Doesn't seem like a good move because the Germans don't hang about like the Dutch, and here they come with the batons and shields and every riot accessory money can buy. There's a split second when I wonder if this volunteer army is going to stand and fight, because this is the old bill. Should have more confidence. The English don't move and the police are getting pelted with bottles and bricks from a small building site and have to stop. There's one bloke down on the floor. With so many England here I reckon they've misjudged things. Played their cards early. It's not chance they're here, but maybe they didn't expect the numbers. Thought it was an invitation-only private party. Fifty a side or something. Dozy cunts. Because the shock wears off and this is a new battle. Adding to the day out.

The older blokes in their late thirties and forties are to one side, trying to get the English organised, and because there's so many different clubs and crews involved it's that bit harder, but there's some well-known faces here and we turn down another street. Skirting the authorities. Taking advantage of natural obstacles, concrete blocks. Piece of piss. We're trotting around the old bill and we're together and sussed and moving well. The old bill have fucked it up and the blokes at the front have been doing this sort of thing for donkey's years. England are in control, making sure we keep the appointment. Two decades of causing chaos across the Continent – France, Italy, Hungary, Norway, France, Luxembourg, Germany, Sweden, Switzerland, Denmark, Spain, Greece, Finland. Everywhere we go, people want to know, who we are, shall we tell them? We're England, putting the Europeans in their place.

We keep going, knowing the Germans will be waiting. Fucking hope so. We slow down. The old bill will be tracking us, but right now we've left them behind. Can't believe they were out-manoeuvred so easy. Shows why we won the war. A classic mix of bollocks and tactics. Slowing right down now, because the Germans should be here. No coppers to hide behind, the fucking slags. We're near a square with flats to one side. Things look quiet. Where the fuck are they? There's a shopping precinct to the left and I can't see it lasting if the cunts don't show. You don't expect the Germans to bottle out. Harris is shouting and going red in the face, where the fuck are they? Fucking German wankers. England fanning out and moving across the square.

After getting back to the Kasbah, Harry had a shower, changed his shirt and hurried to the bars where the English had been drinking since arriving in Berlin, but only found a hundred or so still there. The soldiers were on the move. He swore and kicked a wall. The sex had got in the way of the aggro and he was well fucked off, because apart from spending time seeing the sights he wanted to be there when it went off with the krauts. He couldn't fucking believe it and knew he was never going to live this down. He was a fucking mug, thinking with his knob instead of his brain. He didn't want the others thinking he'd bottled out, because it didn't look good, though they knew him well enough. More important, he wanted to be involved. You didn't want to miss the big dates. No fucking way.

He didn't know what to do next. He went in the bar where Carter and the rest of the boys had been drinking and looked around, but couldn't see anyone he recognised. The familiar faces had vanished and he didn't have a clue where they'd gone. He asked around, but these blokes weren't interested. He swore again and bought himself a bottle of lager and some schnapps, stood outside hoping someone would turn up. The England mob were out on the prowl and he was standing there like a fucking tart. He'd passed the same bar last night with that nutter Ingrid and he should've got out there and then, made sure of today. He really was a cunt sometimes. A right fucking donut. Fucking hell.

Harry's head was still wired from last night, and it just went to show you never knew what was waiting inside the wrapping, with Ingrid dripping by the time they got back to her place, and nothing was a bigger turn-on than knowing a bird wanted the business, and better than that, wanted it off you. Ingrid was a nice girl with white pants, but once indoors she turned into a nympho. She was a fucking raver and Harry made the most of the chance, lifting Ingrid onto a glass coffee table and banging her right there, pumping away till he dumped his load and slipped forward, crashing down through the table and smashing the glass. He looked at Ingrid and her eyes were glazed, and for a second he thought she was dead, skewered by a broken shard of glass, like a fucking vampire.

– Don't stop, she said. Don't finish yet. Come on you pig.

But Harry was over and done and the first thing he wanted after a bit of sex like that, after a bellyful of drink, was to crash out for a while. He pulled back and said sorry about the table, and Ingrid stood up with this dark look on her face, all psycho-like. She said she hadn't climaxed yet and what was the matter with men? Look what he'd done to the table. She stormed into the kitchen, but then came back with a couple of bottles and sat next to him on the couch. Harry took the drink. Who was she calling a pig, the fucking slag.

– Never mind, Ingrid said, fiddling with his cock. We can try again in a few minutes. We have got all night to get it right. My boyfriend won't be back for a couple of days.

Harry wished she'd keep her hands to herself.

– Where's he gone then? Harry asked, wondering about the all-night bit. He was knackered.

– He is visiting his family, Ingrid said. We went to England to sort out some problems we had. He was having sex with my sister and I caught them together. I walked in and they were on the sofa, right where we are sitting now. They did not expect me to come home. It is a hard thing to forget. I want him to know what it feels like.

Ingrid drank half her bottle in one go, and Harry couldn't say he minded filling in for that dozy German cunt, though he reckoned it was a bit iffy being used like some rent-a-dildo party filler, but still, it was decent fanny and he wasn't going to turn Ingrid down. If the girl wanted a portion then Harry was the man for the job, but he didn't want any grief. That was the English for you, get in, do the business, then piss off before the post-mortem starts. He should get going really, but he was fucked.

– Sorry, I shouldn't have said that. I like you Harry. You don't care about anything and you have no manners.

He almost choked on his lager, the stroppy fucking cunt. They sat in silence drinking, Harry narked, and then Ingrid stood up and said she had something that would make him happier.

The night picked up speed, with Ingrid going like a train. After the glass table, they moved to the bed, her mouth, and finally she was greasing her arse and Harry was being forced to run a bombing raid up the Rhine. By this time she'd fed him a

Gulf Boy, and once the chemicals took effect he was doing what he was told, right open to suggestion, obeying orders with Ingrid taking on the role of controller. His head was on fire and he had the vague idea he should be using a rubber, but didn't connect. He was doing what he was told and the Gulf pill made him invincible.

Harry was dead by five in the morning and drifted off to sleep, the next thing he felt a sharp pain under his gut. He sat up and found Ingrid chewing his cock, not sucking but digging her teeth in. It was fucking agony and he tried to get her off, pulling away, but the vampire was hanging on, razor teeth behind his helmet. It was murder and the bed was a war zone, Harry trying to coax the girl off, but she was out of her head and the Gulf Boy had turned their session into a blockbuster video where a soldier forcing a peasant woman to suck him off had his cock bit off and bled to death. It was the perfect revenge but Harry hadn't done anything wrong. The film and the reality merged and Harry was shitting it. He punched Ingrid in the head to get her off, and she went straight to sleep, running on automatic. Harry laid there for a while knowing he should get out, but he couldn't move.

Harry didn't wake up till after two and Ingrid had already gone to work, leaving a note telling him to come and see her later. He left the flat and took a taxi back to the Kasbah, going straight to the shower and washing the blood, shit and spunk from his cock, gritting his teeth as the soap stung cut skin. He stayed under the water a long time and cleaned well, scrubbing away the memory, looking forward to a fresh start.

Now Harry was sipping his lager, more concerned with missing the others than almost losing his knob. The Expeditionary Force was out on patrol and he'd been left behind. He finished his drink and left the bar, went for a wander. His brain was running through old videos chopping at a dead image, thinking of Balti, surprisingly okay knowing the man who was more than a brother was dead and gone, his face blown away by a sad old cunt who'd lost his grandson to leukaemia, and now old McDonald was doing twenty years in another sort of farm, banged up sending his shit through the bars. It was bad news, but what could you do? Nothing at all. You were powerless.

What could you do but walk into the flashing amusement arcade and stand in front of the first machine that took your fancy, in among the pale boys and girls and old prowling perverts who didn't take any notice of the new arrival, Harry wondering if he was faceless, just like Balti, the poor cunt, both of them fucked. But they'd had some good times and that was all you could hope for in life, pulling out the change he needed to play the game, looking for the slot but turning his head when two teenage girls came up next to him and started yelling at a flashing red-orange-blue screen, teenage girls sucked into the chase, blonde runaways in a nicked Porsche accelerating away from the old bill cutting through East German side streets looking for the alley that was just wide enough to squeeze through, escaping through a gap in the wall, because speed was everything on the autobahns, no limit to expansion, they all needed living space, racing all the way to West Berlin.

Everything was easy these days and the English could march right in, when Europe was at peace, it was all so fucking easy, because if you had the cash you could do whatever the fuck you wanted, like that cunt in the corner eyeing the boys and girls and licking his lips. Harry could feel the anger rising because the Gulf Boy had sharpened his senses and the bloke was a fucking nonce, the scum of Europe, the boys had been talking about it in Amsterdam, pulling everyone together with the Cross of St George in the window, all the London geezers and Liverpool scallies and Pompey, Mancs and stray dogs from right across the country, and Harry was trying to pull his thoughts back, telling himself the bloke was probably alright, just wanted to play a game and get away from Berlin and its history, the fucking Berlin Wall and Cold War. Like Harry he wanted to sit pretty and take everything out on someone else, pay an easy target back for all the other bollocks coming his way in life. It was the safe option, picking a soft target and unloading your hatred.

Harry pulled himself straight and looked at the message on the screen, fluorescent green words on a black background, Harry sharp now, feeling his confidence return as he started reading, having trouble, brain ticking, looking sideways at the blondes, not bad really, but young, legal but young, fucking right, too young for a fat cunt like him, looking now at the screen and banging his fist on the control panel because it was ALL IN FUCKING GERMAN.

Fucking cunts. How was he supposed to read that? He breathed in deep and felt his confidence return, because he'd played this game in The Unity back home in London. It was Smart Bomb Parade, flavour of the month, year, decade. It was a piece of piss and he knew the rules, his coin going in the slot, Harry off on a run as the bells chimed and a soft robot voice told him to climb into the cockpit, and he did as he was told looking through the eyes of a fighter bomber pilot, a hero figure, Smart Bomb the biggest seller in Europe, looking through the eyes of Big Bob West the Gulf War veteran from the pub, the original Gulf Boy, but they said he was fucked up on chemicals, illegal substances rotting his brain and breaking down his defences. Harry laughed out loud and the girls looked at him nervously.

It was Flash Harry inside the cockpit preparing for take-off, part of the New Economic Order assault force, Christian idealists ready to take on the might of the wicked General Mahmet in the East, the mighty Mahmet and his conscript farmhands in their vintage killing machines, an evil empire far away over the horizon in a world of medieval cruelty, feudalist perversion, beyond the Slav slave-states, far away on the wisp of a cloud, with a Stone Island bull's-eye in front of his face chiselled into Harry's helmet because he'd paid his euros, feeling the button under his finger and hearing the girls next door, the sound of music and rockets all around the amusement arcade, Harry on a roll forgetting about the football. He was fighting for the NEO, for extended drinking, legalised drugs and cheaper sex. He was ready for take-off, knob red raw, mind wired into the circuits of the European machine.

—I'm scared suddenly in this dead village. I've walked in on Mangler and a crying woman. I ask him what he's doing. He tells me to fuck off and I back out of the room confused and bitter. Bullets explode against the concrete above me so I crouch down behind a broken wall. There's a child's body nearby and I brush maggots from her blonde hair. A small girl, I think, killed by Allied bombers. It's a necessary evil in the struggle for peace. All this evil is necessary if good is to prevail. I have to get the job finished and go home. I try not to think of Mangler and the woman because it is a mistake, my mind turned rotten by the constant destruction. There's a thud on the bricks in front of me, a sniper hidden further along the street. I hear one of the lads firing a mortar and shouting that the fucking flame-thrower isn't working right. I can hear a man shouting something in German. They won't surrender these Germans. They're fighting to the death. We start running forward but I'm not sure where we're going. I'm caught in the panic as a hand grenade blows a hole in the street. I peel away and charge along a small path, catching my head on some wire and ducking down. There's blood coming from my ear but nothing worth worrying about. I turn through the arch of a door and there's a boy in a grey uniform facing me. There's no time to think as I fire into his guts and see the tunic turn black. He stumbles and there's a second of silence as he tries to fight the shock and pain. My heart is pumping and I don't care about this German bastard because all I see is the gun in his hand. I fire again. I don't know how many bullets I drill into his body and I don't hear him scream or even cry. I fire into his head and it explodes. There's blood and brain everywhere and he twitches a lot, struggling in the mud. I stand over him and my mind is frozen. I don't know if it's hate, fear, confusion. His scared expression, shock and then pain are frozen inside me. I know I'll never escape the image, a horror film sitting in the cupboard. I roll him over and there's not much left of his face. I've killed this conscript forced to fight the mad English tommy with the bulging eyes and bloodstained boots. I hear more shouting and firing and run across what was once someone's front room looking for cover. I glance back at the corpse briefly and move forward with the rest of the unit.

We're strolling now. Waiting for the Germans to make their move. The krauts are coming down from a shopping area. It's a bit mixed up in the road, and one or two of the boys must be thinking about the Germans last night, how they had a good laugh. I'm wondering whether it's going to tone things down, and the right-wing lot are going to have their own thing lined up, whether it's political or not, but if it's football then this mob here is ready to go, because the thing is, despite what you read, most of us are just normal everyday patriots out for a punch-up, and while we love the Queen and support the Loyalists in Northern Ireland, we're not political. We just have our views. Because politics is shit. Lines of manky old cunts shouting at each other while they're on the box then it's straight down the bar for a cosy drink. We're English and that's it. And the German crew mobbing up by the railings are starting to look a bit tasty. England are moving and I look at Facelift and almost next to him is Derby and there's no recognition from either of them. Bright is fired up and Harris is straining like a mad man, Mark and Carter, all the boys. Kevin, Crewe and Bolton, Millwall on the left and Pompey on the right next to West Ham, Leeds in the middle, Chelsea everywhere. Strolling towards the Germans. Silent and picking up momentum.

Because it's two World Wars and one World Cup, and the first bottle comes over thrown by someone hiding at the back of their firm, and there's a right old mixture of Germans with smart skinheads and shabby old soulboy-meets-boot-boys with those silly short-at-the-side/long-at-the-back Deutschland haircuts, dodgy tashes and naff trainers. There's even a few scarves, the daft cunts, and I look and see Harris and Bright moving across the street and the rest of the boys follow, a small crew of scousers and a mixture of Midlanders behind, Yorkshiremen through the middle with some Geordies, all moving in together because now it's tightening up and the Germans are pushing forward as they chuck more bottles, the English moving aside to let them land on the ground, glass shattering in among the Deutschland chants, and I catch Facelift's face and the bloke's got a flare gun, the fucking Hayes sniper, moving on from glassing his brother-in-law to firing rockets at Germans.

We're off now fancying ourselves as a fucking commando unit, regiments from every corner of England, steaming straight into the heart of Germany, the English-design Hamburg and Berlin skins coming to meet us and I see the flare flash and that scatters the cunts, better than a fucking fire bomb, this is the fucking war right here with Harris piling in like he's old Bomber himself burning Dresden to a cinder teaching the German scum not to fuck about with the English, and there's waves of English steaming into small mobs of Germans, don't need any orders for this one, and I go full into some bloke and punch him in the head and kick him in the balls and kick him in the head as he goes down with Mark and Carter kicking him again, moving to the next German coming through and hitting him in the head and pulling the cunt forward by his shirt, head down, bringing my knee up and Harris slicing his back, and I get a fist in the face and bounce back, swinging at the German, a massive bloke this one, and it takes five or six English to push him back, head-to-head in the middle of the street with a mass of arms and legs, Facelift's flare sending red-white-and-blue smoke spewing through the air. There's no music now, no soundtrack playing or bands beating up a rhythm for the rows of men getting gunned down, because we're smarter than that, leaving the music behind with DJ Bright lashing out and some of the Germans have started running and we're after them quick as a flash. They've broken into different mobs and there must be a hundred of us going to this wasteland where a German takes out a knife and stabs an Englishman in the face. We circle round and try and do the cunt, his eyes mental flashing murder, knows he's gone further now and if we get him he's dead, but suddenly this little firm think better of it and close round the knife merchant and you can smell the shit as they leg it, moving faster than Schumacher. The bloke with the cut face keeps going and we move back to where there's the main mob of Germans, and they're lobbing bottles and singing this shit song about something or other none of us understands, and the English get together and go into them again.

My head is fucking roaring like a machine tapping into the size of the English mob that's turned out and the fact that we're so far from home in the heart of the fatherland and this is a big one and we're doing the business. Mark's with me, and Carter,

Harris, Facelift, Brighty, Biggs, Ken and Davison's mob and all the other blokes we've been travelling through Europe with, and it hits me that the Germans have their own club differences but that doesn't matter because there's West Ham further along doing some Germans and there's no sign of the old bill. We're fighting smaller mobs of Germans and the English keep together and move in some sort of casual order. The Germans have lost it and we start following their main crew to another square where there's bigger numbers determined to make a stand and I reckon they've been trying to suck us in here, looking to the right and there's a big skinhead mob who are obviously the top boys, some cunt in one of a hundred or so black combat jackets lobbing tear gas, so we back off and let it burn out, milling around as the rest of the English catch up, a nice little breather, chance for a cup of tea maybe. There's a bit of a lull with everyone buzzing, fucking speeding better than that shit last night, better than designer narcotics, a pure fucking natural high this one, an England special.

These skins are the ones we're really going to have to sort out and all of them look the business. They start coming down this grass slope and we fan out still watching the other mob of Germans, all these blokes from both sides of the Channel going to war again and this is a fucking serious row with some of the Germans carrying baseball bats, but you have to keep going and the further in you get the darker it gets and we know there's going to be murders because this is the SS contingent, but the mob to the side have already been run once so we know we can do them easy enough, and when the skinheads come through it goes off with English getting kicked and Germans getting kicked and Mark getting a baseball bat across his arm, sounds like bone cracking, and I see Harris stab the German who did it deep and hard and I fucking hope his heart's not there, more like his gut with his shirt soaked looking shocked dropping the baseball bat, watching the German stagger away glad to see he's alive but hurt and when you lose your concentration you get a slap and that's what happens to me, a fist in the side of the head, except it doesn't hurt much and I do the cunt with the help of a couple of others, but the Germans aren't bottling out, the fighting continuing with both sides standing firm.

A gap appears and this has been going on for a while now without a result and the other Germans have got behind the skins making it more or less equal numbers which is something in itself because fucking hell, lads, this is Germany, fucking Berlin, and we're on their manor and we pile in again like the old boys did in the war going fucking mental tearing up and this time they don't fancy it so much and some start running, the younger element shitting it as the Chelsea and West Ham and Leeds and Millwall and Stoke and Pompey and all the big Northern geezers who are the fucking business when it really comes down to serious street-fighting, the sort of no-nonsense heavy-duty industry nutters who usually hate Southerners but when it's England are united and hard as fucking nails, everyone piles in and thumps the Germans – on their own fucking manor – getting the result – winning the war – living up to reputations – doing our dads and granddads proud – following their example – and it's not over yet because different mobs filter different ways and there's smaller battles now as we go through a row of shops, windows breaking.

The Germans have moved further off so the English start doing cars and buildings, glass made for smashing. The ordinary people are hiding in packs and nobody bothers with them apart from some shouted insults about the war and Hitler and how they killed our women and kids, but it's a coach and these shops that really take a battering, the cars get their roofs dented and the coach its window wrecked, no-one bothering to turn the VWs over and burn them because the colours won't look so good in the light and we've got better things to do. A bit of looting fills in the time and the discipline has gone now. The younger lads are into the vandalism, the spoils of war or whatever you want to call it, and these blokes move forward through the ranks when things get easier and when I look at Mark and the others travelling with me none of us are really bothered about the shops, though it adds to the spectacle and it's something that's going to happen one way or the other, another way of grinding your foot into the Germans because this is part of what they're defending, I suppose, their property and territory.

It's up to the vandals to do what they want. Personally, it's the German mob that counts, but I watch the windows cave in one after the other, racks of vegetables turned over, café chairs and tables broken, moving aside from this old dear who must be eighty if she's a day, a granny who doesn't know any better coming after the hooligans wrecking her cornershop. She's tooled-up with this gnarled walking stick and she catches this scrawny little bloke on the back of the head. He yells and runs away and everyone's laughing because Granny's no bottle merchant, clearing a gap through the English as she marches along lashing out, smacking Harris on the arm hard so he moves out of the way sharpish, grinning with embarrassment as he's put in his place, Granny hobbling after us shouting in German, but the windows have all gone now and she keeps going, chasing a big Northerner who's trying to calm her down and he jogs off giving up saying she's a nutter, and Granny doesn't care, doesn't give a fuck, because she's got the scent and we move away from the shops and onto another big street, milling around on the corner trying to work out where we are.

We look back and Granny's standing there screaming at us saying we're nothing but hooligans, nothing but English hooligans, and she's got a point, and there's some cheering and we're looking round trying to work out which way to go, spotting the Germans up ahead, throwing bricks, Harris saying we're on the right way to the ground where we can have a drink because there's still a few hours till kick-off and there'll be more Germans there, more English as well, but first we're going to have to fight these krauts some more because it looks like they're coming back to have another go, making the most of their big day out, been building up to it ever since the fixture was suggested by the politicians as a show of unity between the two nations and their banking institutions, a sporting event to help promote the new economic order, laying firm foundations for a united Europe.

There's the sound of sirens and a column of flashing lights ahead, so we hang back to see what's going to happen next, enjoying the show. The lights are behind the German mob and there's the slamming of doors and the barking of dogs, a minute of silence as the English stragglers catch up, a few blokes with trays of jewellery shifting towards some flats looking to hide their haul. We wait and see what the old bill are going to do and suddenly they just steam straight into the German mob with their truncheons and that's something you wouldn't get in Spain or Italy, coppers attacking their own kind, and the Germans come running towards us and then realise they're getting chased into another kicking. They shift off to the side moving into the flats and we see the riot police coming at us again and this time they look like they mean business because there's tear gas popping off and it does your fucking eyes in like nothing else. We move back and this gives the old bill the advantage and when I look through the smoke the German mob have seen their chance and are following the coppers through like they're getting a Panzer escort. We've seen it before, where the local hooligans and old bill almost work together because they're all racist against the English, but usually it's the Latins, because Latins and Anglo-Saxons don't mix. They all want to do us and the only difference is the uniform and the fact that the police are legally tooled-up. This lot are just grabbing their chance, though, because the German old bill are like the English old bill and don't play the Latin game. A lot of English get battered by the riot police, but again we don't run and they can't fucking handle this because they don't spend years training in crowd control tactics just to get fronted by a load of hooligans and sheer weight of numbers forces them back along the road.

It's one of those no-win situations and there's enough clever English around to lead the way down another side street, mirroring the Germans who are looking to do the same thing, and when I think about this it's fucking mental, because it's not ending, usually it would fizzle out or the old bill would end things or someone would get done right off, but I suppose the Germans are like us because they're going to keep coming back for more and aren't prepared to give up, specially at home, while the old bill have to deal with all these nutters from across the Channel who don't care about their German laws and aren't too scared about getting nicked. They can't fucking win and we've put ourselves in a situation where sticking together and fighting back means we survive.

No drug does it the same as we run towards the Germans again down another street and the two sides are smaller, people getting lost along the way, filtering off. That's the way they do you, picking off small mobs not paying attention, or people who get unlucky left on their own, and it flares up again with the more dedicated on both sides going for it and there's a couple of English getting done and then it goes back and forward, and with Mark and the rest of the Chelsea boys and another big mix of clubs we run another load of Germans down another fucking street, slowing down not knowing where the fuck we are now, maybe two hundred of us waiting for the rest of the English to catch up, walking now causing havoc, moving through the building blocks, my brain speeding.

Harry was feeling the effects. This was no ordinary war. No ordinary Saturday night punch-up outside The Hide. No midnight runner from the Taj Mahal. No rowing with the bouncers at Blues. No nutting Sunderland coppers. No, this was special. Personal. Because Harry was riding with the soul of Big Bob West, a war hero from The Unity who'd fought in the Gulf and seen so much on his video screen that when he got home his life was fucked, just like the old boys who sat in the corner early evening with their bitter, grey hair and weary limbs, the old soldiers who ran onto the beaches and through the German guns, fighting for England and the English way of life, fighting the Nazis and ready to steam into the Soviets. Old soldiers with fuck all in their pension and a series of governments who stitched them up every step of the way. Businessmen who hid at home telling the squaddies to forget the horror and move on, bow down, do what you're told. There was no gratitude and they were forced to hobble through mean streets to sit in front of prim-and-proper young men and women who hated age and the spirit of former days. Harry had seen the films of Spitfire pilots and commando missions but had also drunk with Bob West, a regular who didn't like the dream.

Harry felt the power in his fingertips, hovering over the buttons. There was a chemical rush through his spine. Tips of his toes to the top of his head. This was the crunch, fighting for the cause from the safety of a seat in the amusement arcade. Jurgen the German giving out change. The boom of engines as Harry soared above the city, high above Berlin, because he was part of the great game now, one more soldier ant fighting for the NEO, a benevolent money-motivated Euro-dictatorship where decisions were made behind closed doors by unelected bureaucrats.

Big Bob burnt women and kids so the Brits and Yanks could march into Iraq, and though these colours don't run it was the politicians who told them to stop before they got carried away and took Baghdad. West said the politicians wouldn't let them finish the job and get rid of Saddam, because he was just a mate who'd gone a bit over the top; and that was all in the past because now the English were in Berlin and the rest of the lads would be near the ground and it would be going off all over the shop, and in among the exhaust fumes of Harry's head he could see the irony, how they were allowed to march straight in and turn the place over while the soldiers obeyed orders and were told to sit tight over the horizon.

Harry was absorbed by the graphics and colour, sucked into a world of heroism where you didn't bruise your knuckles. He was moving into the future at a thousand miles per hour because, like his old mate Mango said, you had to go with the flow, accepting his place in the new super-state and doing his part in securing the borders, House of Commons politicians sneering at the right- and left-wing sceptics, Harry pushing the image of Ted Heath aside because it was changing shape and he saw Balti in the street with his fucking head blown off, all that blood and gore that made him feel sick, refusing to stay with the memory. It was real life and he didn't want real life, because real life was shit.

Smart Bomb Parade was harmless fun and Harry was accepting things for what they were, going forward rather than back, looking down on a futuristic Berlin with its American skyscrapers and American burger chains, the biggest amusement park in Europe built on the site of the Führer's bunker, the laughter of cartoon characters replacing the screams of men and women strapped down to dissection tables and gang-raped by nonces, Harry shaking with rage as he thought of Nicky running for safety, feeling his lungs contract as he gasped for fresh air, wishing those German slags would put out the fag. Harry came through the rocks with a supersonic boom and a biblical city of sodomy and drug addiction was right there, white blocks of stone decorated with marble minarets and tiny ants running for cover going this way and that, circling in on themselves as Harry prepared to teach them a lesson they would never forget.

—I suppose we never learn. It's all in our genes and the images flashed at us through the screen. It seems like another life now and I suppose it was. The Second World War will be forgotten soon and I'll be another rack of bones in a cemetery overflowing with dead, but empty of mourners. My time has passed, but I lived. I was a tearaway when I was young, and maybe I'd have hanged if it hadn't been for the war. Who knows what would have happened in different circumstances. They were hard times to live through but there could never be anything to compare. The war was terrible, but there was a comradeship that has never existed in England since. The working class was given respect by the authorities while there was a war to win and then we went back to normal. I hate war and violence, but the worst thing is that it was exciting. I killed and at times maybe I enjoyed the chaos. Some men like killing and hurting people. A lot of men enjoy destroying buildings and property. The battles were spectacles. The colours and noise of the bombardments were incredible. Hand-to-hand it was hard, seeing the faces of the men you killed but not really taking them in. I've come back from The Unity and everyone's sad because last night they found Bob West hanging in his flat. He committed suicide and didn't bother to leave a note. There were no last words. Denise was crying and says she doesn't understand. He had nothing to say. He never saw the people he killed, just the beauty of the flames and the sunsets. He saw the spectacle and missed the horror. Later he realised what his role had been, but there was no answer and nobody to help. Maybe he killed a hundred people, perhaps a thousand. I saw the charred corpses of men, women and children killed by bombers and I saw the insanity of a concentration camp. I found my wife there, right at the bottom, raped and starved almost to death. She was a brilliant woman. We were happy and I was a figure in the park digging the soil and planting flowers, enjoying the air and work. Nobody knew what I'd seen and it didn't matter. It made me stronger than all of them. You accept your place in the world and the rich take what they want. It's always been this way. The best you can do is stay honest. There was a short time after my wife passed away that I went mad, but I'm okay now and since then I have been content to plod along. You get by. Counting the cost of the heating and going cold at my age isn't right, but there's nothing that can be done. I killed for England. I did it in a uniform and they gave me medals. But I sit with my cup of tea and watch the news and a story of rioting in Berlin. The man on the screen is talking from a London studio. He is very excited. I've heard it before, in a hundred different situations. When he gets tired there are other stories of death and destruction. They can't leave it be. Do the young men I pass in the street learn anything? Or the politicians and media? But old men get bitter and that's not for me. I'll see Eddie and the boys in a few months. I'm going to see the world and go to Australia. That's my decision and I'm sticking to it, because that's all you can really do. I've made my choices and won't complain. Maybe it's better to die with your mates overseas than at home all alone. But there's no point dying young. No point at all.

The youth's taking a hammering from a couple of Englishmen. He's wriggling on the concrete and covering himself. His hair is short and his shirt specked with blood. It's bright red, not black. The thuds are muffled and his fingers cracked from the kicks. The two men take their time and pick their spots. I think of that kicking I got at Millwall a few years back. Then I think of Derby and the time I stood aside and did nothing when Facelift had a go at him. Fitted in and behaved myself. Stood in the shadows. With Millwall I thought I was going to die. Maybe end up in a wheelchair. Or brain damaged. Kicked to death over a game of football. Murdered in some Peckham slum. Chelsea did the business but I was unlucky. It's the luck of the draw. Another kind of lottery. Because a fight's a fight. There's no rules these days. No Queen's regulations. Doubt there ever was. Nothing's different except the wrapping gets more high-tech. They add some colour. It's a load of bollocks. It's all down to what's inside and you make your choices. Have to live with them for the rest of your life. It's personal responsibility.

We're a democratic people. This German decided to have a go at the famous English football hooligans and he's lost out. The mob we've been rowing with has scattered and the rest of the England boys are chasing them for fun. The German on the floor is having a bad time of things from these two. He's pushed himself to get out on the streets with his mates and this is the comeback. It's time for the cunt to pay the bill. Taking the piss having a go at the English. Fitting in with his mates and playing his part. All that mutual respect is shit. Face in the gutter getting the shit kicked out of him by a couple of men ten years older. The bigger of the two hovers around him, stamping on the youth's head. He's deliberate in what he's doing. He wants to hurt this boy. He's trying to crack the skull. Damage that fucking kraut brain. That fucking German cunt responsible for bombing London and Coventry and Plymouth. Fucking slags the lot of them. Kill the boy and walk away with no second thoughts. Leave the body face down in the mud for his mum and dad to identify days later in some regimental morgue. Send the body home in a box. A few miles out of Berlin to some grubby German village. Do the cunt and let his old man sit by the grave crying in front of the wife. Looking soft. Bringing the back of his trainer down on the side of the boy's face.

I walk towards them and hit the one stamping on the German's head. I punch him in the face and I punch him hard. It's a good punch. There's no panic or excitement, but I want to break his nose. I screw my fist in and try to hurt him. He stumbles back holding his head, half from surprise and half from pain. He's the same size and a bit younger than me, but he's a wanker. It's the cowards and the psychos who stand there for hours kicking a dead man. Kicking a dead man to death. I hate that, going on and on when you've done the job and proved your point. These cunts have been hanging back waiting to pick up the leftovers. You never see these slags at the front when it goes off, and they're the first ones on their toes when things go bad. They're a couple of wankers. The kind who in a war torture prisoners and rape women. Scum basically. There's rotten apples everywhere. You have to have standards.

The second man turns round and says they're English. Thinks I've got them mixed up with the krauts. I tell him to fuck off and kick him in the balls. He moves sideways and it only half hurts. He chokes and leans forward, then snaps back as I kick him in the mouth. He's a tart and does as he's told. Not fit to call himself English. He pulls his mate away and they hurry off. I watch them go, then look down at the German. He's moving and trying to crawl away. I turn him over with my foot but he doesn't have a face, just blood from his nose smeared with grit. I think of what Harry was saying in London a couple of weeks ago, when we were getting stoned on some of Rod's dope. Up to your fucking eyeballs on Arab camel dung and Fat Boy's running off at the mouth, going into one. You'd think he'd slow down but he was so fucking chuffed about the coming trip two hours on the herb didn't knock him out. My old mate, new mate Harry going on about how he imagined the face of Balti after he'd been shot. Wanted to know whether you could see the features or just the skull. I didn't want to start thinking about all that because fuck knows with the camel shit. Didn't want the paranoia, but the image stuck. Now I connect everything looking at a face that could belong to anyone.

I lean down and grab the boy round the neck. Hold onto the collar of his shirt and pull him to his feet. He's unsteady at first. His legs are weak for a few seconds but then the messages start coming through as the computer reconnects. He leans into me. Realises I'm not going to hurt him. Probably thinks I'm a local. His weight's on my shoulder as I half-walk, half-carry him to a brick wall. He leans back and shakes his head. Takes a hanky from his pocket and wipes the blood off. Gets his thoughts together. Looks at me again and seems confused. Nods his head up and down. He seems a bit spastic as the current starts firing and I watch the pulse in his temple. I kill time looking down the street to where I can hear shouting and the sound of breaking glass. England are moving along another row of shops and wrecking the place. I can see men running after other men. England are on the rampage but everything has broken up and got confused. I want to get back with the others and enjoy the fun. Make every second count.

I stay for a minute or so. The noise drifts further away and there's nobody but the two of us in the street. It's a fucking ghost town suddenly. Everyone's hurried to keep up with the fighting and left us behind. I look at the youth again and he's got his hands on his knees and his head down. I think he's going to be sick, but nothing happens. There's the blood but it's just his nose. Nothing serious. Fuck knows if they've done his bones or something internal. He stands up, looking better. Starts to say something, but I shake my head, frown and turn away. I jog down the road to catch up with Mark, Carter and the rest of the boys.

— And when you're in that situation in a time of war, as I was, with the world going mad around you, with millions dead all over the globe, you have to make decisions. I saw the German youth crawling and his gun was in his hand. Maybe he was trying to turn, maybe not. I'd killed before and I could have kicked the gun away, but I couldn't be bothered. I'd seen men with their brains blown out and boys with their intestines torn from their guts crying for their mums. I'd seen men with their balls in the mud and exposed hearts filling with rain water. Men castrated by shrapnel and bleeding to death. A lot of them weren't men. I was only a kid myself and I'd seen too much, and when the boy moved I didn't try to think. My brain was heavy and maybe I was insane. I shot him in the head and blew his head open. I shattered his skull with the crack of my bullets. I don't know how many shots I fired but I didn't need them all. I stuck my bayonet into him as well, but by then he had to be dead. I dug it in ten or more times. I killed a boy younger than myself and he stayed in the mud as I moved forward. I doubt he was ever given a funeral. He was probably a brave boy who deserved better from his rulers. I left his corpse to rot. I was mad and angry and would have killed anyone. I lived and thought about everything that happened. I married a survivor from a concentration camp and hated the men who raped her, the men and women responsible for the rapes, murders, tortures and experiments. After the war I thought things through but never really came to a conclusion. I saw Mangler but what could I do? Nobody wanted to know. It was a war and bad things happen. It's not an excuse and I've always wondered about the boy and I still wonder today. There's rubbish everywhere. I did my duty, and things could've been different. I'll never be sure and that's the hardest part. When I see war veterans on the television meeting old enemies and shaking hands I wonder what it would be like to meet that boy all grown up with a wife and children and grandchildren of his own. What would it be like to have a drink with him in a German beer garden? I would be embarrassed and turn my head away when he thanked me for his life.

I pick up my suitcase when the bell rings and open the front door. My daughter is taking me to the airport. I'm excited now and my head is clear. We make our choices, and as a young man you think things will get better, but they don't. It's what we are. We fight and kill and breed to rebuild. It's the English way, but more than that it's the way of the world. When you get older you slow down and realise it's daft, but you can't really explain it in words, and anyway, nobody's listening. People get embarrassed and the likes of me don't count. Life moves on and there's no telling people.

No telling the General in his marble bunker, deep inside stone corridors where nobody hears the prostitutes scream. Nobody heard Balti die in the street, the only witness a woman with the shits who saw everything through glass, and Harry wanted revenge, because life was unfair and the screens all around him were pointing the way ahead. He was powerless, but if he played the game he could have it all. The machine offered a perfect world, where nobody asked questions and an all-powerful state was prepared to crush those animals over the horizon. Harry had to pay his dues and channel his anger in a new direction.

Smart Bomb was a great game and Harry was running up a decent score, watching his missiles hit home, the Gulf Boy mixing his thoughts as he remembered that story from the First World War, when the two sides called a truce for Christmas Day and the English and Germans left their trenches and stood in no-man's land together, had a drink and a game of football. It was a famous story, because after that the two sides stopped shooting at each other. The soldiers had to be replaced and the next year there was no fraternising with the enemy. Harry pumped the button and destroyed a gunship, amazed that the officers were that stupid, because if you saw the face of your enemy and knew him as a person, you weren't going to try and kill him. They were more sussed today, making things easy with smart rockets, conquering the world with consumer goods, and Harry understood this because he could see exactly where Nicky fitted in.

He would go and see her in Amsterdam. He smiled as he pictured Nicky opening the door of her flat and throwing her thin arms around his neck. His knob was aching, but he could trust her. Everyone wanted to return home a hero, Harry aiming at a cartoon tank and shattering its armour, knowing it was just a game – it had to be – the bright red blood of the tank crew seeping through crinkled silver metal.

There's blood on my feet and I'm back with the main mob of English. We're running the old bill. Chasing twenty of the cunts through their own streets. The fighting seems like it's been going on for ever, and there's not so many of us now. We have to watch ourselves because we're on foreign soil, surrounded by people who hate us, but we're doing England proud. Putting on a show the locals won't forget. We're here in Berlin, rioting in the centre of Europe. Maintaining a reputation we've built up through the centuries. Kicking the shit out of anyone who takes the piss. Slowing down now and letting the old bill escape.

We stop at a crossroads and try to work out where we are. Harris has a look at his map, and points the way to the ground. There's some Germans further down the street. As we get nearer they move forward and we pile in, punching and kicking the ones at the front. My fist connects with some bloke's chin and my knuckles jolt. I feel it right along my arm. They don't really fancy it and do a runner. We slow down again, covering the road and walking tall. Going from street to street doing whatever we want, flushing out resistance. Battering the fuck out of anyone who wants to have a go. We're proud to be English and proud of our culture. We're doing the stroppy cunts once and for all.